Helm of Shadows

P.G. BADZEY

DEDICATION

For my parents, who always encouraged me, supported me and gave me their love, no matter what endeavor I attempted.

CONTENTS

ACKNOWLEDGMENTS

The author would like to acknowledge the following individuals for their most excellent contributions:
Eugene Badzey, Dora Badzey and Paul Badzey for their editing prowess, Veronica Badzey for typesetting
The people at Wavecloud for their superior service in generating the incredible cover art for the entire series.

Song of the Grey Riders

Seven they are, the Riders Grey,
who come to serve the Holy Way.
Seven they are of varied flight,
on winged steeds of dark midnight.
The Riders Grey, the warriors brave,
who seek to stem the Evil Wave:
One with sword from dwarves of old
and one fair maiden with hair of gold.
To aid the ones who follow the Three
comes another of the Silver Tree.
One with hawk of sharpened claw,
one forest guide of Christian law.
One small and swift, silent and light;
another the same with magic bright.
North they go to face Cold Fire
to battle the dragon and quench her ire.
When ogre's rage meets its end,
then does their true quest begin.

In tower cold and cavern deep,
the Diamond Eye they now must seek.
For good or evil all must choose
or choosing none, their lives to lose.
When gold to red at passage end,
then halfling toy upward must send.
Golden sorrow, heart's true Love,
pray to God in Heaven above.
That she may see, and all may learn,
what Truthful Eye cannot discern.

Holy relic, giver of life,
meant for tresses of carpenter's wife.

ii

Ancient Evil, Good to slay,
seeks to thwart the Holy Way.
Relic's might of love is wrought,
so evil's will avails it naught.
One Dark Rider fights seven of Grey,
yet Queenly Crown shall win the day.
Seven they were, from varied flight,
on winged steeds of dark midnight.
Seven they were, the Riders Grey,
who came to serve the Holy Way.

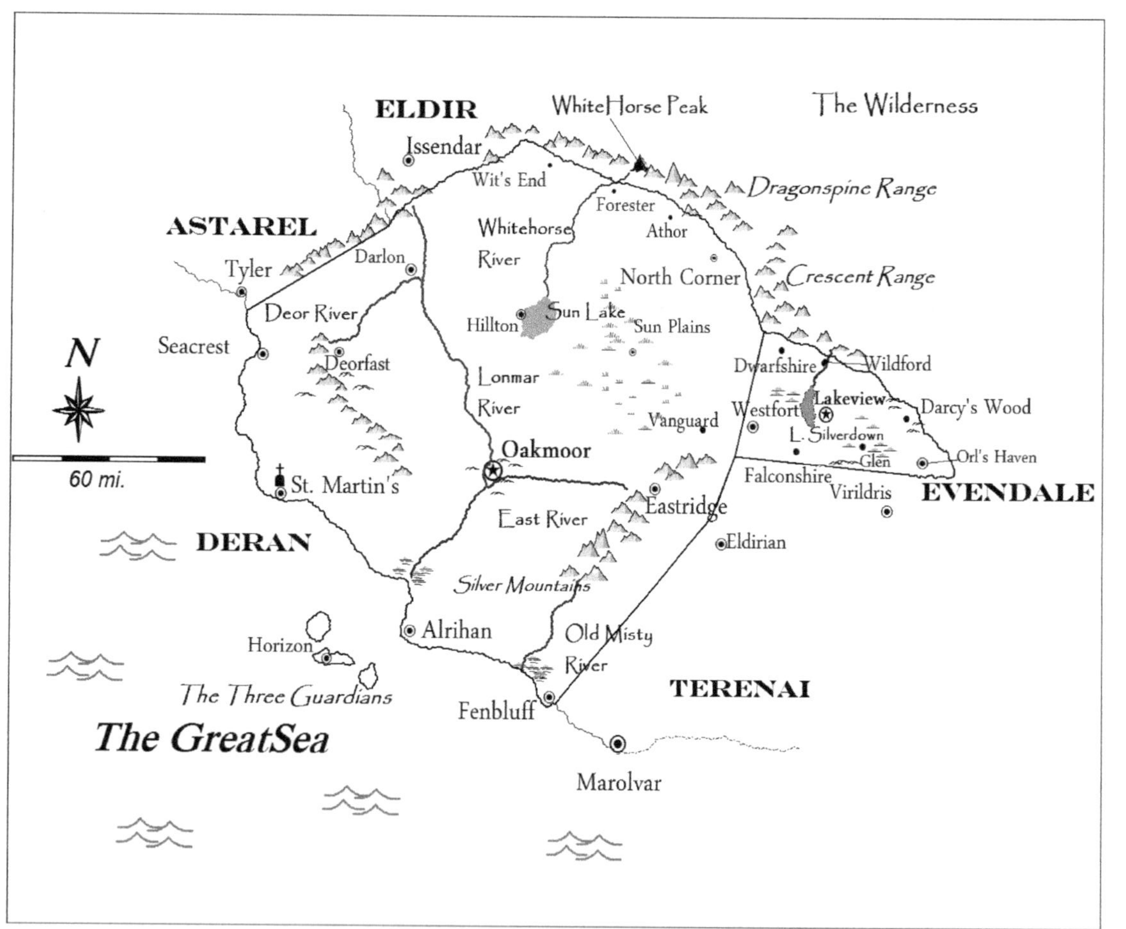

ELDIR
WhiteHorse Peak
The Wilderness
Issendar
Wit's End
Dragonspine Range
ASTAREL
Forester
Whitehorse River
Athor
Tyler
Darlon
North Corner
Crescent Range
Deor River
Hillton
Sun Lake
Sun Plains
Seacrest
Deorfast
Lonmar River
Dwarfshire
Wildford
Vanguard
Westfort
Lakeview
Darcy's Wood
Oakmoor
L. Silverdown
Glen
Orl's Haven
Falconshire
St. Martin's
East River
Eastridge
Virildris
EVENDALE
DERAN
Eldirian
Silver Mountains
Horizon
Alrihan
Old Misty River
TERENAI
The Three Guardians
Fenbluff
The GreatSea
Marolvar
N
60 mi.

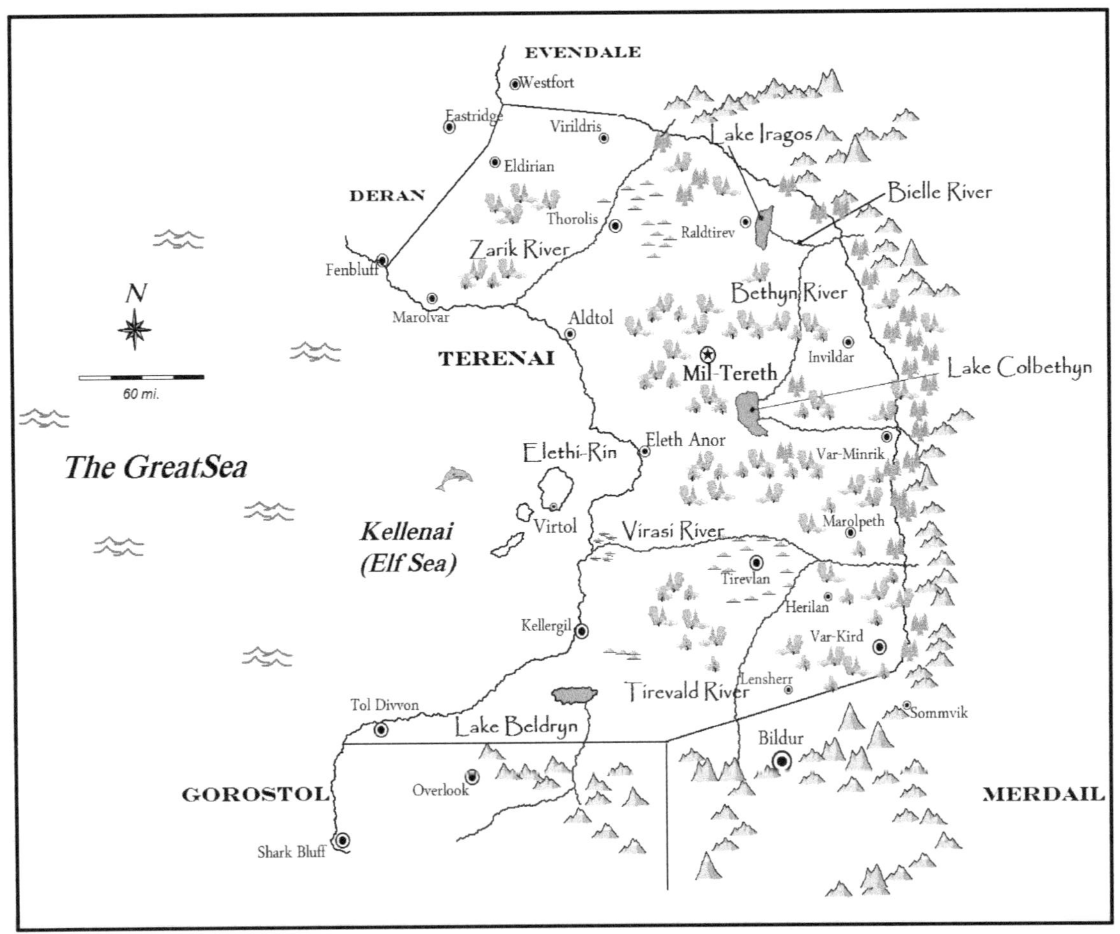

EVENDALE
Westfort
Eastridge
Virildris
Lake Iragos
Eldirian
DERAN
Bielle River
Thorolis
Raldtirev
Zarik River
Bethyn River
Fenbluff
Invildar
Marolvar
Aldtol
TERENAI
Mil-Tereth
Lake Colbethyn
Eleth Anor
Elethi-Rin
Var-Minrik
The GreatSea
Virtol
Marolpeth
Kellenai
(Elf Sea)
Virasi River
Tirevlan
Herilan
Kellergil
Var-Kird
Lensherr
Tirevald River
Tol Divvon
Sommvik
Lake Beldryn
Bildur
GOROSTOL
Overlook
MERDAIL
Shark Bluff
N
60 mi.

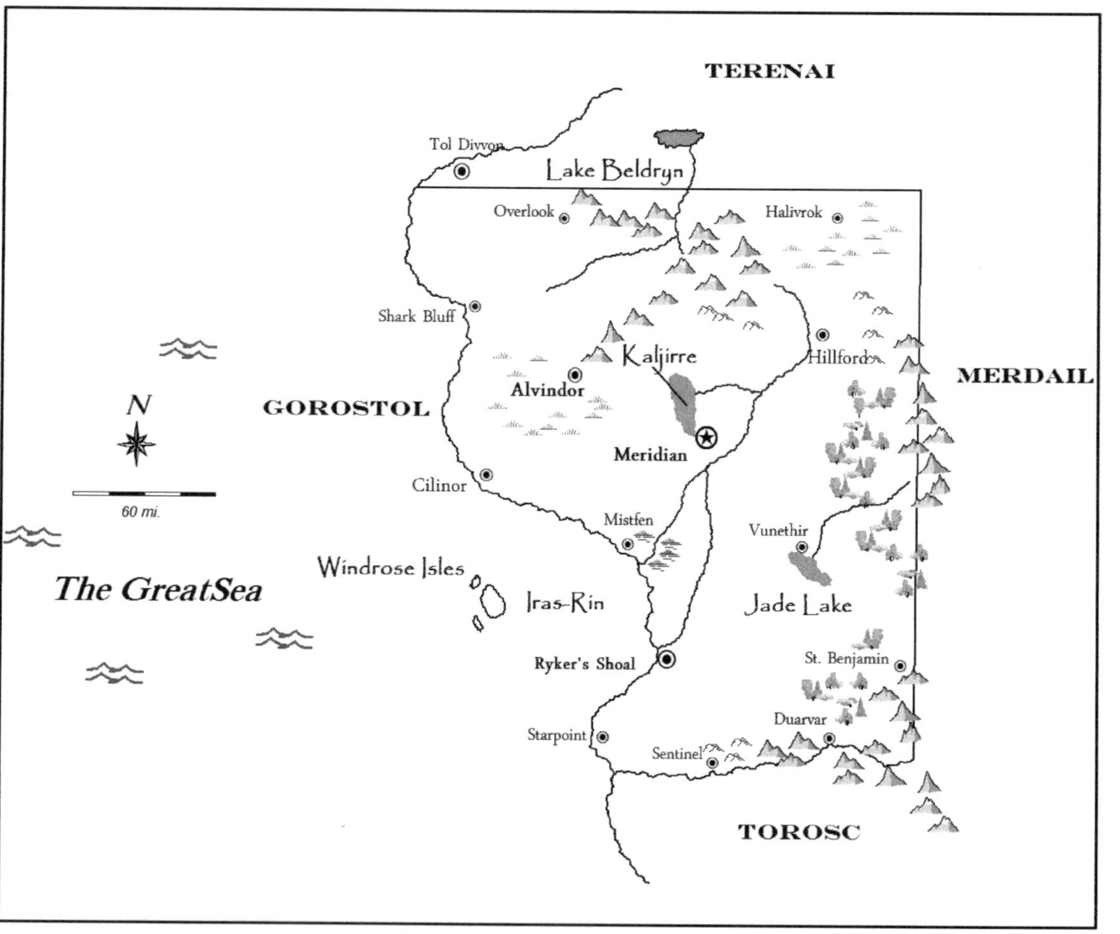

TERENAI
MERDAIL
GOROSTOL
TOROSC
Tol Divvon
Lake Beldryn
Overlook
Halivrok
Shark Bluff
Kaljirre
Hillford
Alvindor
Meridian
Cilinor
Mistfen
Vunethir
Jade Lake
Windrose Isles
Iras-Rin
The GreatSea
Ryker's Shoal
St. Benjamin
Starpoint
Duarvar
Sentinel
N
60 mi.

Chapter One- Red Sky at Morning

Flying horses aren't much good in fog and rain…

Eric Indidarc slowed his coal-black pegasus. He raised a gloved fist overhead to signal the others. A light rain fell around him, wetting his cloak.

"Easy, Niveral," he whispered to the winged horse, giving him a pat on the left wing, folded over his own leg.

Eric put a hand to his sword and scanned the area, his other hand hefting his spear. Other hooves crunched on the gravel next to him.

Dar Cabot slowed and halted his own pegasus and leaned on his saddle-bow. He peered at the ground before dismounting and running a hand over the road surface.

He's found something, Eric thought.

He gave the air a long, careful sniff. He detected prairie grass, heather, oakwood, hartberry and fern, moss and fungus. There was something else, something musty and animal-like. It reminded him of a dog.

Eric kept a careful eye on the tall grass on either side of the road. A couple of gnarled oaks brooded over the path ahead and some bushes clustered near the trees.

"What do you think?" he asked Dar.

Dar Cabot carried a bastard sword on his back. With a shrug, he slid the long scabbard to his side and drew his weapon. "Something's out there. Several somethings. Did you pick up anything with those elven senses of yours?"

"Yes." Eric described what he had smelled on the air and Dar frowned.

A light jangle of harness next to him signaled the arrival of the others.

"Anything going on?" asked Andyn. She shook her head lightly, scattering rain droplets from her helmet. She kept her hands near the maces at her belt.

"Nothing but gawking from what I can tell," interrupted Buck Bydecy from his mount next to her. A pigeon sat on his shoulder, looking none the worse for wear despite the damp. Buck reached a hand to his helmet and swung down a metal arm with a lens at the end. He positioned the lens in front of his right eye, the gemstone within it glittering with many-colored lights.

"Don't bother the scouts," Dar told him, with a wry look, "We, at least, are working."

"Well, I don't see anything with the Eye of Truth," Buck concluded, flipping the arm back up to point the gem skyward. "Of course, whatever is out there might just be out of range."

Another pegasus sidled up next to him. Two small figures, each a few inches over three and a half feet tall, sat in the saddle, one behind the other. Eric could tell them apart by Hlerv's neatly trimmed beard, just visible under the hood of his cloak, and Connor's slimmer but more muscular build.

"This feels wrong," said Connor Lomin, pulling on the reins. Hlerv, seated behind Connor on the pegasus, nodded vigorously.

Dar explained what Eric had found.

"Use your new toy, Eric," he suggested.

Eric put his hand on his shoulder, where a silver brooch lay against his tunic. He whispered a word and the brooch transformed into a brown hawk with black-tipped wings, alighting on Eric's armguard. It watched him with dark eyes.

"Go, Stealth. Find out what's out there." He lifted his arm and the hawk soared up into the mist and clouds.

Instantly, a ghostly image of the surrounding area leaped up in Eric's vision. He saw himself and his friends, the road, and the oak trees. The hawk looped around. He saw other birds and small mammals.

Then he picked up darker, larger shapes moving through the tall grass on both sides of the road, slinking closer. He counted at least ten.

"We have company!" he said. "Both sides."

Buck swung to his right and flipped the Eye of Truth back down in front of his helmet. The gemstone flared red.

"Five over here." He drew a sword that rippled with golden fire and readied his shield.

A chorus of snarling echoed out and armored figures with spotted fur and canine faces hurled themselves at the riders from the tall grass. Eric spun Niveral to face a leaping figure and threw his spear. The creature howled, falling to the ground and taking the weapon with it. It jerked out the spear with a snarl.

Kaftu! Hyena-folk…

A bruising force hit Eric from behind and he almost lost his seat. A Kaftu grappled with him, clinging to his back. Niveral bucked and lashed out with his wings, trying to dislodge the Kaftu. Eric gasped at a sharp pain in his side and kicked free of the saddle, rolling to the left and crouching on the road. His assailant likewise landed on its feet and whirled around. The sounds of battle rang out behind him and he heard the crackle of magic.

Two creatures faced him, the one wounded by his spear and another bearing two daggers, one red with Eric's blood. The Kaftu appeared like large, spotted hyenas— except hyenas didn't walk on their hind legs or wear brigandine armor or use weapons in remarkably human-like hands. Both were female. Strong muscles rippled under their fur and the wounded one yapped something at the other.

Eric felt a rent in the side of his chain armor where the dagger had pierced him. He gritted his teeth against the pain. The edge of his sword glittered with a silvery sheen.

The Kaftu Eric had wounded with the spear threw it back at him. Eric knocked it aside his sword. Leering, the Kaftu picked up an axe from the ground. It lurched forward.

The other Kaftu chanted something harsh and vile.

A whirling cone of air leapt up in front of Eric and he retreated, feeling Niveral behind him, rock-solid. Pebbles and rocks lashed him and he had to drop back, shielding his eyes. He tried to use a counterspell but he couldn't concentrate in the maelstrom.

Niveral neighed and reared, lashing out with his front hooves. Eric heard the impact and shriek from one of the Kaftu. On instinct, he spun to the left, sword out.

A thin bolt of lightning shot through the tiny whirlwind and now he heard a scream of pain from his pegasus.

Now you've done it!

Free from the whirling stones and pebbles, he spied the Kaftu shaman preparing another spell and charged. The wounded Kaftu on the ground struggled to rise, leaning on its axe.

Eric charged the shaman. She gave way, parrying with a dagger, but tripped over the other Kaftu and fell. Eric cut her shoulder with a slash. The prone Kaftu gained its feet and swung. Eric leaped over the axe and thrust down as he went over, driving his blade into her heart.

The shaman regained her feet and barked short words, hand up. Eric focused power in a split second and a glittering shield appeared in front of him. Three fiery darts lanced out at him from the shaman and detonated on his shield with sharp cracks.

He retaliated with a spell of his own, placing a ball of light on her nose. She snarled and yelped, springing to the side. The ball followed her. Eric pressed forward, slashing. He cut her in the leg and when she fell to the side, he impaled her with his blade. Jerking his sword out and feeling the pain in his side, he spun back to his comrades.

Three Kaftu retreated into the tall grass, hurling javelins. One of the missiles stuck in Buck's shield and Connor and Hlerv dodged another. With a final epithet, the hyena-folk raced away, on all fours this time.

Eric went to Niveral immediately. The lightning had struck his left wing and the pegasus whinnied as he approached.

"Easy, Niveral. We'll take care of you."

Eyes wide, the stallion shied away from him. As Eric spoke with soothing tones, he calmed and let himself be pulled close by the bridle. Eric gently inspected the damage.

Damn.

The singed wing and burnt feathers would take days to heal and the pegasus certainly couldn't fly far with that wound. It was a good thing the bolt wasn't very powerful or the wing might be broken. That was a recovery time measured in weeks.

"Everyone okay?" he called to the others.

Andyn walked her pegasus up to him, the mount limping noticeably. "I'm fine. Medianox took a club to the foreleg. I'll have to use magic to heal it. How about you?"

Eric felt the wound in his side. His hand came away bloody. "Damn it… stupid shaman got a knife into me."

"Stand still then." Andyn stepped up next to him and peered at his wound. She let out a deep breath and placed a hand on his side. A mild golden light shone for a second and Eric winced as his wound knit together and stopped bleeding.

"Better?"

He twisted to the side, nodding, feeling only a mild soreness. "Yes, but Niveral is grounded. Took a Lightning Spear to the wing. How about the others?"

The rest of the group joined them. Buck tied a bandage around Dar Cabot's forearm and the scout winced.

"Not so tight, Buck… by all the saints, I'm glad you're not the healer in this group."

Buck grinned. "So am I. Andyn's much prettier."

Andyn Eleandir rolled her eyes. "Enough with the false flattery, Buck. How about the rest of you?"

Buck whistled a merry tune and his pigeon fluttered back to land on his shoulder. Eric eyed the bird and shook his head. *I still don't know how that stupid bird manages to stay alive with all the arrows, swords and magic flying around. It should have been made into stew meat by now.*

He recalled Stealth and the magical construct swooped down to land on his forearm. With another whispered word, it transformed back into a brooch that he pinned to his tunic.

Hlerv lifted back the hood of his cloak, revealing a neatly trimmed beard and mustache, intense black eyes and dark hair. He shook his head. "I'm okay. Damned Kaftu never saw me or Connor. They were so busy with you big folk that we just sneaked around behind one of them and laid her out, then took out another one fighting Dar."

"Mostly females," Dar noted. "Hunting party then. The males aren't taken along unless the tribe is moving."

Convinced that their other wounds were manageable, Andyn set to work on the pegasi.

"We'll check the bodies," Hlerv volunteered. Connor joined him.

Dar nodded to Buck. Eric studied his friend. Dar bit his lip, eyes roaming all over the misty grasslands.

"The borderlands aren't safe anymore. What do you want to bet these Kaftu are like the others?" Dar asked.

"No comment," said Buck, hooking his thumbs in his belt and looking down the road.

"Look on the bright side, Dar," Eric offered. "We avoided an ambush and took out seven of them. That's seven fewer to attack people on the highway or in the towns."

Dar shook his head. "I know Zhinia Margoth is behind this."

"Just because there's a lich princess hunting us doesn't mean that she's behind every bandit attack in Northern Deran," Eric said.

"No," said Hlerv, walking up to them, "But this might. The Kaftu were well-paid. They didn't get all this from casual raiding." He held up two small sacks that clinked with coins.

"And look at this," said Connor, flipping a metal object to Eric.

He caught it and looked at it. Made of pewter, it depicted a fanged skull with a crown of flame.

"Like I was saying," Dar with a look at Eric.

Eric sighed. "Okay, so maybe Margoth is behind this gang too. It just means we have to get to Twinspire Peak before she finds out what we're up to."

Andyn walked up to them, leading Niveral and Medianox. "I think we just have to face up to it. The prophecy says there will be a great battle between us and Margoth. These raids are her attempt to get us before we can find out how to beat her."

Eric inspected Niveral's wing. Aside from a mild scar, it looked undamaged. Andyn certainly did good work.

"Or this could be probing attacks before an invasion," said Dar, not willing to let the issue lie.

Eric felt his stomach tighten. "I'm more afraid of that."

"Well," said Hlerv, hefting the sacks. "We aren't going to figure anything out standing in the road. We have to report this to the authorities and keep moving."

Eric mounted up, feeling the grayness of the clouds and damp weather weigh on his spirit. He shuddered.

"Let's get to Athor. Maybe the town guard there can tell us something."

***

Connor Lomin dropped his saddlebags onto the bunk. "Not too many housing options in this town, but this will have to do."

Hlerv waved a hand. "Just good enough until tomorrow morning."

Eric flopped onto his own bunk. "Do you think the Captain of the guard will be satisfied with what we told him?"

Connor shrugged. "He let us stay in the barracks, didn't he? We should just be glad that he had extra space, with all the troops out on patrol."

Captain Jeffries seemed to accept their explanation well enough. The fact that they were all brevet sergeants in the employ of Lord Nolan of Forester helped, as did the letter of introduction. Connor sensed the captain wanted to ask more, particularly since they appeared to be such a diverse group: two humans, two half-elves, a gnome and a halfling.

Connor sat on the bed next to Andyn Eleandir and looked up at his companions. They looked nervous and unsure, just like him.

He didn't blame them. Their lives together seemed to be moving along a road designed by some unseen hand. They originally joined forces to fight the evil Ja'al cult near Dar's hometown of Forester, a straightforward goal. Now they rode winged horses, mounts so rare and so fast that the prices were beyond the means of most free-lance mercenaries and even some nobles.

Worse still, while battling the Ja'al, they found an ancient prophecy called The Song of the Grey Riders which seemed to predict many recent events in their lives. The most alarming verses told of a climactic battle between the Grey Riders and a Dark Rider. Now they knew that an undead sorceror-princess named Zhinia Margoth had designs on conquering the northlands and she had taken the name of "Dark Rider".

Sometimes it all just made Connor's head hurt, even this many weeks af-

7

ter the victory over the Ja'al at Whitehorse Peak. He found it hard to believe it was summer and autumn approached a few months away.

"It's giving me second thoughts about heading off to Evendale," Andyn Eleandir replied. "I mean, what if the Dark Rider shows up and attacks?"

Buck Bydecy shrugged, unrolling his blankets on his bunk. "There's no guarantee we'd be able to stop her even if we stayed."

They sat quietly for a while. All eyes turned to Dar.

Connor knew why. Somewhere in the wilderness near Evendale, near a place called Twinspire Mountain, lay the clues to the fate of Dar's grandparents who had disappeared when he was a boy.

And it just so happens that the path to Twinspire leads back through Evendale. One of the verses mentioned halflings, so off we go. Back to my family, to my past, to the graves of my wife and daughter.

Dar looked at his friends. "Still sure that my family mystery is the right path? I know that the Song says something about a halfling toy, but that doesn't mean it's in Evendale. We can divert to something more pressing, like stopping the Dark Rider's plans."

Eric shook his head. "There are too many questions that need answering and Evendale is the place we need to go. It's on the way to Shadow Lake and Twinspire Mountain. We can hit two goblins with one arrow."

"So how long do we stay in Athor?" Buck asked. "If we linger, it will be easier for spies to catch sight of us."

Andyn sighed. "I know it will sound odd, knowing how I like a hot bath and nice room, but we should push on right away, in the morning, early."

Hlerv rubbed his beard and rummaged in his backpack for a map. He unrolled it on his lap. "How far can we get in one day?"

Dar shook his head, looking at the map. "Even if we push it, we can't make Dwarfshire in a day. We spent too much time on the road this morning, looking for signs of Margoth's crew and then there was the battle with the Kaftu. We'll have to stop in North Corner and then get to Dwarfshire the next day."

"Unless we skip the towns and camp," Eric offered. "It would be faster and we can just go straight to Glen. The only reason we've been following the North road is so we can get information and now we have plenty of that."

Connor looked up at Eric. "That's a good idea. It's mostly farmland and small hamlets between here and the Evendale border. We won't have to worry so much about an ambush. But can Andyn do without a bath for a few days?"

Eric withheld a grin as their sole female companion shot Connor a look.

"It's not me I'm worried about," Andyn said tartly. "It's all of you. I thought I'd die when we were escaping the dark elves near Darlon, and not from combat, mind you. I should have just stood the lot of you upwind of the dark elves. They would have passed out for sure."

The men chuckled.

"You'll just have to stand it for a couple of days," Buck said with a homespun smile. "In exchange, you can lead us."

Andyn returned his smile. "Deal. On to Evendale."

Chapter Two- Homecoming

Andyn Eleandir reined in Medianox on the crest of the hill and breathed deeply of the summer air. She smelled grass, grain, herd animals, flowers and crops on that light breeze.

Rolling hills stretched away from her towards a city surrounded by a patchwork of farmland. Birds winged by, chirping. She saw a few wagons and riders heading in or out of the town via one of the four winding roads. In the center of the town, a neat arrangement of colored awnings encircled a marketplace. To her right, a stockyard bustled with activity in a cloud of dust. Late afternoon sunshine washed over the scene, casting deepening shadows. She even saw a clock tower near the square, next to an imposing structure which was likely the town hall.

"I like this. Just as I always imagined Evendale," she announced

Dar Cabot pulled Virasi to a halt next to her. He grinned. "What's not to like? Farmland, neat and orderly towns, peace and quiet. They may be on to something."

She smiled, looking down on the town of Glen. "It must have been hard for Connor to leave."

Dar turned in the saddle to look at the other Riders coming up behind them, his face more somber. "No, actually, Andyn, I think it was a relief."

Remembering Connor's tale of the death of his wife and daughter from a witch-plague, Andyn felt a pang of sadness.

"Well," she said, shaking the reins. "Let's make this a more positive homecoming."

She rode down the hill and onto the highway that headed into town from the south. The other Riders joined in behind her and they approached the town gate, two abreast.

As they melded into traffic (a couple of wagons and a rider or two), halflings stared at them with incredulous, wide eyes, whispering to each other. She nodded and smiled but kept looking forward.

At the gates, the town guards sized them up, not appearing aggressive but not loosening their hold on their spears either. One of them, a jolly-looking halfling with a scar running down the side of his face, stepped forward with a hand up.

"Now, I usually don't do this," he said, "But I have to ask your business in Glen, if only for the mounts you're riding."

Connor clattered up next to Andyn, his pegasus prancing. "Family reunion, Sergeant Kirtle."

The guard's mouth dropped open in amazement. "By the Hand of Irial! Connor Lomin! It's been a long time."

Connor smiled. "Which means it's high time I paid a visit."

"Well," the sergeant said, rubbing his chin, "You'll find not much has changed, unless it's the new children and the weddings since you left. You know the town rules well enough."

He motioned the other guards aside and they moved back, one or two of them nodding to Connor.

"Welcome home, Connor Lomin," Kirtle said as he stepped back.

Connor started to drop back towards his place in the line and Andyn stopped him. "Shouldn't you be leading?" she asked. "You're from this country. We're only guests."

He shook his head. "In halfling culture, it would look like I'm leading an armed band of foreigners. You lead. Go to the main square and turn right towards Temple Hill. My parents' home is just at the base of the hill."

More townsfolk came to see them as they rode down the main street. Andyn knew it was the pegasi that caused such a stir. Halflings were used to travelers. Connor had already told her that many free-lance sell-swords passed through Glen every year, either on their way to the wilderness beyond the borders or to more civilized areas in Terenai and Evendale. A pegasus, however, was a rare sight indeed.

To her surprise, she saw more than one building on Temple Hill. Along with the largest, dome-topped structure that had to be the Heather Temple of Irial, she saw an elegant, roofless ring of pillars surrounding a copse of trees that denoted a Verian chapel and, farther back, a blocky structure that looked like a Kurental shrine of the dwarves. She even thought she saw a druid's grove in the woods behind them all.

She turned to Dar with a smile. "Sorry, but it looks like your coreligionists aren't here."

He shrugged. "Father Ander told me there were only a few churches in Evendale, like in the capital, Lakeview. The Church makes allowances for those whose careers take them far from a parish. Besides, God understands."

The Heather Temple appeared not so much an imposing official edifice than a large, comfortable mansion. The grounds looked impeccable, with a manicured lawn, trimmed flowering bushes and shrubs, healthy trees, and a few statue-fountains of Irial heroes. The building itself was made of alternating sections of dark and light wood in a pattern that pleased her eyes. The dome curved above them in golden grandeur, ending with a box-like frame containing a suspended, burning flame.

Andyn liked it immediately.

"My parents' home is there," Connor said, pointing. "It's only a short walk to the temple."

"Convenient," remarked Hlerv.

Connor nodded. "It helps if you have approval from the town to put your home anywhere you want."

They rode around Temple Hill along the winding street to Connor's old home. Andyn gave the place a good once-over. A low, rambling structure painted white with dark blue trim, it stood in the shade of large fruit and maple trees.

The front door opened at their approach and a pair of halflings in their middle years came out to greet them. The Grey Riders dismounted.

Andyn saw the family resemblance. His mother had his fine, even features and dark hair, greying now. She wore a pure white robe with a heather-flower pattern at the hem, throat and shoulder-straps. A golden circlet glittered on her brow, marked with a symbol of Irial: a spinning wheel behind a crossed wheat sheaf and sickle.

She also saw Connor's features in his father: his dark eyes, muscular build and nimble step. The elder Lomin wore dark brown trousers, black boots and a loose-fitting white shirt.

The reaction from Connor's mother startled Andyn. At first, tears started in her eyes, then her jawline tightened. Then her expression became peaceful and benevolent.

Connor cleared his throat. "Mother, Father, I am returned to visit. I hope that I and my friends are welcome."

"Of course," said Connor's mother with a brilliant smile. "Any friends of yours are welcome, Connor."

She turned to regard the Riders. "I am Miriam. This is my husband, Seamus."

Andyn bowed as Connor introduced each of them in turn. For once, Buck didn't launch into his typical, grandiose introduction of himself and his pet. He took in everything with lazy grey eyes. He didn't even mention his pigeon, nestled in the hood of his cloak.

Seamus beckoned to them. "Welcome. Come inside. You must be tired from your journey."

Andyn patted Medianox on the nose. "Wait for me here, girl," she whispered, "Fear not. We are in a good place."

Connor's father led them to padded couches with a smile.

"Your appearance has caused quite a stir," he said, eyes watching Connor. "Pegasi are very rare."

"Yes, they are," Eric remarked before anyone else could say anything. "We were blessed to get them. We had to take several weeks of training just to learn how to control them and they take a bit of extra care, more than horses. These were held in the care of a dragon family for generations, but it's a long story."

"Of course," Seamus replied as he brought in a silver tray bearing fruit, small cakes and a ceramic pot that steamed with a pleasant, invigorating aroma.

He offered Andyn a cup of the steaming beverage and a tiny plate with a cake, some grapes and a small brown pear. She tasted from the cup. It was tea, a mildly stimulating variety with a hint of some kind of flower or fruit. Miriam asked questions of all of the Riders, playing the gracious hostess and including everyone in the conversation.

Andyn sipped the tea, watching the interplay between Connor and his parents. Her friend spoke respectfully enough, asked a few questions of his own, and seemed at ease, yet something was missing. Andyn felt a tension in the air.

Why? Was it his wife and child? I know his parents had their misgivings about Janey, but Connor said they eventually accepted her.

She took a bite of the cake, tasting hints of chocolate, blueberries and pecan. The halfling reputation for mastery of the kitchen came through instantly.

I'm going to gain weight here, I can see that coming.

With a start, she realized Miriam spoke to her. "You will be glad to know that Verian is well-represented here in Glen. The Orchard Temple is just there, on the lee side of the hill. I know the high priest myself, a very friendly and wise elf named Elethor."

"Thank you, priestess," Andyn replied. "I will make sure to pay my respects."

"How long will you be staying in Evendale?" Seamus asked Eric.

"Well, long enough to rest before heading out towards Twinspire Mountain. Since we were in the area, we decided to stop and let Connor visit."

"Twinspire?" Miriam frowned. "That is a dangerous area. Very uncivilized and wild. I daresay you will have an easier time of it if you can fly, and it seems that you are well-equipped as any group that has come through here recently."

She shot a worried glance at Connor. "Still, it is not going to be easy."

"You're right," said Dar, "We hope some of your folk might have information about the area, seeing as how it is not far from your northern border. We should also ask their advice to ensure we have the right supplies for the area in this time of year."

"A sound plan," Seamus agreed, setting down his own teacup. "We can discuss that after dinner tonight. I will inquire around in the meantime."

Miriam stood with another smile. "I am so glad to have met all of you. It is good to see that Connor is in good company and with such an obviously accomplished group. Connor can show you the guest rooms. Our son Brendan and his family will be with us tonight and they have young ones, so you might want to rest up. Deena and Darren are very energetic."

Andyn followed Connor to a guest room, neat and tidy with a small bed (she figured she could curl up into it if she turned just the right way), flowery window curtains, and polished wood furniture. She dropped her saddle bags in a corner and her backpack on the bed.

As she unpacked, she thought over the discussion at their arrival and wondered, both about Connor's family and their interactions with her companions.

For instance, as a rule, Hlerv never spoke to new acquaintances unless absolutely necessary. However, Miriam's habit of engaging everyone in conversation forced him into it and his response surprised Andyn. Although Hlerv only answered Miriam and Seamus in the most basic manner, offering nothing more than what was socially acceptable, he had better manners than Dar and Eric, both of whom had experience with nobility. As a gnome, Hlerv could claim both halfling and dwarven blood, yet he made no mention of his family background, only saying that he came from Oakmoor. Based on everything Andyn knew about the importance of family rankings and social connections in halfling society, this seemed very odd.

We all know Hlerv is hiding something about his past, and his family, but what? Hlerv is not a dwarf or halfling name.

She mulled this over as she removed her armor, changed into something more casual and arranged her clothes in the bureau.

One of the paintings on the wall caught her eye. It depicted the Lomin parents and sons in an earlier time in front of the home. She picked out Connor right away. They all smiled together, the picture of a happy family. Then she realized something.

Since arriving at his family home, Connor hadn't smiled once.

***

She could feel the trees moving in the wind as if she were one of them. Her senses became attuned to every bird in the air, every insect on the ground, every movement of the breeze. Though her eyes remained closed, with her inner sight she saw the hill outside and looked towards the nearby Heather temple. Late afternoon sunshine cast shadows that she could feel, not just see.

Andyn continued breathing deeply and slowly, feeling life and energy within her. The scent of leaves, flowers, grass, earth, and animals drifted to her, amplified by her meditation.

Following the sacred rubric, she centered her thoughts on the things nearest to her heart: her parents back home in Eleth-Anor, then her expectant sister and brother-in-law, her other siblings, then Dar, Eric, Connor, Buck and Hlerv, then the Alenar sisters off on their secret mission far to the south. Her mind drifted to the urgency of their own quest to unravel the Song of the Grey Riders, her worries for the people of these lands, her unease about the signs of rising evil they had seen and the specter of the Dark Rider.

These last thoughts clouded her mind and she forced herself to relax. She focused on the tiled floor underneath her, her hands on her knees, the air on her skin, the gentle breeze.

Letting out a deep breath, she offered it all to Verian and prayed his guidance and protection on them all.

She opened her eyes. A dark-haired elf with sea-green eyes smiled at her from his seat on a bench.

"Did you have any success with the meditation technique?" he asked.

She uncrossed her legs and sat with her hands over her knees. "Yes, in a way. I was able to focus better and feel Verian's Hand on creation around me. I could almost feel what nature was feeling, then, well…"

The elf nodded. "The cares of an itinerant priestess and missionary in the world are more complex than those of a temple priest in a quiet town. Do not be troubled, Priestess Eleandir. The fact that you were able to focus so well is a sign of the god's favor."

Andyn smiled wistfully and stood. "I have had few chances to visit a temple and pray lately. While it is true that there are fewer of our facilities in Deran, I have been very busy and worried and scattered."

Elethor, high priest of Verian's Orchard Temple, walked to her and took her hands. "That is not surprising. Just remember: Verian's voice is to be found in the quiet, not the clamor. Take time to remember that and all will be well. He aids those who are faithful."

She bowed low and pressed her lips to his hands. "I thank you for your kindness and instruction, High Priest. Praise Verian! Please include me and my friends in your prayers."

"Consider it done. Now, though I sense that I cannot ask for the reason for your visit, may I offer what assistance I can?"

Andyn straightened and looked out to the north, beyond Temple hill and towards the Evendale borders, not answering. She stood in silence for a while.

"What do you hear from the borders, High Priest? Are the lands of Evendale quiet?"

He stepped next to her, brow furrowed. "Yes and no. Here in Glen, all seems peaceful, though we have had a rash of burglaries recently. But from the borderlands?"

His voice trailed off.

She nodded. "Let me guess: raiders, unrest among the goblin tribes, Kaftu bandits, slavers, Ja'al or Vardish cults?"

He sighed. "Yes. And I fear something is coming, something dark and malevolent. My auguries to Verian tell me to be watchful and provide help to those who need it."

"Like me?"

He laughed. "Yes, like you, though you don't seem to need much."

She gazed out over the hills and fields, smelling the grass, trees and flowers.

"And what of the Lomin family?"

"Ah, that. Well, I could give you my perspective, but I have only been here for five years and much of what goes on in that family pre-dates me."

"Please enlighten me."

Elethor put both hands behind his back and looked out over the land. "You are doubtless aware that halflings place a premium on family lineage and heritage. In Connor Lomin's case, this is particularly important because of his mother's high position in the Church of Irial. Did you know that she is 6th in the line of authority to the High Patriarch of the entire religion? In any event, Connor's choice of a wife and the way he went about it were not viewed with great favor. As a matter of fact, I believe there was considerable friction between him and his parents on the manner of his relationship to Janey. Of course, after the child was born, all seemed better."

She nodded. "Then the witch plague."

"Yes, the Whispering Death. It caught everyone by surprise really, and opened the nation up to a considerable amount of trouble afterwards. Bandits have an instinct for weakness. When Connor's small family perished, some took it as a sign that Irial was trying to turn him along a different path and didn't approve of the union. I paid it no heed as spurious gossip, and deep down I think his mother was of a like mind, but it seems Connor held it against her that she didn't act forcefully enough in his support. They did not part on good terms."

Andyn nodded. "That is sad."

"It is also only my personal view of the way things stand. It would do you well to acquire other perspectives, if you feel inclined to dig further. It is obvious that Connor has a claim on your heart, as do your other friends."

She bit back tears, remembering their sacrifices to protect her in the torture chambers of the dark elves and their dogged determination to bring her husband's killer to justice. She still felt a pang of regret for all their sufferings, yet knew they would repeat it in an instant to save her. They were her friends and they loved her, each in their own way.

"They are like family."

Elethor smiled and took her hand, giving it a squeeze. "Then thank Verian for sending you such constant and true companions."

She brushed at her eyes.

"Now," said Elethor, releasing her hand and walking towards the altar, "what will you do?" He raised an eyebrow and began to lay out flowers on the altar.

"Well," she said, "We have to find something, a magical toy."

He stopped. "That is an unusual quest."

"It's in the prophecy I told you about."

"Ah. Well, magic toys are not exceedingly rare, but they are not common either. Any number of well-off families could have one. Do you know anything more, such as the age or function?"

"From the Esten Imperial Period and it flies."

He finished laying out the flowers. "That is very specific and rare indeed. Are you sure? If that is the case, you may be better off in Lakeview, the capital. There are scholars at the university who might help."

She nodded. "We knew it was going to be very difficult, but Glen was the place to start. We may have to search elsewhere. I just figured that since we were here already it was worth an attempt."

"Your hosts, then, may be the best source of information here in Glen," he replied. "Speaking of which, I see by the clock tower that it is almost time for you to return to meet your friends."

She looked at the tower and realized that it was nearly six. She bowed low to Elethor. "Then I take my leave of you, Honored One, with gratitude for your kindness and help."

Elethor returned the bow. "Serve Verian well and go in peace."

***

The other Riders arrived at almost the same time as she did. When she stepped up to the front door, almost all the daylight had fled. She hurried to the dining room to find not only a supper laid out on the table, but also Connor's brother and wife and two children as well. Then Andyn saw the warmth and affection she had expected earlier as Brendan Lomin and his wife Cerys greeted Connor with hugs. The two children, Darren and Deena, fairly hopped into his arms with big smiles and laughter.

Still Connor's mother and father stood apart, their smiles not matching the pain Andyn saw in their eyes.

Do they mourn their lost daughter-in-law and granddaughter still?

Connor introduced all his kinfolk to the Riders.

Little Deena, only six years old and a little more than a foot tall, held on-to Andyn's hand. "You can sit next to me, Mistress Eleandir. I can tell you everything about our house."

Charmed, Andyn gave her friends a quick smile and let herself be led to a seat next to the girl. Interestingly, there were larger-sized chairs at their end of the table, which had been adjusted to fit their heights by an ingen-ious set of latches and hinges.

Used to entertaining big folk.

The meal renewed her appreciation for halfling prowess in the kitchen.

Glazed roast pork, carrots, potatoes with herbs, crusty brown bread, honey, beans and leeks, green salad, roasted tomatoes, mellow cheeses, and plump sausages filled the table, accompanied by crystal decanters of dark and light wines. Andyn took care to sample and comment on everything but not stuff herself: halfling desserts were legendary. Deena chattered away, telling her the names of each recipe and asking all kinds of questions about magic and flying horses. Andyn made sure to answer every one.

She saw the shining excitement in Deena's eyes and felt a pang in her heart.

I so wanted to have children with Larad.

"Grandmama is a healer," Deena said, "Are you a healer too?"

"Yes, I am," said Andyn, wiping the corner of her mouth with a napkin. "I am also a mage. But there are others of us who can heal, though they are new at it."

"Who?" asked Deena, craning her neck to look at the other Riders.

With a smile, Andyn nodded at Dar and Eric. "Those two. As scout-rangers, they have to learn some healing in order to take care of people lost and hurt in the wild places. When we were in Darlon recently, they received some training."

Overhearing her, Eric smiled at Deena. "So, if you get a cut on your knee or sprain your ankle or have a bad headache, I'm your man. If it's anything more than that, ask Andyn."

Deena smiled back.

"Everything is so fresh," Dar commented.

"Yes," said Miriam. "It is. On that score, we cannot claim any racial art or advantage. Much of our harvests are kept safe through a Preservation spell, pioneered by Melinor Indidarc, I believe."

Seamus Lomin looked at Eric. "Any relation?"

Eric nodded. "Adoptive father. He found me as an orphan on the streets and raised me."

Miriam made as if to speak, but then only smiled and took a sip of wine. *She knows something.*

Andyn watched Eric, now engaged in an animated conversation with Darren. He gave no sign.

Andyn knew Eric lied about being an orphan. His blood-parents still lived, master and mistress of an assassin's guild named the Crossed Swords. These were the very same assassins who had been hired to kill Larad Fallbrook, Andyn's husband, many years ago.

How much does Miriam really suspect?

Andyn expected at least some comment, but Miriam said nothing, instead chatting with Hlerv about the local shops, especially the herbalist and the magic shop, which seemed to pique his interest.

Connor spoke mostly to Brendan or Cerys, not to his parents.

"So, tell us about these pegasi of yours," Seamus said to Dar as Cerys brought out the pie and teapots.

Andyn listened, taking a slice of peach and a slice of berry pie for herself with a cup of lemony-scented tea.

"It's straightforward, really," said Dar, "A cleric of the Ja'al cult found an ancient scroll telling him that a herd of battle-trained pegasi were somewhere in the region of Forester in Deran, my hometown. He set out to find them, razing a hamlet in the process. We came upon the ruins and were commissioned by Lord Nolan Hanford of Forester to find the perpetrators. By the time we found the pegasi in the charge of a gold dragon named Iron Thunder, the cleric had also kidnapped two dragonlings who were Iron Thunder's grandchildren. We freed the dragons and got the pick of the herd in exchange."

"I see," said Seamus.

"What happened to the rest of the pegasi?" asked Brendan in a soft voice.

That's right. Connor said Brendan had survived the Whispering Plague. Andyn had heard that survivors could not raise their voices and sometimes had trouble speaking.

"In the Royal Air Force of Deran," said Eric. "Instead of buying the herd outright, the Crown gave us riding training."

Miriam's eyes widened. "How many were in the herd?"

"Over forty."

Seamus' eyes flickered to his wife for a second. "That is quite a number."

"We're just glad we have ours," said Buck, wiping his mouth. "They're not much use in bad weather but otherwise, we do just fine."

"Which leads me to my next question," said Seamus, setting down his cup. "You said you wanted to go to Twinspire. I don't have any information here, but a friend of mine down the road is a retired sell-sword himself and might have maps. I spoke to him earlier and he'd be delighted to show you what he has. Shall we go now?"

The meal finished, Dar and Buck exchanged a look and nodded.

"No time like the present," said Buck, rising and taking care not to hit his head on the chandelier.

"Coming with us, Andyn?" Hlerv asked as he rose. "I'm going to see that magic shop Mrs. Lomin told us about."

She felt a sudden tiredness. Maybe it was seeing children and regretting her lack of them, or maybe the comfort of a home, but she didn't want any part of adventures or intrigues tonight.

"I think I'll stay here and entertain Darren and Deena, if that is okay, Mister Lomin."

Seamus smiled at her. "It is an excellent idea. They would be bored within a few minutes anyway."

"Would you like that?" Cerys asked her children, who both nodded, eyes shining.

"Can you tell us stories of your adventures?" asked Deena.

For an instant, memories surged to the surface: the bodies of massacred villagers at Westhaven, the torture chambers of the Dark Elves, a raging hell-spawn bear, and a hamlet ravaged by a frost dragon. She felt a chill.

Not those stories.

She smiled at the little girl. "How about an exchange? I tell you one of the tales of our adventures and you bring me some of your favorite story books and I can read to you."

Deena and Darren raced off.

Brendan grinned. "It appears this will work out just fine."

***

Hlerv spread the map out on the table, following the dim lines carefully. He peered at the column of letters and numbers along the right margin, trying to make out the words.

"This is kind of faded," he noted.

"Aye, that's true," said the portly halfling across the table. "Most of them are, unfortunately. It was a long time ago and we didn't have access to the kinds of papers and vellums you have nowadays."

"These are fine, Mister Wallstone," said Dar. "We realize it's hard to keep these in good condition over the years."

"Yes," said Eric with a slight frown at Hlerv. "We're glad you have them at all."

Hlerv looked up at them and withheld comment.

They show the elevation lines and locations readily enough, but the notes are really what make this useful to us and that's what's most faded. Probably used the maps for wrapping fish or something after he retired.

From what he saw, getting up to the entrance to the fortress would be a tall order. The elevation lines and marked flights of steps indicated a very steep approach, something for which the pegasi would be ill-suited.

Seamus and Brendan Lomin brought a couple of more scrolls to the table.

"Maybe these will show something different," said Connor's father.

Hlerv had his doubts. Kirk Wallstone had led a free-lance group about forty years ago, before Andareth Faldanor and the Four Silvers had made their more famous venture to the area. Much could have changed in the intervening time.

What we really need are Faldanor's records, but good luck getting those. We should have asked for them when we were in Deran. Maybe Melinor could have pulled some strings with the Faldanors.

He held his comments in reserve as the Riders pored over the records. Connor, Dar and Eric took notes of their own, making copies of various pages and logbooks.

Hlerv finally looked up and decided he had enough.

"Well, it seems like everything is in hand here," he remarked. "Mister Lomin, where did you say the magic shop was?"

Seamus looked up at him, face shadowed in the lamp light. "Oh, it's very simple to find," he said, "Go down the road towards my home and turn right at the first street. It's called the Glen Emporium and Apothecary."

Hlerv picked up his shoulder bag. "I'll see you back at the house then."

Without a backward glance, he left, following the route Seamus had described. In the deepening twilight, he passed homes and neat shops with colorful signs advertising their wares. Halflings either nodded or eyed him as he walked along the street. Knowing halfling society, word of the Grey Riders probably made the rounds through the whole of Glen within an hour of their arrival.

The Emporium wasn't hard to find. A drab-looking building with clean windows and a sign with a mortar and pestle marked the destination.

A magical lamp flared briefly as he entered. A middle-aged halfling with a monocle and tiny mustache smiled at him.

"Welcome to the Emporium! I'm George Farfan."

"Fair evening to you, sir," Hlerv replied, making sure to be polite. "Seamus Lomin told me I could find magic items here."

Farfan's eyes grew a little wider. "Oh really? You're a friend of the Lomins?"

"Their son, Connor, is a colleague."

"Ah yes, we all took note of his arrival this afternoon," said Farfan. Hlerv noticed his eyes now became a bit wary. "Well, always glad to help a friend of that most respectable of families. Is there something in particular you're looking for?"

Hlerv shrugged. "I'm not sure. Do you mind if I browse a bit?"

Farfan waved a hand at the store. "Be my guest."

Shelves between the windows held neat rows of items and glass cases on the side walls displayed more items, some of them glittering with magical light. He saw components for advanced spells, some mundane jewelry items enchanted to look magical, a collection of rings in a locked case, wands, scrolls and an entire set of shelves dedicated to potions.

Every doodad, curiosity, gewgaw and bit of magical paraphernalia in this part of Evendale gathered under one roof.

Behind Farfan, another, more expansive glass case spanned almost the entire back wall of the store, broken only by a small door. This case held everything from small swords to bucklers, bags, cloaks, staves and belts, all carefully labelled.

I could look in here for weeks, mused Hlerv.

He took his time, strolling among the items. A clock on the wall ticked slowly in the quiet shop. He examined the items tagged as magical as well as the more mundane items of the apothecary's trade. He left the medicinal rack alone. That was more Andyn's domain than his. However, his eyes lit up when he saw a rack of spices and herbs by the main counter.

He carefully picked out what he needed: black pepper, hot pepper, cinnamon and ground cloves. He hesitated, seeing the essence of swampberry, then picked up a pouch of that as well.

He brought his items to the counter and Farfan smiled at him.

"Will that be all?"

Hlerv's eyes roamed over the items in the case behind the proprietor and lit on one of the bags.

"What is that?" he asked, pointing.

"Eh? Oh, a very special item, that." Farfan moved to the case, did something his hands out of sight. The glass vanished.

Impressive!

Farfan took out the bag and gave it to him. "It's a Quartermaster's Bag. In this form it can hold the contents of, say two large fruit bowls. If you say the keyword, it will shrink in size to no larger than a coin purse, with the contents preserved in exactly the same condition as when they were placed inside."

"Watch," he said. He picked up one of the helmets in the display case and slipped it inside, then whispered a word. The bag instantly shrank down to one tenth its former size. He whispered again and it returned to its original size. Farzan reached inside and pulled out the helmet.

"You see? Perfectly fine." He replaced the helmet.

"Fascinating." Hlerv held out a hand and examined the bag carefully. "How much?"

"Well," George Farfan said, stroking his chin. "Normally, it runs about fifteen hundred, but for a friend of the Lomins I could let you have it for thirteen five."

Hlerv handed it back to him, making sure to keep an impressed expression on his face. "Wow. That's a lot of money. Far too much for me, I'm afraid. But I'll take these."

Farfan nodded, placing the bag into the case but not reinstalling the glass front. He made notes on a pad and wrapped Hlerv's spices in brown paper and tied it up.

"Twenty-five silver."

Hlerv paid him, looking at the bag again. "You don't see too many of those, I suppose."

"Oh, no, we don't. It came from Mister Wallstone. Relic of his wandering days, I expect."

"Well," said Hlerv with a smile. "Thank you. It was nice to meet you."

He put his hand on the doorknob.

"Are you sure you don't need the Quartermaster's Bag?" asked Farfan.

Hlerv turned around with a wistful expression. "I'm sure I will need it at some point, but we have a long journey ahead of us and we have to get more supplies. I'll see you on my return trip."

He knew full well the thoughts running through Farfan's mind right now. How much could he get? How badly did Hlerv need it? What were the odds of him returning? How much did he pay Wallstone for it? How many other free-lancers would come through Glen in the next year, and how many would need such a thing? Most sell-swords wanted armor, weapons, wands: things that made enemies hurt and scored victories. A magic bag was not much in demand.

Hlerv opened the door as if to go.

"A moment, Mister…?"

"Hlerv."

"Ah, yes, um, Hlerv. Perhaps I can make a special discount since you are a friend of Connor's. I treated his wife and daughter before their unfortunate deaths, you know, so I know the family well."

"Really?" asked Hlerv with raised eyebrows. "I didn't know that."

"Yes, yes, well, I did. I could save some of the people, you understand, but a magically-induced plague, well, that's tough for anyone."

"Of course," said Hlerv, nodding. "Your city isn't so very large, so you would have had to fend for yourself, and that's not easy to do with so many falling ill. The town has you to thank for saving many lives."

Farfan blinked and then ducked his head. "Well, thank you for saying so, Mister Hlerv. That's very kind of you. But as to the Quartermaster's Bag, what do you say to twelve hundred?"

Hlerv made a face, pretending to calculate. "Let me think. Well, that would make it too tight. Not enough margin for error, you know. How about a thousand?"

Farfan hemmed and hawed. "Well, how about we split the difference? Eleven hundred?"

Hlerv pretended to think for a long time, then opened his belt purse and sifted through the coins in it. He pulled out another purse and made a show of counting again.

"Well, I think I could get my companions to reimburse me a bit since we'll all see the benefit. All right, Mister Farfan, you have a deal."

The proprietor beamed. "Excellent. You will see the value of this, I'm certain."

I already do.

Hlerv took out the coins, using an assortment of platinum ingots (a few), platinum imperials (a few more), a sizable number of gold crowns, a few excellent-quality garnets and amethyst, and a fistful of silver disks.

Farfan counted them carefully and used a jeweler's loupe to assess the gems. Satisfied, he handed the bag to Hlerv.

The gnome nodded to him and put the item into his shoulder bag.

"Oh, I almost forgot," said Farfan. "Here's the keyword. Don't forget it." He handed over a slip of paper.

Hlerv read the activation word and committed it to memory.

"I won't. And thank you again, Mister Farfan. It was a privilege to meet you."

The shopkeep smiled and nodded to him as he left. "Give my regards to the Lomin family."

Hlerv breathed deeply of the night air as he strode down the street back towards Wallstone's house, feeling smugly satisfied. He knew many things about business and prices and supply and demand, particularly in magical items. A Quartermaster's Bag in a large city would run almost eighteen hundred gold coins, and he had one for almost half that price. An excellent acquisition.

Yes, most excellent.

Handor Lervion, displaced heir to the fortune of the Lervion Mercantile Company of Meridian, Gorostol, smiled to himself and patted his shoulder bag as he walked down the darkening streets of Glen.

***

"Well," said Andyn, putting down the story books. "Those are certainly exciting. I can see why your Uncle Connor became a free-lance."

"Yes!" exclaimed Darren, jumping up and posing as a warrior. "I'm going to be one too when I grow up."

"Ha!" retorted Deena with a toss of her head. "I can still whip you."

To forestall any fisticuffs, Andyn took both their hands and used her most winning smile.

"I'd very much like to see some of the other things you were talking about," she said.

"I can show you my dollies and my drawings!" Deena said excitedly. She ran off down a nearby hallway.

Darren nodded. "I can show you my flitter and my sword and shield!" He ran off after his sister.

A flitter? I wonder what that is.

Andyn sat quietly at the table. Her eyes roamed over the comfortable furniture, vases with flowers, and wooden bookcases. Magical lamps glowed, casting light that made burnished brass and copper seem as if they were aflame.

This is all I ever really wanted: home and hearth and children. Now I'm a free-lance mage and healer, pursued by prophecies and an undead sorceress, of all things. Will I ever have this for real?

She finished her tea, hearing the distant scuffling sound of the children searching for their items. She smiled.

Deena returned with an assortment of dolls under one arm and a folder under the other. She told Andyn all about the dolls, their names and their families, and then pictures she had drawn of them.

One picture in particular stood out. It looked like a cube with a stick coming out of one side. Protruding from the top of the cube was what looked like a shaft topped by four narrow leaves attached perpendicular to the shaft. It made it look rather like a four-petalled flower grew out of the top of the cube. Deena had colored it brown but surrounded it with yellow and gold rays.

"What's this?" she asked.

"Oh that! That's the flitter. Darren and I play with it sometimes."

"Yes!" exclaimed Darren, rushing into the room. "Here it is."

He set down a wooden sword and shield and then a small box. He pulled off the box top and held up an object that looked a lot like the thing in Deena's picture.

Andyn's senses prickled. "May I see that?"

It was indeed a cube of wood. A thick rod protruded from one of the side panels. There were a trio of small holes in one side of the rod, facing her, but none on the other side. On the top face, another rod connected to the four leaf-shaped blades. The whole assembly looked worn and at one time had been covered in a yellowish or gold paint, now mostly faded.

"How interesting," she breathed.

"Yeah," said Darren, picking up his sword and shield. "My Grandpa gave that to me for Winterfest when I was little."

Andyn centered herself for a spell to scan for magic, then made a small circle in the air with her fingers.

"Who gave it to your grandfather?"

Darren shrugged. "I don't know."

Andyn's spell went off. The toy flared bright gold, so bright that she gasped.

"Wow," said Deena. "It's never done that before!"

Chapter Three- Gathering Storm

Megan Alenar looked up as her aunt approached their campfire. "Anything?"

"Lanterns on the road," Daphne Alenar said, nodding. "A couple of wagons."

"Any outriders?"

Daphne shook her head. "None that I could see. It's getting late and I don't think they'll make it to the next town, so I'm sure we'll meet them here."

Megan knew the trail custom: any campfire could be shared along the highway and those who set it first were obligated to welcome any newcomers — as long as those newcomers posed no threat and made no attack.

She unrolled her blankets and sat back against a log. "It will be nice to meet someone on the trail."

Her sister, Brandawyn, smiled. She sat on another log and stirred a pot of stew suspended over the flames. A tiny silver cross sparkled in the firelight from a chain around her neck.

"Riding flying horses in the sky doesn't lend itself well to meeting people, does it?" she said.

Stephen Alenar rose from his seat and headed beyond their camp, towards the sheltering trees where two black winged horses cropped grass. He clucked to them and gently led them back into the shadows, so only their heads and necks showed in the firelight.

"Suspicious?" Megan asked him.

"Cautious," he replied, placing his recurve bow and quiver in easy reach.

Daphne sat at the campfire, facing towards the road and away from the flames, careful not to look into their dancing light. Stephen sat on a log so that he, too, looked away from the flames into the deepening evening. He made a small, looping motion with his right hand and it glowed for a second.

Megan recognized the detection spell. She sat back, making an effort to listen to the wind in the trees overhead.

Just a precaution, she told herself. *Don't be so jumpy.*

"These two have a future, brother," Daphne said to Stephen, sniffing the aroma of Brandi's cooking. "We won't starve with them around."

Stephen just smiled.

Megan's stomach rumbled. "Brandi sure does. This is the third stew we've had and they've all been different and delicious."

Brandi laughed. "It's just some salt pork, herbs and dried vegetables."

"It's chemistry," replied Daphne.

Megan heard the jingle of harness from the road. Her aunt and uncle slid ever so slightly towards their weapons. Her hand crept to her belt, fingering the magic silver dagger given to her by Dar Cabot, so many months ago. Brandi appeared unconcerned, dipping into the stew to taste it.

"Hello, the fire!" called out a male voice.

Daphne and Stephen stood as two wagons drew into view. Large, four-wheeled conveyances with domed roofs, they rumbled along the road into the firelight on muddied wheels. They bore no device or symbol that would mark them as merchants or artisans of a particular stripe, though Megan saw branches of rosemary strung along the sides. Megan counted two men on each wagon, one driver and one crossbowman.

"Greetings!" called Daphne. "Where are you bound?"

"Shark Bluff," responded the driver of the first wagon. A dark-haired, solid-looking fellow, he wore leather armor and had a sword at his side. "We have a load of herbs to deliver to the waterfront."

"It's a long way to the bluffs from here," Stephen said, gesturing southwards. "It's already dark. You are welcome to share our fire."

The crossbowman's eyes flickered over all of them, lingering on Megan and Brandi. He looked at the driver.

The driver gave a broad smile. "It's not quite dark yet, and we need to make all the distance we can. A lot of money riding on our delivery, you know. Thanks all the same. Any word of conditions to Shark Bluff?"

Daphne sat back down on the log, near her bow. "Clear as far as we could tell. A road-warden patrol passed by a while ago and told us of hobgoblin bandits the closer you get to the ocean, but if you have numbers you're in no danger."

The driver nodded. "Much obliged." He clicked his tongue at the draft horses and shook the reins and the wagons headed down the road.

Megan dipped a bowl of stew for herself and watched the wagons from under her eyelashes as they drove away. Two additional men sat on the tailgates of the wagons, armed with maces and short spears.

Her heart began to beat a little faster.

She tried to calm herself and tasted the stew, redolent with the flavors of onions, carrots, sage, wine, pepper and sea salt.

Brandi is definitely better at this than I am.

"Well?" asked Brandi, sitting back against a boulder with a hunk of bread and a bowl. Her eyes looked sharp, like gemstones, in the firelight.

"How much did you pay for the herbs and spices back in Tol Divven?" asked Daphne.

"Four silver."

"Doesn't seem that much in demand based on that price," Daphne mused.

They ate in silence. Megan watched her older relatives as she finished dinner.

"Roads are dry," remarked Stephen, picking up his wineskin. "But their wheels were muddy. They've been off road recently, maybe to avoid the road wardens."

"Could be," replied Daphne.

"And that's a lot of weaponry for herb merchants. The tailgaters were wearing brigandine, as I recall. The drivers both had magical weapons, plus the doors at the back of the wagons are warded."

"And one of them came back to watch us from the brush after they turned the corner," said Brandi. "He's gone now."

Daphne and Stephen exchanged a look.

"Good eyes, Brandi," said Stephen.

Brandi gave him a little smile. "You're not the only one with magic spells. What do you think?"

"Slavers?" asked Daphne.

Stephen nodded. "Vipers, most likely. Wagons looked heavy. Rosemary has a strong scent, to hide any giveaway smells."

Megan felt her stomach clench.

"They have slaves then."

Daphne stood. She picked up her bow and tested the string. "Not for long."

"We'll need to surprise them," Brandi said.

"We have the advantage of aerial observation," Stephen replied.

From under her tunic and armor, Daphne drew out a small medallion on a chain. She placed it on the ground.

"Paractus," she said.

The medallion glowed and warped grew in size until a huge owl stood in its place blinking in the firelight. It towered over all of them. A double-saddle of dark leather sat on its back.

Daphne patted the construct on the side. "I'll be back in a little while." She climbed up into the front seat of the saddle and gave a low whistle. Paractus hopped up and beat his wings, rising from the ground. The pair disappeared with only a muffled whisper of feathered wings.

They didn't have long to wait. She returned just as the others finished packing up.

"There's a camp, about two hundred feet from the road, in an area of dense forest." She leaned down to accept a pair of saddlebags from Stephen. "It's about a quarter of a mile from here."

Megan nodded, swinging up into the saddle on Larinor. Without any further conversation, Stephen vaulted into the seat behind Daphne. Two pegasi and a giant owl soared into the night sky.

Megan shifted to night vision as they flew. The construct didn't give off a lot of heat, but Daphne and Stephen did. Soon, they spiraled down to the ground and landed in a meadow near a thickly wooded area.

"Wait here." Daphne slipped away to scout and returned after a short time.

"I saw an emblem on one of them. They're Vipers all right," she whispered. "Good call, brother."

She said. "We need shielding. Brandi?"

Brandi nodded and moved her open hands in front of her body, facing towards the slaver camp. She murmured soft words. Megan felt a gust of air, then a steady breeze. Now when she looked towards the slaver camp, a screen of moving air wafted between them. She only saw a faint glitter and no people.

Megan created a tiny mage-light in her hand with a word and watched as Daphne used a stick to map the area in the dirt.

"They have two guards watching towards the road and two watching the forest to the west. The wagons are here and here. Of the other four, two are watching the slaves while the two drivers are sitting next to a wagon, looking over a map."

"How many slaves?" asked Brandi.

"A lot," said Daphne with a grim look. "I counted at least twenty, men, women and children. They're roped together at the ankles. All stripped naked to prevent them escaping."

Megan felt her anger stirring.

Stephen stroked his goatee. "Only four guards and not watching all approaches."

"Did we fool them that badly?" asked Brandi. "I don't think so."

Her uncle nodded. "Magical protection is my guess, which means one of them is a sorcerer, probably one of the drivers. We'll have to coordinate this well. I have a plan."

He explained his thoughts and gave assignments to each of them. They decided to use their aerial advantage and loop around to the north, across the road and then back again, ending up on the opposite side of the camp.

They reached their destination quickly. She followed instructions, landing Larinor and slipping to the earth. She whispered to her pegasus and sent him into a thicket with Brandi's Amicus to await their return.

Megan took a deep breath to calm herself, running through her spells and battle plan in her mind.

Brandi waited until they were all together, then placed a silencing spell on a rock and slipped it into her pocket. Megan added a few protective spells of her own: one to automatically heal, one to protect against charms and beguiling and one to defend against evil magic. The four Alenars crept through the woods towards the light of the slaver camp, following Daphne's lead. Megan remembered her aunt's admonition to step slowly and carefully and feel the ground before putting her weight down.

They reached the edge of the camp with only a few waving branches and disturbed sticks to mark their passage. Brandi stepped back four paces and laid down the silencing rock.

Megan kept an eye on the slaves. Just as Daphne said, they crouched on the ground, sharing bits of bread and cups of water. Ropes bound them together at the ankles. She counted five men, seven women and eight children. The black-haired slaver who had spoken to them at their camp sauntered to the other side of a wagon.

Her heart pounded in her chest. *Remember the plan.*

Stephen stood up at the edge of the firelight and held his hands out, then shouted an arcane word. Green and purple symbols on the ground flared bright colors, then vanished.

The slaver guards whirled towards them, shouting in alarm. One with a crossbow raised his weapon and then dropped with two of Daphne's arrows in his chest. Brandi leaped into the camp, twin swords out, heading for the slaves. A pair of guards raced to intercept her. Daphne drew her blade and joined Brandi.

Megan waited for her chance.

Stephen charged in. A guard intercepted him and they thrust and parried, blades ringing in the night. The black-haired slaver came around the wagon at a run. He began chanting and lifted his arms—just what Megan was waiting for.

She rose from hiding and mimicked his motions, but in reverse, to unwind the spell. A glittering net of razor wire materialized in the air over Stephen. She focused her power and it dissipated, falling to a harmless silvery mist on the ground.

The slaver spat a vulgar curse at her and made a quick motion with his hand. A trio of fire-darts lanced out at her. They detonated on her magic shields with sharp cracks and she flinched. Two guards raced towards her.

She made an intricate motion with her hands, then thrust them out at her sides with a whispered word. The air whirled and danced and an impenetrable cloud of silver-grey fog spun around her. She raced forward without waiting as the slavers charged in. She heard them stumble over each other and fall, shouting obscenities.

Megan made a beeline for the slaves and their constricting rope, her magic dagger out. Brandi withdrew her swords from the falling body of a guard and ran to join her.

One of the slave women waved her hands frantically. "No! Look out for the rope!"

The black-haired wizard slaver laughed and motioned with his hand. The ropes grew longer and animated. They coiled and writhed, glowing with magical power. Megan gasped and jerked backwards, her dagger slashing out. Brandi cut into one rope but it looped over her and wound around her waist. The slaves struggled with their own bonds, which seemed to have taken on a great weight.

Megan tried to dodge but a rope caught her arm and pinned it to her side. Another wound around her chest and squeezed. She screamed, feeling the crushing force.

"Oppose the Vipers and die!" shouted the wizard. He began another incantation.

Spots danced before Megan's eyes. She fought for breath.

A figure in armor with a bright sword leaped at the slaver. A blade flashed once.

The headless wizard keeled over and hit the ground. The ropes slackened and went limp.

"You mean 'Join the Vipers and die'," retorted Stephen as he charged off to help Daphne.

Megan gasped with relief and joined her sister in slashing through the ropes. One of the children suddenly screamed and pointed behind them.

The two other guards had found their way free of Megan's cloud trap and hurled spears at them.

Megan fired off a Storm Force spell and it shattered both missiles on their way in. Brandi charged to meet them. The slavers swung maces at her, but she blocked one and dodged the other. Not stopping her motion,

Brandi swung twice, cutting one in the leg and the other in the arm. She whirled, banging aside their attacks and spun, sweeping one off his feet with her outstretched leg. She continued moving, burying a blade to the hilt in the other guard's chest.

The remaining guard leaped to his feet. Megan shot him with fire-darts of her own. Three acorn-sized comets struck him with sharp cracks, hurling him backwards to lie in a smoking heap.

Brandi and Megan turned back-to-back, looking for more enemies.

"Surrender!" commanded Daphne to the lone remaining slaver.

He merely laughed. "I die either way, bitch!" He hurled himself at her and Stephen ran him through.

Stillness fell on the glade, except for the crackling of flames and Megan's thundering heartbeat, which she felt sure everyone in range could hear.

"Well done," said Stephen, wiping his blade in a slaver's shirt.

Megan let out a deep breath.

***

"Widmer's Corner?" asked Megan. She had never heard of the place.

"Yes," said one of the men, tightening the cord on the breeches he had looted from a dead slaver. "It's about ten miles off the main road, north of here by about half a day's ride."

Megan thought back to what she had seen as they travelled the main highway of Gorostol, trying to remember a small hamlet. She recalled a few, but the location didn't jump out at her.

"There's no one there now," said a grey-haired woman, briskly buttoning up the shirt she had taken from another slaver. "They took everyone, all twenty-five of us."

"Twenty-five?" asked Daphne. She looked at the former slaves, picking through the various packs, boxes and containers to find clothing or shoes. "There are only twenty here."

"That's it exactly," said the man, a dignified-looking gentleman who could have been an acrobat in his younger days. "They took the youngest and most attractive away in a separate wagon, heading due west from us, I believe."

"When did all this happen?" asked Brandi, helping one of the smaller children roll up the cuffs of pants too big for him.

"Yesterday morning," replied the woman. "They came to Widmer's Corner pretending to be merchants on their way to Terenai, but killed our town constable and took the mayor prisoner before dawn. When we woke up, most of the men were already captured."

"Who's missing?" Megan asked.

"Two lads and three young ladies. All under the age of twenty but over twelve. Noah, Jason, Amber, Miriam and Cathy."

Megan caught Daphne's eye. Even a day later, she could track the slavers easily.

"Can you make it back to Widmer's Corner from here on your own?" Daphne asked.

The man nodded. "Yes. With the wagons and horses and food, it will not be long before we're home."

"Well," said Stephen, striding over to one of the wagons, "Let's get you on your way. My companions and I will need to get some rest before we start tracking the slavers."

"Do you think you can find them?" asked the grey-haired woman. She looked very worried.

Stephen smiled, but only with his mouth. "Without a doubt."

Chapter Four- Enigma in Bones

"They're not far ahead."

Daphne Alenar stood and brushed off her gloved hands. She indicated a thin track heading off towards the seashore.

Megan looked, shielding her eyes from the sunshine. The trail led through scrub brush towards the GreatSea. She smelled the salty air and heard seagulls call.

"Do you think they just loaded them onto a boat and left?" she asked.

Daphne shrugged. "I don't know this part of Gorostol that well, so anything is possible. But they move much slower than we do and they have unwilling prisoners."

Brandi leaned on her saddle horn. "Do you think we could see them from the air? Why don't we just fly up and take a look?"

Stephen shook his head. "Our mounts are unusual, to say the least. They'd be warned of pursuit and might do something stupid, like kill the slaves in order to prevent capture, then scatter into the wilds."

Megan had to admit he had a point. The pegasi made a distinctly noticeable silhouette in the sky, but Daphne's mount? Well, if flying horses attracted attention, an owl that stood nine feet tall at the head certainly would.

Daphne walked back to the owl, a majestic, grey-and-white barn owl, and gently stroked its wing.

Though Megan knew the giant bird was only an extremely advanced magical construct, she couldn't shake the feeling that it understood everything, especially when it looked at her with those impassive eyes.

"As a matter of fact," Daphne said, taking a silver necklace out of her shoulder bag, "we won't need him any more today since we're in open land with no trees and he can easily be seen. He's done his part to help us catch up this far."

Daphne held out her palm and touched the owl on the forehead.

"Paractus!" she commanded. The owl's form glowed and then warped and shrank until only a small medallion lay on the damp earth. Daphne scooped it up and slipped the silver necklace through a hole in the top, then looped it over her head. She popped the medallion down inside her armor.

Megan looked at her intently. "I've always wondered. Why an owl?"

Daphne smiled. "I like owls. Actually, I can command the pendant to be any bird, like a hawk or sparrow or seagull, but the giant owl form is the largest and most useful for me. Besides, he can travel at night, which is a distinct advantage."

"Should we send the pegasi away as well?" Brandi asked.

Stephen pursed his lip and looked at Daphne. "Well, sister? How far ahead are they?"

Daphne picked up her bow. "Not more than a couple of hours. We can move faster since they have prisoners. It's probably a good idea to send Amicus and Larinor away now. They can find cover in the woods behind us."

Megan dismounted and removed her shoulder bag from her saddle bags, then filled it with items she thought she'd need, including medicine, food and a few articles of clothing from the bandit camp for the kidnap victims.

"Okay Larinor," she said, kissing her pegasus on the nose. "Be safe. I'll call for you."

The winged horse tossed its head and nickered softly. Megan stood back and raised her hand over her head. She pointed skyward and made a wide circle, then thrust her pointing finger at the sky. Larinor backed up, then cantered off to the right and beat his wings, gathering speed and soaring off towards the forest. Amicus followed.

Megan didn't worry about them. No flying beast alive could match the speed of a pegasus. Both would return to them at special signals from their mistresses. Megan used a spiraling purple mage-flame that she shot up into the air.

Daphne took the lead, following the trail through the brush. Occasionally she stopped to inspect a branch or root, then led them on. The land sloped downwards towards the sea. The brush thinned until the terrain gave way to sandy dunes with tufts of tall grass.

Daphne halted them, kneeling to stare at the sand for a while.

Megan waited.

"Did she lose the trail?" she whispered to Brandi.

Her sister shook her head. "Not likely. Aunt Daphne can track a toad in a stream."

Daphne stood. "That way, south along the shoreline."

They followed Daphne through the dunes. Megan watched carefully on all sides. It wouldn't be above slave traders to have someone—or something— guard their back trail.

Their path led down to the firmer sand near the sea, then back around to a higher, rocky cliff jutting out from the land.

Daphne made them wait while she scouted. Megan sat behind a dune, glad for the cooler ocean air to take away some of the late-morning heat. She tried not to fidget. She loved the ocean, but with their current mission and the sense of urgency in finding the kidnap victims, she felt too fidgety and tense to enjoy it.

Daphne jogged back to them. "Well," she said, "they stopped for some reason near the point where the cliff meets the water, next to the rocks. I see boot tracks there. They held some barefoot people, probably the kidnapped youths, away from the rocks about thirty feet, then came back and led them towards the water."

"Did they get into a boat or something?"

Daphne bit her lip. "I'm not sure. We should check it out but the fact that they moved the slaves back away from the rocks means they're avoiding something."

Stephen hefted his backpack. "Then we follow the way they went. And I'll see if I can figure out what's special about the outcropping."

Megan followed the others as they stepped through the shallows. Stephen made the same looping hand gesture he had used back at the camp and stopped them.

"There's a magical symbol etched in the stone, just there. No wait! Two symbols, three, four. Yes, four total."

Megan stared at the large rocks, covered with trailing moss and home to a couple of wary crabs.

If there was any doubt that we're on right track...

They waded knee-deep in the surf to give the symbols a wide berth. As they came around the outcropping, Megan saw a tiny cove with a cave entrance at the back, some twenty feet above the water line. At high tide, she guessed the cave would be half-full with water.

Daphne nodded. "Careful now. I have a feeling there's more to this than just slaving for fun and profit."

Stephen stopped them as they got closer. "Look."

Just inside the entrance, formed stone made an archway. Composed of twisting patterns, it met above their heads in an image of a screaming demon-face.

Ja'al.

Stephen's face became grim. He whispered a short phrase and made a wiping motion with his hand. Three purple symbols flared and vanished.

Megan met his eyes.

"Snaring charms. The ones at the rocks were similar but stronger. I wouldn't be surprised if they were all designed to knock you down and hold you at high tide, when you'd drown."

"We expected nothing less from those vermin," snapped Brandi, her jaw set.

They slipped inside the tunnel. Very soon, inky blackness surrounded them. Megan shifted her vision to sense for heat.

"Hold on," said Daphne. She and Stephen reached into belt pouches and drew out small white rings.

"Better now," Daphne said. She smiled at Megan. "I don't have the heritage that my brother-in-law gave you and Brandi."

Megan smiled back. "We can't all be half human and half elf. Besides, you have more magic toys."

Daphne gave her hand a squeeze, then led them on.

Twice more, Stephen detected a trap and twice more, he erased them.

The second time, he had to ask Megan to join her magic power to his to overcome it.

The Alenars emerged into a larger cavern so suddenly it took them by surprise. A flat stretch of open space stretched away from them, but at the sides, the floor angled downwards into darkness. The roof soared above their heads. At the far end of the cave, flaming braziers illuminated another, bigger archway. Four men in scale mail armed with spears and swords stood guard.

"More slavers," Stephen whispered, his voice barely louder than a breath. "Brandi, use your silence stone so we can get closer."

Brandi picked up a small rock and waved her hand over it. A faint symbol glowed on the rock and vanished. Utter silence covered them.

Despite knowing the spell would keep the guards from hearing them, Megan felt herself barely breathing. She forced herself to relax.

When they drew close to the guards, Brandi tossed the stone behind her and they stepped into the firelight.

"Hold!" Stephen commanded. The guards jerked in surprise.

"We have tracked kidnappers to this complex," Stephen continued, not giving the guards much time to react. "Surrender and take us to the captives."

One of the guards immediately bolted for the archway as his fellows launched their spears and drew blades.

Daphne planted an arrow in the calf of the fleeing guard. He lurched forward but kept limping to the archway. Brandi and Stephen drew their own swords as Daphne dropped her bow and reached for the sword at her hip.

Megan targeted the fleeing guard, her hands moving in a waving pattern. A wave of air rushed by her, carrying a faint, glittering dust. When it reached the limping guard, he collapsed. Megan raced to him.

He slept, just as she intended. She jerked his weapons away and slid them towards a nearby wall. Clanging swords sounded behind her and she heard curses and shouts but she concentrated on her charge. Murmuring arcane words, she pinched two fingers together and touched them to her palm. When she drew her hand away, a sizzling, glimmering cord of magic followed her fingers. She looped the magic cord around the sleeping guard's hands and feet, then turned back to the battle.

The last guard collapsed to the floor as Daphne pulled her sword out of his heart.

"Good work," said Stephen, kneeling next to Megan. "Now, to awaken our little friend and find out what's going on here."

Daphne opened her water skin and dribbled some water onto his face. The man jerked awake and stared around him with a mixture of fear and alarm. Seeing the four Alenars, he opened his mouth but Stephen clapped a hand over it.

"Now, now, we can't have any of that. Wouldn't want your friends to come and spoil our little party."

Daphne looked at Stephen, her expression wide-eyed. "Don't hurt him, brother. He might give us information. Besides, he's rather nice-looking."

Megan inwardly agreed that the guard was mildly attractive but couldn't figure out the sudden change in her aunt's demeanor. Daphne's expression, vapid and wide-eyed, reminded her of girls she had known who played at being stupid in order to dupe unsuspecting males.

The guard's eyed flickered from Daphne to Stephen, then to Megan and her sister. Megan played along; she tossed her head and turned away. Brandi looked unconcerned and stalked off to guard the exit.

"Well…" Stephen sounded doubtful as he drew his dagger. "These Ja'al guards rarely talk, sister. We're better off finishing him."

"Wait! I'm no Ja'al," the man protested.

"See!" Daphne said, pouting. "He's probably just a poor soul, tricked into doing the Ja'al's dirty work for them. Isn't that right?"

She turned an electric smile to the man, who eagerly nodded.

"She's right, sir! She has it exactly right. We were told that we'd just be robbing travelers and farmers. Nothing about kidnapping."

Stephen made a face. "He could be lying to us." He tested the edge of his dagger.

"No! No, no, no," said the guard, trying to wiggle away from Stephen. "I can even tell you where the kids are."

"See? I told you he would help, brother dear." Daphne reached out and touched the man's arm. "He's not one of those devil-worshippers."

The guard smiled at her. "Please, let me go and I'll tell you everything.

Then I promise I'll leave and never come back."

Stephen shrugged. "I guess that depends on what you're willing to tell us."

Daphne scooted closer to their captive, sitting next to him and putting an arm around him. "I'm sure he'll tell us everything, won't you?"

"Yes! Yes, I will."

Stephen looked bored, sharpening his dagger on a stone. "Go ahead. Where are the prisoners?"

Daphne smiled at the guard and nodded.

He licked his lips. "Well, there's another cave farther back. It has two exits. The left-hand one leads to a tunnel that rises up on you. The kids are all in the chamber at the end, in a wooden cage with a lock on it."

"And the right-hand one?"

The guard's eyes shifted from side to side. "I don't know. No one does. It has another archway over it and we're not supposed to go in there. The real Ja'al temple guards say so and so do the wizards."

"Ja'al wizards?" asked Stephen sharply.

"Y-yes. They have Ja'al medallions and they take long wooden boxes in there. We've heard chanting and seen flashes of light. One of the boys asked what it was and the Ja'al guy said he'd have his tongue on a plate for even asking. We didn't ask any more after that."

Daphne patted the guard's hand. "Don't worry about any of that. Just tell us how to get the prisoners out."

"One of the Ja'al guards has a key, and so does one of the wizards."

"Are the wizards here now?"

He nodded. "There's two of them in there, doing something."

Stephen slipped his dagger into its sheath. "Thank you. You have been most helpful."

He murmured a word and touched the man's forehead. His eyes rolled back in his head and Daphne caught him.

Megan pursed her lip, looking at her aunt. "You play the hare-brained woman very well, Aunt Daphne."

Still keeping her wide-eyed simpleton expression, Daphne asked, "Who, me? It can't be. I don't have a hare in my brain." She batted her eyelashes.

Stephen gave a mild snort. "Let's tie up this one with real rope and hide him behind one of the larger boulders. He'll sleep for hours now. The dead we can roll off into the shadows near the walls."

They hid the unconscious guard behind a pair of large boulders and secured his bonds and gag. They slipped under the archway and beyond. The tunnel wound left and right until they saw a faint glimmer of light. They stopped and Daphne held a warning finger to her lips. She slithered forward into the darkness and disappeared into a large open space beyond.

They waited. From the chamber they heard a faint sound like voices and an occasional clack or metallic clang.

Daphne sneaked back to them and led them back to the first guard chamber.

"Sound carries very well in there." She crouched next to her relatives, her voice barely above a whisper. "There are six guards next to another archway. These are *not* Vipers. They have chainmail armor and dark purple tunics with a multicolored patch at the shoulder. Their helms bear the sign of a screaming skull. No bows, though, so that will be an advantage."

Stephen nodded. "Skullhead Legion guards by that description. They won't surrender. Death first."

From her childhood in Torosc, Megan remembered Skullheads. She shuddered. Brutal and sadistic, they enjoyed terrorizing the population and especially taking advantage of young women.

Daphne nodded. "These aren't just common slavers. Something is going on in the chamber with the wizards. But what?"

"Our first duty is to the captives," said Brandi. "Can we take the guards out without setting off a ruckus? We can't handle six of them and two wizards."

They stayed silent, lost in thought.

Megan had a sudden inspiration. "I have an idea from our time with the Grey Riders. Uncle Stephen, you're about the same size as one of the Vipers in the room back there. Get one of the brigandines and put it on and leave your bow with us. Then just walk towards them, maybe pretending to be injured. When they come forward, Brandi can use her silence stone to keep the area quiet while we take them out of action."

Even in the darkness, she could sense her uncle smiling. "A little trick courtesy of Dar Cabot? I like it."

She blushed at the name of her love.

Brandi fidgeted. "I'm not sure. What if one of them escapes?"

"We'll have to risk it. Megan, do you have any illusion spells?" asked Daphne. "We'll need some screening so that the wizards don't notice anything different."

Megan nodded. "I can use a False Mirror to show the viewer what they expect to see. It won't stand up to extensive scrutiny but it will buy us time."

Daphne took Stephen's bow and quiver, leaving her own bow over her back. "Let's even the odds a bit. I'm sure I can get in before the rest of you and hide in a corner. If any of them heads to the exit, I can shoot them first. Brandi, do you have any protective spells?"

"Yes."

"Good. Use them now and let's get moving. No telling how many other patrols or guards may be down here."

Brandi murmured under her breath, holding Eric's silver crucifix in her hand. The figure of Christ glowed with a mild aura of blue that spread and settled on all of them. She changed her chant and now a quartet of tiny gold lights emerged from her hands and settled on each of their foreheads to fade into darkness. Finally, she said a short word and an exhilarating electricity coursed through Megan's body.

"Ready."

They waited while Stephen came back, carrying a guard's leather armor. He removed his own tunic but kept his chainmail on, slipping the brigandine over it.

Megan envied her uncle's armor. Skintight and form-fitting, it was made from a special dwarven alloy containing something called Starsilver. Megan didn't understand metallurgy as well as she would have liked. All she knew was that the armor protected her uncle extremely well and didn't hamper his movements.

Daphne had similar mail and Megan could only guess at the value of it.

"Ready," Brandi said. Daphne ghosted up to the chamber entrance and inside.

"Watch this performance," Stephen said with a wink. The sisters followed him up to the chamber entrance.

Stephen limped forward towards the Ja'al guards as Brandi tossed the silence stone in her hand nervously.

"Hey!" yelled one of the Ja'al guards. "What are you doing away from your post?"

Stephen raised a hand, then bent over, hands on his knees. "Attacked!" he croaked out. "Roadwardens."

"Roadwardens?" The lead Skullhead asked. "Here? How did they track us?"

Stephen lurched forward and stumbled, drawing his sword and using it to prop himself up.

Cursing, the Skullhead guards hefted their swords and axes and trotted forward. Brandi rolled her silence stone towards them.

The Skullhead leader got within six feet of Stephen before he realized he was making no sound. His eyes widened and he gestured to his fellows.

Outside the stone's influence, Megan heard a double twang from a corner of the cave and a Ja'al went down on one knee, two feathered shafts in his chest.

Megan focused her mind and drew forth power, concentrating on the Ja'al leader. Twin rainbow pinwheels spun out from her hands and shot at him, throwing sparks in all directions. He raised his axe in defense. Both pinwheels arced around and detonated. He and two of his companions staggered backwards, their armor sparking and smoking. Their eyes looked glassy and they looked around in confusion. Brandi charged in, swords drawn.

Stephen bowled over the first three Ja'al and engaged the last two. Another pair of arrows hit the wounded guard and he dropped.

Stephen thrust, parried and slashed, driving his opponents back around towards the silence stone. The Ja'al's mouths worked as they screamed in rage and alarm. Then their eyes widened as they realized they were silenced.

Brandi reached the ones dazzled by Megan's spell and attacked. The leader swung at her with his battle axe but seemed slow and awkward. Brandi dodged the blow and thrust a sword into his side. She spun out of the way of a lethargic sword thrust and slashed the leg of a nearby warrior. Megan crept to the edge of the room, waiting for her chance.

Stephen dropped one of the guards with a well-placed thrust but caught an axe-blow to the shoulder from the other. He rolled backwards with the blow and to the side. The guard followed up with an overhead strike. Stephen rolled out of the way. The axe blade struck sparks from the floor.

Brandi rained blows on the last of her three but the guards seemed to have recovered. They waded in, driving Brandi back.

Megan bit her lip. Her sister would be outside of the range of the silence stone unless she did something soon.

Megan focused her mind again and placed her fingers in the palm of her other hand, then made a flinging motion at the Ja'al, hoping Brandi would recognize what was happening.

A bright dot flew out toward the melee, then puffed out into a cloud of shining dust, flying right into the faces of the Ja'al. They staggered, waving their hands in front of their faces. Another double twang sounded and one dropped with a pair of arrows in his side.

Unfortunately, the bright dust hampered Brandi as well. The leader stumbled but managed to slam his axe into her side. Brandi doubled over, then thrust upward, catching him in the shoulder. With another slash, she cut his legs and impaled him as he fell.

Stephen fended off his attacker and managed to force him back towards Brandi.

Megan shot him with Firedarts. The three tiny comets detonated with silence but gratifying effect. The guard lurched and Stephen ran him through.

The last warrior got a sword thrust into Brandi's leg but then dropped with an arrow in the back of his helmet.

Megan raced forward, scooping up the silence stone and rolling it into a corner.

"Brandi!"

Her sister sat up, grimacing. She held her side and blood ran down her leg. "I'm all right… Just need a minute."

"Megan, quickly, the shielding spell," Daphne strode towards them. "I'll help Brandi."

Stephen scooped up a key ring from the belt of one guard. "Go. We have curatives for Brandi."

Megan scooted towards the exit, taking care not to get into the doorway. She put thoughts of Brandi's injuries out of her mind. She had seen her get far worse in the past.

Whispering words under her breath, she waved her hands in an intricate pattern, then spoke a quiet, soothing phrase. A shimmering wall of light sprang up in front of the archway. She knew that anyone on the other side would get the first impression of whatever they had seen there the last time they looked. However, it wouldn't fool a wizard for very long.

She sneaked back to the others, kneeling next to her sister.

"Done," she said with a look at Daphne, who nodded.

Brandi sipped from a small glass vial. A mild light glowed on her sister's leg and side. Brandi stood, flexed her leg, then replaced her swords in their sheaths.

"Better now?" asked Stephen.

Brandi nodded, stretching to the side. "Sore, but I'll manage."

The four dragged the dead guards into corners of the room where a quick glance might give the impression they were sleeping, then headed off towards the left-hand passage, following the Viper guard's instructions. Stephen used magic to detect traps and other mischief but found none.

Megan's heat vision picked up the cage with the prisoners and she hissed a warning. Megan produced a mage-light in her palm and they blinked as their eyes adjusted.

Five teen-agers likewise blinked, holding up their hands against the brightness, covering themselves as best they could with their other hands. All were completely bereft of clothing. The boys both had dark hair while one girl had brown hair, another blonde and another auburn red.

"Noah, Jason, Amber, Miriam and Cathy, I presume," said Daphne with a gentle smile.

The taller of the two boys let his hand down, his jaw dropping. "Wait… who… how did you…?"

"We're not Vipers," Stephen said, inspecting the lock of the cage and drawing forth the key ring. "The people of Widmer's Corner sent us."

"Oh my God," said the blonde girl, holding a hand to her mouth, tears starting at the corners of her eyes. "You're soldiers sent to rescue us? I never dared hope."

Megan stepped closer, releasing her mage-light to float over the cage. "Well, not soldiers, but we're on your side."

The captives forgot their nudity and stared in amazement at Megan's magic light.

"You're a wizard," breathed the red-haired girl.

The lock clicked and Stephen swung the door open. The captives remembered their state of undress and looked appropriately shy, cheeks flushing.

"Here," said Megan, reaching into her shoulder bag. "I found some tunics that might fit you." She began handing them out.

"I don't have enough for all of you though," she said wistfully. "The other townsfolk needed them after we set them free."

"That's okay," said the tall boy with a nervous smile. "The girls can have them."

Brandi smacked her forehead. "I'm such a ninny. We should have grabbed something from the guards."

Stephen made a face. "Well, they're a little messy at the moment so I'm not sure—"

"Oh, don't worry about that," interrupted the dark-haired girl. "We'll take anything. They have only let us have a little bread and water and no clothes for two days."

Megan handed out the three tunics she had brought with her, then drew her mage-light down to Daphne's shoulder and attached it there. She returned to the guard room with Brandi to collect salvageable clothes. Megan kept a wary eye on her illusion shield but it held and there were no signs of anyone else entering the area.

The captives entered with Stephen and Daphne. Megan handed them the clothes and got a good look at them.

The girls are so pretty, and the boys handsome and strong. I could see why slavers would want them to sell.

"Thank you," said the shorter boy, now wearing a tunic and trousers. He put out his hand. "I'm Noah. You can guess who Jason is. The blonde one is Amber, Miriam has brown hair, and Catherine is the red-head."

"Auburn," said Cathy with an acid look at him, then a sweet smile at Megan.

"I'm glad we got to you," said Stephen, handing Noah a pair of boots. "Now it's time to move. I have no idea when they change the guards and we don't want the wizards to find us."

Noah shuddered. "Fine with us. The wizards give us the creeps."

Brandi readied her bow. "Did you see anything about what they were making in there?"

"Something for the special sacrificial ceremony," said Amber in a small voice.

Daphne and Stephen exchanged a look. "Sacrifices?"

Miriam nodded. "Yes. Us."

Chapter Five- Strange Designs

He dreamed and saw them in the darkness, swathed in shadows.

A slim, strong young human male with short dark hair slipped between the trees, his eyes moving left and right, taking in every leaf and bole. He vaulted easily over a fallen tree, a bow in his left hand.

In his wake, a small figure flitted, then scrambled over the tree trunk. He lifted back the hood of his cloak, revealing dark eyes and handsome, carved features. This one, a halfling, stood still, then beckoned over his shoulder. Four more figures advanced in the gloom.

He dreamed and saw a cloud of shadow, lit with red, flaming eyes. It followed out of range of the man and halfling and their company. The presence lashed a ghastly spiked tail.

He tried to shout a warning to the travelers but no sound came out. He screamed in silent rage.

A pale light flared ahead of the group. The man and halfling stopped. The light wavered in the air and danced left and right, then forward and back, beckoning them onward.

In horror, he watched. A pale, clawed hand manipulated the light, drawing the group onward. They followed, heedless of the peril ahead and the danger behind.

He struggled against sleep, fighting against iron bands.

He awoke.

Lying still in the dark, he adjusted his eyes and scanned about for enemies. His chamber remained as always: trophies of goblin and troll tribes hung on the walls, prizes of battle.

He uncoiled himself and extended his neck, sniffing the air. He picked up the familiar, comforting scents of Tholi and Kindri and nothing else.

What was the dream about? Why did he see Dar Cabot and Connor Lomin in a dark forest, stalked by enemies?

The One has sent me an omen. But what does it mean?

He bowed his head in prayer.

"Grandfather?"

Kindriana slithered into his room. With a command, he brought forth a magelight just under the ceiling.

Kindri smiled up at him. "I'm sorry to wake you, Grandfather."

He looked down and smiled back, coiling his tail around her to give her a quick caress. "I was already awake, dearest. What is it?"

"There's an old human at the entrance. It is almost dawn and he sent a Wind Whisper into our home, requesting to see you. It woke me and I came here."

Iron Thunder's eyes narrowed. Wind Whisper bespoke a mage at his doorstep and obviously a very cautious one.

He stood. "I will see him, Kindri. Go wake your brother."

Iron Thunder stalked to his receiving chamber, then towards the cavern entrance. With a muttered phrase, he searched for magical traps but found none.

A single human stood on the flat area outside the cave, looking northward towards Wastrel's Peak.

"I am here. Who calls at this early hour?"

The man turned around. Clad in a robe of grey with a single golden star at the left breast, he bowed low.

"Donnervassilianelikilandra, I am Melinor Indidarc. I hope Your Excellency remembers me."

Iron Thunder's eyes widened and then he smiled. "Young Melinor? I remember a wizard much less advanced in years. Is it really you?"

Melinor smiled back and touched his grey hair, turning white in places. "The flow of time favors dragonkind more than humans, my lord."

Iron Thunder concentrated his power and made it flow over his form, changing him to an old man, with white hair and golden eyes in a white robe.

"How many years?" he asked, sitting on a nearby rock.

"Thirty-eight, to be exact, Excellency."

"That is long in human life I suppose. We have a hard time judging age in your people since you have so short a time to live."

Melinor nodded. "Though they do not live nearly so long as dragons, my elven friends have said similar things."

Iron Thunder sighed and looked out at the Mountains of the Dragonspine Range and the Wilderness beyond. "And yet, though things change, the cycle repeats again and again. How did you find me? This is far from the place of our last meeting."

"My son told me."

"Ah yes. Eric. A fine young man. Very brave and honorable, yet I sensed a touch of Dark upon him."

"Your senses are as keen as ever. But have no fear, Excellency, Eric serves the Light as you and I do."

"I am glad to hear that," Iron Thunder said. "The touch of Dark is something that hunts him perhaps."

"Actually, it haunts him, but I can say no more without his leave."

"Of course. I would never dream of prying. But now, why are you here in the wilds?"

Melinor's brow furrowed. "You see much out here on the frontier. You range far and wide and your magical skills are legendary."

"Thank you for the compliment, but I—"

Melinor fixed Iron Thunder with a piercing gaze. "A great evil stirs. It plans and plots and we know it seeks the downfall of the North, but we cannot discern its plans."

Iron Thunder ran a hand over his beard. "The Ja'al? The Grey Riders put an end to Halkith and his schemes months ago. They are no danger."

"I speak of the Dark Rider."

Now it was Iron Thunder's turn for a sharp look. "From the Song of the Grey Riders? You know the Rider's identity?"

"The Rider is actually Zhinia Margoth, High Priestess of Garon-Zith, Princess of Kher Mardil and sorceress. She is now a lich."

Iron Thunder felt a chill. Ogres, giants, trolls, even other dragons, he could handle, but the undead? He resisted the urge to spit. His very being revolted at the concept.

But now matters made sense. Coupled with the things he had seen in the last few weeks it now increased his anxiety.

"Now much is explained to me. So, the Dark Rider seeks to conquer Deran?" he asked.

"To start with. Beyond that, we know little. I was hoping that you would be able to give me information about anything you have seen in the Wilds."

Iron Thunder stood. "I can do better than that."

He transformed back to his natural state and bent his neck down to Melinor. "Climb on and hold to the two spines at my shoulders."

Humans are so small and frail, he thought as he soared up in the air. He called to Tholi and Kindri and his grandchildren shot up to meet him, swirling around him as he beat his wings. He raced towards a mountain to the northeast, one that looked like a crown of three peaks with one at the center.

The journey took less than an hour, though for a human party in the woods it would have taken more than a dozen perilous days. He selected his favorite outcropping and alighted there. Kindri and Tholi landed on boulders near him.

"Do you see?"

He felt Melinor stiffen. In a valley formed by craggy hills, many fires of varying sizes burned, smoke curling up into the sky. Iron Thunder's keen vision showed him the glint of metal helmets, the flapping of dark standards in the breeze and the motion of many creatures great and small. He smelled a vile incense and heard the whinny of horses and the growl of other, less wholesome beasts.

"How many?" asked Melinor.

"More than ten thousand. Closer to twelve, I think."

"Dear Jesus…"

"Yes, you had best pray to your God." Iron Thunder leaned his head forward. His horned ruff twitched with agitation. "With an army that size, the Dark Rider can drive all the way to Hillton, perhaps to Oakmoor itself. It would take the whole of Deran's army to turn her away and this does not consider the benefits of being a lich. She has access to dark powers indeed, and any who fall on the field of battle may become her thralls. Also, Kindri and Tholi have spied dark elves among their number, but only a few. You and I both know they will not show themselves until the last minute. Where there are only a few, hundreds or thousands lurk behind. Deran may soon be assaulted by an army fifteen thousand strong or more."

"We need to be prepared, no matter where she strikes. This news must get back to the Crown."

"I am sure you will take it there, my friend. I know that there are undoubtedly rangers and spies below who can see us now, but their vision is likely limited and they cannot do anything about us. If what you say about Zhinia Margoth is true, she will inevitably find out who I am and that will make my home vulnerable."

He leaped into the air and soared away to the north, then cut back around the mountains to leave Margoth's army uncertain as to their direction. By the time they returned to his home on Whitehorse Peak, he felt a rumble of hunger but ignored it. His mind spun, considering all that Melinor had told him.

"Kindri, Tholi, make an inventory of the cavern contents. And see how many of the sky-baskets we have."

The youngsters exchanged a look.

"Are we going somewhere, Grandpa?" asked Tholi.

"Very soon," Iron Thunder said grimly. His grandchildren leaped into action, scooting back inside their home.

"And what of the Grey Riders?" he asked Melinor as the dragonlings headed back into the cavern.

"They managed to clear Buck Bydecy's name, in Tyler, Astarel. Buck now has a magical gemstone called the Eye of Truth. It can see past illusion and falsehood and detect evil."

"The Diamond Eye!"

"Yes," said Melinor, starting to pace. "Just like the Song predicted. And there is more. They found out who had hired the assassins to kill Andyn's husband. It was someone from her past life in Terenai, a government official who sought a magical medallion hidden under Andyn's home. It turns out he was working for dark elves, and now we see dark elves in an army of evil."

"How is Andyn?" asked the dragon. He remembered a beautiful half-elven woman with a clear singing voice, a fierce loyalty to her friends, and a deep sadness.

"Her husband is avenged and she finally has peace. Liander Tolin paid for his crimes. But it seems that even he was not his own master. The cult of Arachnia had enslaved him years ago at the behest of Zhinia Margoth. Her webs extend everywhere."

The two, dragon lord and arch mage, stood silently on the mesa.

"Where are they now?"

Melinor put his hands behind his back. "They have travelled to Evendale to see Connor's family, seeking clues about a halfling toy, which is, as you know, part of the prophecy. Liander Tolin's medallion had an image on it of a mountain and a lake. We determined it was a representation of Twinspire Mountain and Shadow Lake."

Iron Thunder jerked his head around to stare at Melinor. "Shadow Lake?"

Melinor looked startled. "Yes. Shadow Lake. Is something wrong?"

Sudden images of a dark wood and malevolent shadows appeared in Iron Thunder's brain. He gritted his teeth at the memory of a clawed hand and a deceptive light.

"Something is very wrong. What do you know of Shadow Lake?"

Melinor shrugged. "Not much. There is an old fortress on the slope facing the lake. The woods there have a dark reputation. Supposedly a Darkwood Drake lives there. Why? What do you know?"

Iron Thunder thought of the Grey Riders - sardonic, intense Dar Cabot, easygoing Buck Bydecy, thoughtful Connor Lomin, cheerful Eric, caring Andyn, the sisters Megan and Brandi…

"A sinister tale told by my people speaks of a horror in that wood, and the Darkwood Drakes worship it. The Riders are in grave danger."

He set his jaw. "I must go to them."

"Excellency?"

"They will need my help. Without it, they may perish."

Melinor bit his lip. "What about your grandchildren?"

That stopped Iron Thunder. Formidable in their own right as dragons, the two children were nonetheless young and impressionable. Margoth, a servant of Darkness, doubtless had many means to seduce and corrupt them.

Iron Thunder looked back to his grandchildren at the cave entrance. They smiled at him and turned back to their tasks.

I can't leave them. Halkith almost killed them and now the Dark Rider…

Melinor snapped his fingers and chuckled. "I have an answer. The Lord either loves me a lot or he has a great sense of humor."

Iron Thunder blinked. Humans sometimes perplexed him, even wise ones like Melinor.

Melinor beamed up at him. "I will take care of your grandchildren. Send them back to my home with me, in Whitepine. Margoth would never think to look for them there."

"Are you sure?"

Melinor now gave a hearty laugh. "Excellency, in my time, I've fostered and adopted a half-daemon girl and a runaway assassin prince. What's a pair of dragonlings after that?"

***

Zhinia Margoth took mental notes, resolving to put certain people in their places after all this was over. It was hard enough carry out an invasion without having to mollycoddle her allies.

Though I doubt if too many people in history have applied the word 'mollycoddle' to Kaftu and ogres.

She turned her gaze to a hulking, muscular Kaftu female standing in the entrance chamber of her tent. The hyena-woman spread her hands to the side and bowed, her long coat of purple patterns swirling around her. Leather straps holding daggers crossed her chest between her teats and in one hand she held a staff of gnarled wood with a glowing blue gemstone. Her spotted fur looked neat and well-groomed and gold earrings winked from her ears.

"Pack-Queen Zirta," Margoth said with a regal nod.

The Kaftu pulled back her lips in a toothsome smile. "Great Highness," she barked out, her Humana heavily accented. "The Shadowrunner Clan is here."

"And I am glad of it." She sat in a tall camp chair and gathered her robes around her. "You have seen the warriors encamped in alliance with me?"

Zirta straightened and nodded. "Many are they."

Margoth lifted her chin. "Your tribe has done excellent work on my behalf in harrying the lowly humans and others living in Deran, and profited greatly from the association, no?"

Zirta nodded again. "Great Highness' help is good for Shadowrunners. We have now much gold from lost ruins in forest you show us. We have meat and loot from raids. Shadowrunners are strong."

"Would Your Highness like to become stronger?"

The Kaftu's eyes narrowed. "How?"

"We have designs on this area. A wide land with plains of waving grass, trees, hills. Plenty of room for all your folk. It beckons to us, Queen Zirta. If you are ready to claim your own land and not have to hide and skulk at the edges of this forsaken human kingdom, perhaps the time is now. We would be pleased if your tribe would govern a portion of the lands we conquer."

She could see Zirta calculating in her head.

"What Shadowrunners do for High Queen so that this happens?"

"Join my army. Send your warriors and witch doctors to me, fight alongside my other allies, coordinate with my plans, and it shall be yours."

Zirta's eyes flickered to Margoth. "We fight soldiers of human king."

"Of course. And the dwarves. Elves eventually, if Queen Ildrisana of Essergil has her way."

Zirta licked her lips at the mention of elves. Then her eyes turned dark. "But we see ogres in camp of High Queen."

Margoth shrugged. "Yes. And the elves and goblins are also here. You know they have no love for each other."

Zirta snarled. "Ogres eat our people."

"On occasion, I have heard that. But there will be none of that in my army. We will work together. If we unite, we will defeat them. If we fight each other, they will destroy us. You will get no land, no meat, no slaves, no gold."

Margoth knew exactly what Zirta wanted. She had gathered intelligence on all the Wilderness tribes long ago. The Shadowrunners were one of the more powerful Kaftu groups and had a long-running feud with the Long-fang clan. Margoth knew that if Zirta had her own territory in Deran, it would boost her standing among all other Kaftu queens. It might even allow her to lay claim to the title of High Mistress.

By assisting the Kaftu in raiding at will and letting them keep most of their winnings with a token tribute to her, Margoth whetted their greedy appetites for more and more. With a chance to wrest territory away from the pesky humans and their allies, she banked on Zirta's ambition.

Yet still the Kaftu queen hesitated.

"Humans and allies are strong," she said, "They have many soldiers. You may win land for a time. They will bring more and push you back. It is not a good thing for Shadowrunners. We lose much and gain little."

Margoth held her temper. "You would give up the chance to plunder Dorn's Hall, Forester, Sun Plains, maybe even Hillton?"

Zirta shook her head. "If we dead, we not plunder anything."

Margoth's eyes narrowed, then she shrugged again. "You have a point. Well, then, I thank the Shadowrunners for their assistance in our past endeavors. I will, of course, retain your tribe to raid and loot here on the borderlands as I accomplish my main mission. I will give your share to Ulgrut."

She stood to go and Zirta's eyes widened.

"Ulgrut?"

"Yes, the ogre chieftain. I'm sure he will be pleased at the increased share."

As expected, Margoth heard a low growl.

Zirta stood with teeth bared, hands opening and closing, her eyes flaring with rage.

"You give our share to those fat worms?" she hissed.

Margoth made sure to sound surprised. "Of course. Who else would it go to? They will fill in the gaps made by your departure and it will be extra work. Naturally they will gain more reward."

The Kaftu queen's eyes narrowed. "That is insult to Kaftu!"

Margoth sighed. "What else am I to do? I need enough troops to take on the Deranese."

Still Zirta hesitated.

Margoth shook her head. "After all, I'm not asking you to be friends with them, or even to fight at their side. You would be supporting the goblins and elves anyway, not the ogres."

As much as Margoth enjoyed using sheer power to strong-arm others into doing her will, she had to admit that manipulating them into it had a certain delicious perversity. Maybe the Ja'al were onto something.

Margoth picked up her staff. "In any case, you are free to keep what you have earned, but do not expect to be part of the New Order. You will have to keep to your areas of the Wilderness as before. I will find someone else to take your place."

Margoth almost reached the tent flap when Zirta spoke.

"Wait, Queen of Kher Mardil."

Margoth smiled.

***

"The flight pattern is always the same," Connor Lomin said, shaking his head. He watched the strange toy as it went through its odd aerial dance. It glimmered in the night darkness. The street lamps of the town shone like fireflies in the streets beyond.

Dar Cabot stroked his chin. "Pressing a button on the bottom of the main section makes it do this. And no one thought it odd all this time?"

Brendan Lomin shrugged and hefted Deena at his hip. The little girl watched the toy with shining eyes and a shy smile.

"Frankly," Brendan said in his light, whispering voice, "No one bothered to scan it for magic. We knew it had special properties when we bought it at the auction so it was no surprise when it flew. We assumed it was one of the many clever magical toys that the dwarves make down in Merdail. Very popular with the children. We think it was bought in Dwarfshire."

"But the flight pattern?" Dar asked, looking at Brendan.

Brendan shrugged, a bit of a smile on his lips. "Yes, it was odd. But so are dwarves. Ever been to Dwarfshire?"

Connor gave a short laugh. "I know what you mean, brother. Enough said."

They watched. The toy floated down to the ground, seemingly weightless, its rotors turning lazily. It landed and remained still. Darren raced to pick it up. He turned it over and pressed the button, then held it up in his hand. The blades on the top of the toy whirred in response, lifting it up. Darren released it. The toy soared up to a height of twenty feet, then stopped in a hover, moved to the side, went up again, then sideways in another direction, then ascended at an angle, then hovered and slowly edged upwards. At that point, the blades stopped turning and it flashed bright golden light and floated down, seeming to weigh only as much as a feather.

Connor shook his head. He knew little of magic—and that mostly from Megan, Eric or Andyn. However, the sheer complexity of the pattern and the toy's small size meant a very skilled craftsman had a hand in its construction.

Dar sighed. "Well, Connor, do you think this is the halfling toy from the Song?"

Connor shook his head, perplexed. "I have no idea. Andyn?"

Andyn put her hands on her hips. "Damned if I know. It is very heavily enchanted. A simple toy might have glowed a little when I used Wizard Scan on it, but not flare as bright as it did."

Connor watched his parents, carrying on an animated discussion with Eric and Hlerv. Buck sat on the grass with a stalk of barley in his teeth, just watching.

"Where did you get it again?" Dar asked.

Brendan set Deena down and she skipped over to her brother. "About twelve years before the Plague, a retired scholar from the capital named Gregory Whicker settled in Glen. He seemed like a friendly enough gent, a widower with three grown daughters living by the Deran border. He kept to himself mostly, but Janey spoke to him more than anyone else. She always told us that there was more to him than met the eye."

Connor remembered old professor Whicker and Janey's conversations regarding him.

"There's something about him, dearest," she had said to him one night. "He's studied in Mil-Tereth, Oakmoor, Alvindor, and Palatine and I think he knows a lot more than he's telling. Why did he come here to Glen to retire? We're just a large town in Evendale."

Thoughts of Janey made him remember the last time he had seen her alive: she lay in the bed quietly, a smile on her face, holding Rose. Then she died in her sleep, followed by Rose not two hours later.

Wanted to be with her momma, people said at the funeral.

The savage pain gripped his heart again and he struggled for control.

I shouldn't have come back! Too many memories.

"What happened to Whicker?" Dar asked, jarring Connor from his thoughts.

"He died in the plague," answered Brendan. "There was an estate sale after the funeral and I bought the toy for the children, after mother scanned it for signs of the plague, of course."

He looked troubled. "That was just before the fire."

"Fire?" Andyn asked.

"Yes," Connor mused. "After the funeral, there were a series of break-ins in Whicker's neighborhood, Goldlawn. The town watch surprised the burglars in one of the houses and a couple of oil lamps broke, catching one house on fire. By the time the brigades arrived, half the neighborhood was in flames. We were so short-handed in firefighters from the plague that it took a long time to knock down, even with the help of clerics from the temples, Mother included. Whicker's house was a pile of embers when it was all over."

Everyone stood quietly in the darkness.

"The question is what to do about this toy," Andyn said finally. "How are we supposed to use it? Where? When?"

Dar gave her an innocent look. "It's in the Song, Andyn. When something gold turns red at the end of a passage. It's simple, really. You're making this much too complicated."

She glared at him and pushed him in the shoulder. He grinned back.

"You should take it," Brendan whispered suddenly.

"Won't the kids miss it?"

Brendan smiled. "Not if you tell them that it's a special magical toy designed to right wrongs and slay evil and that you have to take it to a mystical tower hidden in the wilderness beyond a vile, dark forest. They'll love that and will pester you unendingly when you come back for all the details, so make sure you formulate a suitably exciting story."

Connor watched his niece and nephew, now begging Eric for a game of night tag.

"I think we can come up with something," he replied, then stretched. "But we really should get some rest. Morning comes early and Twinspire is far."

Brendan's smile faded. "You still mean to go there?"

Connor nodded. His brother gave him a long look.

"Watch yourself, Connor. There are rumors."

Connor tried to ignore the sudden feeling of dread. "We will be. It's how we've lasted this long."

They watched the children for a while and eventually everyone trooped back to the Lomin home. Connor decided to follow his brother's suggestion and asked to borrow the toy.

"When we've finished destroying the forces of evil, we'll bring it back," Connor told the children somberly.

Darren looked at Deena and shrugged. "I guess so. You know how to use it, right, Uncle Connor?"

Connor nodded.

Deena bit her lip. "You promise you'll bring it back?"

Connor gave her a hug. "Promise."

She smiled happily and kissed him, then handed over the toy and skipped off to bed.

Connor felt his cheek where her lips had touched him.

"Sweet child," Andyn said, next to him.

Without looking at her, he knew she probably had a wistful look on her face.

"Yes, she is."

That night, Connor dreamed about his doomed daughter, Rose, except Rose was as old as Deena. She skipped and laughed and played with a golden flying toy that blasted evil skeletal wizards into piles of ashes.

Chapter Six- Conspiracy

"Now don't use this unless you absolutely have to," Brandi said, handing a Ja'al sword to Noah. "Wait for an opening and thrust hard, aiming for the armor joints like I told you. Then run."

The teen nodded, hefting the sword. "I always wanted to learn how to use one of these."

Brandi shook her head. "And I'd teach you more, but this is hardly the place."

She turned to survey their group. Using captured clothing from the Ja'al guards and Vipers, the former captives could pass, from a distance, as a group of scouts or skirmishers. The scale mail and chain armor they left behind; their hope lay in speed, not in power.

"Ready?" she asked Daphne.

"Yes, just a moment." Daphne bent her head to listen to Miriam who was finishing a description of the wizards' chamber.

With the teens clothed and armed in a couple of minutes, they decided to move quickly and surprise the Ja'al wizards before they figured something was amiss. Brandi's silence spell and Megan's shielding magic had protected them for now, but they were on borrowed time.

"Here's how it will work," Stephen said. He motioned to their group. "The kids will stay here in the cage, with the lock removed. It will fool any guards for a few seconds if they come in. We'll have to take out the wizards quickly. Daphne and I will go in first. Megan and Brandi will follow after we have their attention."

"Are you sure there are only two wizards?" asked Megan.

Jason nodded. "Only two. They spend all their time poring over charts and books and constructing that, um, thing using the human bones and skulls."

"Are you sure we should stay behind?" asked Miriam, looking nervous.

Stephen shook his head. "If the Ja'al don't see you they won't know that you are free and armed. We want to keep you out of the picture until the last second."

"Please come back safe," Amber said in a small voice.

Daphne gave a wry smile and hugged her. "They're only two Ja'al wizards. We've handled them before. We'll be back in a nonce."

The teens still looked doubtful. Brandi gave them a cheery smile and followed her relatives out to the guard room.

I'm a bit doubtful myself, she thought. Despite Daphne's healing potion, she still felt tired and sore.

She peeked into the guard room. Megan's distortion spell held, a swirling air pattern just outside the entrance to the wizards' room.

"Now, Brandi," said Daphne.

Brandi took a deep breath and centered herself, reaching for what power she had left. She thought of coolness and protection from fire, health and protection from disease, clear thought and protection from insanity. With a word, she passed her hands in the air over her relatives and herself. A glowing fog of intertwining blue, gold and green wisps settled on them, lingered on their clothing for a second, then winked out.

Brandi let out a deep breath. This was very tiring.

Megan likewise added a spell of her own, making sharp gestures at their weapons. With each motion, a silver spark jumped to its target, illumining sword and bow and dagger with a quick white radiance.

Stephen drew his blades. Daphne and Brandi set arrows to their bows. Megan slipped to the side of the archway and, with a small gesture, dispelled the shielding.

Brandi's eyes widened as she looked into the chamber. Despite the detailed descriptions from the captured teens, she tightened her grip on her bow.

A full forty feet square, the smooth walls held bas-reliefs of various Ja'al deities: Gudarti, Arachnia, Neralia, Torvu, and Selaan. Brandi's stomach lurged and she forced herself to look away from the images. To her left and right, dark stone statues of misshapen hounds stood frozen in poses of attack.

Two figures in robes of riotous colors pored over papers laid out on tables near the center. Bones and skulls and stone blocks and orbs littered the floor near them. A bubbling cauldron steamed off to one side. Magical green flames hovered near the thirty-foot high ceiling, bathing the area in a lurid light.

But the structure of dirty white dominating the center of the room was what drew her attention and would remain in her memory for years. It looked like half of a dome, with curved structural members arcing upward to join at a point some twenty feet above the stone floor. Brandi saw human leg bones, arm bones, rib cages and spines somehow welded together in an obscene feat of engineering. Ghastly skulls grinned at her where the vertical members met horizontal stringers. The whole assembly emanated a foul, sickly-sweet miasma. She figured she could easily drive two wagons into it.

Daphne and Stephen stalked into the room.

As attacks go, Brandi thought it could have gone worse. Daphne and Stephen made it halfway to the wizards before the magical traps went triggered. They dodged aside as fire and acid exploded up from the floor.

The wizards spun around at the sound. Ruggedly handsome men with closely-cropped hair painted in multicolored stripes, they moved quickly and with confidence. They gestured and magical power crackled around them. Flaming jets shot out at the Alenars.

Stephen ducked into a crouch. He mimicked the motions of the wizard spell in reverse, then crossed his blades in front of him. The jet of flame lost cohesion and fell apart into harmless tongues of flame sputtering on the stones.

Daphne loosed two arrows in rapid succession. The second wizard ducked. His flame jet sprayed to the side and obliterated one of the dog statues. Daphne reached into her case and drew two more arrows, letting fly again. The Ja'al mage spat a vulgar insult, darted behind the table and ducked. One of Daphne's arrows nicked him in the upper arm.

Both wizards now chanted in unison and two globes of light sprang up around them, one green and the other red. Stephen cast a spell of his own, glowing fire darts arcing out at the enemy. The fire darts struck the green shield and spun away harmlessly.

Daphne let fly again but the arrows struck the red globe and burst into flame.

"Now," said Megan. Brandi slipped into the room with her, heart pounding.

Brandi aimed her arrow at the red-globed wizard, waiting for an opening. Megan murmured next to her, stalking forward slowly, low to the ground. She suddenly stood and shouted a word. The red globe flickered and vanished. Stephen followed with a spell of his own, weaving a silvery net that drifted down over the green globe, extinguishing it.

The wizards struck back, casting thin bolts of lightning at Stephen and Megan. Brandi let fly a little too late and the lightning bolt almost skewered Megan. She rolled out of the way. The bolt scorched her blouse as it zipped past. The other bolt hit Stephen in the side. His armor responded with a brilliant flash of its own and the bolt dissipated. Instead of getting blasted, Stephen gasped and lurched to the side.

Daphne drew her sword and charged a wizard, who threw his hands to the sides. A blast of sound and air hit Daphne in mid-charge, knocking her backwards. She turned her fall into a roll and came up, her sword's edge lit with a blue flame.

The other Ja'al shouted a vile-sounding word and Brandi heard a creaking, cracking noise next to her.

Two of the hound statues moved. Shards of stone fell off their forms. They shook themselves, opening jaws glowing with flame. Each looked just like a normal war hound except for the horns on their heads, the spine of sharp ridges down their backs and their armored, spiked tails. They fixed star-bright red eyes on Megan and Brandi and snarled.

"Back to back," Brandi called out. She felt Megan press up against her. She no longer had eyes for the battle with the wizards.

Brandi drew her swords and one of them flared golden. The hounds charged.

"Clockwise!" Megan shouted. Brandi stepped to the side to match Megan's step, slashing at the hound attacking her. The creature snapped at empty air. Growling, it darted in and out.

She heard a metallic sizzle and the sound of toppled furniture behind her. One of the mages cried out in pain.

Good…

The demon-hound stepped back, then opened its mouth and belched a cloud of purple gas at her. Brandi ducked. The gas turned into a mist, sizzling with acidic intensity where it touched her skin. She winced in pain.

Megan gasped behind her, then spoke a short word. A howl of pain from the other hound echoed in the chamber.

Brandi's hound grinned a horrible human-like grin, then belched again, shooting a tongue of flame at her.

"Breaking!" she called out, rolling to the side and away from Megan. Before the hound could turn to her, she slashed it twice in the legs with her blades.

In fury, it leaped forward, jaws snapping and frothing with a fiery drool. Brandi twisted out of the way and slashed. The hound leaped backwards and jumped at her quickly, nearly catching her left arm. She spun, lashing out with both blades as she whirled. The hound took a cut to the side of the head and yelped. It crouched low to the ground, slavering and growling.

A flare of light and a howl made her look to her sister. Megan lay on the ground, the other hound on top of her. She gripped its shoulders and electricity ripped into it, a network of shiny blue bolts covering the creature. The hound whined and jerked spasmodically. With a cry, she pushed it off and scrambled away. The demon-spawn hit the floor and slid sideways. It wobbled unsteadily as it tried to stand.

Brandi's hound gave a sound like the shriek of a madwoman and charged. She dodged to the side. It bowled her over. She rolled, bringing both swords up in guard position. The hound leaped in the air, jaws gaping and another gout of flame shooting out. The flames singed her arms and face. Brandi gritted her teeth and made sure this time, jamming one sword into the creature's neck and another in its midsection. It let out a choking screech and dropped.

Brandi shook it off her blades, steaming with purple blood, and turned to Megan. Her sister stood and unleashed four fire darts, blasting the other hound into a smoking heap.

A scream sounded from the area near the bone structure. The sisters turned.

Daphne pulled her blade out of one of the wizards as he collapsed. Her own side was bloody.

Stephen leaned unsteadily against the remnants of the table, struggling to support his own weight, his face grey with pain but determined.

The last wizard, his robes cut and bloodied, held the stump of one hand to his chest. He stared at them with astonished, panicked eyes. He spat out a guttural oath and a screen of gold light shone on his boots. He ran towards the entrance, moving at an impossible speed.

Megan's firedarts, a white-hot beam of light from Stephen and a thrown dagger from Daphne arrived at the same time. The attacks slammed into the wizard and he veered wildly off course. Out of control, he slammed into the stone wall with a sickening crunch.

Brandi sprinted to Stephen and slid next to him. "What happened?"

Her uncle grimaced. "Ghoul's Kiss, a Sting of the Scorpion spell, Ghost Hammer and a Fire Finger. Amateur stuff really." Despite his bravado, she could see the pain and fear in his eyes.

She laid him down on the floor as her sister and aunt came up to them.

I don't know if I can heal this. Dear God! Help me heal this...

"Brandi?" Megan asked.

"I'm on it," she replied, shrugging off her backpack. "Get out the green glass vial and the clear one."

She put both hands on her uncle, centering her focus, feeling for his vital signs.

She found his pulse, strong but weakening. She detected major nerve and blood vessel damage in his legs and hips. One ankle was broken.

She concentrated on stabilizing his heart first, closing her eyes and feeling the energy flowing through her. Something blocked her efforts and she recognized poison.

"Clear vial," she said in a strained voice. "Give him the clear one."

She felt him swallow and the poison dissipated. She focused on his hips next, trying to repair nerves and blood vessels. The energy surged through her and she gasped. This was taking all of her strength.

"Green vial!" she choked out the words.

Now she saw the effects of the second potion, a warm, orange glow she could see even through her closed eyelids. With a ragged sigh, she released the remainder of her healing power and sagged forward, hands on her thighs. She knelt there, panting and trembling all over.

"Good work Brandi," said Daphne in an approving voice. She felt her aunt's hands lowering her to the ground.

"Now, one for you," Daphne said, lifting a vial to her lips. Brandi sipped down the potion, effervescent, tart and salty at the same time. She lay on the stone floor. She let the curative work its way through her system and not caring how cold, wet, tired and grubby she felt.

"Well," she heard Megan say. "I'm sure they had their papers all organized, originally. Until Uncle Stephen used that— whatever spell that was— to hurl the table into the wizard."

Brandi heard Stephen get to his feet. "That would be Mens Motus. I'll teach it to you later."

She opened her eyes, surprised she could see at all. She sat up. Megan joined her, holding some papers. She gave Brandi a scroll as she pored over the ones in her hands.

Daphne took a sheaf of parchments herself. "While you are looking those over, I'm going to get the teens. We should all stick together."

Brandi unrolled the scroll and spread it out over her knees. It looked like a design drawing, showing the bone structure and indicating dimensions. A strange, blocky set of runes ran down one side of the drawing. It seemed to her to be list of some kind, since matching runes appeared near various elements of the structure. She examined all four sheets and came to the conclusion that engineering was not her preferred course of study in the future.

Stephen sat with them. "Anything?"

"Design drawings," Brandi said. She rolled the papers up and tied them, then handed them to her uncle. "Not sure what it means, but it looks like the bone structure. There are odd runes on the drawings too."

Megan handed hers over. "This is a set of instructions or a list, but has same runes as the drawings."

Stephen shrugged off his backpack and slipped all the documents into a leather satchel. "We'll send these off to St. Martins. Someone on the Papal Nuncio's staff will know how to direct them for further study."

Daphne arrived with the teens, who looked nauseated at the destruction and carnage. Brandi sympathized. She remembered how she had felt in her first real battle, those many months ago with Eric at her side, fighting goblin warriors near Forester, in Deran.

Daphne handed her sheets to Stephen, who added them to the satchel and replaced his backpack. "These, at least, were in Humana. Personnel lists, pay rates, and attendance sheets, plus a slave inventory."

Jason made a face. "I bet we were on that one."

"You were, but duly noted as virgin sacrifices."

Catherine shuddered. "Let's just get out of here. I want nothing more to do with this place."

"Motion carried," Stephen said, giving her a cheerful smile. "But first, we have to get rid of that thing." He jerked a thumb at the bone structure.

"How?"

Brandi grinned. "We have some nice, big pieces of wood, some large stone carvings and an iron kettle. I think we can come up with something."

Using the remnants of the stout table and emptying the cauldron to use it as a ram, they all leaped into the task with gusto. Brandi noticed that the teen girls, in particular, took a savage glee in ruining the Ja'al structure. With the youths and the Alenars working together, only a pile of bones and twisted metal remained.

Daphne led them towards the exit, weapons at the ready. They approached each chamber quickly and cautiously but no one remained, except the one Viper guard trussed up behind the rock. Daphne checked his bonds, then lifted him to his feet.

"You, my friend, are going to provide information to the road-wardens. Move."

The Viper leered at the teens, especially the girls, but the former kidnap victims glared at him, fingering their new weapons. After a few seconds of this, he saw they weren't intimidated and settled into a sulk instead.

They reached the exit to the beach. Daphne led them out, keeping to the sides of the cove and then turned right at the end of the little ridge. They had waded through the rising tide but made it to the main beach. As they struggled up through the sand dunes, Brandi began to think they were over the worst of it.

Then a party of Skullhead troops came over a near hill.

"Here now!" one of them shouted. "What are you doing away from your posts? Filthy Viper scum! You're supposed to stay on duty until we relieve you."

In answer, Daphne and Brandi let fly with arrows, felling two of them. Stephen unloaded a dazzling beam of light, burning through the armor of another.

"Get them!" a big, bearded Skullhead roared.

"Run!" shouted Megan, waving her hands in a circular pattern. A cloud of fog rolled out from her hands and grew with gratifying speed, filling the area nearby in mere seconds.

Brandi called to the teens. "Follow my voice! Follow my voice!"

One of the girls, Amber, nearly ran over Brandi but she linked hands with her as they stumbled through the mist. Behind them, they heard the crackle of magic and a thump or two, followed by cursing and shouts.

A misty figure came up next to her but it was Stephen leading both boys and Miriam. Amber grabbed Miriam's hand. Behind them, a figure with long hair led another girl.

Brandi headed towards the direction of the coast road, watching her footing and listening for sounds of pursuit. Soon the fog thinned.

Taking up her bow and a special arrow with a sparkly red ribbon, she loosed it straight up.

"Megan, we can take two teens on each pegasus if we stay on the ground."

She looked up into the sky, feeling immense relief as two winged horses approached.

"Megan?"

She turned around. Daphne looked pale.

"Where's Meg?" Brandi asked. A pang of fear grew in her belly.

"Back there," Stephen said grimly, pointing at the wall of fog.

***

Megan saw a shadowy figure in the mist near her and dodged to the side as a blade swished through the foggy air. She ran towards the last location of Brandi's voice.

"Got you!" said a rough voice as another sword-wielding figure loomed up at her. She dodged clutching hands, tripped on a rock and went flying, losing her shoulder bag into a bunch of hartberry bushes. Another man tried to tackle her but she wiggled away and crawled through the grass.

She heard men's voices cursing as they stumbled into each other.

She waited, hearing their voices receding. After counting to five, she stood and ran away from where she thought the ocean to be.

She never saw the club that hit her in the side of the head.

***

Brandi mounted Amicus, her stomach in knots. "We can't leave her in there."

"No, Brandi, we can't," Daphne said, chewing her lip. She put a hand on her knee.

"We'll go with you," said Jason, hefting his sword.

"No," Stephen replied, shaking his head. "That's noble of you, but they're armored warriors with experience and you're not. We didn't rescue you to lose you again. Besides, we have a prisoner to take back to your town."

"If Megan has been taken, follow but do not engage. If they see you, they may harm Megan. Shadow them. I will know how to find you."

Brandi must have looked panicked because Daphne gave her leg a squeeze and smiled. "Megan knows how to handle herself and she's more than a match for a bunch of Skullheads. Just play it smart. As soon as we have the villagers safely on the road, we'll come back after you. Keep Larinor with you, just in case."

Brandi nodded wordlessly and spurred her pegasus into a canter, then took to the air. She kept low above the tree line around the edge of the mist, heading for a rocky outcropping near the Ja'al base.

***

"But which one is she?" asked one of the voices.

"Hell if I know," said another voice. "I only saw them once and the damned Vipers brought them anyway. Wasn't one of them a redhead?"

Megan opened her eyes, trying to ignore the pounding in her skull. When she could recognize shapes, she saw four men hunkered down in the mist near some boulders.

Next to them, her clothes, boots, belt, and dagger lay on the ground.

Please, God don't let them rape me...

She found her hands tied together in front of her, below her waist, and tried the bonds—too tight. She forced herself to control her racing heart and shivered from the chilling mist she had created as it settled on her skin.

Skullheads. I've seen what they do to young women and girls.

Someone knelt down next to her. A rough hand cupped her face, then a shock of cold water made her gasp.

"Awake now, Lieutenant. You want to question her?"

"Not here," said a fourth voice, belonging to a slimmer shadow. "I don't like this damned fog. Bring her along and take her gear. We'll see what the wizards have to say."

The large, muscular man pulled her to her feet. "Don't even think about running," he whispered into her ear. "There's hobgoblins about. A naked girl out here in the hinterlands won't last five minutes with night coming on."

Want to bet? She thought with fierce anger, but kept her mouth shut.

The four moved quickly, staying in the mist. The leader stopped every once in a while to listen for the sound of waves. Soon the magic fog thinned. Megan felt sand between her toes and then they stood on the beach, looking back towards the Ja'al outpost she had just left. The setting sun made the ocean glow orange.

She got a good look at her captors. One stood only a little shorter than Dar Cabot and sported a dark beard and mustache. He carried a club, sword and dagger. He eyed her naked body more than once but his gaze kept darting back towards a burly warrior with a battle axe. He, too, had a beard and mustache, but blond. Her eyes flickered to an insignia on the left breast of the axe-man's hauberk that looked like a skull with a dagger under it.

Another, taller Skullhead warrior carried a sword and spear and he gazed out at the ocean, not sparing her a second glance. She thought his eyes looked dead. He towered over her by almost a foot.

The last Skullhead, a more slender man in scale armor with a sword and shield, stood in the sand. He stroked his shaven chin thoughtfully. She noticed a different insignia on his tunic: two silver skulls.

The axe-man cleared his throat. "Lieutenant Volan?"

"Something's not right," the officer with the twin-skull insignia said. "We find the slaves and those others heading away from the outpost and there's no pursuit behind them. If we hadn't come along to return after patrol, we would have missed all of them. Where are the Vipers? What about Sergeant Lixxan and his team?"

Lieutenant Volan motioned to the smaller Skullhead and the tall spear-wielder. "Vrixus, Tamsan, head to the outpost. See who's there and find out what's going on."

The two warriors gave Megan a backward glance and then trotted off.

Megan stood perfectly still, wishing she was invisible and not daring to breathe. The officer stood next to her, thumbs hooked in his sword belt.

"I'm glad you're being sensible," said Volan without turning his head. "I'd get really pissed off if I had to chase you through the brush after a three-hour patrol. Besides, Sergeant Argus here is tired and he's mighty mean when he hasn't had his dinner."

Argus snorted and eyed Megan, then joined his commander in watching.

If my hands were free, I could use a spell like Tricky Sprite to distract them and then slip away.

After what seemed like years, the other two jogged towards them. "Here they come," said Argus.

"Everyone is dead," Vrixus reported. "All the Vipers, Sergeant Lixxan, his team, both wizards and some kind of hound-things. The structure the wizards were making is totally destroyed. All of the prisoners are gone."

Argus grunted. "The work of free-lancers, or I'm an ogre."

Lieutenant Volan guided Megan forward with his hand. "Only, they lost one of the slaves in the mist after one of the free-lancers used that fog magic. Just our luck."

They think I'm one of the teens!

"Sit down," he ordered. Megan sat, eyes watching his face. Volan had even, handsome features and blue eyes to go with dark hair. He sat in front of her.

"Gentlemen, I know that the prisoners were virgin sacrifices. Are you a virgin, woman?"

Megan said nothing, trying to think of a way to trick him into releasing her.

Tamsan snorted in derision. "Bet you three gold she isn't."

Volan raised an eyebrow. "I have ways to, um, inspect you to find out. Or you can just tell me."

Megan's mind raced, knowing she was on borrowed time and could expect no mercy from these men. Her only chance lay in misdirection and delay.

"I am," she said, making sure to make her voice timid and forlorn.

Volan's blue eyes bored into hers.

"She's lying," Vrixus said, sounding agitated. "Come on, Lieutenant. It's been a long day. We should do her now and get some fun out of it. We can take turns."

Megan's heart skipped a beat and fear clutched her heart.

Volan never took his eyes off her. He gave her a tiny smile.

"No, private, she isn't lying. I know the reaction of a virgin when you suggest violating her and she just had it."

Vrixus crouched in front of her. "Well, so what?" he said in a sullen voice. "Virgin or not, she's ours and we can do what we want."

"Can we? You have amber eyes, darling," Volan said in a soft voice, reaching out a hand to her hair. She recoiled. He persisted and looped her hair over her ears.

"An elf!" Argus said with a chuckle. "Virgin female elf! I know where this is going, Lieutenant."

Vrixus looked back at Tamsan, who scratched his head. "So what?"

Volan stood, pulling Megan to her feet, and Vrixus stood with him. "Vrixus, this girl was one of the prisoners. The wizards wanted virgins for some sacrifice or another. The Vipers picked her out, and Vipers know slaves. Do you know how much a virgin elf woman is worth in the slave trade?"

Vrixus said nothing.

Volan looked back at the others. "Anyone?"

Argus nodded. "A lot."

"Try twelve thousand."

Tamsan and Vrixus exchanged a startled glance. "That can't be! Twelve thousand gold crowns for a slave?"

"Believe it. Elves live long, they're intelligent, learn fast and have great singing voices and can dance like you wouldn't believe. Elven dancing slave? You can bet she'd go for at least that much, especially one that looks like her."

Vrixus wouldn't let it go. He stared at Megan's naked body until she felt more violated by his eyes than the touch of his hand ever could. He seemed like a prowling wolf, light-colored eyes intent and staring.

Vrixus shook his head. "Look at that, though, Lieutenant. I haven't had a woman since that brothel back in Overlook. What a body! That's a fine piece, Lieutenant."

Volan looked at Vrixus with a frown. "You're right, private, which makes her all the more valuable. Think about it. Who's going to pay us now that the wizards are dead? Don't forget we were promised hazard pay for this duty."

Argus cleared his throat. "Sir, the captain said—"

"—said to serve the mages in all things and report back when their task was done." Volan looked back at Megan, then gestured at his comrades. "But now, the mages are dead and their task *isn't* done. Freelancers just took out the whole outpost and freed the captives, except for this one. All the other troops are dead. So, what do we do? Where are we going to take her? The wizards needed, what, five virgins? Where the hell are we going to find four more? With the kidnappings and all that wreck in the village, the road wardens will be swarming around here for weeks."

The others looked at each other but made no answer.

"No," Volan said, eyeing her. To her surprise, she found his gaze almost regretful. "We're owed. Don't you remember our last mission, when it failed and we took the blame even though it was those filthy Kaftu that screwed it up? The captain has put us on the worst duty for months and not even paid us bonuses when we earned them. Well, *she's* our bonus. I know a slaver underground in Shark Bluff who can get us in touch with the right people."

Argus gave Megan a grin, displaying two missing teeth. "She's looking more and more beautiful all the time."

Vrixus set his jaw. "I don't buy it! I've had my fill of this. I want this little whore and I'll have her."

Volan didn't even turn his head. "Sergeant Argus, you have a new assignment. This elf-girl is your charge. No one but me is to come near her. If anyone attempts to molest or rape her, you are to cut off his arms. I will personally heave him into the GreatSea and watch the sharks tear him to pieces."

He turned to Vrixus. The bearded man glared at him with baleful eyes.

"Do you see this?" Volan fingered the insignia on his tunic. "It means I'm in charge. *I'm* the officer. No sewer-scraping private is going to get between me and my due. I've led this unit for six months through idiotic and dangerous missions and only gotten a measly hundred gold. Do I make myself clear?"

Megan held her breath, watching the battle of wills, praying against all hope. Maybe Volan's greed and wounded pride would be her way out.

Tamsan shrugged. "Hey, I'd rather have the gold, Vrixus. Shit, three thousand each? I can have all the whores I want, down in Meridian or in Torosc. I could even start my own mercenary squad."

Vrixus finally looked away. "Damn waste of a hot woman, Lieutenant."

"Only if you ruin her with your filthy hands, Vrixus," Volan snarled. "Keep your mouth shut and follow orders."

He came up to Megan. "What's your name?"

On a hunch, Megan said, "Miriam."

Volan smirked. "I remembered right. There was a Miriam among the virgins. Perfect. You, my little wench, are my ticket to a new life."

He pulled her along by her bound wrists and handed her over to Argus.

"Sir?" asked Argus. "The mist is gone. Shouldn't we go back to the outpost and stay the night?"

Volan shook his head. "Those freelances killed three of us in less than ten seconds and Viper guards and a squad of Skullheads, plus the two wizards. No, once they realize they're missing a virgin, they're going to come looking for her and I don't want to be anywhere nearby when they do."

***

Brandi sat in her saddle, trying not to twist the reins into a knot. She watched as the Ja'al argued among themselves. She witnessed the test of wills between the apparent leader and one of his subordinates, then saw the burly axe-man lead her sister down to the sand and follow the others south, along the shore.

I will watch and wait. Just hurry, Daphne. Or I'll take them all myself if it looks like Megan is in danger.

"Come on Larinor," she said to Megan's pegasus. She trotted the steeds towards the ocean, shadowing the Ja'al and their captive.

Chapter Seven- New Beginnings

Megan sipped from the cup of water, eyes downcast, crouched by the campfire. Volan and Tamsan sat on the other side of the fire, eating their own meager rations. Beyond them, she saw Argus and Vrixus stood watch.

She considered asking Volan again to give her clothes back, then decided against it. The last time she tried it, she'd seen a quick flash of sympathy in his eyes, but then his gaze had hardened. She tried to convince him she wouldn't flee, even suggesting they tie her feet so that she could only shuffle, but he had refused.

"I know you don't like Vrixus and Tamsan looking you over," he said, "But this is the easiest way to keep you from running. If I tie you so you can walk but not run, you'll slow us down. And as for being stared at," he had shrugged then, "you're going to have to get used to it. You're going to be a slave."

She sensed Volan to be the most reluctant Skullhead of all, despite his rank. Vrixus didn't care about anything but his own appetites, Tamsan showed no emotion but she could see a simmering brutality in him, and Argus just fought for whoever paid him.

But Volan? It seemed he wanted out, wanted to sever his connection to the Ja'al.

Maybe I can use that somehow.

Volan reached into his belt pouch and took out a piece of paper, which he unfolded and read. With a snort of disgust, he refolded it and put it back.

Tamsan nodded at him. "Why do you still have that junk? It doesn't mean anything to us anymore. No mages to make us chant it while they do their magic-working on that whatever-it-was they were building."

Volan took a pull from his wineskin. "Because I can't figure it out. It's stupid and weird, but somehow it's tied in with whatever that structure was. I don't like mysteries and I don't like being used as a pawn."

Tamsan shook his head. "Doesn't matter."

Volan stood. "You're right. Let's relieve the others. It's time for our watch."

Volan and Tamsan switched places with Vrixus and Argus, who came to the fire.

Megan chewed and swallowed the last little bit of bread they had given her. She felt a constant gnawing of hunger and knew she needed more water, but they offered her only the barest of rations.

Vrixus shifted closer to her and she shrank back, scooting on her bottom in the soft grass closer to Argus.

The big sergeant smirked. "I'm not much better than him, wench. But I follow orders, I do. And the Lieutenant gave me an order."

Vrixus sullenly downed his supper and swigged from his wineskin. Argus tossed a twig into the fire.

"And if you know what's good for you," he said in a conversational tone, "You'll follow orders too, Vrixus. The girl stays undefiled until we sell her. Then it's out of our hands."

Vrixus stared at her, taking another drink. Megan felt her skin crawl.

"Damn waste," he said with a burp. "Don't see women as fine as her every day, Sergeant."

Argus shrugged. "Three thousand gold will get you a lot of fine women, Vrixus. That's more than four years wages in most countries, even Deran. Just keep thinking about that."

He stood and positioned himself between Megan and the smaller warrior, then lay down and stretched out by the fire.

"Get some sleep." He turned his back on Megan. She warily laid down behind him.

I'll never get any sleep with that rapacious weasel eyeing my body all the time.

She fought to stay awake, expecting Vrixus to slither around to get her at any time.

She awoke from a doze with a start at the sound of something metallic penetrating the ground.

Vrixus froze in place on the ground not two feet from her. A dagger gleamed next to his left hand, stuck in the dirt.

Volan stepped over the sleeping Argus and pulled his dagger out of the ground.

He held up his thumb and forefinger close together in front of his face. "I'm this far from taking off your hands, Vrixus. Try pawing her body parts with no hands. Get back to your place and don't let me see you try anything stupid again."

Eyes full of hate and fear, Vrixus slunk back.

Volan looked down at her and replaced his dagger. "Don't worry wench. He knows I'll do it. Get some rest. You'll need it for tomorrow."

He sat next to Megan, his sword across his knees as he kept watch.

She wasn't sure when she fell asleep. Before she knew it, dawn light broke across her face, awakening her.

Volan stood and offered her a hand. Keeping the persona of a timid young girl, she took it and stood.

He stretched. "We move out in an hour. Be ready."

***

"It's about time," Brandi snapped.

"You're hard to track, you know," said Daphne in a mild tone. She gave a low whistle and her giant owl bent down so she and Stephen could dismount.

Brandi flushed. "I'm sorry. I'm just so worried for Megan."

"I understand," said Stephen, giving her shoulder a squeeze. "We're worried too, but don't forget that Megan has endured much already in her life and is tougher than most people think. How is she?"

Brandi nodded at the Ja'al camp, set among the dunes and tall grasses down the slope from her. From her position among the trees along the ridge-line above the ocean, she could see them but knew they would have difficulty seeing her.

"She's fine, for now. There's been a bit of arguing among them. The tall spearman and the smaller fellow keep eyeing Megan and shifting to get near her, but the big axe-man and the officer are protecting her for some reason."

"Money."

Brandi stared at her aunt. Daphne gave a bitter smile.

"Elven slaves cost a lot of money and Megan is very beautiful. If they sell her, well, that much cash would place them within their commander's good favor, at the least assuming they even return to their duty station."

"How much?" asked Brandi, feeling cold.

"It depends. Twelve to fifteen thousand as a first guess. Those four could retire on that much, split evenly."

Stephen nodded. "Yes. If she's in good condition and undefiled until they sell her off, they maximize their profits. If she's in less than perfect condition, the price drops dramatically. That means we have a good opportunity."

"With the officer and the other guy keeping their eyes on the other two, we could distract them," said Brandi. "We just need a diversion. If we get their attention away from Megan, I can get in there and free her hands. Then they'll get quite a surprise. But what diversion do we use?"

"How about a pegasus?" asked Stephen with a smile.

***

"Vrixus, you and Tamsan scout ahead. I don't want any stupid fishermen to see us before we can get near Shark Bluff."

The other two Skullheads headed off and Megan saw Volan sigh.

"Keep an eye on them, Argus. I don't trust them an inch."

With a snort of derision, the sergeant advanced about twenty yards and hunched down behind a rock. Seagulls wheeled overhead and Megan watched sandpipers play tag with the surf. The sea air smelled fresh and clean, just like from her childhood in Coastwatch. The incongruity of it struck her: the natural beauty of this area appealed to her, yet she was in no position to enjoy it. It was very much like her childhood in Torosc: always in fear of discovery and death, persecuted as a Christian in a hostile, pagan culture and unable to enjoy life.

When will I ever get a chance to slow down and enjoy the sea? Or anything, for that matter?

"Sir?" she asked Volan in a tentative voice.

He glanced at her.

"Sir, why do you do this? You're not like them."

"It pays the bills, wench," he said, turning his gaze away. "It's not like there are a lot of other options for men like me."

Megan sensed her opening. "What do you mean, sir?"

He hooked his thumbs in his sword belt. "Ever wonder how I could figure out your worth as a slave so fast? My mother and father were slavers, Vipers even. That's how I got this job and the commission. They had connections. Can you imagine trying to get any other job anywhere with that kind of background?"

Megan remembered a friend named Eric, with a far darker past, who decided to leave all behind for a chance at a good life: a very good friend, a noble and decent man, and the love of her sister's life.

"You can always have a second chance, sir."

He laughed. "For what? To do something right? I had my chance before and I blew it."

"It can't have been that bad."

"It was."

Acting on instinct again, Megan asked, "What was her name?"

Volan stared at her and shook his head. "You're either magically talented or a really good guesser."

He turned back to the shoreline. Argus waved at them. Volan waved back.

Megan stood silent, feeling more relaxed and hopeful. She almost enjoyed the feeling of the sun and the ocean breeze on her skin.

"Varienne," Volan said. "She was kidnapped by my parents as a young lady, no older than you, really. I was assigned to protect her from the other slavers. She was very attractive and kind. She kept trying to convince me to let her go, that her family would help me and protect me if I helped her."

Megan kept quiet.

"I tried to buy her for myself, you know," Volan said. "My father laughed, saying I'd have to work five years to meet the price for her."

"What happened to her?"

"We sold her to a wizard in Morlan, a mage named George Oxbridge. For five thousand gold. Even if I wanted to, I could never find her or buy her back now. It's been two years."

Now she thought he looked not so much like a hated Ja'al enemy as a forlorn, remorseful young man.

"Maybe not buy her back," Megan said, "But maybe you could free her. And there are others, I think, who might want to help you."

Volan's gaze hardened. "Not much chance of that, wench. I'm a Skull-head."

He straightened as the other three men returned.

"I can see the cave just like you said, sir," Tamsan reported. "Back from the beach in a little cove, north of town by a couple of miles."

"Perfect." Volan took Megan's bound hands and pulled her ahead of him. "Let's move."

Megan's heart sank. *If I can get Volan alone again, I know I can convince him to let me go! He's not as bad as the others.*

She trudged through the sand, following Vrixus and Tamsan ahead of her, racking her brain to come up with a plan. If her hands weren't tied, she could use magic to even the odds.

"By the daemons of Hades!"

She jerked her head up at the sound of Tamsan's voice. Vrixus let out a profane oath.

A single pegasus stood in the tall grass just ahead of them. Even though it had neither bit nor bridle nor saddle, she knew it was her Larinor.

The animal tossed his head and backed up, favoring one leg. He held one wing close to his body.

"Damn, Lieutenant!" exclaimed Argus. "A pegasus! And hurt too, by the looks of it."

Volan's eyes narrowed. "What's a pegasus doing out here?"

"Who the hell cares?" spat Vrixus. "It can't fly. If that whore is worth a pile of gold, a pegasus is worth a mountain of loot!"

"Hold on," said Volan, eyes darting around the area. A couple of small boulders sat in the surf to their right and tall grass led up a slope towards the forested ridge line to his left.

"Lieutenant," Tamsan said as the pegasus took another step back. "We gotta make a play soon. It can't fly but it's still probably faster than us."

"I smell a trap." Volan drew his sword.

Megan's magical senses tingled.

"The hell with it," Vrixus said. He darted towards Larinor. Tamsan leaped forward to join him.

"I said hold, you idiots!" Volan shouted, pulling Megan with him in pursuit.

The tall grass parted and Megan's heart leaped at the sight of Daphne charging out to engage Vrixus. The Skullhead pulled up short with a yelp, parried her sword swing with his club, and drew his own blade. Tamsan whipped around and thrust with his spear. Daphne knocked it aside.

The grass parted again and Stephen stepped out, holding out his hand towards Vrixus and Tamsan. Firedarts shot out, striking them both. They staggered.

Argus roared a challenge and waded in, swinging his axe. Daphne and Stephen dodged.

Volan cursed, dragging Megan with him. A motion from the rocks to her left drew her attention. Brandi hurtled out at them, blades bared. Volan whirled to meet her. Megan kicked him in the back of the calf as he turned. Brandi's sword stroke missed. Her momentum carried her into Volan, knocking him back. He tripped and tumbled back towards the waves, his head hitting a rock in the surf. He rolled to one side, holding his head and groping for his fallen sword.

Brandi cut Megan's bonds.

"Help Daphne and Stephen," Megan said, shaking the ropes loose. "I'll handle this one."

"Are you sure?"

"Go! Watch out for the weaselly one."

Megan held out a hand and pointed two fingers at Volan, casting a smooth blue globe of light at him. It struck him and popped, covering him with a mild blue mist. He slumped back to the sand, then struggled to rise, seeming to move at half speed.

Megan turned back. She wanted to get a spell off into the melee was but wary of hitting her relatives. Stephen cast a spell at Argus's feet, causing a cloud of sand and water to erupt into his face. The axe-man sidestepped and swung, but Stephen wasn't there anymore. The axe buried itself in the sand. Stephen took a long step and swung at Argus's head. The Ja'al sergeant ducked and punched Stephen, who reeled backwards. The great axe rose and struck again but Stephen spun out of the way, darted in and impaled Argus with his blade. The Skullhead gasped and slumped to the sand.

Tamsan tried to keep Daphne at bay with his longer reach and spear, but she timed his motions well and put stab wounds into his thigh and shoulder.

"Surrender," she said.

Tamsan, wild-eyed and panting, charged in. He missed her eyes with the spearpoint, swung the haft to hit her in the side, and lashed out with a kick. Daphne winced but stepped forward, past Tamsan's kick. Before he could turn around, she stabbed him in the side and back.

Vrixus, meanwhile, aimed a flurry of blows at Brandi, who parried each one of them with deadly precision. Vrixus sprang back, eyes wide. Brandi stalked him, aiming blows at his legs, head and chest. He looked panicked.

With a sudden motion, he tossed his club at her head and kicked sand into her face. Brandi dodged back and slipped in the sand, blinking and holding her blades before her in defensive position. Vrixus sprinted to his right, towards the beach.

He saw Megan and scrambled to a stop. Megan stared into his eyes, her hand out with a spell ready.

"You're not a virgin sacrifice!" he spat.

"You have the second part of that right," she retorted.

With an incoherent scream of rage, eyes wild with madness, he charged her.

She unleashed a Lightning Spear and blew his heart out. He flew backwards through the air to thump into the sand.

Daphne and Stephen sheathed their weapons. "Are you okay?" Stephen asked.

"Yes," said Megan, feeling weak with relief. She pointed at Volan. "Tie him up though. Farfield's Lethargy doesn't last long."

Volan leaned up against a boulder in the sand, blood running down one side of his face, groping in the surf for his weapon.

Daphne held him at bay while Stephen got a rope from his backpack and bound his hands.

Brandi searched through the Ja'al gear and handed Megan her clothes. Megan stopped her sister with a fierce hug.

"Thank God you're okay," Brandi whispered, her voice wavering.

Megan felt a lump in her throat, knowing how much Brandi must have fretted and worried.

"I'm fine, Bran. I'm fine. Thanks to all of you."

Daphne and Stephen joined them, smiling and clasping her in hugs.

Brandi wiped a tear from her eye and smiled. "Put your clothes on, you wild thing. The neighbors will think this is a Gariil ceremony."

"Thanks," Megan said with a laugh. "I can't run around naked in Gorostol too much longer."

Brandi went over to the tall grass and whistled for the pegasi. Both Larinor and Amicus came trotting over. Megan smiled, patting Larinor and kissing him on the nose. The pegasus whinnied, seeming delighted to see her.

"Who did the illusion of an injured pegasus?"

"Uncle Stephen. All we did was have Larinor stand there and then pulled him back slightly until the Ja'al came after him."

Brandi joined her relatives in searching the Ja'al, relieving Volan of his pack, belt purse and other gear. By the time Megan was done stamping into her boots, Brandi had applied a healing spell to the Ja'al lieutenant's head.

"He had a mild concussion," Brandi told Megan as she laced up the front of her blouse and slipped into her vest. "Not too bad. It should make it easier to interrogate him."

Megan motioned to her aunt and uncle and they joined her and Brandi. Volan sat in the sand, head down, not looking at them.

"I have a feeling about him," Megan said, binding her hair behind her head.

Stephen stroked his chin. "What kind of feeling?"

Megan told the others about how Volan had protected her from the other Skullheads and even seemed reluctant about the whole escapade. She gave them the parchment that Volan had read from earlier. Stephen put it into his pocket without looking at it.

"Light reading for this evening," he said.

Megan related Volan's background as the son of Viper slavers and his remorse about the one slave he hadn't been brave enough to set free.

Daphne looked thoughtful. "You think he's redeemable?"

Megan nodded. "With the right encouragement."

Stephen handed Megan her shoulder bag. "We'll provide cover for you. You know him better than we do, so we'll go with your best judgement."

Megan came over to Volan and crouched down in front of him. He raised his eyes to her.

He gave a wry smile. "The tables are turned."

Megan nodded. "But thanks to you, I am unharmed."

He shook his head. "No. I was being selfish, for my own gain. I am no hero."

She smiled back. "The fact that you can say so testifies that you know the difference, and perhaps would do things differently, given the chance."

He stared at her for a long moment, then nodded at Brandi. "Your relative?"

"Sister."

He pursed his lip. "And the other two?"

"Aunt and uncle."

"Your sister healed me. She didn't have to do that."

Megan sat in the sand in front of him. "Yes, she did. She's of the Order of Saint Raphael. They heal anyone who will submit to it, even enemies."

"Christians?"

She nodded. "All of us."

"Not many of you in the open in Torosc, but I've heard of you."

"All good I hope."

Volan shrugged. "Mostly."

Megan nodded. "But now the question is what to do with you."

He sighed. "The road wardens will reward you handsomely."

She shook her head. "If we turn you over to them. But I think there's something else in your future, Lieutenant Volan. You're not like the others. Do you want a second chance?"

His brow furrowed. "Why would you do that?"

"Because maybe, just maybe, you'll end up on the same side we're on."

He looked past her at her relatives.

"And you're okay with this?"

Daphne shrugged. "She's always bringing home stray puppies. It's a fault, but it's endearing."

A ghost of a smile flitted across his face. "I see."

"Do you have a name?" Megan asked.

"Altus."

"I'm Megan. Do we have a deal? We free you and you leave the Ja'al and the Vipers behind. Then you get a new life and do it right this time."

He nodded. "Well, Megan, it appears I have no choice."

"No, Altus. You always have a choice. Just think about what you're really trying to do."

She stood, lifted him to his feet and untied his bonds.

"I guess that's part of my problem," he said, eyes downcast. "I'm not really sure what I'm supposed to do."

Daphne returned his weapons and shield to him. "You have command experience and are battle-seasoned. I can think of some mercenary companies of good repute who could use you, here in Gorostol or northward in Terenai. The Black-star Company, in particular. Mention the name of Daphne Alenar to them and doors will open."

"Who knows?" Brandi offered, handing him the belt purses of his slain comrades. "Maybe you'll even make your way down to Morlan someday."

Stephen took a hold of the Skullhead symbol on his tunic and pried it off. The officer looked at his round wooden shield, emblazoned with the Skullhead insignia, and tossed it into the tall grass. Now Volan looked like any other free-lance mercenary.

"A great start," said Megan, handing him his belt purse.

Altus Volan looked down at the purse in his hands, silent. When he raised his head, Megan was surprised to see a glint of tears in his eyes.

"I… thank you. No one has ever done anything like this, nor had such faith in me," he managed, then cleared his throat and stood straighter. "I give you my word I will live up to it."

Megan gave him a bright smile. "Good. I know there's a lady named Varienne somewhere in Morlan who will be very proud to see it."

Chapter Eight- In a Wood, Dark and Grim

He perched on the spire of rock, catching his breath.

The endurance fades after the first three hundred years. In the old days, I d be all the way to Dwarfshire by now.

Iron Thunder inhaled deeply of the mountain air, turning his gaze to the sky. High clouds meandered westward towards the sea, dropping the last of their rain on the plains of northeastern Deran and the Evendale border. Ahead and to his left, the tangled forests of the Wilderness diminished as they met with the patchwork of farmlands, large rectangles of light green in Deran and smaller, darker patches in the halfling land of Everdale. The pride of Evendale, Lake Silverdown, glittered in the afternoon sun to the east. Farther to the north, another lake hid among mountain peaks.

He sighed, then forced himself to relax. Darkwood drakes stood between the Grey Riders and their objective now. However, he had time. From what he knew of Darkwoods, they wouldn't strike until their prey had been softened up and tormented.

Base cowards.

Iron Thunder turned his gaze eastward, towards a mountain peak with two spires and a shining body of water at its feet. He drew a deep breath and spread his wings. With a final prayer to the One that he would be in time, he launched himself into the air, winging towards Shadow Lake far away.

***

Dar held still in the undergrowth, filtering out the familiar scents of leaf and earth and animal. He listened for small sounds in the brush and trees. Slowly, he identified all the normal creatures and plants.

His eyes flitted left and right. Not fifty paces from him, hidden in the brush and wearing a cloak of mottled green and brown camouflage like him, Eric crouched behind a boulder.

Well, something made the wildlife go quiet a while ago. Everything is normal now, but what was that all about?

Behind him, in the forest, he knew that Buck and Andyn waited. Ahead of him, flitting through shadows, Hlerv and Connor scouted.

He smelled something odd: a faint, sour and strangely metallic odor. It drifted on the breeze like a wisp, only just strong enough for him to detect but not identify.

A small figure slipped through the underbrush towards him and he and grinned.

I must be getting better at this. They used to be able to sneak up on me and make me jump.

Connor slipped next to him. Eric joined them.

"Well?" Dar asked.

"Thick brush up ahead, but it thins out a bit to the north. There's also a pathway, but it feels wrong. For one thing, no one lives out here and no hunters will go near this place so why would there be a clear pathway?"

"Did you send up Stealth?" Dar asked.

Eric fingered the brooch affixed to his tunic. "Yes. Nothing lurking along the pathway I could see but the trees are still thick, despite the pathway. Even using Stealth's eyes, it wasn't easy."

"A pathway," Dar mused. "Anything else?"

"Some of the plants look different. Not any species I've seen before. Maybe Andyn can identify them."

"Let's get back."

They picked their way back to the others. Hlerv conversed with Andyn and Buck, all three likewise cloaked in camouflage.

Connor repeated the results of his reconnoiter.

Hlerv stroked his beard. "I found lots of rocky ground to the south and very large trees with impressive roots. Very tough place to fight. This pathway, now, it makes me wonder."

Connor nodded. "It looks like it heads towards to the fortress. It bothers me that it wouldn't be completely overgrown after all this time."

Dar gazed up through the branches and leaves of the trees, towards the slope of Twinspire northwest of their position. The crumbling towers, balconies and walkways of an ancient fortress brooded on the steep slope of the mountainside.

"How far?" asked Buck.

"With pegasi, not ten minutes. Through these woods? An hour at least."

Andyn made a face. "I still say we should have tried to land closer."

Eric shook his head. "And if we couldn't, then what? We'd need to spend a lot of time trying to find a landing area in this tangle and we're plenty noticeable up there silhouetted in the sky. We'd have alerted the Darkwood drakes that we're here and they'd have plenty of time to work mischief."

Hlerv shrugged. "What about landing on the fortress somewhere?"

Eric put his boot up on a fallen log. The surface of the wood crumbled in rot underfoot. "You saw the condition of that place. I sent up Stealth and there are no places to land one pegasus, much less four. Imagine getting a pegasus with a broken leg *and* the drakes coming after us. It will be a chore climbing up there on our own, never mind the pegasi."

"He's right," said Dar. "As much as I don't like slogging through the woods, there's too much risk of being seen flying right up to the fortress. The pegasi are safe where we left them."

"Of course," said Buck, hefting his pack. "They have Puup to look after them. They'll be fine."

Andyn rolled her eyes at the mention of Buck's pigeon but said nothing.

Dar slung his bow over his back again. "One thing I can tell you is that bows and arrows won't matter in here unless you're an uncanny shot. Too many branches and leaves."

Silence reigned,

The other Riders lifted their eyes to the fortress.

Nobody wants to be the one to loose the first arrow.

"We can go back to the lake shore, to the camp from last night, and plan something else," he offered.

Andyn exchanged a look with Connor. Buck made a face.

Eric gave a wry smile. "No, Dar, we're just postponing the inevitable. This forest is sick and twisted, and I'm sure the drakes are the reason. We know they'll track us down and find us eventually, and we'll have to deal with them. Melinor said as much. We should just head out. It will be worse when night falls."

Dar nodded. "Well, then, you magical people should get us ready."

Andyn and Eric reached into shoulder bags. Andyn drew out a rod of burnished wood, about as thick as her thumb, set around the perimeter near the tip with tiny gemstones in a variety of colors. Eric laid out a bundle of cloth on the ground and unrolled it, exposing a multitude of small pockets holding glass vials.

"Stand together," Andyn said, pressing the green jewel. She held the rod overhead and made a circling motion.

A rush of magical energy swirled around, then Dar felt a faint pressure on his skin as a dark green mist descended on them.

Andyn repeated the maneuver again for each of the colored gems, seven in all. When she finished, Dar felt oddly secure and safe but a bit dizzy. He told her so.

Andyn smiled. "It's a lot of magical energy to use at once on someone. It will fade."

Eric handed out potion vials, four to each of them.

"The first three you can use now," Eric said. "The last one, the dark blue, is if you feel yourself fading and losing consciousness. Keep that one handy."

Dar tucked the dark blue one into a belt slot. He opened the yellow, clear and pink ones in succession and downed the contents.

"Holy saints," he coughed after the last. "Peppery, orange, chocolate, salty, lemony and minty, one after the other. I bet Melinor makes those flavors just to laugh at people after they drink them."

Eric tried to talk in between coughs. "I know he spends a lot of time trying to get the flavor right, whatever that means."

Andyn put the rod back into her bag. "The protections should last for a couple of hours, or until overpowered by magic, whichever comes first."

"Is that what it says on the warranty?" asked Hlerv with an innocent look. She made a face at him.

"Come on, let's move," said Connor, giving Hlerv a nudge towards the fortress. "The drakes are probably laughing at us right now."

Dar hesitated. "The pathway still bothers me. When we get in sight of it, stay to the side until we can figure out what's going on."

Eric replaced the cloth with the vials in his backpack and they set out in the same pattern as before: Hlerv and Connor scouting with Dar and Eric shadowing them and Buck and Andyn bringing up the rear.

They followed the direction Connor had indicated towards the clear pathway. Boughs and branches reached towards them, seeming more like clawed fingers. Noisome, deep purple ivy ran up the trunks of some of the trees, and Dar didn't like the look of some of the spiky bushes.

Connor's hand went up. Dar and Eric crept next to him. The halfling nodded towards a pathway.

It appeared to be made of interlocking white and grey stones. Dar stared at it for a while, a vague, disquieting feeling growing in him. With a start, he realized what was bothering him.

"Look at the pattern," he said as Andyn and Buck slipped next to them.

Andyn gasped. "Skulls…"

The tiles formed a pattern that showed two skulls side-by-side, then a band of grey, then two skulls, then another band. It stretched off into the dark forest ahead.

"I don't like this," said Eric.

Connor shook his head. "But get a load of the foliage around it. I like that even less."

Dar got the creeping feeling they were being herded. The pathway, ominous as it seemed, was hemmed in by some dusky brown creepers with pale yellow bulbs, probably closed flowers. Worse yet, blood-red roses with black leaves grew among the creepers in some weird symbiosis

"Ghost creepers," whispered Andyn, "And Vampire Roses."

Dar looked at her. "That's what those things are?"

She nodded, looking grim. "If you get close, they will attack. The Ghost Creepers have the power to weaken you and will hold you down while the

Roses slice you to shreds to get at your blood. Don't look directly at the roses. They are magical and will try to hypnotize you into coming closer."

Hlerv muttered an oath. "Attack plants? Now I've seen everything."

Buck removed his backpack. "Nothing that a little fire won't cure."

"No!" Andyn hissed. "You might get away with burning the roses, but the ghost creepers will start wailing. If the drakes are around, they'll hear for sure."

Dar felt his frustration building. Their scouting revealed this was the only route available to them but now?

Think, Cabot, think!

He snapped his fingers. "Buck, use the Eye of Truth."

Buck looked at him. "It shows truth through falsehood, Dar. I'm not sure what else you'll learn."

"When you found it, you were able to see an aura surrounding each of us, right?"

Buck nodded slowly. "I see what you're aiming at." He flipped the arm down on his helmet. The Eye of Truth glittered with rainbow colors.

"Hmm…" Buck peered at the pathway and forest around it. "There's definitely evil, but you've already figured that out. However…"

"What?" Dar said, trying to keep the edge out of his voice.

"The righthand eye-socket on each skull in the first row has a red glow. The same glow is on the left-hand socket on the skulls in the second row. Then back to right, then left. It repeats as far as I can see."

"The Eye of Truth doesn't lie," said Dar. "I'm willing to gamble that the red glow is a trap. If we don't step on those stones, we should be safe."

Connor hefted his bow. "We don't have another way forward, so we have no other choice. Stay sharp."

They got about fifty feet down the pathway when the first of the ghost creepers started waving at them. Dar drew his sword, keeping a wary eye on them. The vines moved more as they advanced, groping around as if searching for them.

Dar's throat clenched. *We are so dead if those things start shrieking.*

"Quicker," he hissed.

They hurried along, trying to watch the forest, the path and the vile plant life at the same time.

When the roses came to life, he knew they were in serious trouble. The branches reached out across the path and he had to duck and step over them while avoiding the deadly eye-sockets on the pathway. His breath came in gasps and his heart pounded in his chest.

"No good!" Connor spat out from the lead position. "They're forming a wall ahead of us."

"No choice now," Eric muttered. He raised a hand and spoke over his shoulder. "Fire away, Andyn."

Eric spoke a hissing word and flame shot out from his hand in a jet, crisping the creepers and roses on each side. The fire immolated the plants nearby but burned out after only a few seconds. He moved forward, setting flame to a wall of roses in front of him. Dar shot a look behind him.

Andyn fired a similar jet of flame at the plants nearest her. The burned roses and creepers made no sound, but their fellows farther back in the woods stirred. Dar heard a faint moaning, rising in volume.

"No use in staying on the path anymore!" he called to the others. "Off the path to the right, and follow Eric and Andyn."

As one, the Grey Riders stepped off the pathway of bones and into the forest, following Andyn and Eric as they cleared the deadly growth. Ashes drifted around them. They heard only their labored breathing and the crackle of flames and the eerie moaning of the Ghost Creepers.

So suddenly that it surprised them all, the creepers and roses gave way to a vast open space under giant trees. Thick roots bulged up from the ground all around them.

The wailing died down.

Dar felt the hackles on his neck rise. A sinister chill filled the air. Then he heard the voice. It sounded like the rasp of a tomb door.

"So, what comes to our forest, dear sister?"

Dar whirled towards the voice, only to see a wisp of shadow wind itself sinuously between two giant trees and off into the gloom.

"Small ones," said another, voice, lighter in tone but with the same malice. Dar turned towards that sound and caught a glimpse of four, close-set, glowing green eyes in a fog of darkness. "Small ones who didn't like our welcoming plants and pretty pathway."

The eyes faded back into the darkness.

"They seek the fortress," said the first voice. "Just like the others."

"Maybe they will reach it," replied the second. "Or maybe not."

"Circle!" Dar shouted and the Riders formed a circle, weapons facing outward. "Identify opponents as they appear."

"They are disciplined," said the second voice. "Pity. So seldom seen in mercenaries."

"Stop hiding, if you are not cowards!" Dar said. "Or is it true that Darkwood Drakes cannot do so for fear of repulsing others with their ugliness?"

He heard Connor's exasperated sigh behind him but didn't care. He wanted the drakes to show themselves.

They did.

A draconic form slithered out from the trees, sinuous and snake-like, with six legs and a horned head and spiked tail. Four luminescent green eyes blinked at him and the fanged maw split in an eerie grin. Its scales seemed like glittering smoke, if that was possible, or shining black fog. The drake pulled its thirty-foot length from the shadows and regarded them.

Despite his fear, Dar was mesmerized. It had a certain seductive, silky beauty, like a black widow spider.

"Is that so?" hissed the drake, eyes narrowed. "What do you say now?"

He shook himself. "I was wrong. How are you called?" he asked the drake.

If a dragon could smirk, this one did so. "So polite now, little one. I am Ziskar, sister and mate of Thulrin, spawn of Ridanmir. I will not ask your name. It is unseemly for food to have a name."

The other drake slipped out of the shadows, larger and with less horns on its head. "But it is not unseemly for food to die."

"Ah, brother, this food can bite back. It will provide good sport first."

The drakes split away from each other, circling the Riders. Dar kept his sword up and ready, praying that all of Melinor's magical protections would hold.

"But can they see what they attempt to bite, sister?" asked the larger drake, Thulrin. He breathed out gently. A cloying darkness spread out and filled the area.

"Andyn!"

"Working on it."

A ball of light winked into existence over Dar's head. They stood in a dark cloud, surrounded by a misty white light but unable to see the great trees any more. It seemed like they walked in night time, in a fog.

Ziskar's voice rang out at them, seeming to come from everywhere at once.

"They have magic too! Excellent. Then their treasure will be valuable as well. It is best when food can pay its own way."

"Buck! Where are they?"

"Right! Both right, in front of Connor!"

Dar swiveled that way, leaping in front of Connor, who darted back.

They heard Thulrin's voice. "Interesting. They have more than the usual magic, sister. One of them has an ancient talisman, I see. Let us have a wager: the one who eats the owner gets to keep it."

"Deal, brother."

Ziskar's head darted out of the fog, snapping at Dar. He dodged, slashing at it. The drake retreated into the fog as swiftly as she had emerged.

"Eric? Any ideas."

"Hang on."

Dar shot a look at him. Eric pulled a roll of paper out of his shoulder bag.

"Cover me."

The male drake snapped at Buck. He held firm behind his shield and took a swipe at his eye with Khelios. The sword flared with golden light.

"More magic!" said Ziskar, sounding delighted. "Now whoever eats him gets the blade as well."

"No fair," pouted Thulrin. "You can only get one toy per meal."

Eric spoke magic words. Soon, a fresh breeze filled the glade, sweeping away the dark fog.

"I don't like the way this food behaves," growled Thulrin, drawing back into the shadows of the trees. "It cheats."

"Behind you, Dar!" shouted Buck.

Dar whirled around as Ziskar rushed at him. He dodged to the side, leaping over a slashing claw. He brought his blade down on the creature's back. The blade clanged off with sparks flying.

Ziskar snapped at Andyn, who rewarded her slamming the drake in the head with her two maces. Ziskar hissed in anger and lashed Andyn with another claw. Andyn tried to sidestep, tripped and went flying, landing painfully on a great root. Ziskar slithered over to her but Dar stabbed her in the leg, getting better results this time. Glittering white blood showed on Ziskar's leg.

She shrieked and lashed her tail at him but three fire-darts tore into her side, fired by Eric. Hlerv suddenly appeared at her side, stabbed her in the neck with a dagger, and flitted back again.

Ziskar backed out in irritation.

"Cursed beasts," she fumed, slipping back into the shadows. "This will be more work than I thought."

"Here!" called Buck.

Dar whirled around. Thulrin towered over Buck and Connor, swinging at them with his claws and trying to bring his spiked tail to bear. Dar drew his handaxe and hurled it. The enchanted weapon buried itself in Thulrin's shoulder. He grunted, then took a stab from Khelios and roared in anger.

He, too, slipped back into the shadows.

"Foul fiends!" he growled. "You are right, sister. They bite harder than I thought. We will have to use sterner measures."

"Reform the circle," Dar told his companions. He controlled his breathing. If this was a preview of things to come, it was not a good day. Hitting Ziskar's scales felt like hacking at stones.

I'm not all that enthused to see what 'sterner measures' mean.

Both drakes suddenly vanished.

"Buck?"

"Nothing! Damn it! Where did they go?"

"Must be out of range," said Andyn.

"Up!" Hlerv shouted frantically. "Up! They're in the trees."

Dar looked up in astonishment. The trees were either sturdier than he thought or the drakes had an amazingly light structure for all their toughness. Ziskar and Thulrin perched on large boughs, winding their sinuous bodies around the trunks of trees above Buck's line of sight.

"Die, creatures," Ziskar hissed. She and Thulrin opened their mouths and breathed.

A cloud of glowing green mist shot out at the Riders from each drake. Worse yet, as the fluid mingled with the air, it burst into flame.

Dar crouched down, huddling under his cloak and praying to Saint Kira that the magic would hold.

Heat surged around him. He lost sight of his friends in the cloud of fire. Some droplets of the green mist landed on his exposed skin and he felt it burn and sear. A sudden weakness hit him and he fought to breathe.

A flare of magical light surrounded him twice, once with blue and once with yellow. The flames surged around the light and the green mist vanished.

Dar stood, his breath returning. He gripped his sword amid the small fires lit by drake-fire on the bushes and exposed tree roots. The weakness faded and he felt magical energy leave him as Melinor's protections absorbed the damage and neutralized the poison.

"What?" shrieked Ziskar. "This is beyond the pale! Where did they get such magic?"

With an incoherent scream, Thulrin launched himself from the tree, landing among the Riders as they scrambled to get out of the way. He lashed out with claw, fang, spiked tail and jets of flaming, poisonous fog. Buck and Eric took the brunt of it, dodging, striking and getting hit. Dar saw flares of magical red and green as Melinor's protections absorbed damage and winked out.

But Dar had eyes only for Ziskar. As he guessed, she waited until Thulrin landed to wreak her own havoc. She gestured with a claw and ghost creepers surged up out of the ground near Hlerv. The gnome disappeared in a writhing mass of plants. Dar leaped forward and slashed at the roots, pulling creepers away with his hands. He grabbed Hlerv by the shoulder and dragged him out by sheer force.

"Hlerv!"

The gnome looked pale and wan. "I'm all right. Give me a minute."

Connor darted in at Ziskar, stabbed her in the foot, leaped over a claw swipe, jumped onto her shoulder, stabbed her in the back, avoided a tail strike, rolled to her other side and poked her in the neck before scurrying under her to return to her other side. She lashed out and bit him, clamping her jaws down around his midsection.

Connor screamed. Andyn fired a ng at the drake, striking her in the chest. Ziskar reeled backwards, dropping Connor. Andyn leaped forward to drag him back. Ziskar snarled and crept forward but a trio of light balls darted in at her and she recoiled, snapping at them.

Hlerv leaned on Dar, his face determined as he sent another trio of light balls at the drake.

"Pull us back to the others," he hissed.

Dar joined Andyn and Connor and together, they stumbled over to Buck and Eric. Buck limped noticeably.

"We will roast you, little ones," Thulrin fumed as he prowled just outside of sword range. "You will rue the day you set foot in this place."

"Yes, brother, but we will use other fuel to stoke the fires," said Ziskar, her voice cunning.

Dar felt a chill.

Ziskar turned her head and breathed her fiery poisonous mist again, but not at the Riders. She aimed for the trees.

"Ha!" laughed Thulrin. He too fired a stream of burning fog at the forest. He raked the wood with flame, surrounding the Riders.

Dar's stomach knotted.

"They're going to broil us in here," Buck said. "Or we'll die from lack of air."

Dar's brain whirred, trying to think of something.

"Andyn?"

"I have something. Hang on."

Andyn Eleandir turned towards a section forest to their rear, back the way they had come. She moved her hands in a waving pattern, then wiggled her fingers and brought them down in front of her. Dar felt the air turn dry, then a deluge of water showered down on the forest behind them, putting out the fires.

"Now!" said Andyn.

The Riders darted for the opening. Both drakes shrieked in fury and surged to meet them.

Dar charged Thulrin, slashing and stabbing and not caring if he got hit, desperate to cover his friends' retreat. Buck and Andyn joined him.

For the next few horrifying seconds, Dar thought his life was over. Buffeted by heavy drake paws, he felt Melinor's magical protections vanish one by one. He was slashed by talons, nearly decapitated and punctured by tail spikes, he was forced to spend every ounce of effort keeping the drake at bay. Finally, he dropped to one knee, feeling Andyn's arm around him. Buck lay on his side next to him, unable to rise.

"I can't feel my legs," Buck said. Andyn knelt next to him, giving him a potion to drink. One of Andyn's maces lay broken on the ground next to her.

Dar's vision blurred and he pulled out the healing vial from his belt, downing it. New energy surged into him and he straightened, sword up.

Thulrin limped back away from them, bleeding sparkling white ichor from several wounds.

"Food can't be this strong," he seethed.

Ziskar joined him, bleeding from her legs and chest as well and looking murderous. "They will die, brother, and then we will feast and heal. They are nothing."

She breathed poison-fire at the trees branches over their heads. The wood flared into a flaming mass.

Dar felt suddenly weary. *When will this end?*

Then a warm wind surged into the glade.

"What means this?" roared a new, yet familiar, voice.

Drakes and Riders gaped as a golden-amber, winged creature dropped down through the flaming trees and landed in the glade, scattering burning branches and leaves.

"Oh my God," Eric breathed.

"Grandpa?" asked Andyn in a tone of disbelief.

A golden-brown dragon flicked his tail and glared at the drakes, then turned a smiling face to Andyn.

"I told you I would be there when you needed me, dear one."

"What means this?" demanded Thulrin. "This is our forest and our demesne! You are trespassing!"

Iron Thunder drew himself up to his full height, towering over even the impressive height of Thulrin. His scales glowed with majesty and his eyes glittered.

"I am Donnervassilianelikilandra of the Sunfire clan. You are unlawfully attacking these creatures and this will stop now."

Ziskar's eyes darted towards the Riders and back to Iron Thunder. "What do you care, Dragon of the Sunfire? These lower creatures are not worthy of your attention. Look you: a halfling, two humans and there are half-spawn among them as well, to add to the insult. They are mere food to be done with as greater beings see fit."

"You have a strange outlook on the way that dragons should treat others," rumbled the dragon. "We are not meant to lord it over those weaker than us. In addition, these are clan-friends."

Dar could have detected the shock and disbelief of the Darkwood Drakes if his eyes were closed.

Thulrin positively sputtered with rage. "Clan-Friends? Them? This is outrageous!"

"Speak not against these people!" snapped Iron Thunder. "They are Clan-Friends and if I had my way they would be accounted Allies as well. They have done a great service to me and mine and I *will not* see them eaten. They are more worthy of honor than the likes of you. Stand down."

The Darkwood Drakes eyes narrowed to slits and Dar's heart skipped a beat, seeing them change color to red.

This can't be good.

"Then by the Dark Death," Ziskar hissed, her voice taking on a sinister, vicious tone, "Clan Battle is declared upon this Dragon of the Sunfire, lover of lower beings."

"So be it," said Iron Thunder in a cold voice that Dar had never heard from him before.

Without even another word or sound, the drakes launched themselves at Iron Thunder.

To his dying day, Dar would remember that battle between drake and dragon, in the dying embers of a flaming forest, at the root of an ancient fortress in the wilderness. He stood in awe, the pain of his wounds and exhaustion forgotten as three members of ancient races clashed in savage combat. The drakes swirled around Grandpa, using the shadows to their advantage, striking from odd angles, using their poisonous flaming fog, spiked tails and speed. Iron Thunder, for his part, used one hand to cast spells of light, lightning, cold and fire while staying on the move to counter the drakes' greater speed and agility. He appeared unhurried, unconcerned and completely focused.

"Why doesn't he use his fire breath?" asked Hlerv through gritted teeth as he dragged himself up to Dar's side.

"He's afraid he'll hit us," Andyn said. "The drakes move so fast and they're putting us in line with Grandpa's attacks to keep him from using it."

"And they don't attack us?" wondered Eric.

"Probably don't consider us much of a threat compared to him," said Connor. "Or they know Grandpa would pummel them if they tried it. Let's back up."

The Riders moved back as surreptitiously as they could.

Dar had never seen such an amazing display of raw power, unearthly quickness, devastating strength and magic. Iron Thunder lashed his tail at Ziskar, only to miss and shatter a large tree through the trunk. Thulrin narrowly missed taking out Grandpa's left wing with a tail strike himself, only to get a tremendous whack to the chest from a claw that sent him spinning into the darkness. Ziskar responded by leaping on Grandpa's back, claws raking and jaws snapping. The gold dragon responded with a remarkably human-like move. He reached up over his head to grab her by the shoulders and flip her forward, pulverizing two flaming trees as she crashed into them.

"We have to help him!" Dar said. "Get your missile weapons ready. Go after the eyes."

He drew his bow and readied an arrow.

Ziskar swirled back into the shadows, the flickering flames casting an eerie light on the scene. Dar found it hard to pinpoint her location.

Thulrin charged at Grandpa, ducked a claw swipe, slammed his tail into Iron Thunder's leg, and leaped for his throat. The gold dragon gripped him by the shoulders and shoved down, using his greater weight. He opened his mouth and Dar heard a roaring like a furnace.

And Ziskar struck, hurtling out of the shadows. She clamped her jaws on Grandpa's neck.

"Now!" Dar let fly, set another arrow in place, and let fly again. Arrows and sling bullets shot out at the drakes.

Grandpa breathed a hellish cloud of flame onto Thulrin, who shrieked in agony and writhed like a giant deadly snake. The spiked tail hit Grandpa in the head and he lurched to the side. Thulrin wiggled out of his grasp and Iron Thunder stumbled, trying to get Ziskar off his back.

Dar's first arrow hit Ziskar's facial armor and the second planted itself in one of her eyes. She uncorked an unearthly scream just as one of Andyn's bullets hit her in the mouth and another arrow punctured another eye.

Hlerv muttered an incantation and slung a bullet into her open mouth. She gagged. With a loud pop, an explosion burst inside her head, blowing teeth out of her mouth and snapping her head back.

Buck and Eric planted two arrows into the exposed, softer armor at her throat and she reeled back with a gurgle.

Grandpa thrust his claw to the side, dislodging her, then clouted her in the head with a massive strike. She sailed back through the air, crushing another tree.

Thulrin raged incoherently, horribly burned. He turned into a whirling black cloud of fangs, claws and tail. Iron Thunder reeled under the assault, stumbling over tree roots.

Hlerv and Connor leaped onto the drake's back, small swords stabbing. Eric charged, impaling Thulrin in the side. Dar hurled himself into the fray and drove his blade down into the drake's neck near the base of the skull.

With a gurgle, Thulrin thumped into the ground.

Dar straightened and yanked his sword free, staggering, pointing the blade in the direction of Ziskar.

To his relief, she didn't move.

Iron Thunder lay in the clearing, bleeding and breathing heavily. Slowly, he turned to regard the Riders with impassive eyes.

Dar shook so badly he wondered how he was standing.

The dragon raised his head. "Your help is appreciated."

Dar leaned wearily on his sword. "We're Clan-Friends, right? All in a day's work among the clan, then."

The ghost of a smile showed on Grandpa's face. "Indeed."

He made a motion with his claw and his form shimmered, then shrank until a white-haired old man in amber robes stood before them. He closed his eyes, a mild yellow light whirling around him as injuries faded.

"Now," he said in a tired voice. "We are all in need of healing. Andyn, please lend your skills."

Limping a little, he led them back to Buck, still lying crippled in the glade. Andyn and Iron Thunder knelt next to him.

"Tell Puup that he is the heir to all my possessions," said Buck, flopping back.

Dar broke out laughing, and all the Riders with him.

Iron Thunder chuckled. "You have a second career as a jester, Buckminster Bydecy! Now, let us do our work."

Dar found his companions had used all their blue vials. He sat on a giant root, waiting for his turn and inspecting his injuries. He felt bruised and sore all over. He counted nine puncture wounds from claw and tail spikes and three slashes on his arms and hands. None appeared to be serious, though they certainly hurt.

Andyn crouched in front of him as Eric and Iron Thunder helped Buck stand. "For once, Connor and Hlerv didn't get mauled. It looks like you're the last in the infirmary."

He smiled. "I didn't think we'd make it there for a while. How did Grandpa know to find us?"

She took a tiny jar of glittering ointment from her backpack. "He says he talked to Melinor a couple of days ago and found out we were coming to Shadow Lake. While flying overhead, he saw the trees on fire and heard the sounds of battle and guessed it was us. Apparently, you could see the flames for miles."

Dar watched the ointment glow white as it healed his wounds. "I'm surprised that the entire forest didn't go up. We'd be just as dead as if the drakes killed us."

"Grandpa says the forest is suffering from a form of rot, almost like a fungus, and it is rather moist and doesn't burn well. That tells you something about the power of the drakes' breath and Melinor's protections in keeping us alive this long."

Dar nodded and closed his eyes, feeling the renewing power of her ministrations. Gentle hands lay on his head for a few heartbeats and he heard her whisper a prayer to Verian.

He felt warm and peaceful all over, then the feeling faded.

She smiled at him. "Almost like new."

Dar felt a surge of affection for her, a woman who had thrown in her lot with such a ragtag band of castoffs and misfits and yet remained their faithful friend through it all.

He stood and clasped her in a quick hug. She returned it, then held him at arm's length.

"Ready?"

He nodded.

"Good," Iron Thunder said, striding up with the other Riders in tow. "Now, these two likely had a lair nearby. I need to find it."

Dar and Eric conferred, then set about back-tracking the drakes from the site of the initial confrontation. Dar concentrated hard and looked for the smallest signs of disturbance in order to follow the trail, and they lost it twice. Still, having Iron Thunder there to watch their backs made it easier.

"Well, this is ugly," said Eric as they stopped short near a twisted, tangled mass of trees and shrubs. It looked as if some giant had grabbed all the trees in the area, bent them down to form a sort of hut, and intertwined the branches and roots to bar the entrance. Fully forty feet high and twice as deep, it could certainly have held both drakes comfortably.

Iron Thunder pursed his lip, then pointed a hand at the entrance, moving his fingers in a sideways pattern. The branches and brambles glowed sky blue, then parted.

A yawning, dark opening stared back at them. A horrible, sickly sweet stench emanated from it. Dar resisted the urge to gag.

Hlerv muttered a word and created three magical light balls, sending them into the darkness.

Coins, gems, jewelry and other precious items glimmered in the light of Hlerv's magic.

Buck started forward but Hlerv stopped him. "Wait," said the gnome.

The lights floated farther into the darkness and Dar went cold. A tenfoot-tall statue of a woman stood at the back of the lair. She wore only a filmy robe decorated with vile symbols in red and purple. Statues of a spider and scorpion stood next to her. With one hand, she beckoned to them and the other held a dagger tipped with lurid green. Her gemstone eyes looked sultry and vicious all at once.

"Arachnia!" hissed Andyn.

Iron Thunder nodded. "This is what they worshipped. This is what gave them the power to poison the forest."

He looked at Dar. "They may have eggs or young in there. Search the treasure for anything useful while I check."

"Shouldn't we come with you?" asked Buck.

The dragon looked grim and sad. "No. This is my task alone."

The Riders cautiously entered, Andyn and Hlerv casting spells to check for traps. Finding none, they sifted through the drakes' treasure hoard. In among an astonishing mound of silver, copper and gold coins mixed together, they found necklaces, rings, a mace, a short sword, a shield, a jeweled belt and some crafted items.

"Dar," said Buck. "Look at this."

The others crowded around Buck. He held a silver medallion in his hand, with a symbol that they all recognized: a crowned, fanged skull.

"Margoth's men, here?" said Hlerv, casting a nervous look around.

"Not any more," said Eric. He knelt and sifted through the black leaves, bones and sticks. He pointed to a skull still attached to a collarbone and one shoulder. An identical silver pendant hung on a dirty chain around its neck.

"Maybe there are others," mused Connor, using a dagger to search through the junk on the floor of the cave.

Dar held up a third medallion on a chain when a gurgling shriek echoed in the lair, making him jump.

"What in the Nine Hells was that?" Buck asked, looking pale.

Andyn shook her head. "Don't ask. Just bring some of this stuff outside."

They took the singular items, the medallions and some of the gold with them and waited. Eric used a spell and determined that the sword and mace radiated magic.

"The mace is rather strong," he said.

"Good," said Andyn. "One of mine is broken."

Iron Thunder emerged. Dar had never seen him look so haggard and it alarmed him.

"Grandpa?"

The dragon-man shook his head, sinking down to rest on a nearby rock. "I have never seen such horrid abominations. Twisted beasts, a profane insult to dragonkind and vicious. They attacked immediately. I had no idea Arachnia could warp creatures so badly."

Andyn and Dar exchanged a look. "Grandpa," Andyn said gently, "If those were drakelings, they were the spawn of Thulrin and Ziskar. They referred to each other as, well, brother and sister."

Iron Thunder's mouth opened in horror and he looked like he would vomit.

"Has dragonkind fallen so far?" He slumped down, elbows on his knees and face in his.

"You know better than I do that Arachnia's evil is insidious," replied Andyn, placing a hand on his arm. "She convinces people that all restrictions on their behavior are mere illusions, contrived by the forces of good to keep them from true power. Many have fallen under her sway, many elves. I feel your anger and pain. I have seen her effects on my people in, er, similar ways."

He shook himself and gave her a warm smile. "I forget that evil corrupts without prejudice. Come, let us see what you have found."

He inspected the items and seemed especially interested in the sword and mace. The Riders showed him the medallions. He sat on a boulder and pursed his lip, turning one over in his fingers.

"So! Servants of Margoth enter this forest, only to find Darkwood Drakes in the service of Arachnia and then are slain. Why were they here? And do Margoth and Arachnia now battle each other? I thought the dark elves worshipped that foul goddess and yet were allied with Margoth."

"It can mean only one thing, Grandpa," Dar said. "Margoth sent them here to get the Helm of Shadows. The problem was that the Drakes had taken over the forest in the meantime, and they didn't care what Margoth's plans were."

Iron Thunder nodded, still lost in thought. "Yet Margoth and Arachnia are supposed to be allied, through the service of the dark elves. So why wouldn't the Drakes just simply let them pass? Could it be that some other, more sinister plan is at work here? Could Arachnia actually want Margoth to fail, for her own purposes?"

Dar shook his head. "Now you're making me dizzy, Grandpa. If it's evil demigods and lich queens doing battle over some obscure goal, I'm lost.

We have more practical things to worry about."

The dragon gave a wry smile and tossed the medallion to him. "Good point, Mister Cabot. I will discuss such matters with Lord Melinor later. For now, let us see what else you have found."

He held out his hand. Andyn gave him the mace and Eric the sword. Iron Thunder sat with one on each knee, eyes closed and murmuring under his breath.

Finally, he opened his eyes and smiled up at the Riders. "You have good fortune. Both of these are mighty weapons."

"This," he held up the sword, "is named Shriek. It is a sword of stealth and can help its wielder to blend into shadows. It does great harm to the undead."

Dar examined the blade, curious. Named weapons were rare, and one that had an added enchantment against the undead rarer still. The blade curved a bit at the end and the guard had an intricate pattern of flames. A white gem winked at him from the pommel.

Hlerv exchanged a look with Connor. "Dice you for it?"

Connor waved a hand. "I think you should get it. I've seen you try to sneak around."

Dar didn't know what he was talking about. He found both of them annoyingly stealthy.

Hlerv nodded, accepting the sword from Grandpa. "I'll take both the barb and the sword. The sword is far sharper than your snide comments."

"And this," continued Iron Thunder, handing the mace to Andyn amid the laughter of the other Riders, "is named Eleison. It means 'Mercy' in Ecclesia, the language of the Christian Church. It is mighty against evil and can amplify a person's healing powers."

"Maybe one of you should have it," Andyn said, looking at Eric and Dar. She held out the weapon, silvery metal with a smooth, spherical head. Dar saw a band of tiny crosses etched into it.

"No," Eric said with a smile. "It suits you. I'd be honored for you to have it."

She blushed and took the weapon.

"Now," said Iron Thunder, rising, "I have to return to Melinor. The things I saw today need to get to the proper authorities. And you have a fortress to enter."

Dar stepped forward and bowed. "Once again, thank you, Iron Thunder. We owe you our lives."

The dragon transformed to his natural state and smiled down at him. "And Kindri and Tholi are alive because of you, Clan-Friend."

"What do we do about this thing?" Eric said, pointing at the lair.

Iron Thunder drew himself up to his full height, eyes flaring. He opened his jaws and Dar saw the light of his fiery breath kindle. The dragon unleashed a jet of flame, setting the warped branches alight at the entrance. He looked pleased as they burned merrily.

"I'll think of something."

Chapter Nine- Allies

Gorlak held onto the rim of the steel-encased chariot. The vehicle rattled beneath him as he rode with King Vorquul towards the camp of Zhinia Margoth. Other goblins raced alongside on giant lizards or misshapen badgers.

The vast encampment of the Dark Rider flashed past as a fell-bear pulled the chariot through the pathways. Gorlak smelled campfire smoke, incense and roasting meat as well as offal, waste and other more unwholesome scents on the air. His eyes darted around at the troops who stood at their approach, watching them with wary eyes or smug looks.

Ghai-zhal, Gorf, Umchak and Urmum, he thought, eyes flicking over the humans, ogres, Kaftu and elves he saw in the host. *And yet, Margoth needs the Za-Arak to make her war.*

In the late afternoon shadows cast by the westering sun in the mountain valley, an enormous tent loomed. It brooded like some dark idol, dead black with eight white skulls embroidered at even intervals around the top. The standard of a fanged skull wearing a crown of flame, fluttered in the breeze near the entrance. Odd red and pink lights danced within the tent and a cloying black fog clung to the ground amid blackened grass and weeds. Gorlak smelled something metallic and sharp. He wrinkled his nose in distaste.

King Vorquul grunted a command at his driver and the chariot slowed, stopping about fifty feet from where two figures sat in camp chairs of teak wood. Gorlak identified a male human and female elf.

"Ah, I see that worms crawled up out of the ground this night," said Vorquul. The other goblins in the chariot grinned and chuckled.

"Who you see there, Captain Gorlak?" the king asked. He hooked his thumbs in his belt, next to a silvery glowing mace and scimitar with rubies in the pommel.

"The man is a human servant of Ja'al," Gorlak replied, "He is probably high priest. Has good armor and weapons and I see rings and a necklace that could be magic. The woman is one of the *Faal Urmum*, maybe priestess or queen from her robes and jewelry. They are commanders of other parts of Margoth Army, I think."

Vorquul gave a grim smile. He adjusted the platinum circlet on his head and straightened his chainmail armor.

"Very good. You see much. Bad for Halkith he dead and you live. Good for Whiteskull you return to serve us. Maybe wizard-ways grow on you, no?"

Gorlak inclined his head. "I glad to serve King Vorquul."

Vorquul nodded. "And serve you will. For now, you stay with chariot. See that none of the other rabble approach but do not fight unless I order it."

"Yes, my king."

Vorquul dismounted and stalked over towards the others waiting for Margoth. The human priest stood and bowed but the elf woman made no move to get up.

Gorlak pretended to be bored but made sure to catch every word from the leaders' conference.

"Hail Vorquul of the Whiteskull tribe," the human said, smiling behind an impeccable mustache. "Pleased you could make it."

The elf sniffed but said nothing.

Inwardly, Gorlak seethed, not so much for Vorquul's pride but for his own. Dark elves and goblins hated each other almost as much as they hated dwarves. The insult from the dark elf woman made his blood boil.

Vorquul gave the human a curt nod. His eyes lingered the elf. She pointedly ignored him. The king fingered the milky white gemstone on a chain around his neck.

"You are Zanlor of the Ja'al?" he asked the human.

"Zanilor. And yes, I am representing the Ja'al high council."

With a grunt, Vorquul plopped down into a third camp chair and Zanilor resumed his seat.

Silence reigned. Gorlak heard only by the occasional clink of armor as the dark elf guards and goblin guards regarded each other warily.

"The training goes well?" Zanilor asked.

Vorquul scratched his chin. "Well for now. Not enough ogres yet. How we train with them if not many here? And only a few Kaftu. Army not complete, I think."

"Train?" said the elf with a distasteful look. "I'm not so sure you can train with the Kaftu. Just as likely to chase a rabbit as to follow orders."

Zanilor smiled and leaned back in his chair. "But no disdain for the ogres, Queen Ildrisana?" he said with a sidelong glance.

Ildrisana smoothed her dress, bringing her stunning figure into sharp relief. "I can only have disdain for those of sufficient wit to detect it."

"I see." Zanilor smoothed his mustache and waited but she said nothing further.

Gorlak's eyes drifted to the dark elven troops on the opposite side of the clearing in front of the tent. The soldiers stood at ease next to a giant scorpion with a black-and-gold striped carapace.

A motion made him jerk towards Margoth's tent and he started in surprise. Unseen and silent, a pair of skeletal servants in chain armor bearing halberds now stood next to the tent flap. Tiny purple pinpoints of light glimmered in their empty skulls.

Gorlak suppressed a shudder. His former employer, the late and unlamented Halkith, could occasionally change skeletons into automatons with a magic spell. However, those moved mechanically, like machines. These, well, these had a fluid grace about them, not to mention the lights in their eye sockets.

He smirked, thinking of how jealous Halkith would have been at Margoth's handiwork. He had heard through the grapevine that Margoth kept another skeletal servant minding her fortress somewhere in the wilderness, a former lover whom she had promised would never die.

The promise was not all he thought it would be.

The entrance to the pavilion burst open so quickly that Gorlak jumped and cursed himself in irritation. A skeletal figure in a purple robe strode out. She swept towards Zanilor and the others. They stood.

Margoth fairly radiated irritation to go along with a palpable feeling of dread and overwhelming magic power. Gorlak fought the urge to flee. With a sidelong glance at the king's guard, he saw his troops fighting a similar panic.

Zanilor bowed first. "Your Highness."

She regarded him with pinpoint firelights in empty eye sockets. "Zanilor."

Vorquul bowed next.

"High Queen of Kher Mardil," he said.

"King Vorquul," she answered. "Your flattery is appreciated but I am not queen yet."

He straightened. "There are none left of your line. In my eyes, you are the ruling queen."

Margoth's mouth twitched. With interest now, Gorlak watched her. He could almost feel her calculating whether Vorquul was currying favor or being honest.

"Quite so," she said, turning her undead gaze to Ildrisana.

The dark elf queen curtseyed, barely moving enough to qualify as such but just enough so that she couldn't be accused of an affront.

"Your Majesty," said Margoth, bowing. Similarly, she moved just enough for courtesy and no more.

Gorlak pondered this. Margoth was not a queen; Ildrisana was, yet she bowed to Margoth and seemed to take orders from her.

He shook his head. Despite his service to sophisticated figures like Halkith, Gorlak's brain whirled from trying to figure out the political maneuverings of Margoth and her allies.

The lich withdrew a ball of marbled black stone from her robes and cast it at their feet. Before it hit the ground, it levitated up to waist height. At a word from Margoth, it glowed. A projection map of the surrounding area sprang up before them like a painting.

Gorlak's jaw dropped. Yes, Halkith and his mistress, Aalre, had more power than a typical witch doctor or shaman, but this? The detail in the image astounded him. He saw the charred ruins of Westhaven, caravans traveling the Border Road, boats on the Whitehorse River and the waving of grain on the plains south of Forester.

Margoth pointed a bony finger at one particular area northeast of Whitehorse Peak.

"We are here." A large red dot glowed.

She pointed again due north. Another, smaller red dot glowed, surrounded by tiny purple dots.

"Here is Ulgrut."

Vorquul snorted. "He late? Why?"

Margoth set her mouth in a firm line. "They were to travel here with the siege engines and the bulk of his warriors when some troll bandits decided to have a go at them. Ulgrut obviously insulted their mothers or something because now a tribe is attacking them."

Ildrisana pursed her lip. "Losses?"

"Many trolls side, some ogres. Ulgrut has made good use of the funds I sent him. His troops are better armored than the trolls and have good weapons. I received word that they are just now breaking down the remainder of the troll tribe and will be here in the morning, using forced marches."

Zanilor nodded. "How will this affect our time line?"

Margoth gestured impatiently. "It will make us late by a few days, but at least they will be here for the training sessions."

She glared at them. "I expect that we will all work hard to make up for lost time, yes?"

All three of her allies nodded.

She waved a hand and the stone ball leaped to her palm. She swept it into her robes.

"The council will meet again after Ulgrut has arrived and we have had a time to coordinate training. At that time, I will describe our plan of action."

She inclined her head at the three and stalked back into her pavilion.

Zanilor clapped his hands together. "Well, there is no plan that ever survived the day of battle… or training, it seems."

Ildrisana shook her head. "A waste of time in my opinion."

Vorquul nodded to Zanilor. "Ogres are needed. We wait them. I go to my camp. Until tomorrow."

Without so much as a glance at Ildrisana, he marched away off to join his guards.

Gorlak sprang down and lowered the steps for the king to mount the chariot.

"To our side of camp," Vorquul ordered the driver.

Gorlak maintained his silence all the way to the goblin headquarters. They stopped in front of the king's hut, a large construction of specially cured hides inscribed with warding spells in goblin runes. Sacred poles carved with various goblin deities and heroes stood guard at the entrance.

Two of Vorquul's wives opened the door and emerged, bowing. They wore bone-white skirts and leather brigandines with bright silver studs that glowed with magic power. Each had a sword on her back and a dagger in her belt. One of them eyed Gorlak with enticing dark eyes.

Vorquul dismounted. "Take chariot to holding area. Feed the bear dwarf-meat and elf-meat," he ordered.

With a measured look at Gorlak, he motioned to his hut. "You follow, Captain."

Surprised, Gorlak bowed and followed the king inside. The smell of roots and herbs suffused the air. They stopped at an antechamber. A shaman in brown and black hides and a deer-skull helmet chanted and cast spells. Gorlak felt his arms and legs strengthen as the magic power wafted over him.

Why I get such an honor? he wondered. Normally only the king's advisors were permitted to receive the blessings of the shaman.

Vorquul stumped into the central chamber and held his arms to the side as his wives removed his armor and clothing, robing him in a black and orange mantle. Gorlak stood absolutely still, watching shadows dance in the flickering torchlight.

A complete dwarf skeleton slouched in a cage next to Vorquul's throne, garbed in the tunic and trousers of a fool. Its brightly colored cloth contrasted starkly with the darker shades of the king's chamber. An enormous bear rug dominated the floor. Two ornate tables of white wood sat on either side of the throne, holding stone decanters, silver cups and statuary of goblins and fell wolves carved out of solid turquoise.

Gorlak smelled roasting meat, wine and ale and his stomach rumbled.

Vorquul nodded to the women and they departed. Gorlak kept his eyes averted from the one who had stared at him earlier.

"You know why you here, Captain?"

Gorlak inclined his head. "To serve King Vorquul."

The king poured from a stone decanter and mounted his throne, silver chalice in hand. He drank silently, eyes measuring Gorlak.

"You here because of talents, Captain."

Gorlak bowed. "I thank Mighty King…"

"No. Stop with bow and scrape!"

Gorlak straightened, surprised.

Vorquul pursed his lip, his polished horns glowing in the firelight. "I know about you. Mother and father killed in fight with *Urmum*. You brought to Irontooth tribe. Brothers die in raid against *Ghai-zhal* in Athor-town. Then you serve Halkith of Ja'al."

Gorlak nodded, wondering what was coming next.

Vorquul twirled the chalice in his fingers. "Now you serve me. I hear of you work with Halkith. I see you command goblins. I know you survive Grey Riders and come to Whiteskull tribe. I see you command raids against trolls, slay fell-wolves, steal treasures from ruins. I make you captain. You have skills."

Gorlak shifted uncomfortably. "I was not advisor to Halkith. Just corporal to Aalre the *Urmum*, then sergeant when Grey Riders kill Grand Sergeant Choorg."

Vorquul nodded. "But why *Urmum* wizard choose you? Why Halkith not kill you after dragons freed? I know. You smarter than average goblin. You see things they not see. Halkith know this. Why you have this skill?"

Gorlak shrugged. "I not know. I know to serve kings and lords, that is all."

The king's eyes narrowed. "That is true. I have task for you."

He stood. "I will give you special medallion. It hides you from mind-magic. Your thoughts your own. You watch *Urmum* and *Ghai-zhal*. Wait for chance for *Za'Arak* to take control."

Gorlak started in surprise. "Take control? How? Margoth in command."

Vorquul made a half-smile. "You too smart. You see how *Urmum* and

Za'Arak enemies but work for lich? You also see how *Umchak* and *Gorf* hate each other but not fight unless Margoth commands? What if Margoth gone?"

The captain's mind spun. "Where she go to?"

The goblin king turned slowly to a carved wooden box. He placed his hand on it and the top glowed, then vanished. He reached inside, removing a parchment.

"Grey Riders." He handed the parchment to Gorlak.

Too late, Gorlak caught himself while reading. Most goblin troops didn't know how to read, even many officers. He looked up at Vorquul, who smirked and nodded.

"That say Grey Riders defeat Margoth. You remember Grey Riders, yes?"

Gorlak remembered them well. He saw them again in his mind, marching down the forest path with the rescued dragonlings. He remembered how mighty they seemed, vanquishers of the hated Aalre and slayers of many powerful hobgoblins and with dragons to help them. He had fled into the forest, knowing that in a second his life would end by arrow or dragon-fire.

And he also remembered their voices…

"…just some of Halkith's goblins… we can take 'em…"

"Come on, Buck, they're running away. They can't hurt us now. No use in killing for killing's sake."

"But they might have treasure…"

Then a woman's silvery laugh. "How much do you need, Buck? We have plenty and they probably don't have any. No, let them go. They can't harm anyone."

He remembered the slimmer, shorter Grey Rider with the big sword as he looked back over his shoulder. This Ghai-zhal had lowered his weapon and let Gorlak escape, watching with dark eyes that had… sympathy?

He still wondered why the Riders let him go. If the roles were reversed, Gorlak would certainly have cut them down, for vengeance if nothing else.

Why?

He still had no answer, even this many weeks later.

"Yes, Great King. I remember them," he answered Vorquul.

"That paper is *Ghai-zhal-ik* prophecy. Most of their prophecy is trash.

But this one, if true, means power for the *Za'Arak*. You watch. If Margoth thrown down, our people take chance. We attack *Urmum*, take lich crown, take staff, take magic power. Then others serve *Za'Arak*."

Gorlak looked at his new king and wondered. Even if Vorquul could master Margoth's crown and staff—and there was a decent chance of that, as Vorquul had personally trained all his own witch doctors and shamans in magical arts—could he overpower the elves, ogres and Kaftu?

Vorquul held out his hand and Gorlak returned the parchment.

"How king get prophecy?"

Vorquul sneered. "Margoth think *Za'Arak* stupid. When she meet us for first time, she show me and Zanilor page with prophecy, then take away. I memorize. Write down when I return to camp."

"Now," he continued, replacing the page in the magic box and taking out a dull pewter medal on a silver chain, "you my agent. I give you magic cold iron dagger. Cold iron against evil *Urmum* is poison deadly. Special weapon for slaying *Urmum* queen. You hide. If time right, you strike."

Gorlak nodded. "What of *Za'Arak* army? *Urmum* will attack. Many will die."

Vorquul shrugged, handing the medal to Gorlak. "Cost of war. With queen dead, we win."

Gorlak felt a chill, thinking of Ildrisana's personal guard. He might be able to get in a strike, but then Gorlak himself would become a tally mark on the ledger of 'cost of war'.

Vorquul downed his chalice of liquor. "You have orders, Captain. Do them. You serve Whiteskull. You serve me."

Gorlak looked into the king's face and suppressed a shiver. His eyes looked exactly like Ildrisana's.

He bowed. "I exist to serve, great king."

***

Brandawyn Alenar landed Amicus on the crest of the hill behind the copse of trees. The city of Meridian, Gorostol, shone in the distance. The sky cast long shadows of early evening on the walls and towers of the city. Meridian was built into the crest and side of a massive hill at the shore of the great lake called the Kaljirre, or the Skymirror. Three large highways stretched from the visible gates of the city, one reaching north, one south and one west, towards them. Beyond the grassy hills before them, about two miles away, she saw the western road and its traffic of wagons and pedestrians hustling to make the city gates before nightfall.

"It will be great to have a real bed and a bath," said Megan, reining in Larinor.

"You don't like bathing in the streams, Megan?" asked Daphne. Her giant owl preened its feathers.

Stephen hopped down from his seat and gave Megan a rascally look. She made a face at him.

"It's a stream, not a bathtub. I mean a real bath with hot water and soap instead of pebbles and bugs and leaves."

"She's too picky," her uncle said to Daphne.

Daphne grinned, then dismounted. She returned Paractus to his medallion form.

"Truth be told, brother dear, I understand exactly what Megan is about."

Megan blew her aunt a kiss.

Brandi shook her head. "Where do we go then?"

Stephen pointed at a suburb sprawling on the city's western edge. "Kenwall. It's close to the University, where we're going to start our search. There's an inn there called the Red Swallow. We've been there before. I think Megan will be very pleased."

Brandi thought of a hot bath and a good night's sleep and she sighed. Not having to worry about dawn watch and keeping an eye out for hobgoblin raiders appealed to her.

"I will be right behind her."

Megan and Brandi likewise dismounted. Brandi rummaged through her saddlebags to get what necessities she thought she would need for the next few days.

Megan looked wistful as she closed up her saddlebags and finished loading up her backpack. Brandi kissed Amicus on the nose and stepped back, making the circular motion with her hand and pointing to the sky. Megan did likewise and soon the two pegasi winged away to the northwest, flying low over the trees, heading to some safe place they knew only by instinct.

As much as Brandi would have liked to ride Amicus into town to avoid the four mile hike, it was out of the question. Flying mounts, and pegasi especially, attracted all kinds of attention. Not only would the city's air defenses be alerted, but the sheer value of a single trained pegasus marked them as targets by unsavory elements that always lurked in large cities. Even if the Alenars proved to be harmless from Meridian's point of view, they simply couldn't afford the attention.

Besides, their errand demanded secrecy. Just as they were agents of the Northern Alliance and the Christian Church, spies from Torosc and Jered would also be sprinkled among the population. Gorostol shared a border with Torosc. The more they could do to avoid attention, the better.

Daphne shouldered her pack and led them through the tall grass towards the highway. She set a brisk pace. Stephen likewise marched along, unconcerned. For her part, Brandi's thighs and calves burned a bit by the time she got to the highway.

Need more hiking and less flying, I guess.

Daphne led them into the flow of people heading towards Meridian.

Megan eyed the city as they approached. "An, um, interesting mix of buildings."

Stephen nodded. "Just like the nation of Gorostol. The whole country depends on dwarf, elf, halfling and human working together, so the architectural styles sort of intermingle. But in a nice way."

Brandi let Daphne do all the talking when they arrived at the guard post. She opened her pack for inspection by a sharp-eyed gnomish woman officer, then joined the stream of people and conveyances into Meridian.

She took in the different types of architecture and landscaping. Brandi had to admit that the city planners somehow made a combination of dwarven walls, elven towers, halfling inns, and human market bazaars look compatible.

Daphne pointed ahead towards a market square about a half-mile away. The trees of a massive city park loomed in the background.

"We turn left at the park. Kenwall is close to the western gate and is predominantly human, though some elves and halflings live here too."

Brandi nodded, too engrossed in taking in the city to respond. Megan elbowed her with a smile.

"Try not to look too much like a tourist."

Brandi elbowed her back with a smile of her own. "You're the one who wanted the scented bath water."

They moved through the crowds. Daphne expertly guided them past merchants hawking all manner of wares and various inns and taverns. At the turn, they continued on a slightly upward slope as the traffic thinned out. Now the dusk deepened and city workers moved along the street, using long poles to remove the light covers from the street lamps. Covered sewer trenches ran down the middle of the street. These held potted plants on top of them at intervals, an attempt to make an unpleasant aspect of city life somehow a little more attractive.

A lot like Darlon, she thought.

Daphne finally stopped at an ornate iron gate with two guard shacks. Beyond it, a well-manicured lawn, flowerbeds, a fountain and a driveway for carriages sat before an impressive two-story edifice of grey stone and red wood. A set of double-glass doors beckoned to her, lit by magical lamps on either side. A sign hung over the door, made of a silvery metal with three red swallows painted on it.

Brandi smiled. The swallow images actually flitted from one side of the sign to the other and vanished for a moment. Then they reappeared and repeated their flight.

Megan looked impressed. "I like this already."

The lobby held polished tables, glass figurines, pots with colorful plants, flowers in vases, carpets from Evendale, tapestries from Eldir, and two smiling attendants. In no time, they had the Alenars in a two-room suite with a balcony overlooking the city, magically secured doors and two separate bathing rooms. The hotel piped water into the bathtubs—magically heated for a small fee, but Megan and Stephen's spells made that last surcharge unnecessary.

After unloading her pack, Brandi lowered herself into the hot bathwater and sighed, feeling the tension melt out of her body. Her level of tiredness and stiffness surprised her despite so much experience traveling and living outdoors. The aforementioned scented bath water both lifted her spirits and soothed her. She floated serenely in the warmth until she felt herself drifting off. With a pinch on her cheeks, she sat up and scrubbed all the grime and sweat away.

She took her time washing her hair and combing it out afterwards. She sat naked on a padded chair in front of a mirror, letting her body cool down and dry slowly.

A rather serious-looking half-elven woman with red-gold hair, violet eyes and a toned, athletic build stared back at her from the mirror. The brush strokes in her hair slowed and stopped.

She sighed. Not exactly the princess of a man's dreams. Oh, she knew that people called her pretty. Eric certainly spoke often of his admiration of her physical charms, but most people paid attention to Megan first.

She stood, picking up a towel and patting her damp, but combed and clean, hair.

Will Eric like me this way? she mused. *I'm not a willowy, slender thing and I've never been called graceful.*

An image of her love came to mind and she imagined his reaction if she even asked the question. He would probably chuckle, pinch the end of her nose, and kiss her soundly, then tell her not to change a thing.

A pain of longing hit her and she felt suddenly morose.

If I see him again.

With an irritated shake of her head, she set the towel down and reached for a clean shift, blouse and trousers.

Stop thinking like that.

She heard a knock at the door to the bathroom. "Hey Eran, are you ready? We're starving."

She smiled at the sound of her sister's voice and hurried to dress.

Dinner at the inn's tavern proved to be just as satisfying as their comfortable rooms and the refreshing bath. Brandi took her time, appreciating the beef in wine sauce, baked stuffed tomatoes, crusty bread with butter and honey, leeks in cream sauce and apple tart.

"However you get the money for this," Megan said, lounging back in their private booth overlooking the garden, "I say you keep it up and don't tell us where it comes from."

Stephen saluted her with his wine goblet. "Done."

Daphne sighed. "It almost makes all the danger worthwhile."

They all sat quietly for a while, lost in their own thoughts.

"Speaking of danger," said Stephen, "let's see what this is."

A glass ball of swirling colors sat on a tin holder in the middle of the table and he tapped it three times with his room key. A shimmering field of energy curved up and over the booth.

He took out a scrap of paper from his belt pouch and opened it on the table. "Now we won't be overheard," he said.

"Well," said Daphne, "It looks just like any number of bits of Ja'al propaganda I've seen in the past."

Stephen nodded. "Very similar to other screeds."

Brandi looked at Megan. "We thought the Song of the Grey Riders was just a bit of lyric poetry, Uncle Stephen. Now we know better."

Stephen waved his hand. "That was different. I assure you, I've seen things like this before."

Brandi read:

"Rise together with bloody blade
Together Ja'al will rule the age

Cross and Hearthstone, Stone and Tree
They know not what fools they be

Font of Life and Vale of Tears
Lie in death ten thousand years

Gate of Stars and Dome of Glass
Pay the Toll and you may pass

Daemon heart is red and black
Through Gate of Skulls this world attack

Rise together with bloody blade
Together Ja'al will rule the age

Power of good thou pitiful fool

Power of evil this world will rule.”

"Honestly," Daphne said, putting a hand on Brandi's. "It's nothing. Just a chant to send the followers into a frenzy so they can work their dark deeds."

"Then why did Lieutenant Volan have a copy of it?" asked Megan.

Silence.

"He's not a Ja'al priest," she continued. "He's not even a Ja'al. He hated them and he was just a hired hand. And he said that the wizards made them chant it while they constructed those structures. And what's all this about an attack by daemons? Have you ever seen anything like that before?"

Daphne glanced at Stephen. He pursed his lip.

"Sometimes. Ja'al chants often have some dire predictions of doom for their enemies or hymns to the glorious tyrannical rule that awaits the faithful."

Brandi nodded. "I have to say that the bone structure looked more like a hut of bones rather than a gate of skulls. This whole thing makes me nervous."

"Will they have anything on this in the library in Meridian?" asked Megan.

Stephen shook his head. "Not likely. We'd need ecclesiastical resources, like a Verian or Irial institute or one of the Nuncio's people."

Brandi handed the paper back to him. He folded it back up and tapped it in his hand.

"Well, we do have some dispatches to send to Saint Martin's Town. Why don't we add this to the package with whatever we find in Eldermain's private library?"

Brandi nodded, still feeling uneasy. "I'm sorry I'm so jittery, but after all we went through with the Grey Riders, I don't discount anything."

"Don't mention it," said Daphne, picking up her goblet. "You're never sure what is going to be significant in this business. After this much time, I know enough to trust people's instincts."

Stephen put the paper away and tapped the glass ball again. The shimmering field disappeared.

They passed the rest of the meal in relative silence, weary from their travels and wondering about their latest adventures.

Brandi felt the weariness hit her full force as soon as she took off her clothes and laid on her lovely pillowy mattress, not even getting through all of her night prayers before slipping off to sleep.

An image of a grinning skull and a swirling vortex lingered in her dreams until the morning.

***

"Are you sure this is authorized?" Brandi whispered to Daphne.

Her aunt put a finger to her lips.

Great, thought Brandi. *I'll bet it isn't. That's all I need: to be dragged into court accused of grave-robbing.*

They crouched in the shadow of a giant stone grave marker that soared up above them, nearly twelve feet tall and half as wide. The statue of a dwarven warrior on a giant lizard perched on top. Brandi mentally thanked whoever had been ostentatious enough to erect such a large monument just where they needed it.

Of course, this didn't make her feel any less uneasy. Visiting a cemetery was not unusual, but doing so in the wee hours of the morning with armor and weapons certainly was.

Dew glistened on the lawn and flowers nearby. Stephen knelt in the grass near her. He bent his head over a small red leather book with a faded gold star on the front cover.

Brandi knew the little book well. The ghost sage, Damion Eldermain, had gifted it to her and Megan as thanks for helping him gain release from this world. It seemed like ages ago but had only been spring.

Stephen motioned to them and slipped to the next memorial, a stone edifice almost as big with the figures of two dancing halflings on the top.

Darting between grave markers seemed ridiculous to Brandi. When she found out their plan, she had objected, but to no avail.

"We can't go sneaking around a cemetery in broad daylight," she had told Megan. "Someone will see us and start asking questions."

Megan had arched an eyebrow at that. "You'd prefer to go at night?

That won't seem suspicious, will it?"

Brandi had no answer for that one.

Stephen finally stopped at a small building with a peaked roof and ornate stone carvings. She was about to ask him what he was up to when he literally picked up a section of grass, revealing a hole in the ground. He disappeared into it.

Daphne smiled back at her and winked, then also slipped down into the darkness. Brandi and Megan followed.

A set of stairs led down. At the end, Brandi saw the shining light of a glow-globe held by her uncle.

"Should I put the cover back?" she whispered.

"Yes," said Stephen, "But wedge it open a bit with something. And get Megan to put a sentry spell on it."

Brandi slipped back out of the hole, found a chunk of loose masonry in the side of the mausoleum, and used it to prop the trap door open. Megan whispered an arcane word and the door sparked yellow.

"This way," said Stephen, leading them down a dark passage. Brandi followed, hands on her sword hilts.

The passage opened up into a burial chamber with no exits. The Alenars looked all around the room. Ornate but faded carvings of harvest and village scenes decorated the walls. A sarcophagus sat at the far end, inscribed with a faded name: George Eldermain.

"Well," said Daphne after a few heartbeats, "This can't be it."

"Now if I was trying to hide a secret library, how would I make sure only I could get in?" mused Megan.

Brandi shook her head. She scanned the walls, looking for anything significant. She ran a gloved hand over the carvings. One of the scenes caught her attention: villagers at Christmas time, standing around a Nativity scene complete with a star hovering over the stable.

Brandi absently touched the star. The last time she had celebrated Christmas was with Daphne and Stephen back in Terenai. That was before she had come north with Megan and met the Grey Riders—and Eric.

She choked off further thoughts in that vein.

She stared at the carving, then blinked.

"Star! Uncle Stephen, a star! Bring the book here."

Her uncle joined her. She showed him the artwork.

"Well done, Brandi," Daphne said.

"If I read the book right," replied Stephen, "This will do the trick…"

He turned the book and placed it over the star, cover first. The tome flared bright red, then faded. The wall flared an equally bright red and vanished.

"Neat trick," Megan breathed. "I'm going to have to learn that one for my house. Whenever I get one."

Beyond, a large room beckoned. It held a table, six chairs and wall shelves filled with books. Once inside, something flared red from behind them. They spun around.

The wall had returned, with a bright gold star in the center.

Good.

"Damion Eldermain's secret library," Megan said, looking up at the shelves with shining eyes.

"All right," said Stephen, rubbing his hands together. "Let's see if your sage friend had anything interesting in here."

They went to work. Brandi stifled a sneeze from the dust she stirred up while removing a book from a shelf.

"Magical paints and coatings," she read. *Probably not.*

They examined the shelves, trying to read the faded printing on the spines of the books. More often than not, they had to pull them out to read their titles. Brandi started at the low shelves first, going through the tomes methodically, not quite sure what to look for. She came away with one book about military orders in the Paragon Era and another about Paragon heraldry.

She sighed and straightened, looking at her relatives. Daphne looked pensive, Stephen thoughtful and Megan irritated.

"Anything?"

Megan shook her head. "I don't know. Why go through all this trouble? We could have found these books at any university."

Stephen nodded. "You're right." He dropped two volumes on the table with a decisive thump. "This isn't it. It's too easy. Eldermain is playing a trick on us. There's something else going on, I'm sure of it. Ignore the books and look for something unusual."

"Like this?" asked Megan. She pointed at something odd on the front of the shelf. It looked like a knot in the wood, but very regular, almost like a button.

"Hmmm…" Stephen and Daphne exchanged a look.

"Check it," Daphne said, "Just in case."

Stephen held his hands out, palms up, then murmured a phrase and flipped his hands palm down.

"No traps that I can see," he reported.

Megan pushed the button with her thumb. The entire section of wall rotated out about two feet.

She blinked in surprise. Beyond lay a small chamber with a table, a glowing lamp of blue light on it. Glass cases held scrolls, books and some odd-looking, spindle shaped stones.

"This is more like it," said Stephen, looking satisfied.

Daphne rolled her eyes. "He's going to be insufferably pleased with himself for a week," she whispered to Brandi.

Brandi hid a smile as they entered.

Stephen closed the door behind them after making sure there was a matching button on their side. Brandi peered into the case holding the spindle-shaped stones. She opened it and gently drew one out.

It looked a lot like a child's top, except that it was made of a smooth grey stone with black and red flecks. The top had a narrow shaft that a child would use to spin the top in his fingers if it had truly been a child's toy, but around the shaft, a channel had been cut in the top surface of the stone.

Brandi found, to her surprise, that she could insert her pinky finger up to the first knuckle into the channel. She also saw tiny holes cut into the bottom of the channel at regular intervals, all around the circle.

"What is this?" she breathed.

Stephen actually gasped. "Amazing…"

She gave it to him.

"A Heritage Stone!" He said, turning it over in his hand.

"What's that?" Megan asked.

Stephen turned it in his hand. "It was a means to prevent succession wars in the time of the Paragons. If someone claimed to be a member of a royal or aristocratic line, a couple of drops of their blood would be dripped into the channel. Then, you spin it like a top and it shines with a specific color to indicate the level of association with the family line."

Brandi shook her head in wonder. "Who came up with that idea?"

"Dwarves and halflings, I think. Their level of sophistication in those days was jaw-dropping."

"Look at this, Stephen," said Daphne.

They all crowded around the table as she spread out a large sheet of vellum.

"A map," said Megan. "It looks like Torosc."

"And look at the nations on it," said Stephen, running a hand over the surface.

It indeed looked like a map of Torosc, but with different provincial borders. Unfamiliar names leaped out at Brandi.

Tielo, Loemin, Turis Rhi, Kadar…

"Alenar?" Brandi read in disbelief. A chill raced down her spine.

"Oh my God," whispered Megan. "Alenar? Does that mean that's the nation our family is from?"

"Very likely," replied Daphne, tracing the outlines of the region near the northwestern coastline. "Very, very likely. People were often named for the regions they came from and this looks, well, this could be our homeland. It's along the coast, and there's a city where Coastwatch is now."

"Except it's called Tor Haldin," mused Megan. "Why does that sound familiar?"

Stephen nodded. "The original home of Saint Alyssa. Let's see what some of these other items are," he suggested.

They sifted through the other books and maps.

Finally, Stephen put his hands on his hips. "I think we have enough here, but it will use up all the teleport seals we have to get it back to Saint Martin's. Agreed?"

They all nodded. They placed a letter of explanation and the Heritage Stones into the magic bag first. Just before Stephen attached the medallion, he paused, then shrugged and added the parchment they had taken from Altus Volan with the Ja'al ritual poetry. The medallion flared and the bag vanished. In a few minutes, it reappeared.

They repeated the cycle four more times. When they finished, the library of Damion Eldermain stood empty.

Megan looked wistful. "We've certainly raided his library. It feels kind of lonely now. Does anyone else feel a little guilty?"

Brandi remembered Damion's ghost, his heroism in defending his adoptive people in the elven town, his loyalty, and the look of peace on his face when he finally attained his rest.

"No," she said quietly. "I think he's actually glad that all his knowledge is going to someone who can possibly use it. He might be rather proud."

The magic bag glittered back into being on the table. Her aunt reached inside and brought out two letters.

Brandi's heart skipped a beat when Daphne gave her a wicked grin.

"Is it…?"

Megan snatched up the first one. Daphne nodded, holding out a similar letter to Brandi.

"Thank you, God! They're alive…" Brandi breathed as she opened the letter.

Dearest Bran, she read, *I hope and pray this letter finds you well. Dar is sending along his own letter to Megan…*

***

"Holy Eminence?"

"Yes, Detlef, what is it?"

Edward Simpson, Cardinal Metropolitan and Papal Nuncio to Damora, looked up as the door to his study opened. A blond young half-elven man with sea-green eyes peeked around the door.

"Begging your pardon, but a teleport satchel has arrived. From Colonel Alenar."

Edward smiled. "Very well, I'll be down to the library in a moment. Let me finish this."

"Yes, Eminence."

Edward turned his attention to a sheaf of papers, sent to him from every major area of the known lands, from cities and seaports and sparsely populated areas in between. The picture they gave him left him ill at ease but without a specific pattern he could identify.

The late morning sunshine illuminated the room. It shone on the dark wood of his desk and made the small chamber brighter and less confining. He smiled, looking at his favorite wall. A cork board held pictures drawn by children, children who always made pictures for him in all the towns and cities he visited. He made it known that he especially appreciated pictures.

He ran a hand over one of them, a drawing of him talking to a group of students under a towering tree. A little dwarven lad had drawn that for him months ago and it was still one of his favorites; stick figures never looked so good except when drawn by school kids whose depictions of faces included only smiles and brightly colored eyes.

A sharp pain hit him in his midsection and he put a hand to his side with a sharp breath. He felt every one of his ninety-two years but knew he didn't look it. If he gazed in a mirror (and he only had one in the vesting room to make sure he didn't look like a fool with something misplaced before receiving official visitors), he would see a grey-haired man in his late sixties.

Time passes differently here. Has it really been twenty-five years? And now, reaching the end of it…

He sighed. This was no time for wool-gathering, no matter what the cause. If Alenar had sent something, it was probably important.

He left the study and descended the stairs to the library, where Detlef awaited. The tall windows of the library showed a spectacular view of Saint Martin's harbor with puffy white clouds overhead and ships floating on the waves. His eyes went immediately to a long table laden with scrolls, books and some odd, spindle-shaped stone objects that looked like toy tops used by children.

"Well," he said, putting his hands on his hips, "When the good colonel delivers information, she does not hold back. It would have been nice of her to hand it over by less than a wagon-load, but I guess I should be grateful for anything I can get."

Detlef nodded but Edward saw a little smile on the lad's face.

"Is there a summary sheet?"

"Yes, Eminence. It said to read the smallest paper first."

Edward pursed his lip as he selected a small, stained paper. "Did you send back the bag?"

"Yes, Eminence. It has only one charge left."

"I presume you sent along my letter with my next instructions."

Detlef nodded.

"Excellent. Did you include the letters from Indidarc and Cabot to the young ladies?"

Again Detlef gave an almost-smile. "Yes."

Edward lifted the paper, but Detlef interrupted him. "It was nice of you to send those along."

"Oh pshaw," Edward waved a hand. "Ellen Hanford's idea, weeks ago. I played innocent when she asked if I knew anything about the Alenars but I swear that woman can read minds."

Detlef chuckled. "If you don't mind, Eminence, I will return to the catalogs."

"Of course." Edward read slowly, carefully, first from the summary sheet, then from the small paper.

Ja'al propaganda. Not the first I've seen and certainly not the last.

But Stephen's letter contained some of the details of the finding of this Song of Kudath. Those details made him pause.

Of course, anyone could see a connection between a Gate of Skulls in the Ja'al verse and the odd structure the Alenar's reported. But what did it mean? A planetary gate? To Hades?

Edward sat back in his chair, stroking his chin. The Alenars reported the structure was not complete when they destroyed it. Even if it were a means to bring in daemons, the threat ended there. Even if they hadn't managed to ruin it, a Gate to the home of the daemons could only bring in a limited number. Celestial spies on Damora would scent them out in a matter of minutes.

At that point the Elohir of Celestia would open their own hidden gates in response and the battle would be on. Native Damoran forces would lend their efforts to supplement a Celestial task force. Any attack from the Dark World would fail quickly.

So, what did the Ja'al hope to gain, even if they had more than one Gate? Or was this all another ruse in a much more complicated game?

He considered what he knew of recent events: unrest in many capital cities under the surface veneer of tranquility, tales of raids on the borderlands of Terenai, Deran, and Merdail, this rather unsettling business with the pegasi of Whitehorse Peak. In addition, there had been proposals in various levels of government to repeal laws against prostitution, indentured servitude, drug use and smuggling, and various alarming trends in the arts to attack traditional societies.

He recalled the reports from the Servants of Mindra and the Order of Saint Thomas. Their efforts to counter the repeal of existing laws resulted in legislative support and early success, he still felt uneasy. He shifted in his chair, feeling a growing agitation but unable to put his finger on it.

He shook his head, puzzled, then stood and walked to the dining room. There, he poured a tiny glass of elven wine and looked out the window at the plaza outside the Nuncio's residence, watching the trees and the flowers. He stood there for quite some time, thinking.

The door opened.

"Ah, Detlef, just the man I need to see."

"Eminence?" Detlef said with a quizzical look.

"Please contact Lord Melinor by magic mirror. We need to convene a meeting of the Order of the Three Magi."

Chapter Ten- Opening Move

Conversation in the antechamber of the pavilion died out as she entered, replaced by a somewhat tense silence.

Zhinia Margoth, Princess of Kher Mardil and priestess of Garon-Zith, swept her velvet robes about her. She leaned her staff of black wood against the side of a chair. The tiny, horned skull at its top gleamed white in the glow of magical lamps. She adjusted the crown on her skull and let her undead eyes roam over the others in the room.

Margoth waved a hand at her black orb on the floor in the center of the room. A shining disk of green light swirled horizontally in the air, about two feet off the ground. In a heartbeat, it resolved to her detailed map of the Wilderness. Forester, Wit's End, Dorn's Hall, Athor and even Hillton stood out in various colors of brown, grey or black. The Whitehorse River frothed, foamed and surged southwards, towards Sun Lake. There were even tiny caravans, horseback riders and boats on the river.

"The time is ripe," she said, joining the others watching the map. "My spies report that the Grey Riders are not in the region. Lord Nolan has sent them on a mission to the south, doubtless seeking if we will attack there. We will not disappoint him, but that will come later."

She waved her hand again and pointing a skeletal finger at the map. A red circle popped over Dorn's Hall.

"This is our first target. The dwarves will be a tough nut to crack, but they have slightly more than five hundred citizens and we have easily twenty times that number."

She saw Vorquul's eyes glint at the mention of dwarves and Ildrisana only raised a haughty eyebrow.

She conjured a second circle, farther south and to the east, along the Frontier Highway. "Here, in Athor, we will set our first diversion. A battalion of goblins, two companies of Kaftu and two companies of Ja'al regulars will encamp five miles from the town. Their mission will be to launch probing attacks and raids. I will send a messenger bat to the commander of the Ja'al when it is time to attack the town proper. A second bat messenger will alert them that it is time to break off the attack and move southwest."

"Our second diversion," she continued, "will be to the northwest. Here, a battalion of Ja'al, a company of ogres and a battalion of dark elves will overrun Wit's End. Their objective is to menace Darlon and the towns near it. Once another bat is sent to the commander of the dark elves, they are to wheel southeast."

Ildrisana's brow furrowed. "Why the diversions?"

A third circle appeared over Forester. "This is our real prize," Margoth said. "It controls the direct route to Hillton and we need the road for the siege engines. We would lose valuable time travelling the plains. If Deranese cavalry catches us on open ground we will lose most if not all of that equipment. We have to root out Hanford and his troops if we want to get on the Hillton Road. They will expect a direct attack, so sending the other two formations on hooking routes will make them pause to see if our real object is somewhere else."

A big red circle appeared over a large town next to Sun Lake. "Here, the northwest attack group and the southwest attack group will meet the main force. We will level Hillton and use it as a base of operations to move on to Oakmoor."

Zanilor, the Ja'al high priest, stroked his mustache. "Hillton will not be easy, Highness, and Oakmoor? There are almost half of a million people in the city and suburbs. How do you propose to destroy that?"

Margoth smiled. "We don't. By causing Phillip to come out with his army, we will draw him into battle and then cut off the head of the snake. Phillip is the prize. Without their king, the Deranese will sue for peace. I will take central Deran as my fiefdom and trade it to your high command for the properties in Kher Mardil, as promised."

Ulgrut frowned. "How to kill King? He has many warriors about him, and the Queen is a wizard. Holy warriors are in his court and army. It is not possible." His question affirmed her opinion that his intellect surpassed most of his people.

"Ah, Ulgrut," she said with a smile. "It is possible. I just have to be within a certain distance of him. I can move next to him with a picked force of assassins before he knows it and take him out."

"How will you do that?" Ildrisana asked.

"I constructed a magical helm long ago," Margoth said, sweeping back to the throne. "It is a helm that allows teleportation in the shadows: a Shadow Helm. It has the ability to bypass most wards and protections. Even now, my agents are on the way to retrieve it."

"Why you not have it now?" asked Vorquul.

Margoth suppressed a rising irritation. "It is in hiding. I cannot get it but my agents can. The Helm will obey anyone who wears it. As soon as they touch it, I will know. As a matter of fact, if anyone other than me touches the helm, I can summon it and all persons in the vicinity to my side.

"I had to keep its location a secret because a certain person had a medallion that gave him a clue to its whereabouts," she continued, "This person was using the medallion as blackmail against me, threatening to give it to my competitors for the favor of the Ja'al. Happily for me the Grey Riders eliminated him and the medallion is no longer. My servants will get to the helm and touch it and I will have it again. With the Helm I can get near Phillip on the battlefield, eliminate him and make it back to my forces without incident, thus achieving victory and spoils for all of us."

The command team absorbed the map silently and she watched them. She purposefully arranged it so that the ogres and Kaftu were not in the same theater of operations. Similarly, she made sure the Ja'al were on hand to keep the elves and goblins from tearing each other to pieces. They would be at each other's throats in a blink of an eye and as for the others? Well, ogres liked the taste of dog and the Kaftu sometimes attacked on a whim or went off in an entirely different direction.

Ildrisana tapped her chin. "What if something goes wrong? Suppose the

Deranese get wind of this and move armies to intercept us?"

Margoth eased into her throne. "I have prepared for contingencies. I have a battalion each of light and medium Ja'al cavalry to allow for quick reaction in case the force at Athor or even at North Corner decides to sally forth. I also have a battalion of Kaftu rangers available. Fifteen hundred warriors are more than enough to slow down any Deranese army units in the area."

Ulgrut shook his head. "King not stand still while this happens. He will attack."

"Yes, Lord Ulgrut. And the main force will be ready for him. The only truly large garrisons are at North Corner and Hillton."

"What about the dragon?" Zanilor asked. His eyes measured her.

Margoth shrugged to hide her uncertainty. It helped that she no longer had a face to betray expressions. "My spies tell me he has left the area. A team observed him flying away with his younglings not two days ago."

"He will return," said Ildrisana. "He has an alliance and sympathy with Deran, based on what we already know."

Margoth shook her head. "With his younglings in tow? Unlikely. He won't risk them in battle. They are not of age to have undergone combat training."

"But he could bring King's army," said Vorquul, scowling.

Margoth felt her patience wearing thin. "In two days? I think not, Highness. It will take weeks for the main army to move. By that time, we will have surrounded Hillton and leveled it."

Zirta bared her teeth. "How so? Hill-town is far."

Margoth smiled. "We move today, Pack Queen. We attack today."

***

"Captain, you have to see this."

Captain Oldur of Dorn's Hall slipped up next to his sentry. The dwarven soldier pointed.

"There."

Oldur stroked his beard. Lines of goblins and Kaftu filtered through the trees and brush of the far hill, accompanied by human horsemen and a few slinking creatures he couldn't identify.

"That's a lot of goblin-meat," he agreed.

He rose from behind the brush-blind and helped his trooper set it back into position.

"Tell the squad to move out."

Oldur gathered his team and trotted off into the forest, heading back to Dorn's Hall.

***

"How many?"

"We saw at least two companies, milord." Captain Oldur stood at attention in the Father's Hall, a scout by his side. "Mostly goblins and Kaftu, but well-armed. They had scouts probing the area ahead of them and some creatures in their train. I think they might have been fell-bears."

Jalek Dorn, Fifth Lord of Dorn's Hall, turned around to face him. He held out his arms to the side so his orderly could tighten the straps on his plate armor.

"Did you see anyone else with them? A cleric of the Ja'al or a wizard?"

"No, milord. Some Ja'al cavalry scouts accompanied them but we saw no high cleric or mage."

Jalek stood quietly as the orderly finished.

"Thank you Ivrin." The orderly bowed and left the room to see to his own arming.

Jalek moved over to a side table, picked up a marker and stared down at a map. With deliberate calmness, he made a few notations, not speaking.

"Jalek?"

A dwarven woman entered the hall and he smiled. Her auburn hair bound up on the top of her head, she carried a helmet under her arm and wore chainmail armor herself. A short sword swung at her hip and a crossbow was slung over her back.

"Yes, Riti?"

Lady Riti of Dorn's Hall strode up to her husband and gave him a firm kiss. "All is ready. We can move as soon as you give the order."

He stroked her cheek with the back of his hand. "What would I do without you?"

Her eyes twinkled. "A lot worse."

He turned back to Oldur. "Come look at the map, Captain."

Jalek indicated the markings he had just made, then pointed to three others. Together, they formed an arc advancing on a silver crown next to a mountain. "The two companies of mixed troops you saw are here. Then, over here, other scouts reported human Ja'al levies and over here, dark elves with giant scorpions. Oh, and I forgot the platoon of ogres over there."

Riti nodded. "How many all told?"

Jalek stroked his beard. "Two battalions at least. Some of the ogres pulled light catapults and battering rams. And this is just the vanguard. More scouts report similar groups from the northwest and southeast. It is no raid. They want the Hall."

Oldur gave him a sharp look. "An attack on the Hall? Why? And why are Kaftu and goblins and ogres working together?"

"They have a leader," Riti said grimly. "Is it this Dark Rider that Lord Nolan of Forester warned us about?"

Jalek pursed his lip. "It could be. Or it could be a feint to mask their true intent. With Ja'al you never know. One thing is certain: it is no mere raiding or probing. If it were just the two battalions of those ruffians, we could handle them in short order. From all the intelligence we have…" His voice trailed off.

He felt Riti's eyes on him. "How were their formations?" he asked Oldur.

The captain shrugged. "Not a mob, I am certain of that. They maintained good order, with the Kaftu ranging ahead in skirmish with the goblins following in columns. Their officers and sergeants kept them under control. The human cavalry seemed to be providing a control function, to keep them focused on the path ahead."

Jalek planted a hand on the map. "Organized and disciplined, like the other groups."

"How many all told?" Riti asked.

"With all the formations? Five thousand," Jalek murmured. "And that's a conservative estimate."

Oldur paled.

"Five… *thousand?* We only have five hundred and thirty-one people in all of Dorn's Hall, and that's counting noncombatants. If we can get three hundred soldiers on the field, we'll be lucky."

Jalek nodded, feeling a tightness in his stomach and a hot anger in his heart.

"What do we do?" whispered Riti.

Jalek took a while to speak the next words, so bitter did they taste. "We evacuate the Hall."

Riti's eyes flared. "And retreat before those… spawn of the Dark One? Our halls, our homes, our livelihoods?"

"Riti," he said, calmly meeting her gaze. "I know when to fight and when not to. If I ask for help, Nolan will send it. But he has only five hundred men with him, and over two thousand civilians to protect. Against this large a number, we will bloody them, but we will lose *everything*. Retreating gives us a chance to return and rebuild."

Riti stood silent for a while and finally nodded, her jaw clenched. Knowing his wife's fiery temper and sense of justice, it was the best he could expect.

"Captain, send a runner to Forester, immediately. Give the evacuation order, assemble the regiment and set the countermeasures. We will make a fighting retreat."

Oldur bowed and left the room at a run.

Jalek took Riti's hand and gave it a squeeze. "A lot less than five thousand will make it to Forester, I guarantee that."

She squeezed his hand back. "I will send the children with the first evacuation, no matter how much they protest."

Jalek could only nod.

***

"Ready, milord."

Jalek nodded, feeling the weight of his great sword on his back and the crowned helm on his head.

"Remember the plan, Captain. Make sure the lieutenants see the signals."

Oldur saluted and trotted off.

Jalek turned to a dwarf standing at his left, armored in scale mail and carrying a mace and sword. "I will leave the use of the countermeasures in your hands, Fendir. Seli and Trana, I trust to your judgement to use your magic when it is most advantageous."

Fendir gave him a wry smile. A holy symbol of Kurental, a silver anvil, lay against his armor. "I am looking forward to using Lady Ellen's toys. Praise Kurental and be valiant!"

A pair of female dwarves in leather armor stood next to him. Each bore a staff with a blue jewel at the top.

"Praise Kurental," Jalek responded almost absently.

"We will prevail," said Riti at his side.

He nodded. "Kurental Himself will sustain us. We will return to the Hall. I know it."

The lead elements of the enemy force emerged on the opposite side of the clearing, one hundred yards away. The Kaftu loped through the brush and grass, startling birds and insects. Behind the hyena-folk, dark lines of armored figures marched with spears and shields shining in the sun.

One of the Kaftu hurled a knife at an escaping bird, impaling it. The bird fluttered down to the earth. The Kaftu pulled its knife out and sneered, then left the animal dead in the dirt and ran on. Jalek felt his anger stir.

I will return, by Kurental's favor, or die trying and go to the Everland to be with Him.

"Here we go," he said to his team. The Hall Guard, twenty dwarves in plate armor with battle axes and spears, lifted their steel shields and nodded.

Dwarves armored in chainmail or scaled armor stood in three companies under the trees, shields up, one group in front of him and one each to his left and right, over three hundred strong. To Jalek's left, the ground rose up sharply, pines interspersed with large boulders, a difficult area to traverse. To his right, the forest grew more thickly, impeding movement. He had chosen the place carefully, knowing that the Ja'al force would want a clear and quick path to the Hall that would allow the ogres to pull their siege weaponry along. This area, the easiest pathway for miles around, would funnel the enemy in to an area of his choosing and limit their ability to use their superior numbers to encircle his smaller force.

Deliberately, Jalek left a fifty-foot wide gap between each company of dwarves. He hoped the enemy would notice.

The lead Kaftu stopped, sniffed the air, then spotted the dwarves. Her lips curled back in a leer and she let out a laughing howl. The other Kaftu took up the strange, wavering call and charged.

Jalek's faith in his commanders was well-founded. The dwarves held position until the Kaftu were only a hundred feet away, then the front rank knelt down behind their shields. Crossbowmen in the back rank loosed their shafts and Kaftu dropped under the hissing bolts. The company mages, one per group, cast their magic, making the grass and brush come to life, entangling Kaftu warriors.

More Kaftu made it through the fusillade and reached the front rank. The dwarves raised their shields and thrust forward with spears, impaling hyena-folk, knocking down swords and bashing their enemies. For a moment, combat swirled as the dwarves laid about them and the enemy tried to hack their way through. Several dwarves dropped, to be pulled back out of the fight by the crossbowmen. Behind the Kaftu shock wave, goblin troops marched in disciplined lines, spears and shields up, chanting a dark melody as they advanced. Some of the Kaftu detected the gaps in the dwarven line and gleefully charged through, howling.

Fendir waited until a good number of them had passed into the gap, then raised his hands and shouted a word. Blue stones, hidden under the dirt and leaves, vibrated, then leaped upwards to a height of four feet. They detonated with sharp cracks, blasting the Kaftu with magical fire and hot shards of stone. When the smoke cleared, a few Kaftu remained, racing towards Jalek and his command, blades held in their teeth as they went to all fours.

Jalek drew his blade and waited. The Kaftu crashed into his guard, who dispatched them with spear and axe. The two mages, Seli and Trana, added darts of glowing fire to blast down those Kaftu who caused the most damage. Jalek turned his attention to the main battle.

The Kaftu suddenly retreated, moving behind the advancing goblins. At a bawled command from their sergeants, the goblin soldiery spread out in a vast line, four deep. Behind them, another group of equal size formed up in identical fashion.

The more mobile of the wounded dwarves helped their comrades move towards Jalek as the defenders reformed their units. The goblins charged. Goblin warriors with short bows unleashed a hail of arrows at the dwarves, who hunkered down behind their shields, crossbowmen and spearmen alike. Most of the goblin shafts struck trees, bushes or shields, only a few hitting their mark.

The dwarves popped back into their formations with the goblins only fifty feet away. Dwarven mages shouted spell words and each crossbow bolt came alive with red fire. The dwarves loosed, their bolts sizzling out at the enemy, trailing tails of flame. They blasted through goblin shields to strike down the soldiers behind them.

Then the wave hit. Another maelstrom of steely weapons erupted before Jalek as he watched carefully.

"Team one left!" he shouted and ten of his guard leaped forward. They hurled themselves into the fight on the left flank where the press of goblins threatened to overwhelm the defenders.

The goblins kept away from the gaps between the dwarven companies, fearing another magical onslaught.

That will last until they get their own mages up here.

Seeing the center wavering, Jalek hefted his sword.

"Team Two to me! For the Hall of Dorn!"

He led the assault personally, leaping into the fray. Goblins snarled and lashed out at him, focusing their efforts on the Lord of Dorn's Hall. His weapon glowed with golden fire. He knocked aside spears and scimitars, slashing through goblin armor and stabbing. Riti fought at his left, guarding his blind spot. She leaped, dodged, and thrust, taking out a goblin with each stroke.

The wave broke and the goblins retreated in good order, moving back to join the next wave.

Jalek took a deep breath and gritted his teeth. Not enough time had passed.

"Back to Rally Point Two," he commanded. "Leave the dead."

The dwarven officer nodded and echoed his command. Shields up, the dwarves moved backwards, faces at the enemy.

Jalek rejoined Fendir and the mages. The priest of Kurental moved among the wounded, healing those he could save and giving final blessings to those he couldn't.

"To Rally Two."

Fendir looked out at the retreating dwarves and mass of goblins beyond them. "Well, we slowed them down."

Jalek shook his head. "Not enough. We move now."

"On the double-time! Turn and repel at fifties!" his lieutenants called. The dwarves turned as individual platoons and trotted back towards Jalek, passing beyond his command force. After fifty paces, they all wheeled as one to face the enemy and, seeing no pursuit, turned again and trotted away.

The goblins saw this and surged forward, entering the treeline. They halted and loosed arrows, but the trees and bushes spoiled their aim. No shaft found its mark.

Using an overlapping pattern with one dwarven company retreating while Jalek's command and the other two companies guarded them, they moved away from the goblins towards their second rally point. The goblins sent squads forward to harass and harry, trying to goad the dwarves into attacking, but the discipline of Jalek's army held firm.

He gave a grim smile. Living out in the Wilderness taught the dwarves of the Hall self-reliance, self-control, and dependence on one another. They would not break just because of hooting goblins launching arrows.

Jalek assessed their progress, calculating how much time it would take for them to get back to Dorn's Hall via the secret woodland path. If they could hold the enemy here long enough, they could easily return to the Hall and mount an even stiffer defense. This would give the retreating civilians more time to get to Forester and Jalek knew he could tie up even this large a force in the tunnels and halls of his mountain home.

"In place, milord!" shouted Oldur from behind him. He turned with his command, Riti at his side.

Here the area opened up and widened a bit, but Jalek had prepared well: a series of barricades blocked the way. He led his team through the winding path, careful to avoid certain places. He arrived at a rise, allowing him to look over the maze of wood and bracing at the enemy advance. To his right, the forest led off into a dark hollow and wet, spongy ground. Attempting to flank would result in a mess for the Ja'al.

"Casualties?" he asked Fendir.

"Sixteen dead and twelve wounded," the Kurental priest answered, wiping his sword. "Of the wounded, only three have trouble walking. They have volunteered to hold the side nearest the hollow with the other wounded."

Jalek's heart both swelled with pride at the valor of his people and fell with sorrow for the ones already lost.

"Prepare for the assault!"

The mass of goblins ahead sifted through the trees and brush. Seeing the barricades, they stopped.

"Crossbowmen at the ready!" shouted Oldur.

Goblin sergeants halted their forces and appeared to confer with their officers. Soon, other goblins appeared, holding what appeared to be round clay pots on the ends of ropes. Smoke curled up from the top of each pot.

Goblin soldiers led the way, shields up, guarding the grenadiers. Oldur gave the command to loose and more bolts sang out at the goblin force. Some dropped but others came on. Twenty paces from the barricades, the ground suddenly gave way and entire sections of the goblin advance vanished as pits opened beneath them. Dull thuds signaled the detonations of whatever they carried in the clay pots. They heard screams and shrieks from the goblins that fell in. Flames and smoke poured out of the pits.

The dwarves cheered as one. Some of the remaining goblin grenadiers hurled their pots. They broke against the barricades and exploded, showering the wood with sticky flaming goo. The barricades quickly flared up.

Fendir stood forth, raised his hands, and chanted. The air became dry and a thick cloud appeared over the goblin force, swathing the trees in a mass of grey. With a final word, he released the spell. A sudden downpour lashed downwards, fat raindrops pummeling the goblins and inundating the area. The flames faded and disappeared in clouds of steam.

The goblins screeched in rage and drew back.

Jalek sighed, glad for the respite. He had Oldur keep an eye on the situation while he and Riti went among the troops, encouraging them and checking their morale and equipment. They visited the wounded where they lay crouched among the brambles and stones, watching the boggy ground.

Riti whispered into his ear. "Something is not right."

He nodded, waiting for her to continue.

"We've drawn them away from Dorn's Hall. Look at their force. If they really wanted to capture Dorn's Hall, they would have split off some of their force to get there before us. They don't know about the secret way, so they think they have us cut off and isolated. So why are they following us?"

He looked at her. She met his gaze.

"They don't want the Hall," she whispered through gritted teeth. "They want *us*. Dead. *All* of us."

He felt a chill.

A runner came to them while they were with the wounded and brought them back to the command post.

"Look," Oldur said grimly.

Large, shaggy bear-like shapes with bulging, burning red eyes and dripping maws stalked through the goblin lines. Their paws ended in wicked, curved talons and spiny ridges ran down their backs. Intricately tooled leather harnesses lay over their backs, allowing the spines to show through. On each side of the bear-thing, a basket of wood and metal held one goblin. These bore shields and held wands in their hands. The bear-things numbered ten.

Jalek gaped. "Hell-spawn bears! But they eat goblins. How are they allowing them as riders?"

A sudden fear gripped him. Who could command such discipline and order?

Oldur swore under his breath. "This doesn't make sense. Kaftu might be able to ride them but not goblin mages. Something is terribly wrong."

"This is Margoth's work," Riti spat.

"Make ready!" shouted Jalek.

No sooner had the order gone down the line when the hell-spawn raised their muzzles to the sky and roared. The sound was so full of malice, savagery and hatred it made Jalek's skin crawl. It took all his will to keep himself from cowering. Then the creatures surged forward.

Crossbows twanged. The goblin mages chanted from their baskets and screens of purple light leaped up in front of the bears. Most of the crossbow bolts bounced off the screen, only a few making it through to strike the hellish mounts. The creatures snapped and growled but their riders viciously jerked on their harness and held them under control.

The mages shouted again and pointed their wands. Sickly green balls of light shot out and struck the foremost barricades. The barriers sagged and grew brittle and rotten, then collapsed. Snarling, the bears charged, the goblin army in their wake.

"Entropy globes!" exclaimed Trana. "There is a high wizard at work if they have learned to use those."

Jalek knew there were more pits behind the barricades, but the bears simply gave great leaps and hurdled over them. Fortunately for Jalek, the mages couldn't concentrate while sailing through the air and his crossbowmen took advantage, riddling two bears with bolts and dropping them.

"Countermagic!" Fendir commanded. Seli and Trana raised their staves and the blue gems flashed. Shafts of light seared into a pair of hell-spawn and their riders, burning holes into them. The goblins shrieked and died and the bears writhed on the ground, but the enemy mages turned their attention to Jalek's command group. A veritable storm of fire darts shot out at them.

Jalek tried to dodge but no less than seven darts hit his armor. The sharp detonations made him reel backwards. Riti collapsed under the onslaught and he hauled her up. Seli lay dead at his feet, hit by six of the magical missiles.

"I'm okay!" Riti protested. To prove it, she levered a bolt into the throat of one of the goblin mages.

"Target the mages!"

Bolts and firedarts flickered between the forces. Without a missile weapon of his own Jalek could only watch as the goblins and dwarves peppered each other. By the time the bears managed to rip through the last barricades, only three remained and one had no riders. They laid into the dwarven line with savage frenzy. The dwarves maintained discipline, held their shield-wall and methodically hacked them down.

With a shout, the remaining goblin force charged, heedless now of the barricades and pits. Jalek felt a sinking dread as he saw Kaftu in their wake. The goblins met the dwarven line and slashed and fought and died among the barricades. Dwarves dropped and either lay still or were pulled back by their comrades.

"Lord Jalek!"

One of the wounded troops hobbled up to him.

"From the fens, milord. Dark elves! They are using wooden boards and magic to cross the bog!"

Jalek couldn't believe his ears. "What? Elves? And goblins working together?"

Riti looked up at him, her face showing the pain of her injuries and a growing despair.

Jalek gritted his teeth. He ran to the boggy area. As he watched, dark elves laid down wooden boards on the soggy earth. Elven mages cast spells and the boards anchored themselves down firmly into the bog, forming a wooden road. The wounded dwarves retreated, loosing bolts at the elven combat engineers. A few dark elves dropped from bolts, but the others loosed arrows of their own. Three of the wounded dwarves fell dead.

"Fendir! Get us out of here! Full retreat!"

"Jalek, no!" shouted Riti. "We can still…"

"No!" he shouted back, lifting her up and half-dragging her backwards. "This fight is done, Riti! They are too many and have too much magical support. And with dark elves? No, we have to leave."

"Milord!" Fendir stood with them. "Now would be a good time."

He thrust both hands skyward and shouted. A thick black fog surged out from his hands, engulfing the enemy forces in a matter of seconds. Trana, tears streaming down her face at the loss of her sister, screamed aloud. Lightning flared from her hands, tiny bolts spearing into the blackness. Shrieks of dying goblins and Kaftu and elves rang out in the glade.

Trana turned sheet white from expending all her magical power and Oldur grabbed her, lifting her onto his shoulders.

"Now!" Jalek yelled. "Rally to the hot point! Per the plan! Move, move!"

Supporting Riti with him, he retreated from the battlefield as the Ja'al forces struggled to get past the bog, barricades and cloud of fog.

The dwarves ran, jogging at a good pace but not too fast. The wounded soldiers vociferously urged their more able fellows onward, pledging to slow the enemy so they could escape.

Jalek felt tears of rage and anger at such brave men and women sacrificing themselves for him. He wanted to run back and lay into the enemy but he knew it would make their sacrifice in vain if they lost everyone. He forced himself to support Riti and run onwards.

The next two hours were a blur. A couple of times, Kaftu runners caught up with them, but the dwarves dispatched them with no losses. By the time they saw the towers of Forester, they were exhausted, dirty, thirsty, wounded and demoralized.

The Forester guards gaped at them in shock and amazement but threw the gates open. The Christian priest, Ander, stepped to his side immediately, joining Fendir in healing what wounded he could.

"My lord Jalek."

He turned to see the familiar form of Nolan Hanford in full armor striding up to meet him. The Baron of Forester bowed low.

"My people and my town are at your disposal milord. We heard from your scouts what you faced. We were preparing to sally forth to aid you."

Jalek returned the bow. He straightened, looking at the ranks of Forester guards, civilian levies and sellswords gathered in the main square. He set his jaw.

"My lord Nolan, your assistance is greatly appreciated. However, it comes too late and in short supply. The enemy force is great and has many weapons at its disposal."

Lady Ellen Hanford bowed to him. "How so, Lord Jalek?"

He explained about the goblin mages, the entropy globes, alchemical grenades and dark elven combat engineer battalion. He described the methodical, disciplined Ja'al battle plan and their refusal to break despite casualties. Oldur listed off the known enemy force composition.

Lady Ellen looked grim. "Hell-spawn bears ridden by goblins? Dark elves and goblins working together? I agree with Lady Riti. This has Margoth's hand on it, my lord."

Hanford looked off into the distance. "How many?"

"Thousands. At least three, probably five. We gave a good account, but probably only dispatched a tithe of them."

Jalek and Hanford stood silently, looking over the dwarven survivors and the assembled army. With a dull feeling, Jalek realized he had lost a third of his force.

"Did you send the civilians south?" he asked instead.

Nolan nodded, his eyes steely. "Your advice was heeded and your counsel wise, as usual. We are in your debt."

"We cannot defend Forester." Jalek removed his helmet and wiped his brow.

Ellen looked at Nolan. The lord of Forester nodded slowly. He watched Father Ander tend to an unconscious Trana.

"How far behind are they?" he asked.

Fendir stood up from tending a wounded soldier and moved over to Riti, bringing out healing salves. "Probably no more than two hours. The spell I used was Fog of War. It not only obscures vision but confuses the mind. Unless they have a powerful wizard, they won't disentangle themselves for a while yet. Based on what we saw, they are likely reforming as we speak, and marching on."

Nolan turned to an armored knight next to him. "Sir Colin, give the order. The gates are to be barred and countermeasures set. The entire force will gather up the travel provisions and leave by the south gate immediately. I want cavalry units watching our back trail."

The knight saluted and wheeled his horse around.

"Will they catch up to us?" asked Riti. "On the plains south of here, their superior numbers…"

Ellen gave a wry smile, her dark eyes glinting. Her smooth, dark-skinned face looked both lovely and deadly. "I have some surprises that will slow them down, Lady Riti. And I have means for monitoring them as we retreat to Hillton."

"We have carts for bringing your wounded, Lord Jalek," said Father Ander with a smile. He and some of the guards began gathering up the injured.

Jalek put his arm around Riti as Fendir finished administering a healing potion to her.

"Lord Jalek?"

He looked up. Lord Nolan still faced northwards, towards the unseen enemy.

"We will reconquer the Hall. Your people sacrificed for our protection.

We will see to it that your home is returned to you and rebuilt."

He turned steel-grey eyes to Jalek. The dwarven lord saw resolve, anger and respect. "It is a promise."

Jalek believed him.

Chapter Eleven- Into the Dark

"What this place must have been like in the old days!" said Andyn Eleandir.

Buck nodded. He turned and surveyed the balcony as they caught their breath from ascending the stairs. The late afternoon sun shone down on them and the clean mountain air felt crisp. "Excellent view of the lake and forest around. On a clear day you can almost see all the way to the pass by Darcy's Wood," he said.

Hlerv stopped next to them. "I don't know how this place fell, but from the looks of it, it must have been a hell of a fight."

Andyn remembered their slow clamber up the broken steps to this landing, some fifty feet above the highest tree. Along their way, they found dented shields, rusted weapons, scorch marks, arrow heads and an occasional bone. At places, they had to completely detour and use pitons and rope to make their way up. It helped that Connor and Hlerv were so nimble and agile. The rough traverse guaranteed that their initial assessment was correct: there wasn't a place to land a pegasus, let alone five of them.

Even a thousand years can't completely erase what happened here, Andyn thought.

"Can you read this, Andyn?" asked Dar, peering up at an inscription carved into the rock over the open doorway on the mountain's side of the balcony.

"I think it says 'Fort Aldric - the Eagle's Perch'... but it's kind of faint," she replied after perusing it for a while.

"Definitely Elven though," added Eric, joining them.

"Well," said Connor, hefting his backpack. "It's getting late and we've already had a time of it. Let's find a place to make camp."

Hlerv examined the doorway with careful hands and alert eyes. He shook his head. "No traps, which is a good sign. If there was anything still active, it would mean someone has been here recently."

Andyn entered the room with the other Riders. Open windows, now with only a few bits of glass along their edges, stared out at the magnificent view on either side of the doorway. The room beyond sported two arched exits.

With Connor and Hlerv leading, they stepped into a passage. the remaining afternoon sunlight gave them some visibility for a little while but soon Buck stopped them. He reached into his pack and pulled out a metal clip with a crystal sphere dangling from it. He shook the sphere and it glowed bright white, illuminating the area around him. After flipping down the Eye of Truth, he attached the sphere to the top of his shield using the clip. A soft white glow suffused the area to about twenty feet away.

Andyn shifted her vision, wishing that Dar and Buck could see in the dark like the rest of them.

Hlerv and Connor led them into the fortress and they followed as silently as they could. Andyn knew a spell that would help them move without noise but it would also make conversation impossible. In her present state of tiredness, she wasn't sure she could get it off anyway.

Their path led to a larger room with one entrance off the main corridor. Connor motioned them forward.

"It looks clean."

Buck held out his dwarven sword, Khelios, watching for the tell-tale golden glow that signaled the presence of evil. Nothing happened and they all entered.

"We need to rest," said Andyn, feeling the fatigue of the trek through the Darkwood and the battle against the drakes. Her eyes grated in their sockets. She ran a hand over her face, trying to banish some of the weariness.

Connor nodded, setting his pack on the floor. "I'll go out with Hlerv and scout the corridor and see what's nearby."

He and the gnome disappeared into the dark shadows.

Andyn set down her pack and removed her helmet, shaking out her hair. She flopped down and pulled out a wineskin and some rations.

"Too bad we can't cook here," said Eric. "I was looking forward to what Dar could make from what we have." He held up salt pork, way-bread and a dried apple.

Dar looked thoughtful. "I might be able to do something with that. Why don't you run down to the forest and get me some sage and rosemary?"

Andyn took a bite of her rations, never imagining that a dried piece of fruit could taste so good. "I don't ever want to go back there, but Iron Thunder seemed confident the forest would heal eventually."

"So long as those drake-things are gone," said Buck, plopping down on a stone bench.

They ate in silence after that, pausing only when Connor and Hlerv returned.

"Nothing out there for quite a distance," the gnome reported. "I set a few magical alarms at the intersections just in case. We should be okay for a while."

Something silvery flashed in the magical light and Andyn saw Eric fingering a tiny crucifix. His eyes looked a million miles away.

She gave a wistful smile.

He sat back, caught her eyes, and realized she had been watching. "Is it that obvious?"

Her smile grew. "Of course, you jester. Same for Dar. You miss her."

He tossed a pebble up against a wall. "The distance and time away wear on me. And we've only had a couple of letters from them."

She sat next to him and offered her wineskin. Dar sat next to the light globe, reading a letter. Eric took a drink and tossed another pebble. Dar looked up at the sound and she smiled at him, beckoning him to join them.

"You need me closer so Eric can actually hit me with those rocks?" he quipped.

Eric handed the wineskin back to Andyn. "If I wanted to hit you, you brush tramp, I would have."

"What does Megan have to say?" Andyn asked, nodding at the letter.

Dar folded up the letter and put it back inside his belt pouch. "They are well. Daphne and Stephen too. They're praying for us every night. They can't tell us anything about their mission for fear of the letter getting intercepted. Basically, what you'd expect. And no, I'm not telling you the parts that you could use against me later."

Andyn laughed. "As if there was anything untoward in there. Although I have to admit, if I found out her pet name for you, I'd use it mercilessly."

"That's why I'm not telling you."

She nodded. "Where were they when they wrote the letter?"

"Southern Terenai, near the eastern border. The postal mark shows Tirevlan."

They sat in silence for a while. Andyn knew Tirevlan, a large town near the borderlands, deep in the forest. It had a particularly beautiful fountain in the center of town.

Eric spoke up. "They liberated a ghost."

Andyn almost spat out her wine. She stared at him. "What? I have to hear this one."

Eric smiled. "Brandi says they found a ruined village. The only resident remaining was the ghost of the town sage who couldn't leave this world until the survivors were rescued. I'm not sure why Brandi and Megan were in the town to begin with but the sage seems to figure into it somehow. Anyway, Daphne and Stephen weren't with them, so Brandi and Megan searched for the survivors. It turns out the elves had escaped but were prisoners of something called a hell-wisp, an evil undead sprite. The sisters freed the elves and stayed with them for a while. The ghost apparently had been waiting for all the villagers to come back because when they returned, he, kind of, went away. From there, they stayed in a town called Marolpeth before going to Tirevlan. Nothing more."

"I'd like to send something back to Megan. But we're so far away," Dar said, sounding morose.

Andyn nodded. "But you can always do that via Lady Ellen in Forester. She will find a way to get them delivered. Until then, we can only send prayers. Besides, we don't have anything new to report until we find the Helm, or your grandparents."

Dar sighed. He stared at the far wall for a long time.

"Andyn, it's no use pretending. This place, the area nearby, the forest—

nothing has been here for years. There's very little chance that they're alive anymore."

She sat very quietly. "We can't be sure."

Dar shook his head. "My grandmother was a great scout. If they didn't return for some reason and were forced to hole up in here, she would have detected us and come out as soon as we approached. If they made it this far, they're dead by now."

She put her arm around him. "I'm sorry, Dar."

He shrugged. "I think it was always the most likely possibility, and I knew it. Just facing it now and realizing it's probably reality…"

Eric also put his arm around Dar. "If we can find them, we'll bring them out and give them the proper burial back at Forester. Father Arder will say the blessing over them."

"How will you know them, though?" asked Andyn. "We've seen bones and skulls and weapons but all those are much older."

"My grandmother had a map-case, a special one with slots in it for charcoal pencils and ink pens and different compartments. She let me play with it when I was little. It had a silver clasp in the shape of a dove."

Eric looked at him. "Is that unique enough?"

Dar gave a little smile. "The clasp only opened if you touched the dove and said *Spiritu Sanctu*. I think that's pretty unique."

"Hey, I don't mean to interrupt the threesome," said Hlerv, coming over to them with a smirk. "But if you want some rest, you'd better get it now. Connor and Buck have first watch."

Eric, Dar and Andyn all tossed pebbles at Hlerv, who deftly blocked them with his palms.

"Not fast enough," he said with a grin.

"He's right," Eric said. "Time to rest."

Andyn was still sore from the battle in the forest but also so bone-tired she knew she wouldn't have any trouble falling asleep. She was right.

***

"You've been a bad boy!" his mother said with a sneer. "Or rather, you've been a good boy. Either way, you'll pay for it…"

161

She raised a whip crackling with red lightning.

Eric's eyes popped open with a start and he momentarily lost track of his surroundings. For a panicked second, the darkened chamber looked like one of the holding cells in the complex of the Crossed Swords assassins' guild. Then he remembered the forest, the Darkwood Drakes, the trek to this ruined fort and let out a deep breath.

My past life must have been something awful, he thought, *when a battle against evil dragons in a poisoned forest and a night in an abandoned ruin seems comforting compared to home.*

Even as he thought it, he forced himself to relax and remember his other home, his adoptive family: his foster father, Melinor, his late foster mother, Anne, his adoptive sister, Saren, his brother-in-law Terenil. He imagined of their faces, feeling his pulse slow.

I have a real family now.

A glow-globe shone with a mild light, illuminating the Dar's face. He sat with Andyn Eleandir near the doorway, keeping watch. Andyn yawned.

She needs more rest.

He stifled his own yawn and sat up. Picking up his bow and case of arrows, he slipped next to them.

"My turn," he said.

Andyn rubbed her eyes. "I have half a mind to argue with you. But only half."

She moved off to find her sleeping place. Dar looked at him with bleary eyes of his own.

"We keep hearing noises, down farther in the fortress. Nothing I can identify though. It sounds like something moving, but then it dies off. Sometimes it seems like whispering. Maybe I'm going mad."

Eric gave him a tired grin. "Too late. You're already crazy."

Dar sat quietly for a while, then turned to pick up his bow and case. "Bad dreams?"

Eric nodded. "You too?"

"I see the ruins of Westhaven, the burned homes outside Forester, Elaine lying dead near her parents' home. Not good images for falling asleep. You?"

Eric sat with his back to the doorjamb, casting his more sensitive vision out into the passage beyond.

"My parents' house," he said curtly.

Dar didn't reply, but instead clapped him on the shoulder. "We're with you, my friend." Then he too went to his bedroll, taking the glow-globe with him.

Eric tried an old scout trick, shifting his position slightly every one hundred counts to avoid stiffness and stave off fatigue. All the time, he listened and watched. Only an occasional rat or spider glowed with heat as he kept an eye on the corridor.

Something vaguely like a moan reached his ears but he wasn't sure he had heard it. A little while later, he thought he heard clacking and a rustling sound. It echoed faintly back to him through the corridor, so faintly he had to remain very still to ensure he wasn't hearing things. Some time later, he thought he heard a whispering sound.

Nothing moved. He risked a spell, using one to detect evil creatures, but it showed nothing.

Still, he couldn't shake the vague feeling of unease. He kept his vigil, occasionally shooting a glance back at his companions, seeing their warm forms under their blankets. Andyn stirred restlessly.

Based on her past and his own dreams, he was willing to bet she was reliving her husband's murder and the torture chamber of the dark elves.

Dawn sneaked up on him, bringing a pale glow of light from the passage they had used to enter this place from the balcony room. He waited until he could make out his companions' outlines, then crept back to wake them.

Connor snapped to wakefulness with his hand on his sword, then relaxed as he recognized Eric.

"Sorry. Had a bad dream."

Eric made a face. "I think we all did. There's something in this place, something bad."

Hlerv's tense expression and Buck's wary eyes confirmed his suspicion that they, too, had been haunted by ill dreams.

They rummaged in their packs for breakfast, eating quietly without speaking. Finally, Eric stoppered his wineskin and stood.

"Well, Hlerv, let's see what you mapped out yesterday."

The gnome pulled a parchment from his shoulder bag. "Connor and I were able to get pretty far without anything attacking us."

He indicated a square on the map. "This is us now. If we go this way, turn left and then right, we'll end up in a long corridor with a series of openings. Connor thinks they were a barracks. There's an iron door at the end."

Andyn nodded. "If I were going to hide something as powerful as the Helm of Shadows, I'd put it deep in the mountain, as far away from the outside world as possible."

"What about here?" asked Dar, pointing at another set of corridors.

Hlerv shook his head. "That actually curves around and leads to a set of stairs that go up to another balcony room. We stopped there and came back. I agree with Andyn. We go deeper."

He rolled up the parchment.

Eric hefted his spear. "Let's move then. The sooner we find the Helm, the sooner we can break it and get out of here."

He led the way with Connor, Dar and Hlerv following behind. True to Hlerv's map, they found the passage with the many openings and he had to admit it looked like a type of barracks, with enough space in each chamber to hold four people. In one he saw the remnants of a bunk.

As they went deeper, the area grew darker so Buck used another glow-globe.

"I only have a few of these left," Buck muttered. "I hope we don't run out."

"You can hold my hand and I'll lead you," said Eric.

"Into a pit you'll lead me," Buck retorted.

"Quiet now," hissed Connor. "The door is just up ahead."

Eric waited while Connor examined the door, its handle, and the edges. The halfling finished and pointed at the right and left edges. He made a 'writing' gesture with one hand.

Detonable runes, thought Eric, examining the edge of the door. A barely perceptible pattern was etched there. *Reasonably new, too.*

He set his spear to the side and let out a slow breath, then pointed at one of the symbols. Speaking low and deliberate words, he traced the symbol, watching it glow purple and disappear.

He concentrated on the second symbol, repeating the process.

He finished and let out a breath. "There," he whispered. "Whoever put those there knew what he was doing. I think—"

He didn't get to finish his sentence as a third symbol above the door flared red. He just had time to bark a warning to everyone else and duck. A low boom sounded in the hallway and searing fire shot out at him. He rolled backwards, singed by the flames.

"Look out!" Connor shouted, tackling him as the iron door groaned, tottered and fell at them. Eric and Connor landed in a heap at the feet of their retreating companions.

With a thunderous boom, the iron door slammed into the floor, its edge not a foot away. Simultaneously, short explosions rang out along the hall, hurling small bits of metal and stone at them. Eric hid his face under his cloak. He winced at shrapnel lacerations and bullets of metal pinged off his helmet.

The dust cleared and Eric peeked out. The other Riders had taken hits from the traps, bleeding from minor wounds and looking mildly scorched.

"My fault," said Connor in a shaky voice. "I thought they'd trap the area around the door, but never that they'd use the door itself to kill us."

Eric shook his head. "No. I should have been more wary. The symbols were strong, all right. They were so strong that they took all my attention and distracted me from the symbol up above. And we were so focused on the door that we didn't even bother to look for the auxiliary charges along the passage."

Misdirection and treachery: hallmarks of the Ja'al.

Dar shook his head. "We have to be more careful."

Andyn nodded. "It's Verian's own grace that we're not dead."

"One thing is for certain," said Buck, flipping down the Eye of Truth. "That is sure to alert someone."

Hlerv drew his new sword and stared at it when a ripple of white light raced over the blade.

"Didn't Grandpa say something about it being a weapon against the undead?" he asked.

Eric gritted his teeth and retrieved his spear. "Stay sharp."

He and Connor led the way through the opening. It led into an empty antechamber, then a large area that looked like a meeting room. A huge stone table lay on the floor, three of its massive legs broken. Remnants of chairs littered the floor, as did bones and complete skeletons, some still gripping rusted weapons and wearing armor.

"Evil, " Buck whispered.

A chill raced up Eric's spine. "Where?"

"Everywhere."

Khelios' golden fire lit up the room and Andyn's new mace flared to brilliant life.

The skeletons rose and moved with fluid grace, as if they still possessed flesh and muscle. Their eye sockets glowed with a vile pink light. Most of them were human-sized, but one stood distinctly shorter than the others, about the size of a dwarf.

Eight of them advanced on the Riders, the first three lifting swords and forming a shield wall. Three more with spears advanced behind them and two marched in the rear, their hands glittering and glowing with magic.

Andyn's voice rang out in a prayer to Verian and an arc of golden light raced past Eric. It struck the skeletons and they shuddered, drawing back. One of the spearmen vibrated furiously and then fell apart.

Dar moved up next to Eric on the left and Buck did the same on the right. Connor and Hlerv darted to the sides. The enemy surged at them, magic crackling through the air as the skeletal mages dueled with Andyn. Buck and Dar leaped forward.

The dwarf-sized skeleton stabbed a sword at Eric and he blocked it with his spear. He turned slightly to get leverage as the undead swung its shield around to bash him. He waited until the shield got within range, then skipped backwards and used the spear tip to swing the shield wide. He stepped in, striking the skeleton's shield-arm with the haft, then using the butt to poke at its head. The skeleton almost dropped the shield. It weaved out of the way of Eric's spear, countering immediately with a sword swing at Eric's head. Eric blocked the attack with his spear haft as the skeleton's weapon flared bright orange He dodged quickly to avoid a leg slash. The dwarf-skeleton pressed forward and he weaved out of the way of another thrust, then blocked a slash.

He felt a cold sweat. These were not the simple automatons he and his friends had defeated at the Battle of Forester. These were something different entirely, and this one had a magical weapon.

A spearman joined the swordsman and Eric spent a few desperate seconds blocking spearpoints, sword strikes and shield bashes. Turning so he put the spearman behind the charging dwarf-skeleton, he held his spear like a bar in front of him, pushing against the shield and driving the undead back into his fellow behind.

Eric leaped backwards, raised a hand, and blasted fire-darts at the spearman. It staggered. A small, shadowy figure slipped in behind it and a glittering blade slashed once, twice. The skeleton fell, its skull hacked from its neck and a leg cut in two. As quickly as he had appeared, Hlerv slipped away.

The swordsman spun towards the gnome, stabbing out with its blade. Hlerv parried with his sword and Eric stepped in, grabbing the shield with his free hand and pushing down with all his strength. He swung his spear around, striking the back of the thing's skull with the bladed head. With a crack, the undead's skull jerked to the side. Hlerv leaped forward, lopped an arm off, then split the skull in half down to the jaw.

Eric whirled around and narrowly missed a spear to the kidneys. A skeleton charged past. Eric fired off a lightning spell. The bolt of electricity hit the skeleton in the breastbone and it flew backwards.

Andyn shouted and Eric felt a wave of heat behind him. The room came alive with flickering firelight and he heard the clash of swords and armor. Connor cried out in pain.

Eric's opponent thrust, swung and lunged. Eric blocked all the attacks, drawing back just enough to give Hlerv an opening. The gnome leaped forward, cutting through a thigh bone as easily if it were a loaf of bread, then split the skull in half.

Eric spun around. Flaming skeletons lay on the stone tiles. Buck stood over an assemblage of bones that had once been a pair of skeletal warriors. Dar helped Connor limp over to Andyn. The halfling had taken a spear in the thigh and was bleeding profusely.

"Damn it," Andyn cursed as she slid to Connor's side. She removed her gloves and pressed a hand to the wound, a mild glow covering him.

Connor looked at her, face pale and sweaty. She took the mace in her hands and closed her eyes, murmuring a prayer. She extended a hand to

Connor's injury.

Eric's eyes widened. Her hand seemed to be made of golden light. She touched Connor and he stiffened, then relaxed. She removed the spear.

Connor blinked, color returning to his face. He fingered the hole in his armor and found no scar.

"Good God…" breathed Dar. "How did you do that?"

Andyn shook her head. "It was Eleison, the Mercy-Giver."

The Riders sat in the room for a while, shaken. The rapidity of the attack and the skill of the undead gave Eric an uneasy feeling. He stood next to Andyn.

"Those were no normal skeleton servants," he whispered to Andyn.

"No. They weren't."

"Any ideas on what could craft those?"

Andyn looked at him. "A powerful high priest or a greater undead, like a mummy or vampire or … a lich."

"Not Margoth…"

"No," she murmured. "Not Margoth. If she were here, it would be over and we'd be dead already. But Verian knows what's been in and out of here in the last thousand years. We'll have to watch our step. Someone is taking pains to make sure intruders don't get very far."

Eric pursed his lip. "One of them was the size of a dwarf."

Dar came over to him, a strange look on his face. "Which one?"

Eric showed him the ruin of the dwarven skeleton, watching his friend, lost in thought.

"What is it, Dar?" asked Connor.

Dar shook his head, kneeling down and inspecting the other junk on the floor. "I remember something."

Eric caught a glance from Andyn and shrugged.

Dar picked up the sword. The blade glowed orange for a second.

"Skeletal servants with magic weapons?" asked Hlerv.

"Bring the light globe closer," said Dar, motioning to Buck.

In the light of the magic globe, Dar peered at the weapon. "Buck, I know Khelios helps you read dwarven."

"Yes."

"What does this say?"

Buck knelt down, his eyes glowing faintly. "Hmm. It's a name, spelled in dwarven runes on the handle. Killian Ware."

Dar sat back on his haunches and hefted the sword, face grim.

"You know this Killian Ware?" asked Buck.

Dar nodded. "Killian Ware was a dwarven spy, an agent from Merdail and a friend of my grandparents. I remember him because he was Christian, one of the few dwarves I've met who were."

Hlerv's eyebrows rose and he gave Eric a sidelong look. "Christian dwarves? Now I've heard everything."

"You think this was him," Eric said, watching Dar.

His friend nodded. "I remember my grandmother talking about his sword. It could detect different types of metals. This sure looks like it."

"I'm sorry, Dar," said Andyn with a look of compassion.

He gave her a weak smile, replacing Killian's sword in its sheath and slipping it into his backpack. "Thanks. He was a good person and always treated me kindly. At least his bones are at peace now."

Buck let out a deep breath. "Let's keep moving. Maybe we'll find something else."

Eric and Connor took the lead again, watching for anything suspicious. The door on the other side of the room hung on its hinges, so they stepped through and into the passage beyond.

Every ten paces or so, a small alcove sat in the wall at about chest height, littered with the remains of some kind of statue or display. Shards of ceramic glittered with gold inlay and silver and small gems in the light of Buck's magic globe.

Another door at the end of the passage beckoned. Mindful of the Song of the Grey Riders, Eric kept a weather eye out for any signs of a "red to gold at passage end" but the stonework looked grey or black.

At the door, they paused as Connor examined the edges in detail. This time they left nothing to chance and asked Hlerv to use a magic spell on the top of the door.

"Clean," he whispered to Eric. "But the door is locked, so I'll need some time to get it open."

The Riders waited while Connor took out a belt with a set of tiny tools and went to work. After what seemed like forever (but was likely only a minute or so), they heard a faint click.

Connor replaced his tools and they entered.

Twin pillars arched gracefully up into the darkness overhead, giving the impression of a tall, elegant chamber though they couldn't see the roof. The walls held tall, inset book cases, now filled only with moldering remains of tomes and scrolls, festooned with spider webs. A giant wooden desk sat directly across from them, behind a table with four chairs, two of them overturned. Behind the desk were the remnants of an inlaid carving, made faint by the slow pace of time. The room smelled of mold and rot and sewage.

A bright glow sprang up behind him.

"Evil." said Buck. Hlerv drew Shriek, the blade flaring white again.

Eric went on guard, his spear out. "Where?"

Buck shook his head, looking both scared and frustrated. "I can't tell. Something is playing with the environment in the room… I can't get a direction."

Unbidden, the image of a magical trap above an iron door entered Eric's mind and he looked up.

A pale man with fangs and glowing red eyes hurtled down at him out of the darkness, his face twisted with malice and rage.

Without thinking, Eric thrust with his spear. Almost too fast to follow, the man slammed the weapon aside, twisted around and slashed at Connor with claw-like hands. The halfling parried with his sword but the blade only made a thin line on the man's wrist. With a hiss, the man swooped aside and shot back up into the darkness.

"It can fly," said Dar.

"Buck, can you locate it?" asked Hlerv.

"Not yet," said Buck. "But this will help." He flipped down the Eye of Truth.

"No fair!" snarled a voice from the darkness. "Magical trinkets are not permitted here. At least, not ones that don't belong to me!"

A ball of light popped out of the darkness, landing squarely on the Eye of Truth. Buck cried out, averting his gaze. He flipped the arm up on his helmet and the light ball remained stuck to the gemstone.

"Whoever you are, dark and nameless undead, show yourself!" shouted

Andyn.

"Nameless?" said the voice. "I am not nameless, little elf-girl. I am Janos Durant, commander of the legions of Fort Aldric, now in the service of Galchimor the Great! He gave me my current form and eternal life and made me crave the blood of the living."

"Galchimor?" Eric glanced at Andyn. "Wasn't that the wizard killed by the freelance party years ago, Andareth Faldanor's group?"

"Ah!" said Janos. "So, the old goat met his untimely end! Excellent. I was wondering why I hadn't received a summons for some idiotic task in a while. My compliments to this Andareth Faldanor then. This leaves me free to do what I please. And I please to kill you and make you my slaves."

Eric cast his eyes up, down, all around.

A whooshing sound alerted him. He spun to the left just in time. The vampire swooped down and slammed Buck to the side. The warrior flew through the air as if hit by a stone from a trebuchet and crashed into the wall.

Eric dashed forward, stabbing with his spear. Janos dodged again and attempted to backhand him but Eric spoke a word and clamped a hand on the vampire's arm. A network of tiny lightning bolts sizzled as they raced all over Janos' shoulder. This earned Eric a punch in the ribs that drove the wind out of him. He dropped to one knee, gasping. Andyn stepped up with her new mace flaring to golden life.

Her swing connected with Janos' leg and he shrieked. He pointed a hand at her and a gout of flame hit her right in the chest. Her magic armor flared with silver light and the fire bent around her, but she stumbled backwards.

Hlerv jumped out of the shadows with his new, glittering sword. Janos leaped up and flew back into the shadows.

Eric drew a sword and crawled to Andyn's side. Her armor smoked and she grimaced.

"Good thing our armor is enchanted," she managed.

"It won't be for long with another assault like that," gasped Eric.

Buck staggered up to them, holding up his shield and fiery Khelios. "We need to pin him down so he can't fly," he muttered, wincing with every motion.

Dar stepped into the middle of the room. "Janos!" he called in a sing-song voice reminiscent of a child's playground taunt. "Janos! Come out and play, you coward! Or are we big kids too much for you?"

"Dar," hissed Andyn. "What are you doing?"

Janos' voice floated down at them. "I do not trifle with lower beings, worm!"

"Ha!" retorted Dar. "You're too afraid to fight us all where we can see you, you weasel! Who's the worm now?"

"Andyn, Hlerv," Eric said in a low voice. "Be ready. I think I know where this is going. Dar knows what weapons you carry."

"You are the whore-son of a goat and a dog!" roared Janos.

"That's what your mother said when you were born!" Dar shot back.

An inarticulate shriek of fury echoed in the chamber and Janos shot out of the darkness, heading straight for Dar. The ranger pointed his sword at Janos. When the vampire twisted to the side to avoid it, Dar let go and tackled him.

"Now!" he yelled. "Andyn and Hlerv, now!"

Janos spat out a vile oath. To Eric's horror, a horrid purple flame covered both of them. Dar screamed.

Andyn and Hlerv leaped forward. Janos' eyes widened in terror at the sight of Eleison and Shriek. He struggled to get away but Dar retained a death-grip on him.

Andyn struck, breaking one of his arms. Janos twisted away and the purple flame died.

Hlerv stabbed him in the leg. He let out an unearthly, echoing scream. Dar went limp and Janos hurled him away. Andyn and Hlerv pressed forward, striking again. Shriek lopped off Janos' right hand, then his left arm. Eleison landed straight on the crown of his head. With an explosion of golden light, his skull burst into a thousand fragments.

Andyn darted to Dar's side.

"Dar! Can you hear me?"

Dar's armor looked blackened and burned, as did his skin. When he opened his eyes, Eric gasped. The pupils burned with a pale pink flame. His breath came in faint wheezes.

"Oh Verian!" said Andyn. "It's Tombfire!"

She took off her pack. "Quick! Find the clear potion from Melinor!"

"What will happen to him?" asked Connor, sounding anguished.

"He'll become a skeletal servant or worse…"

They only had two potions left. She fed them to Dar and held his hand, eyes closed in prayer, holding Eleison with her free hand.

Eric knelt in prayer too.

The mace glowed again, just like before when she had healed Connor. This time it gained the brightness of daylight. The scents of a green forest meadow and clear streams and wildflowers filled the room, banishing the more noisome scents.

Andyn slumped forward as the glow vanished. Eric caught her. He held her in his arms. Her eyes rolled back in her head and she went limp.

Jesus, no!

Dar moaned. His skin looked pale but normal.

They found a healing ointment in Andyn's pack and used some on Dar's remaining burns. Andyn remained unconscious. Without knowing which of her potions might help, Eric decided against trying any of them.

Buck knelt next to Dar, placing his face close to his ear. "Dar! Can you hear me?" he asked in a loud voice.

Dar managed a weak chuckle. "Ow! Yes, I can, you big oaf. I'm not deaf yet."

"How's she doing?" asked Connor, helping Dar sit up and scoot closer to Andyn.

Eric shook his head. "I don't know. It looks like she just lost consciousness. Maybe the magic power of Eleison was too much for her."

Buck joined them as Hlerv stood guard at the exit.

"What do we do?" asked Connor. "We can't cart her around with us and we can't leave her here."

Eric racked his brain. "I don't know. We'll have to think of something."

Left unspoken was the realization that the quest stalled here in this room if they couldn't find a way to get her on her feet. They would be without her considerable magical talents.

"Our only healer," said Buck.

"No, not really," replied Dar with a sideways look at Eric and a wince of pain.

Buck raised his eyebrows. "Really?"

"Really," said Dar, wincing again as he shifted his weight and took Andyn's hand. "Scouts, particularly march-wardens and rangers, have to be able to heal travelers on their own. Not serious healing magic like Andyn or Father Ander, but more minor things, like sprains, minor cuts, bruises, headaches, mild fevers."

"We spent some time in training in Darlon," added Eric, "while you and Connor were out carousing."

Buck looked impressed. "And here I thought you were writing mushy love letters to Brandawyn."

Connor shook his head. "I don't see how any of that will help Andyn."

Eric watched Andyn breathe, trying to remember something Melinor had taught him.

"What?" Buck asked.

"I'm trying to remember something Melinor taught me about mage exhaustion," Eric said, "It's when a mage uses too much power or uses magic for too long. You get quite a headache. I think that's what happened to Andyn."

Connor sat next to Andyn. "It doesn't look like a simple headache."

"Well, the part of the brain that stores magical energy gets stressed and tired and it affects the other parts of the brain. Sometimes they shut down. In most extreme cases, the mage dies." Eric checked Andyn's pulse

Dar put his head in his hands. "I see where you're going, Eric. I don't know if I can help you."

"What are you talking about?" Buck asked.

"The part of the brain that is the center of magical energy, the *fons magicae*, is susceptible to stress and inflammation," Eric explained. "I think Andyn's probably overheated and caused her to go unconscious. If I can bring down the inflammation with a spell for headaches, she might wake up."

"Can you help at all?" He asked Dar.

Dar gave a tired nod. "I can try."

They placed their hands on Andyn's head. Eric closed his eyes, concentrating on the magical formula for the healing spell. He could feel her pulse against his pinky finger where it rested at the base of her head. He extended his senses and knew that his original guess was correct. He found inflammation in exactly the area he thought was affected.

He released the healing energy and felt Dar sag next to him as he did the same. He opened his eyes to see Buck catch Dar as the scout lay back weakly.

"I don't know if I helped much," Dar panted. "But I gave it a try."

Eric sat back with his friends, watching Andyn carefully. He made Dar lie down with his eyes closed and took out his wineskin.

"How long do we wait?" asked Hlerv after a while.

"Wait for what?" asked Andyn.

"Thank God." Eric helped her sit up. She put a hand to her head.

"Woo! Dizzy. What happened? No, wait, I know what happened!"

She looked around for Dar, but he put an arm around her.

"Now I owe you, friend," he said.

Andyn smiled and wiped a tear from her eye. "We're not even. I still have a debt to pay from the prison of the dark elves."

Dar smiled back and she hugged him.

Hlerv let out a deep breath. "You had us going there for a bit."

She smiled at him. "Good to be back."

"Can you stand?" asked Eric, offering his hand. She took it and rose to her feet, wobbling a little. He steadied her.

"One thing is for sure," said Buck, "If a gang of juvenile goblins shows up demanding our cash, I'm going to open up my bag and tell them to help themselves. I don't think we could whip cream in our condition."

Eric looked at his friends: tired, dirty, wounded, weak and nervous. He had to smile at Buck's words. They needed a place to rest and recharge. They had only just risen from sleep a couple of hours ago and ironically, here they were, trying to find somewhere to hole up again.

"Yes," he agreed. "Dragon hoards are pretty safe from us right about now."

"How about this place?" asked Connor.

Dar shook his head. "It gives me the creeps. Let's see if there's another exit. If we can't find one, we go back to where we stayed last night."

Fashioning torches out of chair legs and cloth wrappings, Eric, Connor and Hlerv scouted around while Buck stood guard over the door and Dar and Andyn tried to gather their energy.

After a period of searching that somehow fatigued Eric more than he thought it could, Connor spoke. "Dar?"

Connor knelt next to the desk. He stood and held out an object in his hands. It was a map case, with a dove-shaped clasp of silver. He brought it to Dar.

Eric's heart skipped a beat. He looked into the eyes of his friend, seeing a mixture of sadness and relief. Without taking his eyes from Eric, Dar touched the clasp.

"Spiritu Sanctu," he whispered.

With a mild click, the clasp released.

Dar held the map case in his hands, running his fingers over the surface.

"I'm sorry, friend," said Buck, laying a hand on his shoulder.

Dar nodded. "Thanks. I knew this was the most probable outcome after all."

"Does this mean that they were among those skeletons?" Hlerv asked, then let his question trail off.

Dar shook his head. "Aside from Killian, they looked like soldiers, not freelancers. My grandma and grandpa had very distinctive gear, special armor and items like this map case. I don't see any of it here."

Andyn leaned against him. "Let's see if we can find where they are, Dar."

He nodded, looking weary. Eric gave his shoulder a squeeze, then returned to his search. H wished e could come up with something wise and comforting.

"Hmm. What's this?" said Hlerv, peering at the faded mural behind the giant desk.

Eric joined him. "What?"

"You see those human-like figures?"

"Yes. They're standing next to an archway."

Hlerv reached into his belt pouch and removed a couple of tiny tools. He pointed with one of them.

"That's not an archway. It's a door. And this is the keyhole."

Amazed, Eric looked closer. In the flickering torchlight, he saw a small keyhole next to the inlaid pillar that formed the right side of the archway.

"But the door! It would have to be only four feet tall."

Hlerv looked amused. "What, you can't stoop down?" He inspected the mural carefully, muttering a spell under his breath, then took his tools and tinkered with the lock. Eric heard a soft click.

The archway of the mural popped outwards, then slid to the side noiselessly.

"Wow," said Connor. "I'm jealous. Nice work, Hlerv."

The gnome shrugged but Eric could tell he was pleased. "Anyone could have found it."

Eric shook his head. "Not just anyone, Hlerv."

He brought Dar, Andyn and Buck to join them. They agreed to let Connor and Hlerv go first as they were the shortest, followed by Andyn, then the others.

"What the hell is this?" breathed Buck when he entered the area beyond the secret door.

Eric shook his head. "I don't know."

A long, clean-swept hallway stretched ahead of them. Elegantly carved crown molding in the shape of birds decorated its smooth surface. The door at the end looked brand new, a light golden wood with a silver handle and hinges.

"Buck?" he asked.

The warrior flipped down the Eye of Truth and shook his head. "I'll be damned. Golden light. Everywhere. How was this behind the mural all the time with Janos out there? When I see gold, it means good."

Connor looked at him. "Simple. Janos never found it. And if what you're saying is true, he wouldn't have gotten very far."

He led them down the hall to the door.

Something seemed different to Eric. He couldn't quite put his finger on it until he turned to Andyn to ask her. Andyn looked fresh and alert, nothing like the exhausted woman who had brought Dar back from the brink of the grave. He realized his fatigue and apprehension had disappeared. He looked at his other companions. They all looked rested and refreshed.

"This is weird," he whispered to Dar.

Dar nodded. "Yes. I feel it too. I just can't explain it."

"Well?" asked Hlerv with a look at Connor. In response, the halfling took a coin out of his pocket and flipped it.

"Heads."

He looked at the coin and grinned at the gnome. "I lose."

Before Eric could do anything, Connor opened the door.

The passage vanished behind and around Eric. Instantly, he stood in a long, wide hallway with a mild white mist around his ankles. Tall walls, seeming to be made of glass, soared up overhead. The passage looked like it trailed off into infinity.

He searched for his friends and saw them standing in between high glass walls of their own. He looked at Andyn to his left and Connor to his right.. Connor licked his lips and shook his head.

The glass walls turned opaque and a figure approached him out of the mist ahead.

It was a woman, dark-haired, with the most piercing and intelligent blue eyes he had ever seen. She wore a simple white robe with a golden cord. Eric eyed her suspiciously.

She smiled. "Greetings, Eric Daniel Hylar Indidarc. You are expected."

Chapter Twelve- Forester

"It has begun, Your Majesty."

Phillip II, Lord of Oakmoor, Sovereign Prince of the House of Kalar and King of Deran, sat back in his chair and steepled his fingers in front of his face.

"You are certain?" Terenil DeMey nodded. Saren stood at his shoulder, looking grim. He pointed at a relief map on the table and three red pins inserted along the north-eastern border of Deran.

"Yes, Majesty. In the north, Wit's End has been completely overrun. Reports indicate about five hundred mixed human and dark elven troops supported by a company of ogres are the attacking force. His Grace the Duke of Darlon is sending a quick-reaction battalion to intercept. The 155th Regiment of Darlon is mustering as we speak and will try to turn the attackers north into the mountains. Astarel has offered support from Issendar."

Phillip sat without speaking.

"Have we invoked the North Alliance charter?" asked Queen Ahlana, standing at his elbow.

The king shook his head. "Not at the moment, but I am considering it. If we face a major invasion along the borderlands I will. Astarel's 1st Legion is in Issendar and could break any attack there."

Terenil pointed to the north-eastern border. "Athor is besieged but holding. The attackers appear to be at least a battalion of goblins, two companies of Kaftu and two companies of Ja'al. Lord Hardy in North Corner has sent two companies to attack from the east and relieve the pressure on Athor, but spies indicate there are another pair of companies in the woods, including hell-spawn creatures and fell wolves."

King Phillip listened, mind whirring as he looked over the map. He considered available forces, possible enemy motivations, and known Ja'al patterns of behavior.

Queen Ahlana pointed to the center north border. "What about here?"

"We received word today that Dorn's Hall has fallen to a mixed force of goblins, dark elves and Kaftu, at least three thousand strong," Saren answered. "Lord Jalek has sent his civilians to Forester, but this morning we received a message from Lady Hanford that Forester is now evacuated and all non-combatants are heading to Hillton, by way of Sun Plains. They may get some respite there but I doubt it. Not against that many."

Queen Ahlana sighed. "Margoth. With that many Ja'al and races that usually fight among themselves, it has to be her. She's the only figure with enough power to weld them together and keep them in line."

Terenil nodded. "It certainly fits."

"But what is her eventual objective?" asked the queen. "What does she hope to gain by all this? If she's as canny as legends allow, she knows she cannot conquer Deran by force. What is the estimated size of her army?"

"Somewhere between twelve and fifteen thousand," said Saren. "Lord Indidarc and the dragon Iron Thunder felt that was a good estimate, based on the visible forces and known dark elf populations in the area."

Phillip's brow furrowed. Fifteen thousand was certainly more than enough to overwhelm his smaller towns and even cause trouble in North Corner and Hillton. However, the Deranese army had five full-strength divisions and three regimental attack teams at hand, plus almost twice that in reserves. Two companies of medium infantry stood ready at Sun Plains to harass and slow any advance into the heartland. Lord Degrance had more than a thousand regulars and twice as many reserves to call up in Hillton. Zhinia Margoth couldn't hope to conquer the entire country with even twice her numbers.

"She can use the slain as an undead force to augment, Majesty," mused Terenil.

Phillip shook his head. "Not enough. Priests from the Allied Faiths can turn them to powder without too much difficulty. No, she's after something. But what?"

"If she gets to Sun Lake and encircles it, she can cut off the water supply to the farmlands, hoping to starve us," Queen Ahlana suggested.

Phillip gave another vexed shake of his head. "She has to know that the other nations in the Alliance will come to our aid. Then she'd be facing ten times her number in enemies and be quickly reduced. Lich and sorceress or no, she can't conquer an entire nation by herself. She's working with the Ja'al, so this could be some enormous diversion or something else."

He stood. "Where are Iron Thunder and Lord Indidarc?"

Saren looked at Terenil, who placed a hand on her shoulder. She looked worried.

"Iron Thunder headed to Evendale a couple of days ago to assist the Grey Riders," Terenil replied. "Some sort of omen or portent he received, I believe. Lord Indidarc is taking care of the dragon's grandchildren; he sends word that he believes free-lance mercenaries will attempt to capture them to hold hostage to ensure Iron Thunder does not get involved. He assures us the dragon will help when he arrives, but even a dragon can be brought down by a lich, especially if she has help, and her army is undoubtedly heavily augmented with magical abilities."

Phillip leaned on the table, then looked up. "I need a task force to try to figure out what Margoth could be after. In the mean time, I will send the Lord and Lady of Tallemar to assist Lord DeGrance in cutting off Margoth at Sun Lake. Who can move out immediately?"

Ahlana pursed her lip. "Thanks to Lord Melinor's warning, the Fire Eagles are ready to move at a moment's notice. The Blue Ravens are on the road even now, heading to Darlon for maneuvers. I will alert them to divert and take the road to Hillton. Saren, please contact the Cardinal of Oakmoor and ask him to send some of his medical corps and anti-undead troops to assist."

Saren bowed. "Of course."

"Thank you," said Phillip.

Terenil joined her and the couple left.

Queen Ahlana joined her husband as he gazed at the map. She took his hand and intertwined her fingers with his.

***

Caridan Jas kept still. Not that the figures moving in towards the town below would notice, but he didn't leave anything to chance, not with a rumored lich on the prowl. There was no telling what kind of detection magic she had available.

Besides, if I don't survive to give the report, I won't get my bonus, he thought with a grin.

Files of goblin infantry approached the tree line to the north of Forester. They assembled there just beyond bow range. Though he knew the force composition from what Lord Jalek said, he also had to report on anything new.

Kaftu ranged around the edges of the tree line, accompanied by humans: Ja'al clerics in their riotous-colored vestments of red, purple and violet. Now and again, he saw the flash of magic, and one of Lady Ellen's diversionary traps disappeared.

A suspicious lot, these Ja'al. Then again, if I was taking on Ellen Hanford, I'd be careful too.

Caridan extended his elven senses, using smell and hearing as well as sight to assess the enemy.

He identified the musty scent of bears and wolves, tainted with the odor of brimstone that marked them as hell-spawn. He saw dark elves, worshippers of Neralia or Arachnia, and resisted the urge to spit.

Then several heavy thuds made the air pulse. As he watched, some of the trees back in the forest, swayed, then toppled. A few seconds later, he heard rumbling voices, then a high-pitched whine and another set of thuds. More trees fell.

Caridan took out a small ivory medallion of a sparrow on a chain around his neck and held it in his hand. Breathing a soft word, he touched it. The medal glowed and a small bird sat in his palm, regarding him with beady eyes.

"Let's see what they're up to, Alicia."

He released the magical bird and it winged away, careful to keep out of bowshot from the forces in the trees. Instantly, he saw through the bird's eyes as it soared far above the woods and town of Forester.

He gritted his teeth. Behind the enemy force, a swath of ruined forest extended back towards Dorn's Hall. As he watched, huge forms dragged wheeled catapults and mangonels towards Forester. The lead trio of creatures halted next to a set of dark elves and Ja'al priests. The ogres and Ja'al moved next to a copse of trees barring the way to Forester. Sparks of magic lit the shade under the trees, then the enemy drew back about forty paces. With a dull, triple boom, something detonated near the roots of the trees, right at the level of the ground. The blast ripped through them with a flash of light and a cloud of smoke. The severed trees leaned over to crash into nearby vegetation. Some of the huge forms, now recognizable as blue-haired ogres in scale armor, parted from their fellows. They dragged the fallen trees away from the pathway and the siege engines advanced.

Not only was this a shameful desecration of the forest for evil purposes, but it took less than a minute. Caridan recalled his sparrow, changing it back into a medallion.

Well, you're going to find a surprise soon, Margoth.

He looked back towards the walls of Forester. Spears and helmets glinted above the wooden palisade.

A nice surprise indeed.

Within a few minutes, a pathway to the forest edge stood clear and ogres pulled their siege weaponry into range.

Caridan slithered down out of the tree. After casting a spell to detect for invisible creatures and enemies, he slipped back towards the town. Using all available cover, he ghosted between trees and bushes. He arrived at a set of stones to the west of town just as the Ja'al began cranking back the gears on their machines and loading glowing orbs of stone.

He knelt next to the rocks and placed a hand on top of one of them. A series of inscriptions glowed in the rock and he pursed his lips, watching the Ja'al.

Fire first, I think.

One of the best things about being the apprentice to Lady Ellen Hanford was getting to use her toys.

He pressed a dark blue symbol as the Ja'al loosed their first projectiles.

A shimmering screen of blue light leaped up in front of the town walls. Glowing stone balls, trailing fire, slammed into the screen, detonating with fiery explosions. The town walls stood unscathed.

He pressed a black symbol and the spearpoints waved up and down and armored hands raised in jubilation. He heard a hearty cheer from the town walls.

The Ja'al shouted curses in multiple languages and reloaded. Another salvo hit the blue screen with similar results.

Forester's main wall towers were actually massive trees with wooden platforms, holding troops and ballistae. He pressed a green symbol. Glittering ballista bolts shot out at the enemy siege engines. They struck the axles and wheels, slicing through the machines with shining steel edges. The siege engines tipped to the side. A couple of them actually fell over, trapping ogres beneath them.

Shouting officers whipped their troops forward, dragging another set of machinery to replace the damaged ones. They loaded different ammunition and launched it.

Caridan pressed a red button. Spinning wheels of flame leaped out from points in the walls to slam into the incoming missiles. The catapult shells detonated in clouds of ice and snow. Some of the bombs made it through, exploding on the walls, covering them with thick ice. Spearpoints and helmets in those areas vanished.

The Ja'al cheered. As the engineers reloaded, the goblins, Kaftu and elves charged, loosing a storm of arrows at the town. Teams of soldiers carried ladders with them, guarded by shield-men.

Caridan pressed a white symbol. Arrows shot out from predetermined positions on the palisade, skewering goblins, elves and Kaftu alike. Fire darts shot out as well, dropping the attackers. Still they charged on, howling and shrieking.

Well, I suppose it could have gone worse.

He had hoped for a longer delay, but he wasn't able to guess the Ja'al moves before they implemented them. He had done well to prevent the walls from burning.

Two frost-projectiles from the Ja'al force struck one of the trees, sheathing it with ice and snow. More spearpoints and helmets disappeared.

Ogres charged with their fellows, roaring and carrying battering rams with steel tips glowing red. The Ja'al forces hit the walls, ogres bashing at the wooden supports with the rams. Sections of wall caught fire.

Caridan re-animated Alicia and sent her up. The north attack, apparently, wasn't the only one. More Ja'al attacked from the east.

He put his hand on the stone in front of him and pressed a golden symbol.

Time to go.

He slipped away from town heading to a place where a fast horse awaited. In Alicia's eyes, he saw the enemy breach the walls and pour into the town.

An empty town.

Goblins, elves, humans and Kaftu raced through the openings, weapons ready to kill anything that moved. They saw only illusions of spears and helmets on the walls, illusions that faded out as he watched.

Realizing their danger, the lead Ja'al clerics called for a retreat as Ellen's last traps went off. Symbols flared orange and searing light shot into the Ja'al, dropping attackers left and right. Stones leaped up from hidden spots under the dirt. They detonated chest-high and lacerated elves and goblins with hot shards of stone or blasted them with fire. Magical charges launched spears of orange fire into ogre armor, dropping the massive creatures. The Ja'al scrambled back through the rents in the wall.

Caridan reached his mount and recalled Alicia, sending her ahead of him to scout his path back towards the main evacuation force.

Grimly, he added up the enemy casualties and all he had seen. He knew he had slowed them down and cut their numbers by more than a hundred, but also remembered the teeming masses behind them.

This was going to be a long fight.

***

Margoth stepped over the smoking corpse of her field commander and surveyed his successor, a Ja'al cleric with red hair and grey eyes.

"I trust you will be a little more thorough in your attack plan?"

Eyes veiled, the cleric nodded. "Yes, Highness."

"Good." Margoth lifted her chin and surveyed Forester, trying to control her seething anger. Being called up to the front on a simple clearing task was humiliating when she had to be elsewhere, implementing other aspects of her plan.

Being duped by Ellen Hanford was demoralizing to her force, but she had the upper hand still. All the booty in this town, like Dorn's Hall, belonged to her allies—all the booty, that is, except items that could be used to press her attack, like the dwarven mining charges used to clear the forest. Those were hers.

"Could the defenders be waiting in ambush south of the town?" asked Prince Darogir. The dark elf, one of the children of Ildrisana, watched Forester, dark eyes tinged with a red glow.

She shook her head. "Not enough cover there, unless Ellen Hanford decides to use another set of illusions. That would be quite a feat of magic even for her, to hide five hundred troops in open hills and plains. No, I think the town is deserted, except for traps."

She chafed at the delay, but keeping her force coherent was her top priority, and she couldn't keep them together if they had no loot. She motioned to both sides of the town.

"Send your clerics and mages east and west. I will open a path through here personally, then they can move in and clear those areas. When I give the word, you may send in the troops."

The new Ja'al commander bowed.

Margoth strode forward, her staff held before her. Reaching into her magical reserves, she gathered power, siphoning life force from the beings around her. Those nearest her wavered and stumbled. She didn't even spare them a sneer.

Margoth crafted their stolen energy into a vibrating field of power. She layered dispersions, jamming codes, force fields and countermeasures into the wave. With a loud cry she released the spell and a blade of black energy leaped forth, shooting out at the town. Blue light flashed and white fire blazed. Stone mines detonated with sharp cracks under the dirt of the town square, and magical symbols flared and winked out.

She waited, extending her senses. Satisfied, she nodded. "There. Now you may enter. The town and its contents are yours. Remember that every allied group gets an equal share, so make sure to deposit everything in the town square for the commanders to assess. I do not take incompetence or failure lightly, so bear in mind that attempting to cheat each other will be most unhealthy."

With a significant look at the charred corpse of her former northern attack commander, Margoth swept back to her command group. A coal-black horse with a ghostly white stripe on its face and fiery green eyes waited for her. It growled and whined at her approach, lowering its head with its twin spiral horns. She tapped it on the head and it pulled its lips back, exposing wicked fangs.

Margot vaulted into the saddle.

Despite this minor problem, all went well. Dorn's Hall was looted of its treasures, the spoils well-distributed to her allies, and now the richer plum of Forester lay open to them. Beyond, they faced Sun Plains, Hillton and eventually, King Phillip.

She turned to Zanilor. "Are the newest recruits ready?"

The Ja'al cleric smiled with a glance at a column of shuffling dwarven corpses next to them.

"Of course, Highness. Though I don't know why you didn't use them to set off Hanford's traps."

"Ellen Hanford is too smart to fall for that one," she replied. "Her traps were probably keyed to evil living beings and wouldn't react to undead. No matter. I need our little pets for their psychological effect on our enemies farther south. Everything in its time, Zanilor."

***

"I'm sorry, Milady, but I didn't slow them by more than an hour or so. There were a lot of them and the only thing that really drew them in was your illusions on the walls."

Ellen Hanford smiled at Caridan. "Don't blame yourself. You did well to implement a difficult set of defenses that are a bit above your ability right now. Any time at all is a bonus. Go and report to Sir Colin."

"Yes, milady." Caridan turned his horse and rode off.

Ellen rested her hands on her saddle horn. A stream of refugees headed south on the royal highway. People pulled carts, rode livestock, carried children and hefted packs as they hurried away from Zhinia Margoth's invasion force. Dwarven and human troops marched on both sides of the road next to them, weapons at the ready and eyes alert. Riders ranged on the grasslands nearby, casting about for signs of pursuit. The warm sun shone down on them and a swirl of dust from their passage clouded the road behind.

She looked to the north, towards her home, steeling herself for what she knew she would see. A billowing cloud of smoke reached into the sky from Forester.

Her home burned.

We'll see who burns last, Margoth.

"Milady."

Nolan rode up next to her. She wheeled her mount to meet him and forced a smile, holding her hand out to him.

He lifted it up to his lips. "We will rebuild, Ellen."

She remembered all the hard work his father had put into building the town and making it a haven and refuge on the borderlands. She remembered working alongside the citizens in raising walls, planting gardens, celebrating weddings and baptisms, burying the dead, enduring bad weather and rampaging illness. Amy and Timothy had been born there.

She blinked away a tear. "I know. I have no monopoly on sadness, my lord. There are many who gave more than property to make Forester a home."

He smiled back, giving her hand a squeeze. "And we will repay their faithfulness and sacrifice by making it better than ever."

A scout called to him and he rode off. Ellen ranged up and down the stream of refugees. She took time to speak with them, encouraging them, assisting those who needed help, giving rides to fussy toddlers, subtly urging everyone to make their quickest pace without letting them give in to panic. She raised her head to the south. The distant outlines of the town of Sun Plains beckoned, not three miles away, their next refuge.

Another scout beckoned to her and she gave a small child back to his mother, then gathered the reins and cantered over.

"Milady, there is an attack force approaching."

Her stomach tightened but she nodded. "Tell me everything."

"The attackers are Kaftu rangers and light infantry, heading from the northwest. They broke from the border west of Forester, using the woods as cover; even now they race through the plains towards us. Lord Nolan will strike them from the east to drive them away as they approach the column but asks you to organize a defensive line against any attempts to wheel back and flank him. He requests Caridan's assistance."

She nodded. "Have the sergeants attend me and take Caridan with you. Ask Lord Jalek if he will join us. And find Father Ander."

The dwarven lord of Dorn's Hall nodded as Ellen told the commanders her intentions. "Aye, we can help hold the line."

"Thank you, my lord. I hesitate to ask more of your people who have already lost so much."

Lady Riti gave a wry smile, her eyes sad. "We have much to repay the Spawn of the Serpent, Lady Ellen. It will be a privilege to join you"

Ellen felt a surge of affection for the feisty dwarven lady. "You are a credit to your House, Lady. Thank you."

Riti's eyes regained some of their spark and she inclined her head.

"I will need you to come with me, Father Ander," Ellen said to the priest, who nodded. "Also, I will need such freelancers as are available. We have another mission."

The soldiers moved out, organizing their numbers to guard their western flank and thinning their numbers on the east.

Ellen rode to the head of the refugee column and waited on her horse with Father Ander. Soon, a sergeant and a dozen riders of different races joined her. She addressed the freelancers as the sergeant rode off.

"Kaftu in service of the Ja'al will attack soon. Scouts report that they will strike from the west. Lord Nolan and the cavalry will deal with them and the dwarves and infantry will dispatch any that come near the refugees. But I know the Ja'al. They will try to get at the column from the east in some way. Father and I and the freelance mages will set detections in the grasslands to the east as we go. The peril will likely come from the northeast. Watch carefully. When that attack comes, we must counterattack immediately. We do not have enough troops to defend both sides of the road. Be aggressive and convince the Ja'al that they face a much more powerful force."

One of the freelancers, an elven scout, nodded. "We will make it so, Lady."

"Good."

"Look!" A human female, an agent, pointed towards the grasslands.

A column of cavalry with Nolan at its head charged off towards dark figures in the plains. Kaftu leaped out of the grass to grapple with riders, hurl javelins or cast spells. A glow of magical blue light surrounded Nolan, leading their charge like the prow of a boat slicing through water. Nolan's light shield deflected spells and arrows as if they were mere wads of paper. Spears, swords and axes flashed in the summer sun. Caridan rode outside the range of the battle, picking off wounded Kaftu with magical fire-darts or bolts of electricity.

"We're being attacked!" cried a woman in the refugee train in a panicky voice.

"Yes," Ellen shouted, so as many as possible could hear. "The Ja'al advance, but we are prepared for them. The best you can do is quicken your pace, keep a weapon at hand, and pray. Look, to the south. The town of Sun Plains lies before us. There is safety for a time until our journey to Hillton. Make Sun Plains your goal. Hasten and do not panic!"

She wheeled her steed away as the mass of refugees surged forward, moving faster towards Sun Plains.

She did not know if her brave words would inspire them to do the right thing or not but she had to see to the eastern defenses. She and Ander and three freelance mages set detection spells to the north and east.

Father Ander reined in as she rode up. "We're ready but I don't see anything. Nothing. Only grass grown tall in the summer."

Ellen sat her horse quietly, chewing her lip. She watched the mounted freelance warriors, mages, scouts and clerics range out on the plains, scanning the tall grass and horizon for any sign of an attack.

A feeling of dread gnawed at her heart. The Ja'al had their attention to the west. It was the perfect time for the enemy to attack their weak side, but how?

"We can't fight what we can't see," said Ander, twisting his reins in his hands, looking frustrated.

A chill of fear struck her. "What we can't see! Oh my God! Father Ander, you're a genius!"

She cast her hands to the side and stood up in the stirrups, shouting an arcane word. A loud cracking sound broke the stillness. All around them, a shimmering field wavered and vanished. Dark elves stood among them with bow and blade looking dumbfounded, armored in black-enameled chain mail. One of them stared in amazement at a shattered crystal on the tip of his staff.

"The enemy is here!" Ander called, spurring his horse forward. "Attack for Deran!"

Dark elves swarmed at them. Some broke for the refugee column and others aimed bows, spears and javelins at Ellen and her team. Ellen cast up a projectile screen. A glimmering sphere of energy surrounded her and Ander. The spears and arrows struck the globe and glanced away, landing in the high grass.

Then the free-lancers attacked the dark elves. For a few frantic seconds, all was a whirling storm of steel, light, flame, lightning, screams, thuds and clashes of metal. Ellen used Storm Force to hurl dark elven warriors away from her, stabbed through chain armor with Lightning Spears and blasted enemy mages with firedarts. She burned Margoth's troops with Flame Fan, and used her staff to knock away weapons and strike Ja'al soldiers. She vaguely knew that she got hit several times by spell or blade but she had eyes only for the foe, trusting in the enchantments of her armor and her own spell protections to see her through. Sharp pains wracked her body but she gritted her teeth and fought on.

Father Ander rode the battlefield like an avenging angel, blinding Ja'al with balls of light, striking down enemies with a fiery white mace or using counterspells to blunt the attacks of enemy wizards.

One of the dark elven wizards shouted to his fellows and they all began heavy-sounding chants.

Father Ander used his own magic to cancel one spell, but the other wizards continued their incantation. The ground trembled. The priest's horse reared as giant, stony hands erupted out of the earth and pummeled the mount and her rider. One fist slammed Father Ander out of his saddle and he landed heavily.

Ellen sent a Lightning Spear through one of the stone hands, blasting it into pebbles. The others pounded Ander as he stood up. He shattered one of the hands with his mace but another slammed him in the chest. He staggered.

"No!" Ellen screamed. In a fury, she spurred her mount forward. Two dark elven lancers leaped in front of her, stabbing her in the leg and her mount in the shoulder. Her horse reared, striking out with her hooves. Ellen leaped from her back to avoid being thrown. She had the sense to land on her good leg but stumbled anyway.

Lancers charged. She muttered a phrase and swept a hand in front of her. Twin swirling dust devils leaped up, throwing dirt, sand and tall grass at the dark elves.

A quick application of Flame Fan turned them into shrieking, walking torches that her troops quickly dispatched with sword thrusts.

She ran to Ander as he crushed another stony hand and fell back to the ground under the onslaught of the remaining constructs. Using a reserve of power she didn't think she had, she blasted the remaining hands and one of the wizards with a Storm Force spell so strong that her vision blurred and darkened.

I will NOT fall!

Fairly growling with rage, she clamped a hand on Ander's collar and dragged him back towards the road.

"To me!" she called. "To me, warriors of Deran!"

To her amazement, she heard not only an answering shout from the freelancers near her, but from the dwarves and civilians by the road.

The dark elves redoubled their assault, trying to finish Ellen and Ander. The freelancers tore into their flank with savage ferocity, four of their number falling but the others turning back the attack.

Then the citizens of Forester and Dorn's Hall swarmed around her, sweeping away the remnants of the dark elven company. She stood to join them but her leg buckled under her. Now she felt the pain of her wounds and fatigue and fear overwhelm her. Ellen Hanford dropped to her hands and knees in the dust.

She tried to force her eyes open and saw two pairs of boots in front of her. She struggled to stand and one of the pairs of boots moved to her side.

"Steady, my lady," said an alto voice next to her.

She focused on Lady Riti of Dorn's Hall. The dwarven woman held Ellen up with one hand while the other gripped a reddened short sword. Riti's tunic showed rips and blood aplenty.

"Try and take her, you foresworn cowards!" bellowed Lord Jalek Dorn from Ellen's other side. He held a great sword overhead and pointed at the enemy force. "Let Margoth the Swine Queen know the humans and dwarves stand together!"

"Thank you, milord, milady," managed Ellen in a voice that sounded strangely distant to her ears. The world spun.

"I have you, my lady," said another voice as strong arms bore her up. "Ready to move, Lord Jalek."

"We'll guard your back," said Riti.

Ellen looked dizzily at the man carrying her back to the road.

"Who…?"

"Cortin, the weaponsmith, my lady," said the man, giving her a tight smile. "You're safe now, Baroness."

"Father Ander?"

She felt herself lowered into a cart but shook her head and pushed hands aside. "No, no, no, I can stand. Where is Father Ander?"

Jalek looked at the weaponsmith and shook his head. Cortin's mouth set in a firm line and she saw tears in his eyes. "There, lady."

Father Ander lay in another cart, one of the free-lances working on his wounds. His breath was shallow and he looked up at the sky with distant eyes. One side of his chest looked oddly flat and his right hip canted at an unnatural angle.

"Father!" Ellen slid next to him. "Can you hear me?"

His eyes lighted on her and he smiled. "Lady Ellen. Good. You are well. And the dark elves?"

"Defeated. But don't worry about that. We have to heal you."

She shot a glance at the freelancer, a halfling acolyte of Irial. The halfling shook his head, muttering under his breath, a glowing hand laid on Ander's side.

"Lady," Ander said as if he were discussing an upcoming harvest. "There is no healing for me now."

"Nonsense, Father," Ellen retorted, feeling dizzy herself but pushing it aside. "We'll have you on your feet in no time."

"My lady, I can feel nothing from the neck down, and my breath comes shorter each second. Please, allow me this then. The people are safe to continue to Sun Plains, yes?"

Her vision swam with tears. "Yes," she managed.

His smile grew more peaceful. "Then all will be well. I am not afraid. My Lord and Savior awaits me."

"No!" a sob escaped her lips. "Father, please! Don't leave us."

"Leave?" he looked at her with surprised eyes. "No, dear child, I do not leave you. I will be with you always. I can help you now more than ever."

She held his hand, looking at the Irial cleric with pleading eyes.

"Too many internal injuries," the halfling said, hands clenched in frustration. "I just don't have enough skill!"

"Do not blame yourself, friend," said Ander, closing his eyes. "You have done your best and are a credit to your Church. I myself could not have healed this, nor, I believe, could any other high churchman."

"My ladies, my lord?"

Ellen, Riti and Jalek looked up to see one of the freelancers ride up to the wagon, a burly human in plate armor with a reddened battle axe in his hands.

"The enemy has been wiped out. The field is yours."

"There, you see?" said Ander, opening his eyes again. "All is well indeed."

"Father?"

He didn't respond, looking off to the sky.

"Father Ander?" she choked again past her tears.

He spoke next as if he hadn't heard her. "Yes, Lord. I come to do Your will. Thank you for bringing my parents with you. I am glad to see them."

"No!" Ellen held his hand to her breast and wept.

"Lady," Ander said, giving her hand a weak squeeze. "Do not grieve. Times of great hardship and valor and glory await you, and beyond, a golden age of light, free from darkness. Generations yet unborn will hear the tales and give praise to God. Farewell."

He closed his eyes and let out a last breath.

"Ellen!" She heard Nolan's voice and felt his arms around her.

She sobbed twice before the darkness closed in.

195

Chapter Thirteen- All Must Choose

"How did you know my name?" Dar asked.

The slender young man before him smiled. "I have known your name all your life, Darius Richard Cabot of Forester. Have you not heard my voice before?"

Dar had the funny feeling that the man was right: he had heard his voice somewhere, but he couldn't place the face among his acquaintances.

"Have we met?" he asked.

In answer, the man turned and started down the hallway. "Come and see."

Dar followed him cautiously. The fact that the Eye of Truth had detected no evil should have given him confidence, but Dar couldn't shake an ominous feeling.

"What do you see?" asked the man as Dar followed.

"Mist, you, glass walls."

"Ah. Well, keep looking."

At first, Dar didn't notice anything special. Then, shapes and colors formed on the glass walls to his left and right.

The images grew clearer and more detailed. To his left, he saw himself and his friends, the Riders. The figures of his parents appeared, as did the folk of Forester. His eyes widened. The figures, no bigger than his hand, looked so lifelike and realistic he imagined he could speak to them and they would reply.

He shot a look at the right-hand wall. A similar image showed on that wall, except that he and his friends marched away from the people he knew, their faces grim.

Dar stopped. The man stopped and turned back to him.

"What is this place?" Dar asked.

The man inclined his head. "The Chamber of Decision."

Dar felt a chill. "What kind of decision?"

"What does the Song say?"

Dar's chill raced down his spine. "Song?"

"Come now, Dar, you know the line from the song. 'For good or evil, all must choose'."

"What does this have to do with this place and why we're here?"

The man looked a little disappointed yet amused. "So many questions. Come with me and look. All will become clear to you. You are in no danger."

Dar continued on. The images warped and transformed.

On his left, the Riders met with figures bearing weapons in their hands and hatred in their eyes: dark elves, goblins, Kaftu, ogres, trolls. They emerged victorious. As they progressed, their opponents fled before them and they soon faced hulking, demonic creatures out of nightmares. Boldly, Dar led his friends and they soon appeared in a rich audience chamber, speaking to evil wizards, daemons and dark powers.

Why aren't we fighting them?

In a similar scene on his right, the Riders fought against dark forces. With a quickening heartbeat, he saw the figure of Megan Alenar and her sister. But here, the Riders fought against a rising tide, desperately trying to stave it off while heading for a shining golden light that beckoned up ahead.

To his left, Dar saw the Riders now commanding the wizards and daemons to do their bidding. They marched at the head of mighty armies, destroying other dark hordes, putting all to the sword and torch. Then, they reigned over nations, sitting on jeweled thrones. They ruled as right-hand vassals to an assembly of shadowy figures he knew from their shapes to be the gods of the Ja'al. Dar was in charge of a fiefdom, held under his iron grip.

With a feeling of horror, he saw Megan approaching him. She begged him to turn away from the Dark. His image spurned her as unworthy of his attentions any longer, a pale and powerless thing. His attention diverted by power and wealth and the seductive lure of gorgeous half-daemon women, he turned away and she left in tears. Dar reigned over his dominion, destroyed all rivals, and became mighty in the eyes of the world and the Powers that ruled it. He kept both Andyn and a daemoness as mistresses. Dar's stared in shock at the sight of Andyn, his caring, compassionate friend, changed into a conniving and vindictive servant of Arachnia. Her beauty had turned to depraved seductiveness.

Dar saw himself oppressing those who opposed him as he ruthlessly sought the order his lands demanded and the security he required. He became a dark king, pitiless and efficient. He suppressed chaos with those Powers that supported him, firm in the conviction that to be feared was greater than to be loved. His own family remained safe, but he saw their tormented expressions and guilt, depression and fear.

Dar turned away from the images, sickened by the implications.

On his right, he saw no less discomfiting scenes. The buildup of dark forces grew unabated and peaceful dales became ruined battlefields, littered with the dead. He watched in dismay as first Brandi, then Megan succumbed to the assault of a torrent of enemies, perishing valiantly and fighting to the last. Tears sprang to his eyes at the sight of Megan lying dead atop a hill of enemies. Crows circled above her. He saw Forester in flames, Hillton leveled, and Oakmoor besieged. Swarming, teeming masses of evil creatures surged over hill and dale, razing villages, slaughtering soldier and peasant alike. Dar felt tears stream down his face as his parents and brother fell, as did Buck's father, Connor's family, Lord Nolan and even Saren and Terenil. The Riders pressed ahead, relentless, slipping through traps, slaying their assailants and reaching towards the golden light. Just short of the light, Andyn, Eric and Connor fell, and Dar saw himself carrying her body into the golden glow.

Then his form emerged from the light. The luminescence grew brighter, more potent. The wave of evil creatures shrank and shriveled before the light, retreating as he advanced. In that bright wake, the tortured land healed. The wounded arose, trees and animals returned, and villages and towns rebuilt. Eventually the darkness melted away and a peaceful land fairly shone in the sunlight. He stood with bowed head before a still form on a bier in a beautiful chamber, lit by the multicolored lights of stained glass windows.

The images on both walls faded and vanished.

Dar turned a tear-streaked and anguished face to the man in the white robe.

"What does this mean? Why have you shown me this?"

The man fixed him with a sober gaze that yet held comfort. "You and your friends will have to choose, and soon. The actions you take will seal the fate of many. 'For Good or Evil, All must Choose'. Isn't that what the Song of the Grey Riders says?"

Dar turned away from him, miserable. "I wish I had never heard of the Song."

He felt a companionable hand on his shoulder. "Strife and struggle are part of this life, and yet also are glory and joy. Do you see the options set before you? Will you choose lordship, power and wealth or sadness, loss and the eventual victory of good? Will you pay the price it takes to do what is right?"

He shook his head. "The price is paid by those who do not make this choice. My family, my friends, Megan. They have no part in this choice."

"But they do, Dar. What choice do you think they would have you make, if they were here?"

That stopped him. He looked up at the man in the robe and knew the answer.

Setting his mouth in a firm line, he stepped towards the right wall and placed his hand on it.

"They would want me to choose this even if it meant their lives. They couldn't bear the thought that my love for them could make me to become… that." He nodded at the left-hand wall.

The man smiled and Dar felt a wild, fierce joy well up in him.

"Then you have made your choice. Be at peace. All will be well."

***

Buck stared at the glass walls as the images faded away. He looked at his guide in shock.

A golden-haired woman in a tan robe raised an eyebrow. "Well?"

Sudden anger rose in him. "Well? Well what? As if I could do all that, as if I could affect the events of the world in that way to cause…" His voice trailed off.

She smiled and he felt a wave of sympathy and warmth. "But you can. You are in the unique position of someone who can control the fate of many with his choices. You know what the Song says. Choose."

His anger grew. "I choose neither one! Why do I have to choose one or the other? Why can't the balance just continue as it has?"

She shook her head, lip pursed. "No, Buckminster Bydecy. That is an illusion. Ever and always, evil will seek to destroy and good to preserve. Even were you to attempt a middle path, the dark will destroy you. They do not compromise and seek no co-existence, only their own will and power. Choose."

"Neither!"

Her expression appeared mild but she sighed. "Have you forgotten the verse? 'Or choosing none, their lives to lose'. Ruin awaits you. Think on it. Think of those you care about. What would they have?"

Buck stared long and hard at her in defiance but she merely met his gaze with deep brown eyes. Finally, he spun away in frustration, clenching his fists.

"All I wanted is to be left alone!" he raged.

"Evil will never leave you alone," she said quietly. "Even if the Light would, the Dark will never suffer it. They seek to make you a willing ally or a slave or a corpse. Nothing more, nothing less."

With a sinking feeling, Buck realized she was right. All his experiences with the Grey Riders, all his adventures and indeed, his whole life, brought it into stark relief. Those who followed the Light, like Eric and Dar and Andyn, would leave him to his own life in peace and respect his decision. Those who followed the Dark respected nothing.

He set his jaw and very deliberately stepped over to the right-hand wall, touching it.

"I choose."

She bowed, her face radiant. "So be it, Buckminster Horatio Bydecy.

Your choice is made.”

***

Sobbing uncontrollably, Andyn leaned her head against the right-hand wall.

“I choose!” she wailed, images of her dead parents and sister and brother-in-law and little niece and nephew still fresh in her mind. “Verian help me! I cannot do otherwise!”

She felt the arms of her guide, a blonde-haired woman with amber eyes, encircle her in a warm embrace.

“You have chosen well, as your heart leads you. Love is an act of the will, Andyn Josette Fallbrook Eleandir, not an emotion. You have shown your will to be strong. Be faithful and do not give up hope.”

Andyn collapsed in her embrace.

***

With a shaking hand, Connor reached out and touched the right-hand wall.

“Is all this fated to come to pass?” he asked the young halfling in a golden robe in front of him.

His guide smiled. “Nothing is fated irrevocably. The images show actions and consequences and possibilities, but not certainties. The only certainty is the nature of each path. One is Dark and one is Light.”

Connor nodded. “Then I stand by my choice.”

His vision blurred at the memory of the image of little Deena’s broken body lying among the ruins of his parents’ home.

The man put a hand on his shoulder. “Be not afraid. You are guarded by Agents of the Light even now. All will be well.”

Heart full of misgivings, Connor could only nod.

***

Eric smiled despite the raw emotions surging through him. He moved towards the right-hand wall.

"This is your choice then?" asked the woman in the white robe.

He held down a flood of despair and sadness that threatened to overwhelm him.

I'm so sorry, Brandi.

"If I serve the Dark," he said in a voice remarkably steady. "Brandi will never forgive me. I could never live with that. Besides, I have seen the Dark most of my days in my mother's and father's house, and I reject it utterly. It is empty and shallow."

He let out a deep breath. "If thus is my life to be, then so be it. I will never choose that other way."

The woman took his hands, looking into his eyes. Her own eyes filled with such compassion and kindness that his vision grew misty.

"You have chosen well. Fear not. The High God watches over you. He will not leave you orphaned."

He felt her arms encircle him as he wept, seeing the images of the bodies of Melinor, Saren, Terenil, Megan and Brandi lying in state in a church bathed with light from stained glass windows.

"I am not strong enough," he managed.

"Your strength will come from Him," she said.

***

"Suppose I don't choose," Hlerv said, carefully watching the gnome woman in light blue robes.

She gave him a sardonic smile. "You have to. The Song says so."

"The Song doesn't rule my fate."

"That's what you think," she replied. "But even you will allow that there are things in the larger world that affect you without your agreement."

He felt his irritation growing. "I didn't ask for this. I refuse it."

"I don't think you understand," she said again. "You aren't in charge here. The only thing you can control is your reaction to what is placed before you. What will be your choice then? How will you act?"

Hlerv turned away, mind racing.

There's always a way to game these things. I just have to find out how. I won't allow this stupid prophecy to run my life. It's fine for the others, but I don't believe as they do and I have more important matters to deal with.

He hesitated, running through various strategies in his mind.

"Take all the time you need," the gnome said. He could hear the smile in her voice. "I'm not going anywhere."

Hlerv decided. He moved his hands in front of his body in a subtle pattern, out of her view, murmuring quiet words. He felt an exact copy of himself superimposed over his form. Without moving, he cast a spell of invisibility on himself. Then he made his fake self turn, shrug at the woman and touch the right-hand wall.

"I guess I have to," he made his illusion say in a resigned voice. "Let's get this over with."

Her voice came to him. "So, your choice is made then."

"It is," he made his illusion say. "May I go now? I have things to do."

"I'm sure you do," she said in a voice suddenly stern. "Very well, Handor Lervion. Go your way. Only know this."

He made his illusion stop.

"Choosing none, their lives to lose."

The mist and the glass walls vanished. He used an Air Mirror spell to look behind him but he only saw a smooth-walled chamber with a door of golden wood on the other side. No one appeared to him.

With a sigh of relief, he turned around.

Boy, that witch was irritating! No stupid Song is going to dictate anything to me, I guarantee you. I don't have to make any choice between Dark and Light! I choose my own way, like I always have! I am master of my own destiny!

"Oh, one moment," said a male voice behind him.

He spun around, hand flashing to his sword.

A male gnome in dark grey robes with a black corded belt bowed from the waist. "I see you have managed to outwit the simpletons in the Chamber of Decision."

Hlerv said nothing, watching him for any hostile moves, his hand on Shriek.

The man fixed him with dark, glittering eyes. "It takes quite a bit of skill and determination to defeat the guardian. For such skill, there is reward."

"What kind of reward?" asked Hlerv.

The man smiled. "I know you seek a means to free your sister. I can provide it.”

“How?”

The smile broadened. “How about learning to control the Helm of Shadows? I think it would come in very handy for a man of your abilities.”

***

Dar looked around, startled. The glass walls, the man in the white robe, the mist: all had vanished. He now stood in a smooth-walled room with a golden door at the end.

“Dar?”

He turned and Andyn ran to him and hurled herself into his arms.

Eric joined them, clasping them to himself in a fierce hug.

He looked into their eyes and knew.

Buck stepped next to them, Connor and Hlerv following.

“I’m guessing we all saw the same thing,” Buck said, laying his arms around their shoulders.

Andyn nodded, sniffing and embracing Connor. She held out a hand to Hlerv.

The gnome hesitated, then gave her an awkward smile and took her hand. She pulled him into their circle.

Dar sighed. “I can guess what you all saw, and I can guess what you chose. I don’t speak for anyone else, but I will not turn from my choice.”

Connor nodded, eyes bleak for a moment, then resolute. “There is no going back.”

The Grey Riders stood silently in the room for several heartbeats.

Dar wanted to say so much, to ask so much, but didn’t have the heart now.

Maybe later, he promised himself.

“Hey,” said Hlerv, touching Andyn on the arm. “Let’s get going. The Helm of Shadows isn’t going to just jump out in front of us.”

She laughed at that. “You’re right. Lead on, friend.”

Hlerv gave her an answering smile, but his eyes didn’t match it. Dar wondered.

I can only imagine what visions it gave him. We know so little about him or his fam-

ily or past.

The gnome led them towards the golden door. It opened readily and they entered a smooth passage of dark grey stone.

"Look." Buck pointed to the ceiling. A thin strip of pure gold led away from them into the shadows.

"When gold to red…" Eric breathed.

Andyn gasped and the others turned to look. She pointed behind them. The door had vanished. Only a stone wall greeted their eyes.

Connor arched an eyebrow, then joined Hlerv in scouting ahead. As they went along, they needed to use another light globe from Buck's supplies. The passage became rougher and they saw remnants of the fortress' violent past: a skull here, a bone there, a rusted weapon or bit of armor. Still the passage continued, with its golden band glittering overhead. Several, larger, side passages beckoned, but they stayed on the path with the gold strip.

"Well?" Connor said, raising a hand. The passage ended at an intersection. The gold strip led straight into the wall.

"This doesn't make sense." Dar scratched his chin. "The passage has ended, but according to the Song, something red is supposed to be here."

"We could try going left or right," suggested Buck.

"No," Eric said, shaking his head, "There's no gold stripe leading either way. Something needs to happen here."

They regarded the gold strip, lost in thought.

"Connor," said Andyn in a shaky voice. "What's going on in your backpack?"

Dar's mouth dropped open. Reddish light leaked out from the halfling's backpack.

Connor shrugged it off and withdrew a glowing red object. It was Deena Lomin's flying toy. Only now instead of having a faint gold color, it fairly glowed with a ruby-red light.

"By the Earth Mother!" Buck said. "It was gold and now it's red."

"Send it up," said Eric.

Connor pressed the button to make the toy fly. It soared upward, mimicking the pattern they had seen previously. However, it flew directly to a part of the ceiling and hovered there. As they watched, the wall ahead of them rumbled. It slid aside, revealing the entrance to an octagonal chamber. As soon as the door opened, the toy flew forward, heading for the center of the room.

They stepped inside and the door slid shut behind them. Above their heads, the gold strip had turned as red as the halfling toy.

A glowing ball of magical light hovered just under the ceiling. The room held eight figures of winged humans carved in white marble, set up before each wall. Each stood over six feet high and they were entirely naked, four male and four female. Hands held before them in prayer, their eyes looked heavenward in worship, as if seeking help. Dar felt no embarrassment or discomfort, only awe at the skill of whichever sculptor had created them. They made him think of beauty and peace and holiness.

The toy continued on its path, stopping in a hover below the ceiling. A tiny door, not bigger than a dinner platter, opened above it and the toy soared upward out of sight.

They could hear the mild whirring of the propeller blades, then silence.

They waited.

"Now what?" asked Hlerv.

As if in answer, the floor vibrated. They felt themselves rising upwards.

"Where are we going?" said Buck, putting his hand on the hilt of Khelios.

Dar shook his head. "I have no idea. Wherever it is, it's up."

"I thought the best direction for this Helm of Shadows was down," Buck replied.

Andyn shrugged. "Let's see where this leads."

The sensation of upward motion ended and the ceiling split in two, the halves moving to the left and the right. The halfling toy floated down towards them transformed back to its faded golden color. Connor retrieved it, putting it in his pack.

The floor vibrated again and they rose up until they stood in a much larger chamber.

Dar watched in wonder. Globes of white light hovered just under the domed ceiling, shining on walls inlaid with combinations of gold and rubies. Around the edges of the walls, near the ceiling, intricate patterns wound around the room. He thought they looked like writing, but unlike any writing he had seen.

"At the risk of repeating my original question and getting something else to happen," offered Hlerv with a wary eye on the room. "What do we do now?"

"What does the Song of the Grey Riders say?" asked Connor.

Andyn brought out a scroll from her mapcase. "Golden sorrow, heart's true Love, pray to God in Heaven above, that she may see and all may learn what Truthful Eye cannot discern."

"Buck?" Dar looked at his friend.

Down came the arm on Buck's helmet and the Eye of Truth slipped in front of his right eye.

He turned in a full circle, scanning the room. "No evil I can see, and nothing hidden. No illusions, nothing. Just an empty room."

"I know it says to pray, but what do we pray for?" Dar asked Andyn.

She shook her head. "I'm not sure. Guidance? The triumph of good? Discernment? Help?"

"My vote is for discernment," said Eric. "We have to try something."

"I'm not the praying type," said Hlerv, "In case you're wondering."

Dar gave him a warning look. "If we want out of here, you'd better learn. I don't see any exits."

"Come on," said Eric, dropping to his knees. "Let's try praying for discernment on what to do."

Andyn joined them, but Connor stopped her. "It says that 'she may see and all may learn'. I don't think you're included."

She looked confused. "But…"

Dar nodded. "It definitely says 'she'. You're the only woman here, so whatever we're supposed to see, only a woman can see. The implication is that the men have to pray while the woman discovers something—whatever it is."

"Who do we pray to?" asked Buck. "Connor is Irial, or was, anyway. I'm a follower of the druids, you are Christians and I have no idea what Hlerv follows, other than spare change."

Hlerv gave him a withering look and Dar grinned despite the tension. "Let's pray to whomever we want, whoever is most comforting."

He joined the other men in praying. After a while, he opened his eyes.

Andyn looked frustrated. "Nothing."

Buck let out a sigh. "First time I've prayed to anyone in a dozen years and nothing doing. I need to practice or something."

Andyn turned to them and pulled out the copy of the Song.

"Sorrow… heart's true love…"

She snapped her fingers. "I have an idea. I'm willing to bet that even Hlerv falls into this category. We all have someone in our life whom we love, someone whom we miss dearly— golden sorrow for our heart's true love. Pray for your true love."

The image of Megan Alenar's face flashed in Dar's mind immediately.

I have a lot of practice at this. I pray for her every night and every morning.

Dar nodded to the others. "Hlerv, we don't know anything about your past, but I'm guessing Andyn is right. Pray for someone you love whom you miss."

They again bowed their heads.

Midway through a prayer for Megan's safety and their reunion, Dar heard a gasp.

With an effort, he kept his eyes closed.

"Don't move, guys," said Andyn.

After a few heartbeats, she said, "Now look."

He opened his eyes and gaped.

Andyn held her hands cupped under a golden spinning jewel in the shape of a teardrop. It hovered in midair and gave off a glorious yellow light.

"Sweet Jesus," breathed Eric. "Golden sorrow…"

Andyn looked at them. "Ready?"

"For what?" asked Buck.

She closed her hands around the gemstone. The world turned to a sea of stars and spinning galaxies, whirling all around them in a streaming blaze of light and dark.

Chapter Fourteen- Fire by the Lakeside

Terenil DeMey, Knight of Saint Michael and Earl of Tallemar, reined in his horse. To his left, the sparkling waters of Sun Lake glittered in the sunshine next to the walled city of Hillton. The Deranese Plain stretched ahead to the north and east, a vast expanse of waving tall grass, wheat, corn and barley, heavy with grain and ready for the harvest. The farms now stood deserted and shuttered, their occupants safely behind the outer wall of the city proper.

No time to get all the harvest in, he thought with a pang of regret.

His lady, Saren, sat her own steed at his side, watching the road leading north to Sun Plains and Forester. She wore her trademark black brigandine of leather with dark metal stars, the back of the outfit open to allow her wings room to unfurl if she so chose. They watched a long column of wagons, horses and people wind towards them, not two miles away.

Terenil's eyes strayed farther northwards. A cloud of black smoke rose high into the air like a dark pillar holding up the blue sky. At its base, flames leaped and danced.

The town of Sun Plains burned.

Smaller fires scattered around showed that Zhinia Margoth's forces had used the torch with enthusiasm. It surprised him at first that they left anything intact, until he remembered whom they fought. Margoth was not an idiot. She knew she would have to feed her troops though she herself did not eat. What better larder to use than Deran's own breadbasket?

Three enormous, orderly columns of figures marched towards Hillton. Their forms glittered with metal. Large conveyances and the blunt, squat forms of siege engines rumbled in their wake. Some of the creatures in the van looked very large and bulky like ogres or trolls. Terenil counted fifteen different standards but the distance prevented him from distinguishing the markings. Less orderly mobs of skirmishers ranged out in front of the main force.

Terenil looked again at the refugee column and pursed his lip.

"Captain Navarre?"

A blonde woman in banded armor rode up next to him on a barded horse. Her white surcoat bore the figure of an eagle of flame, the symbol of three stars just under her collar and on each sleeve.

"Yes, milord?"

"Take the Beta Company down and greet the refugees as they arrive. Make sure to um, discourage, anyone who tries to interfere with their arrival."

Her green eyes gleamed. "With great pleasure, Excellency."

Terenil watched as Captain Navarre joined her cavalry. They formed up into a long column of their own, three abreast. The Fire Eagles galloped off, two hundred strong. Above them, the flag of Deran—a crown and cross of gold on a white field surmounted by three stars—snapped in the wind alongside the regimental standard.

The troops reached the lead refugees in a matter of minutes. Captain Navarre remained at the head of the column, conversing with one of her officers while her sergeants arranged a rear-guard. Margoth's skirmishers slowed their advance. Individual dots scurry from one band of to another as the enemy commanders conferred.

"At least Margoth didn't burn it all," said a voice next to Saren.

Terenil bowed to Marcel DeGrance, Count of Hillton. "We have reason to believe that the Dark Rider will leave the remainder of the harvest as it is," he replied. "She needs to feed her force and they are much more numerous than the stores of Forester and Sun Plains could have sustained at any rate."

Lord DeGrance shook his head, his mane of grey hair waving in the air. He looked both mournful and angry.

"Burn my towns and fields, will you?" he muttered at Zhinia Margoth's horde. "And steal our daily bread?

He glowered darkly at the scene. "How many are they?"

Saren bowed in turn. "Estimates range between fourteen thousand and sixteen thousand now, erring to the high end. The Kaftu do an excellent job of hiding among the fields and tall grass so they are difficult to count. We are certain that Margoth has, shall we say, manufactured allies from among the slain."

DeGrance stroked his neatly trimmed mustache, dark eyes narrowing. "Yes, and she'll pay for that too, the lousy witch."

"Do we have any information that will disturb our battle plan?" asked Terenil. "The war council this morning has several contingences prepared but there is nothing to indicate that we should change our first approach."

DeGrance shook his head. "No. But I've been reading up on this Zhinia Margoth. She won sixteen major battles during the Paragon Wars, only losing ten times, three times to Saint Alyssa of Tor Haldin. Of course, it was that last one that sealed her fate, so to speak. We need to watch out for all manner of devilry. Expect a surprise in almost every engagement."

Terenil nodded. DeGrance seemed an impeccable, almost fastidious man upon first glance, but his attention to detail in his appearance matched a tendency to research a problem to death—hence his extensive library.

With a thunder of hooves and a cloud of dust, a rider joined them. A dark-haired human man wearing black surcoat with the figure of a blue raven saluted.

"Colonel Greystone reports the Blue Ravens are in position and await Your Excellency's orders."

DeGrance nodded. "Tell the Colonel to send some scouts with signal mirrors in boats to the north shore of the lake. I want as many perspectives on this as I can get."

The messenger saluted again and rode off.

Terenil and Saren had gladly received a blessing in their trek to Hillton to reinforce DeGrance: the Blue Ravens, First Regiment, First Deranese Division under the command of Caridan Meraloy. Originally scheduled to travel to Darlon for joint maneuvers, a hastily-dispatched courier bird from Oakmoor diverted all one thousand to Hilton. They consisted of heavy infantry, heavy cavalry, and, most importantly, artillery to Hillton. Moving by forced marches, they arrived late the previous afternoon, rested through the night and faced Margoth's army fresh and ready to fight.

Terenil watched the refugees and their escort. The speed of the enemy scouts virtually guaranteed a pitched battle right in front of Terenil, at the base of the hill. The Fire Eagles and Blue Ravens evened the odds considerably in their favor. Now there was a good chance that the people fleeing the fighting in the North would get to Hillton unharmed.

Counting the Hillton regiment of one thousand and Terenil's own personal company, DeGrance now had slightly more than thirty-two hundred fresh troops. With the remnants of Lady Sarith's company from the town of Sun Plains, the Hillton County militia, the surviving dwarves of Dorn's Hall and the border legion from Forester, the defenders numbered fifty-five hundred troops in arms. Measured against the massive force of the Dark Rider, they looked small enough

However, Terenil knew they had three factors on their side. First, their position near the city made a siege a very difficult proposition. As its name implied, Hillton sat on a hill that jutted out into Sun Lake from the eastern shore. Two rings of walls faced the plains, the inner one of stone with ten towers. Second, the Blue Ravens and Fire Eagles comprised some of the more highly trained units in Deran's army, each company and platoon supplemented by spell-casting mages and healers.

Third, unknown to anyone except Terenil, Saren and Lord Degrance, King Phillip and Queen Ahlana approached from Oakmoor with the entire Second Deran Division. They came with air support in the form of pegasus and griffon riders. They would arrive in two days.

Margoth had bitten off quite a hunk of trouble.

Something nagged at him though. Terenil was quite certain that Margoth knew she had a daunting task in front of her. This made him wonder at her real game. She wouldn't spend a large force in assaulting an entire nation when she knew her enemies had more than enough resources to wear her down to a nub.

A group of riders detached from the refugee column and hustled towards Terenil's position. As they drew closer, Terenil recognized Lord Nolan, Baron of Forester, and Lord Jalek of Dorn's Hall. Alongside them rode

Mary Sarith, Lady of Sun Plains, wearing a tan hauberk with an orange sun. Count DeGrance nodded and his herald rode forward to meet them.

The trio bowed when they reached Terenil.

"Your Excellency," the herald announced, "their Lordships Nolan Hanford of Forester and Jalek Dorn of Dorn's Hall join Lady Mary Sarith to request sanctuary and aid from their enemies."

DeGrance bowed, as did Terenil and Saren.

"Milords and milady are welcome to Hillton and will of course be given every courtesy, aid and comfort," he announced.

The three lords looked a sight: tired, worn, dusty and bloody. Their armor bore dark stains and dents.

"Now that the formalities are done," DeGrance said, "Do you have any intelligence to add that is above and beyond what your advance couriers told us?"

Lady Mary removed her helmet and shook loose her dark brown hair. "The Dark Rider's forces are using undead now. She raises shamblers from the corpses of the slain without discrimination and sends them as an attack force. As they advance, her siege and archers attack from range before the Kaftu sweep in. Whatever is left is assaulted by the goblins, ogres and dark elves. The Ja'al levies she has held back for the most part. This makes me believe she is using them to police the other troops."

Terenil didn't doubt it. Margoth couldn't have picked a more volatile mix if she tried: goblins and dark elves detested one another, ogres fed on Kaftu if they could catch them, and the Ja'al loved to play off their rivals against each other to gain maximum advantage. She was a strong commander indeed. He was also willing to bet that she would alter her attack pattern as soon as she reached Hillton.

"Hillton is open to receive casualties and those in need of special care," DeGrance said. "Will Lady Hanford be escorting them?"

Lord Hanford stiffened. "Lady Hanford will be one of those needing care."

Terenil felt a pang of dread.

Saren paled. "What has happened to Lady Hanford?"

"My lady was wounded in the fight along the way to Sun Plains." Lord Nolan wiped his brow, eyes veiled. "She was poisoned and also infected with some vile disease."

Terenil nodded. "But Father Ander is with you. He is learned in the sciences of medicine and magic."

Nolan dropped his gaze. "Father Ander is with God, Excellency. He was mortally wounded in the battle defending the refugees."

Saren gasped and bit her lip, tears welling up in her eyes.

Terenil felt a lump in his throat, remembering the steady, calm kindness of the town priest.

In war, losses are to be expected, but not Ander!

Terenil always felt that, no matter what, Father Ander would remain at Saint Anne's church in Forester until the day he died, ministering to all who approached him.

In a choked voice, Saren said, "May angels sing him to his rest."

Terenil made the Sign of the Cross, taking Saren's hand and giving it a squeeze in comfort. They had both known Father Ander for years.

Hanford looked up. Terenil saw the pain in his eyes. "I would ask that one of the healers be assigned to assist Lady Ellen."

"I will see to it personally," said a voice next to Count DeGrance.

A rotund human male rode up on a grey dappled steed. He was grey-haired and balding with a mutton-chop mustache. He wore a rose-colored skullcap and a white surcoat with a silver cross.

"Bishop Bannister," said Terenil with a bow.

Arthur Bannister nodded to them. "My lords will forgive me foregoing the customary courtesies. I heard of the injured and have brought with me healers from the Orders of Saint Francis and Saint Raphael. With your permission?"

DeGrance nodded. Lord Nolan looked relieved, the first real sign of hope Terenil had seen from him. "They are just there, Excellency, being brought in the lead wagons."

"My Lords and Lady." Nolan rode off with the Bishop towards a group of clerics wearing brown or white robes.

Terenil sat his horse quietly. The refugees arrived at the base of the hill. Their drooping shoulders straightened at the sight of the Fire Eagle infantry and the Blue Ravens, arrayed in battle formations alongside the road. Some of the refugees smiled. The children's eyes brightened and some laughed and cheered at the soldiers.

Safe for now.

"Look," said Saren.

Apparently fed up with playing a positional cat-and-mouse game with the Fire Eagles and now infuriated at the sight of their prey celebrating their escape, some of Margoth's advance units now darted in and out at the Deranese rear guard. They launched occasional javelins or arrows, trying to get the Fire Eagles to break formation.

Captain Navarre's unit retreated in good order, shields up at the enemy. They backed their steeds towards Terenil.

At some unseen signal, all of Margoth's skirmishers charged, unleashing a swarm of missiles. Several of the Fire Eagles sagged in their saddles, hit by arrows or javelins. Their fellows bore them up and led them back towards the hill. The cavalry maintained position until the Kaftu and goblins were within fifty feet, then at a shout from Captain Navarre, split into two sections with a gap in the middle. The enemy hurtled right into the gap and the cavalry wheeled about, slamming into Margoth's troops from the sides. The plain turned into a dusty, swirling chaos of white surcoats, metal armor, flashing blades, dark furry figures, black spears and crackles of magic. Lightning lanced out from several of the Eagles to strike down goblin or Kaftu leaders. Witch doctors from the enemy side retaliated with noxious clouds of gas and whirling black spiny disks. Fighters fell on both sides.

Saren stirred restlessly in her saddle. Knowing her daemonic heritage, she probably spoiled for a chance to lash out at Margoth's raiders but held herself in check.

Margoth's forces found their advantage in numbers reduced as the horses and armor of the Eagles hemmed them in. The rearmost units attempted to flank the Deranese, but determined charges from squads of horsemen broke up their formations. Finally, the bulk of Margoth's remaining force disengaged and withdrew, shield-men guarding bowmen and javelineers as they dropped back.

The refugees cheered, seeing their tormentors defeated and in retreat. The cavalry acknowledged the cheers with a sword-salute and rode towards the city.

"The ogres, Kaftu and goblins retreat in good order," mused DeGrance.

"The Dark Rider has trained them well, and they work together."

"They are very well-equipped," said Saren. "Most of the weaponry looks relatively new. No tribal-forged swords and axes there."

Terenil nodded, watching the fight ebb to nothing as the Fire Eagles re-formed their lines. They gathered their dead and guarded the rear of the refugee column.

Soon, the remainder of the refugees had passed Terenil's position. By now, the bulk of Margoth's army marched only about a mile away. He got a good look at them.

Armored ogres pulling siege engines: light catapults and trebuchets for the most part, not heavy artillery, which implies some form of magical ammunition. Ja'al cavalry and heavy infantry in banded mail or scale mail, plenty of archers and pikemen. Cadres of Ja'al clerics and mages. Lord, even the goblins wear brigandines or scale armor. Weapons look to be standardized, not like the motley arsenal of a mob or tribe. How much could it have cost her to outfit them?

Dark elves marched in formation, a sinister-looking force in black chainmail or black plate armor. They wielded pikes, longbows or shield and sword. Giant scorpions or spiders stalked next to the commanders of the dark elves, exoskeletons glimmering in the sunlight.

He sighed. "This is going to be messy."

"Plenty messy," said Saren. "Look at the rear of the formation."

A single rider advanced, surrounded by shuffling ranks of walking corpses. It wore a flowing purple robe and a golden crown that shone with a sort of dark energy. Even at this distance, Terenil felt the power radiating from the figure and imagined bright, purple flaming eyes glaring at him.

"Zhinia Margoth."

An honor guard of heavily armed ogres, dark elves and Ja'al accompanied her, as did one of each of the five races in her force, undoubtedly their commanders or liege lords. Her standard flew boldly in the wind: a black, fanged skull wearing a crown of purple flame against a bone-white background.

DeGrance snorted. "Well, we'll see how she likes fighting against those who aren't outnumbered fifty to one."

***

They found out later that afternoon. With a minimum of fuss and an efficiency Terenil found impressive, Margoth's army arrayed itself into orderly units. Then, without warning, they attacked.

She decided to move towards the less daunting of the Deranese forces facing her, directing her troops towards the Hillton County Guard on the lakeshore. Ogres led the attack, roaring and hurling rocks or spears. Ja'al infantry and dark elves marched behind them to the roll of drums and the skirling of shrill pipes. Margoth's banner waved in the wind overhead.

Margoth's catapults hurled sizzling ceramic globes that burst into green fire when they struck. Warriors dropped to the ground writhing in pain until healers could drag them out of danger. DeGrance's commanders retaliated with ballistae bolts, arrows or magical fireballs. They shattered or crisped some of the catapults, but the enemy came on, leaving at least a score of smoking ogre corpses on the field, impaled by bolts or arrows.

The attack reached the Guards and all hell broke loose. Ogres flailed away with hefty maces or giant swords, slamming soldiers into the dirt or lopping off limbs. Mages blinded the ogres with balls of light and the Deranese leaped in to hack them to pieces.

The Ja'al and elves arrived next, trotting into the fray, spears down, but were met by a hail of arrows and a stiff wall of pikes. The attack stalled for a moment, then the forces of the Lich Queen overbore the defenders, driving them back. The Ja'al pressed forward, heading for the northern wall of Hillton. Siege engines rolled in behind them, undead corpses guarding the sides.

DeGrance had his herald raise a blue flag and the Blue Ravens leaped into action. Heavy infantry marched towards the flank of the attacking force, singing a hymn. Cavalry accompanied them, walking their steeds. When the herald waved the flag, the infantry charged. The archers behind them sent a blistering wave of arrows into the Ja'al and elves. The cavalry galloped into the remaining ogre warriors, bowling them over or running them through with lances. Magic spells or ogre swords unhorsed some of the Ravens, but the Deranese gave better than they got and the assault started to unravel.

Then a howling mass of goblins and Kaftu surged at the northern flank of the Blue Ravens. Archer and mages supported them with a hail of arrows and magical missiles of cold, acid or fire. The Ravens turned in good order, the archers loosing their arrows at the seething companies, slaying many. Margoth's troops reached the press of cavalry and infantry, Kaftu leaping to take warriors out of their saddles.

DeGrance had his herald run up an orange flag next and the Fire Eagles wheeled as one. They charged into the side of Margoth's flanking force, turning it towards the lake and into the first force of her troops. Confusion reigned as Ja'al, goblins, Kaftu, elves and ogres intermingled in a mob. Their commanders tried desperately to reform the lines and hold their troops together.

Terenil stood up in his stirrups. A small team of Ja'al raced forward towards the undead fighting the Blue Ravens near the catapults. They carried something in a metal frame that glowed purple. "What are they doing?" he asked in alarm.

DeGrance shook his head, looking grim. "I don't know, but it doesn't look good." He signaled to the herald. "Run up the black and white, quickly!"

A black and white checkered flag went up and a group of freelance mercenary warriors, mages and clerics rode out towards the enemy.

They arrived too late. The enemy reached the undead and slammed the iron frame into the ground. One of them slapped something on the top before the group raced away. The freelancers reached them as they withdrew and a melee ensued, but the device activated.

A vile purple light flared. From Margoth's position, an answering light glowed. A writhing, luminous cord snaked out from the lich queen to the iron frame.

Terenil watched, horrified, as the zombies on the field were sucked backwards towards the purple light. They slammed into each other, melting and welding together to form what looked like a giant man-like figure.

"What is that?" Saren gasped.

"It's a magical construct," DeGrance breathed. "A zombie-golem."

Without another word, Saren leaped from the saddle. Ivory bat-wings grew out from her back and ivory horns peeked out from under her black hair. Her body, already trim and fit, grew more sleek, taking on a seductive aspect. Saren's dark eyes swirled with rainbow colors. Her beautiful face seemed unnaturally alluring.

"It's time Margoth learned a lesson or two. Keep the others away from me," she said in a sexy, slightly husky voice. She smiled and showed the tips of her fangs.

"My lady!" cried out Lady Sarith in shock. Terenil remembered that she had never seen Saren in her natural form.

Without taking his eyes from his wife, he addressed his personal guard.

"We guard Lady Saren," he said, drawing his sword and setting his shield on his arm. "See to your magic supplements."

He whispered a spell and his blade glowed red, then his shield and armor glowed blue. He recited another spell and a white mist wafted down over him and his steed, vanishing as it touched them. His guards applied similar protections, reciting spells from scrolls or downing potions from tiny vials. Armored in plate mail and carrying steel shields, their swords shone with magical light.

The zombie-construct had now reached mammoth proportions. The Fire Eagles and free-lances hacked down the shambling corpses but to no avail. The golem stood over twenty feet high. Orange flames burned in artificial eye sockets and a grey mist swirled around it. The Deranese soldiers closest to it coughed and stumbled, falling under the weapons of the zombies. They were soon sucked up into the golem. Their fellows retreated. The enemy force roared its approval and swept forward, driving the defenders back.

The construct crushed a catapult with a giant hand. The smashed siege engine glowed with orange light and it transformed into a flail of fire. Terenil spurred his horse forward as Saren took wing, soaring high in the air over the battlefield. She shot down at the golem, unleashing a hail of lightning and ice attacks at it. The golem reeled back, lashing at her with the flail. An arc of flame shot out at her. Saren wheeled away.

The golem aimed the next arc of flame at the Deranese defenders, scorching them with fire and driving them back. The flail struck some of the soldiers and they sailed through the air to land in flaming heaps. The Blue Ravens and Fire Eagles closed ranks, beating a fighting retreat towards the hill where DeGrance and his personal guard waited. Every time they halted the enemy, the zombie-golem swept out an arc of fire and the Deranese retreated, leaving their dead on the field. Deranese mages used lightning and fire spells but the zombie golem made sure to stay out of range. Only the iron discipline of the elite army troops kept it from becoming a rout.

Saren looped in again, launching a fireball at the construct's head-shape. With a roar, the fireball detonated, enveloping the thing in a halo of flames. It staggered.

The Dark Rider's army turned its attention to Saren, sending up a veritable storm of arrows, magical lightning and fire darts. She whirled away from the attacks, spinning and darting in the sky like a hawk. The enemy roared in anger and redoubled their efforts to bring her down.

Terenil saw his chance. He spurred his mount forward, leading his platoon of guards. He aimed at a group of Ja'al archers and mages targeting Saren as she danced and swirled in the air.

His small force slammed into the enemy before they knew what hit them. He cut down two archers and a mage before he took his first hit, a Lightning Spear to the shield that rocked him backwards. With his shield-hand, he placed a light globe on the offending wizard's eyes. One of his guards lay her out with a sword thrust.

He rode among the enemy, slashing with his blade, maneuvering his steed to knock down warriors or ruin magical attacks at Saren. He paused, watching her progress. She still dove at the zombie golem like a sparrow defending her nest against a cat. Every time her spells damaged it, the golem simply repaired itself with a nearby corpse.

This is going to be a problem, Terenil thought, blocking a sword strike and running a Ja'al warrior through. A trio of enemy mages advanced, casting up a shimmering magical screen that crackled with energy, forcing him back, shield up. He tried to think of a counterspell.

Then voices sang behind him. Terenil's company and their enemy turned as one to look.

Bishop Bannister walked a dun horse towards the battle, wearing plated armor and carrying his crozier. A squad of episcopal knights accompanied him. Behind them walked the monks, priests and nuns of the Franciscan and Raphaelite orders singing a *Gloria.* A nimbus of white light surrounded their robed forms.

Margoth's warriors ran towards the clerics. Ja'al priests gesticulated, casting tongues of black fire at the advancing clergy or conjuring nightmare creatures out of dark fogs. Bannister and his lead priests countered the magic with spells of their own, deflecting the bolts or dissipating the illusions. A few monks fell but the remainder advanced.

Saren broke away from the battle and hovered in mid-air. She pointed at the clerics, then soared away.

"Disengage!" Terenil shouted to his force. "Protect the Bishop!" He and his troops cut down a few remaining enemies and retreated towards Bannister.

The prelate nodded at him, his face serene as he led his force towards the zombie-golem. Terenil trotted his steed next to Bannister, watching Saren.

Unconcerned with her attacks by this time, the golem ignored her as she stopped high overhead and cast a spell. The earth under the golem's feet churned and fell away, forming a deep pit. The golem tripped, then stumbled and fell over on its side into the pit It struggled to rise.

The Deranese cheered.

"Benedicamus Domino," said Bannister in a loud voice. His companions began a chant in Ecclesia.

The very air around Terenil grew brighter, cleaner and more wholesome. The monks and nuns raised their hands to the sky. The light grew brighter and larger.

Terenil's raised a hand to shield his eyes. A brilliant shaft of white shone down around them and a warmth suffused his bones. It was almost like awaking from a long sleep after a hard day's work. He felt energized and renewed.

Bannister pointed at the zombie-golem and the clergy followed suit. The shaft of light pivoted around and focused on the golem.

It threw up its hands and arms, but the light penetrated everything. Zombie parts disintegrated, shredding in the light like leaves blown in the wind. The golem lost both arms, then its head, then collapsed into a heap of bones and ash.

DeGrance's force cheered. Bannister slumped in the saddle and Terenil spurred forward to hold him up. "Excellency?"

Bannister looked up at him. He looked old and wan. "We must …leave this place," he gasped.

Indeed, Bannister's group all appeared spent, hands on their knees or clinging to their fellows for support.

He nodded. "We will escort you back."

An unearthly shriek split the air from the enemy side and Terenil shuddered involuntarily.

Margoth and her command team rode toward the fight. A cloud of black mist followed her, low to the ground.

Terenil's guards hoisted the clerics to their saddles and they rode off, away from the fight. He cast a look over his shoulder.

Margoth gestured at the battlefield as she rode. Touched by the black mist in her wake, dead Kaftu, men, elves, ogres and goblins rose up from the ground, groped for weapons and shuffled off to follow her.

"How is he?" asked DeGrance as Terenil rode up with Bannister in tow. He looked concerned.

Bannister waved a hand. "I will mend, my lord. However, I would counsel a retreat to the city. The Dark Rider's forces have been worn down but she now swells her ranks with the dead, and it has been a long, hard fight already. We cannot stand and hold them here."

DeGrance nodded. "I agree."

He turned to the herald. "Show the striped flag."

The herald raised a black-and-blue striped standard. Commanders reformed their units as best they could and the defenders retreated to Hillton.

A shape from the sky landed nearby and Terenil held out his hand to Saren. She vaulted into the saddle behind him, wrapping her arms around his waist.

"Damn it," she seethed. "I wanted to go after Margoth, but she was watching me the whole time. I know what spells she probably has ready and I couldn't get a clear shot."

"We got the golem anyway."

"Yes," she said, sounding mollified. "But we've only delayed the inevitable. Margoth will lay siege to Hillton. I don't know how long we can hold her off."

He lifted one of her hands to his lips. "The King arrives soon with an entire division, and air cavalry. We just have to wait until then."

He said no more, sensing the frustration and tension in her as she returned to her human form. They with her at the city gates, watching the retreat. Margoth's army seemed content to harry and harass, not mounting any more assaults as DeGrance's army left the field.

Why? Why not press us while she raises an army of undead?

He had no answers but comforted himself with the knowledge that reinforcements were on the way.

"Yes," he repeated, "We just have to wait. The King will end this."

Chapter Fifteen- Holy Relic

Eric soared in a starfield of whirling light, lost in the sparkling splendor. With a dull thump, his feet hit something solid. He staggered. Nausea churned his stomach. He leaned forwards, his hands on his knees and heard someone cough next to him.

He blinked to clear his vision. He stood in an open, domed gazebo made of white marble. Ornate, carved pillars held up the ceiling. Between them, he saw mountain ranges, snow, a far green wilderness, and a lake in shadow below him. The air seemed chill but fresh and clean. The nausea faded.

We're on top of Twinspire Mountain!

"I can't believe we're all the way up here," said Connor in a tone of wonder. "How did this happen?"

As if in answer, a silvery bell rang. Golden light flashed from the dome's inside surface overhead. It swirled and darkened until it showed a night sky spangled with stars. A beam of radiance shone down and struck the marble floor in front of Eric.

He gaped. Words failed him.

An incredibly gorgeous woman stood in front of him. Over six feet tall, her tanned, flawless skin seemed to glow. Soft golden hair cascaded down onto her shoulders, framing a heart-shaped face set with jewel-like, sapphire-colored eyes. She wore a short, sleeveless tunic that reached to mid-thigh, her waist encircled by a silver belt. Beautiful white wings tinged with tan unfurled from her back and she carried a short sword in a scabbard at her side. She was barefoot.

Eric couldn't take his eyes off her. Her figure was flawless: strong, slender and shapely, as if God Himself had taken a page from His book of Creation entitled "Woman". In his eyes, she personified grace, strength, vitality, and pure femininity.

She smiled and Eric felt all his tension, despair, grief, anxiety and anger fade from him.

Elohir...

Eric knelt. "High Servant of God, I greet you."

Her voice reminded him of woodland streams and birdsong. "I greet you in kind, Eric Daniel Hylar Indidarc of Deran. Kneel not before me, nor before any creature, but only before the Most High."

Gentle hands lifted him up by the shoulders and he rose. Her touch seemed like his foster mother, Anne, had reached from beyond the grave to smooth his hair and give him a hug.

Tears stung his eyes.

"Sweet warrior," the Elohir said, "Grieve not for your mother. She is at peace and she is so proud of you. You have done well."

She smiled at the other Riders. "Welcome. I was charged to listen for the ringing of the bell that signaled the arrival of the Chosen. You are the Grey Riders, foretold by the church of Irial."

"Please, lady, what is your name?" asked Dar.

She inclined her head. "Darius Richard Cabot of Deran, I am Melissa in the service of Kelson of Celestia."

"Why were we brought here?" asked Andyn, "Is there something to do with a crown?"

Melissa laughed. "You certainly are impatient, Andyn Josette Fallbrook Eleandir. But I understand your need for haste. You will need to move quickly before the day is ended."

She turned and held out her hand. A light glowed in her eyes, then faded. A pedestal now stood next to her, holding a box of polished red wood bound in gold.

Her expression turned somber. "What is within must be used to destroy a great evil, one you already know, one that hunts you. This item is proof against all things profane."

She opened the box and drew forth a crown, very much like a tiara. Made of a silvery metal that Eric guessed was platinum, it brought to mind soaring cathedrals, stained glass windows, rainbows, and the sparkle of sunlight on the water. Seven points surmounted it, the center point capped by a cross. Two chains of platinum hung from the left and right sides, as long as his thumb, ending in rubies. A single diamond in a triangle-shaped setting glittered from the center, where the wearer's forehead would be.

"The queenly crown?" breathed Connor.

Melissa smiled. "Correct, Connor Tiberius McLoemin. This is the Crown of Saint Alyssa, Queen of Tor Haldin, mortal enemy of Zhinia Margoth."

She offered it to Andyn. "It is for you."

Andyn turned sheet-white. "What? Me?" she squeaked.

Melissa raised an eyebrow. "You are the wife of a carpenter, the late Larad Fallbrook, are you not? The Song says this is meant for the tresses of a carpenter's wife. And you are the only woman Rider here present."

"The Song? Well, yes," gasped Andyn. She took a step back. "But… that is the crown of a Christian queen and a saint! I thought we were to deliver it to someone else. I'm not worthy to even touch it…"

"Which is precisely why you are one of the few who can."

Andyn looked at Dar and Eric for support. "Saint Alyssa is someone from your faith, not mine. What do I do?"

Eric watched Melissa, who returned his gaze steadily. He waited a long moment before speaking.

"No, Andyn," he said quietly. "It really is for you."

Melissa smiled at him. Andyn took the crown in trembling hands.

"How do I use it?" Andyn asked.

Melissa smoothed the hair from Andyn's brow and stroked her cheek. "Just put it on, dear sister. The saint will guide you. The evil one is on the move and your time is at hand."

Her eyes rested on each of the male Riders in turn. Her eyes lingered on Hlerv, who averted his gaze. Eric thought Melissa looked sad for a moment.

Why? What is going on with Hlerv? Eric had a sudden sense of foreboding.

"What are we supposed to do?" Buck asked.

"Remain steadfast, Buckminster Horatio Bydecy, aid Andyn, and follow always the Light. Remember that. The Light will guide you." She motioned with her left hand and a chest of dark wood with a golden clasp appeared next to her.

"I was also bidden to provide you tools for this quest and future toil against the Enemy. I see that Andyn, Buck and Hlerv bear mighty weapons already, and that is good. To aid the others, however…"

She knelt down and opened the chest. She rose with a short item that looked like a spear grip with a long, bladed spear point at one end and a metal sphere at the other.

She handed it to Eric.

"What is it?"

She smiled. "It is a special weapon crafted in the time of the Paragons. Its name is Fidelis, for it is ever-faithful and will return to you when thrown, whether it flies true or not. It is endowed with added range and strikes against dark and faithless things with holy light. Speak its name."

"Fidelis."

The spear transformed so quickly Eric almost dropped it. It lengthened and extended to the same size as any other spear, with notable differences. Elven runes ran along the haft, which bore inlaid silver patterns, and the spearhead glittered with orange light.

"I don't know what to say. Thank you, my lady."

"You are very welcome, Eric. Bear it well. Speak its name again and it will return to its smaller size."

She knelt again, then rose with a short, broad sword in a red scabbard. This she handed to Connor.

"This is right-wise named Tiuz, which is the ancient Elven name for fire. When you speak its name, its edge will come alive with holy flame. Yet it is real fire and can be used to both illuminate and set things aflame. Use it wisely, for the Holy Fire is only used for good and not selfish things."

Connor took the sword and pulled it from the scabbard. It rang with a silvery sound and red runes marked the blade.

"I cannot begin to thank you," he said.

"I know you miss your wife and daughter. Make Janey and Rose proud of you," Melissa said. She bent down and cupped his face in her hands. Eric thought Connor looked likely to burst into tears. "That will be thanks enough."

Melissa knelt again and held another scabbard in her hands. This one was dark blue, with tiny enameled stars along its length. It looked like a bastard sword, similar to the one Dar used.

"This is for you," she said, handing it to him.

Dar reverently accepted the weapon and drew it out of the scabbard. To everyone's amazement, the blade was dead black.

No, not dead black, as Eric noticed. The stars of the night sky glimmered in the dark metal.

"What is it?" breathed Dar.

"Ah this," said Melissa. "This is a special weapon, one made in my homeland. I will not tell you its true-name, for that would give you knowledge of its forging and such knowledge is not for your folk, not yet. Know that its last bearer, an elven sword-maiden, named it after her mother. In the Elven tongue it is called Rindara, or Bay-sprite. Others have called it The Starblade. You may call it what you wish."

Dar slid the sword back in its scabbard. "Rindara Starblade."

"A fine choice. It strikes with special power against those from Hades and they cannot abide its presence. It is proof against those things corrupted and twisted. Use it wisely and well."

She faced the Riders now, looking satisfied. "Yes, you are ready to carry on. I have done what I can."

"But we don't know how to get down from here," said Buck, looking exasperated.

"I think I can help you." Melissa waved a hand and another golden teardrop gemstone appeared in front of Andyn, spinning as before. "This will take you back to the Room of Awaiting and then to the Levitator. Once you get back, face the wall as you did when you first used the halfling toy, then go to the right. You will find what you seek."

She looked at Dar with sympathetic eyes. "There comes a time when we must release the ones we love. You will understand later."

She unfurled her wings and the ceiling began to glow. The wooden chest at her feet vanished.

"I have a feeling we will meet again," she said with a wink at Eric. "Remember, have faith."

As quickly as she had appeared, Melissa disappeared in a shaft of golden light that faded into the domed roof of the gazebo.

Andyn carefully placed the Crown of Saint Alyssa into her shoulder bag, then latched it shut. With a deep breath, Andyn closed her hand on the glowing gemstone.

***

Eric decided that if he ever learned a spell to teleport, he wouldn't use it. It just wasn't worth the nausea and disorientation.

"You look like you're going to puke," said Buck.

Eric opened one eye. "You look like you already did."

"Come on," Hlerv groaned. "If we keep moving it will fade away."

He and Connor led the way out of the octagonal room and they released the toy to open the doorway. They headed down the passage just as Melissa had instructed.

The effects of their return trip dwindled as they walked. He and Connor took the lead, alert for any tell-tale sign of a trap or ambush. Only the sound of their boots echoed in the stone passage, their way lit by one of Buck's light globes.

Hlerv tapped Connor on the arm and they stopped.

Eric slipped up next to them. "Something wrong?"

Connor glanced at Hlerv, who nodded.

"The color of the stone is a little too even," the gnome said, rubbing a finger along his mustache. "It's been pretty variegated so far, but here?"

Eric waited with the others while the pair of agents investigated. Finally, Connor beckoned to him.

"Tap your spear right there, butt-first," he said, pointing.

Eric did so. At first, nothing happened. Then, with a faint groan, the floor swung down and away. The doors slammed into the side walls with a loud bang. A pit spanned from one wall to the other, blocking their path.

"Nice job," said Dar.

The Riders peered into the pit.

"Well," Andyn remarked, "no one is going that way. Or rather, someone already did, with unfortunate results."

Eric nodded. About twenty feet down, long metal spikes sprouted up from the floor, their rusty lengths festooned with ribcages, skulls and fragments of armor. Bones littered the floor near their bases.

"That tears it," said Hlerv, brushing off his gloves. "We can't go that way. The pit is fifteen feet wide and at least twenty across. I can find a way across, but I can't get all of you over there. Does anyone have a flying spell?"

Eric shrugged. "I sure don't. Even if I did, it would only affect one person. There's no way we'd all get across."

"It's a spell called Eagle Magic," Andyn said, "but I my talents are more in combat and healing magic. Flying spells are more of a utility."

"Besides," Dar said with a lopsided grin, "You have a flying horse. Why would you need a flying spell?"

"Now what?" asked Connor. "We have to go back."

Hlerv scratched his beard. "This Melissa must have made a mistake."

Eric stared at the pit. Something didn't seem right. He knew Elohir were fallible but their knowledge was also legendary. To make an error like this seemed out of place.

"Buck," he said on a hunch, "Use the Eye, would you?"

Buck flipped down the eye of truth and grunted. "Good guess, Eric."

"What?" asked Andyn.

"It's an illusion. There aren't any spikes or bones. It's a pit all right, but it has a ladder on each side and there's a door in the right wall. Someone went to a lot of trouble to make sure no one went that way."

Eric whistled. A permanent illusion spell like this one took a skilled practitioner.

"Sure looks real," said Hlerv.

"It isn't," Buck said. "I'll prove it to you."

Without another word, he stepped to the edge, grabbed something and began climbing down. With every step, the walls of the pit shimmered. Eric saw the ghostly image of a metal ladder.

He smiled. "I'll join you."

As he descended, the spikes and bones seemed more insubstantial, ephemeral. At the bottom, he pushed his hand through four spikes and wiggled his fingers inside an illusionary skull.

Andyn laughed. "All right, we get the idea."

The other Riders soon joined them at the bottom.

"One thing is certain," Andyn cautioned as Hlerv opened the door in the pit wall. "If this is the way to the Helm, Margoth probably set it up, which means she'll have someone or something guarding it. Stay sharp."

Again, Connor and Hlerv led them forward, watching the walls, floor and ceiling for traps. Eric used a spell to detect magic, hoping for some kind of clue as to their destination. He saw nothing but a dusty passage.

Buck's light globe flickered. A little while later it went out completely.

"Last one," Buck whispered as he activated another.

They turned a corner and Connor's hand went up. The Riders stopped and he came back to them, leaving Hlerv to watch.

"Room ahead," the halfling said. They crept up to a yawning opening under and archway of skulls.

A square chamber opened out from the passage, its roof soaring above to a pentagonal-shaped ceiling. Eric tried to figure out the structure and architecture of that and failed.

Bones and bits of equipment littered the floor. In the light of Buck's globe, a layer of dust obscured everything, some patches thicker than others.

"Be careful," Eric whispered. His eyes narrowed. "Some areas have been recently disturbed... at least, more recently than a few hundred years ago."

They stepped inside. Something at the back of the room glowed brightly in Eric's eyes.

"Look! It's—" he began, his heart beating faster.

"We see it," said Andyn.

On a pedestal shaped like clawed hands, a helmet glimmered with a faint purple light. It seemed to shift and warp. Just over the eye-slits, the symbol of a fanged skull with a crown of flame mocked him.

Connor and Hlerv picked their way into the room, but the rustle of bones stopped them.

The blade of Eric's new spear shone brighter. The other Riders drew weapons. Khelios cast bright golden light all over the area, Tiuz flamed,

Shriek glittered and Eleison flared white. Dar raised his new sword, the shimmering stars in the blade bright as diamonds.

Two forms rose up from the bones nearest the pedestal. They were made of utter blackness, vaguely human-shaped, with bright red stars for eyes. A wave of chilling cold swept over him and Eric felt it to the marrow of his bones.

One of them spoke. "Who trespasses in the chamber of the Helm?" it demanded in a stern, commanding tone.

To his amazement, Eric Dar's mouth dropped open and he lowered Rindara Starblade.

"Grandmother?"

***

That's her voice!

Dar shook his head, mute. The wraiths hovering in midair over a floor littered with bones. The one on the left seemed smaller and it hesitated. It turned to the larger one.

"Is that you, grandfather?" Dar whispered.

"What means this?" the larger wraith asked, its voice hesitant.

"It's me, Dar, your grandson."

The smaller wraith shuddered. "No. We have no children, no grandchildren. We serve only the helm and its creator."

How did this happen? God, how could you let this happen? Despair clutched at his soul.

"You're wrong," he pleaded. "I am Dar, brother to Lawrence and Mark. Our mother, Elizabeth, is your daughter. Don't you remember?"

"All is shadow and flame," said the taller wraith. "All who trespass within are doomed. We have been given our charge. Defend the Helm."

Dar shook his head. "The Helm is evil. You and grandmother were never evil, not once. You cared for me when I was sick, taught me to track in the woods, told me stories of adventure. You lived in Wit's End, near Forester."

The wraiths paused.

"Dar?"

He turned. Andyn and the others stood behind him, bathed in the light from their weapons.

"Dar, you can't let them hold us back," she said. "That's the Helm and we have to destroy it. If they're defending it, they have been turned."

"I have to try!"

He turned a pleading gaze to the wraiths. "Don't you remember anything? Grandma? Grandpa?"

In answer, the helm at the back of the room flared purple and the wraiths surged forward. They soared above the Riders, sweeping at them with clawing hands.

Buck lashed at one, Khelios flaring bright. The dwarven blade passed through the wraith. It shuddered but struck the warrior in the shoulder.

Buck let out a strange, keening sort of sigh and went on one knee, face pale.

"So cold…" he managed.

Andyn leaped next to him, holding forth Eleison. The wraiths spun away, pursuing Dar's companions but not coming near him. Only Shriek, wielded by Hlerv, seemed to do anything to them. After a couple of slashes from the gnome, the wraiths avoided him as well.

Dar darted from one of his friends to the next, interposing himself between them and the wraiths. Dar's grandfather slapped Eric and he and went down on hands and knees.

Andyn held up her silver tree symbol of Verian. A sphere of misty white light surrounded her and the wraiths hovered outside of its range.

"Stalemate," said Connor.

"Please, Grandma, Grandpa! You don't know what you're doing! You are not yourselves! If you could only remember!" Dar felt torn in two, afraid for his friends but aghast at what his grandparents had become.

"We serve the Helm now," the wraiths said in unison. An unbelievable wave of cold pulsed out at him.

"Dar," called Andyn. "Tell them who they are!"

"I did!"

"No, use their true names."

Dar set his jaw. "Robert and Kelly Marek, I name you! You are the parents of my mother, Elizabeth! Return to me!"

Both wraiths recoiled, holding spectral hands to their heads. They moaned with a sound that made Dar's bones hurt.

"I name you!" he shouted again. "Robert and Kelly Marek, I name you! Return from darkness!"

For a wild, crazy moment, he thought something would happen to magically change them back to human beings. Then the wraiths lowered their hands.

"We hear you, Darius," said his grandmother's wraith. "We hear you, beloved. But we are not free. The Helm's magic guardians slew us as we tried to lay hold of it, even as we slew them. We are now imprisoned this room until we are destroyed or the Helm returns to its creator."

Dar's heart skipped a beat. "But—"

His grandfather's wraith nodded. "There is no hope for us, child, to return to the land of the living. Our true names have returned to us our memories, but now we long for peace."

Kelly Marek's wraith nodded. "Release us, grandson."

Dar felt tears streaming down his face. "No! I can't…"

"You must. The Helm holds us here, but your sword can set us free. We can feel it."

He heard Andyn's voice. "Can't you just stand aside and let us get the Helm?"

"No, friend-of-Dar. If we allow you to draw near, it will command us to attack again. We can only hold on for a little while. Please, son, release us."

Dar's heart sank but he set his mouth in a firm line and hefted Rindara Starblade. "I understand. Please forgive me."

Both wraiths straightened. "There is nothing to forgive," said his grandfather.

Dar gritted his teeth and swung Rindara, sword of Celestia, in a broad arc. The magical weapon flared with white light as it slashed through first one wraith, then the other on the backstroke.

With shrieking sighs that tore his heart in two, the black forms of his grandparents burst apart into shreds of darkness.

Dar bit back a sob. Then he gasped, eyes wide. The light of the stars on his blade filled his sight. In that light stood two people, translucent and filmy. The woman looked a lot like his mother, dark-haired and dark-eyed, smiling as she held a tall, blond man with a neat mustache. They blew him kisses, then looked up.

Dar blinked and they vanished in a cloud of stars.

The light from Rindara faded. Only the flame of Tiuz lit the darkness in the chamber.

"You had to do it, man," said Buck, placing a hand on his shoulder.

"Did you see?" Dar asked.

"See what?" asked Connor.

"My grandparents."

Eric put a hand on his shoulder. "Dar, we just saw you slash through them, then they dissipated and you stood there, looking at where they were."

Dar sighed. "Andyn?"

She shook her head. "That's what I saw. What did you see?"

He bit back his tears. "They were as the last time I saw them alive, in a ghostly sort of form. Then they looked up and a bright light covered them and now they're gone."

Andyn put her arm around him. "Then they have achieved their true destiny. They are with your God now."

Dar stared at the floor numbly. *How do I tell Mother?*

"Hlerv," said Connor in an odd voice, "what are you doing?"

Dar jerked his head up.

Hlerv stood next to the pedestal. He turned dark eyes to them. "What I have to. You don't understand now, but you will later."

He reached for the Helm.

"What are you doing? No!" screamed Andyn.

Hlerv picked it up. It flashed with pink, purple and red light. A deep, dissonant gong boomed somewhere in the distance.

***

Zhinia Margoth stood bolt upright in her stirrups. A thrill of exhilaration coursed through her.

"Your Highness?" asked Queen Ildrisana. "What is it?"

Zhinia laughed. "The Helm of Shadows is found! It calls. I will answer!"

She spoke a long, rolling word full of the harshness of the lash and the bitter pain of grief and the soul-killing poison of lust and thrust her hands skyward.

236

Chapter Sixteen- Queenly Crown

The ground shook and trembled. "Stay together!" Dar shouted.

Andyn felt a surge of panic, then remembered the Crown. She pulled it from her shoulder bag, then held it in one hand and Eleison in the other.

Dar and the other Riders formed a circle around her, weapons drawn.

"Hlerv!" shouted Eric as the ground heaved. "Drop that thing! We have to destroy it!"

The gnome shook his head. "It's my only chance! You don't understand. I can control it!"

"Are you crazy?" yelled Buck. "What are you talking about?"

Hlerv crouched next to the dark pedestal, clutching the Helm of Shadows. In a swift motion, he pulled a sack out of his leather jerkin. He popped the Helm into it and whispered a soft word. The sack shrank to the size of a common belt purse and he slipped it under his armor again.

A sudden, sickening wave of evil surged at them from Hlerv's location. Fighting to keep from retching, Andyn squeezed her eyes shut and leaned into Eric's shoulder.

In a flash of green light penetrated her eyelids. The world lurched. Andyn staggered against Eric. The universe warped and twisted. She felt herself falling, then suddenly landed on her feet.

She blinked. The earth seemed unsteady she walked in a fog of confusion.

They stood on a hill outside a fortified city. The fields nearby showed the wreck and carnage of battle: goblin, human, elf, dwarf, Kaftu, and ogre all jumbled together in the last sleep of death.

A wave of nausea hit her and Andyn's mind reeled. She tried to concentrate and focus her eyes.

Hulking ogres hauled siege engines towards the city as smoke from many fires on the field blew past them in a hot wind. Nearby, horrid walking corpses shuffled forward, joining ranks of infantry wearing the screaming demon-head livery of the Ja'al. Twisted, misshapen bears and wolves snarled and prowled among the wreckage, their eyes glowing with hate.

Nearest her and her friends, a fearsome band of enemies approached. An ogre chieftain hefted a massive battle axe in guard position, baring his fangs. A dark elven princess or queen stood next to him, eyeing them as she fingered a wand in her belt. Near her, a Kaftu female with a twisted staff topped by a shining blue gemstone snarled and crouched beside a haughty-looking Ja'al officer in plated armor. A goblin chieftain wearing scale mail wielded a dagger and a sparkling silver mace, eyes darting around. Next to him stood an oddly familiar little goblin with piercing eyes.

"Um, this is a problem," managed Buck, sounding like a man who had just had a few too many dwarven whiskeys.

But Andyn's heart stopped when she saw a figure riding on a dark, horned horse behind them. A skeleton in rotting robes guided the steed around the command group, then dismounted with fluid grace. She held a staff of twisted wood topped with the skull of some alien creature and wore a crown on her head. Instead of eyes, vile purple stars of baleful intensity glowed from within her eye sockets.

Margoth!

"Ah," said Margoth in a remarkably sultry voice. "You must be the Grey Riders I keep hearing about. I am Zhinia Margoth, Princess of Kher Mardil. So nice of you to stop by."

Andyn struggled to think, still overcome by the nausea from the Helm. The waves of pure malice radiating from Margoth chilled her soul and clouded her mind.

"What, no clever response? No announcement of my doom?" the lich mocked.

Think, woman! The Crown…

Andyn looked dumbly at the Crown of Saint Alyssa in her hand. It flared with bright golden light and her nausea, confusion and dread vanished.

Margoth halted. "What is that?"

Andyn found her voice. "Don't you recognize this?"

Margoth's face twisted in a horrid spasm of rage and she slammed the butt of her staff into the ground. The skull glowed deep purple and a hail of shadowy arrows lanced out at the Grey Riders.

The crown in Andyn's hand glowed bright white and an orb of misty white energy leaped up, covering her. Her friends tried to dodge the shadow-arrows, rolling or hurling themselves to the side. The missiles ripped into the earth. Buck's shield was hurled from his arm and he tumbled to the side, grimacing in pain.

The dark arrows pinged off Andyn's globe of light.

"Pitiful fools!" shouted Margoth. "You cannot escape me!"

As one, Dar, Connor, Eric and Buck loosed arrows at her. Margoth contemptuously lashed her staff before her and the shafts broke into splinters before they could reach her.

"Andyn!" Eric yelled. "Use the Crown! Don't worry about us!"

"Never!" cried Andyn, emotions raging between panic and horror. "Come close to me! I can't leave you!"

Dar looked right into her eyes. "You have to get her, no matter what."

Andyn couldn't breathe.

"You dare defy me? You dare raise a hand to me?" Margoth shouted. Her mouth worked in a spasm of rage and she spat out vile, horridsounding words. With each word, a blast of colored light in sickly green, lurid red or swirling purple shot out at the Riders.

The first blast tore into Hlerv and Connor and hurled them backwards. The second caught up Dar and Eric and slammed them into the ground. The last knocked Buck head over heels.

All of the Riders lay still. Dar looked at Andyn for what seemed like centuries as the light faded from his eyes.

Andyn ran to Eric and Dar, feeling their necks for a pulse.

"No! No, no, no, no…" she whispered. A deep pain wrenched her heart.

They were dead.

***

Terenil and Saren stood in shock with Count DeGrance on the ramparts, watching the impossible unfold. Soldiers, clerics and wizards alike stopped their tasks and froze, dumbfounded.

When Margoth's wave of death magic struck down all the Riders except Andyn, they gasped.

"Eric?" whispered Saren DeMey. "Dear God, no... not Eric." She gripped her husband's hand, tears running down her cheeks. She felt the blood drain from her face and her heart clenched.

He held her wordlessly.

Such pain as she had not felt in half a dozen years coursed through her and she heard someone scream in agony: her. A white-hot demonic rage seized her.

She fought against it. *No! I have to maintain control... I can't...*

She saw Eric in her mind's eye, the way he had appeared when he first came to Melinor's house in Whitepine, ragged, sad, yet timidly hopeful. Again, as a free-lance, wearing his own armor, using his own skills, with his own friends. She felt anew her pride at seeing what he had become.

And now...

The agony seared her again. She pushed Terenil away, feeling a blood-red haze swim before her eyes.

"Zhinia Margoth!" she screamed as the troops on the battlements stared at her, wide-eyed and shocked. "I will destroy you! I will see you roast in Hell, you misbegotten Whore of Satan!"

"Saren, don't! Don't give in!" Terenil held her hands tightly, looking deep into her eyes, his gaze pleading. "It's what Margoth wants!"

The haze intensified and Saren felt her wings and horns come in again. A savage, vicious hatred coursed through her.

"She killed my brother," she snarled in a husky voice. "I will have her head on a plate with her miserable guts as decorations!"

With a surge of power, she pushed her husband back and launched herself into the air.

"I'm coming for you, Margoth! Daemon versus Lich! I will grind your bones to dust, you bitch!"

Terenil uttered an unknightly curse and passed a hand over his body. He leapt off the battlement.

"My Lord!" called DeGrance. "Where are you going!"

The Eagle Magic spell lifted Terenil DeMey into the air and he soared after his wife.

***

Tears streamed down Andyn's face.

"No!" she screamed in agony. "This can't be! No! Dar! Buck! Get up! Get up! Eric!"

She stared at the bodies of her friends lying still on the withered grass.

Margoth snarled at Andyn. "How is it that you resist me? I see the crown, but you are not Alyssa, that thrice-cursed simpleton from Alenar."

Something snapped at the sound of Alyssa's name. Andyn's terror, indecision and sorrow vanished, replaced by resolution and strength. Andyn Josette Fallbrook Eleandir placed the Crown of Saint Alyssa of Tor Haldin on her head.

"I am not even close to being as holy as Alyssa," she replied. "But I have faith. And I have been given leave to wear her crown and thus, I am your doom."

A mild, calming feeling drifted over her. A series of symbols drifted in the air before her eyes, etched in gold.

She knew them. They were names of spells, mighty magic that she would need to study for years to even attempt.

Margoth's face twisted in disgust. "Idiot. You will die like these pitiful male-things."

Andyn pointed at one of the symbols.

Time slowed and stopped. Margoth froze, a shocked expression on her face. A dome of web-like golden light covered the battlefield, curving over Margoth, Andyn and the dead Riders. The inside surface of the dome looked reflective, like very clean glass. Andyn touched another symbol and faint nets of light blue wafted down on each of her friends.

"Well done, Andyn Josette," said a voice in Andyn's head.

"Who are you?" she thought back. Margoth appeared frozen in time, as did everything else on the battlefield.

"I am Alyssa," said the voice.

"Alyssa! Your Majesty, forgive my presumption to wear your crown."

The voice laughed. "Do not be afraid, dear sister. I have no use for it any longer."

"What do I do?"

"The symbols before your eyes you might recognize," Alyssa continued, "Use these magic tools in the crown to defeat Margoth. Remember that she cannot abide truth, nor love, nor forgiveness. She knows only pride and hatred and greed."

"Yes, Majesty."

She heard the laugh again. "No longer, Andyn. There is only one Majesty, and He alone I serve. I am henceforth Alyssa to you."

Margoth struggled to move, then hissed an angry word and slapped the skull at the top of her staff. With an effort, she stumbled forward.

"Who are you speaking to?" she demanded in a harsh voice. "Don't stand there gawking like an idiot! Answer me!"

Andyn heard Alyssa sigh. She thought the saint-queen sounded sad. "She has not changed, even after all this time. Stop her, Andyn. Let her see the truth."

***

Saren DeMey knew Terenil followed her, and the part of her battling against her daemonic nature loved him for it. She sensed him flying after her, throwing caution to the winds in a desperate attempt to save her from herself.

Fortunately, the battle on the hill transfixed Margoth's army with amazement just like the defenders of Hillton. Saren flew unopposed to the hill, arriving just as a dome of golden light covered it.

She arrowed down at Margoth and bounced off the dome as if she were a pebble thrown at a castle wall. She tumbled though the air and righted herself with an effort, beating her wings and stopping in a hover. Gritting her teeth, she shot down at the dome again with the same result.

Surprise and confusion gave her the advantage for a split second and she mastered her daemon-rage with an effort. She stared down into the dome, watching Andyn Eleandir square off against the lich sorceress.

Dear God! What is this? she thought with a sudden, unwarranted thrill of hope.

Some part of her replied: *Yes, it is of God.*

She didn't even resist when Terenil swooped next to her and gathered her in his arms.

"Saren?"

Despite seeing her Eric lying dead on the blackened soil, she felt peace. "I'm okay, lover. Everything is going to be okay."

***

"That trinket will not avail you," Margoth said haughtily. She eyed Andyn imperiously. "You do not have power enough to challenge me."

Andyn smiled. "Of course not. The crown is merely a channel, a tool of faith. You probably don't know what that means, do you, Zhinia Margoth?"

"As if I would take lessons from you, a gutter harlot of a half-breed elf slut?" sneered Margoth.

Andyn shrugged. "If your magic is as effective as your insults, this will be over soon."

Margoth's eyes narrowed and she gestured with her hand, casting a stream of tiny, bright stars at her. Andyn pointed at one of the symbols in her vision and stepped backwards. She moved her hands in a complicated pattern, slapping the stars aside as if she were swatting flies. They sizzled into the ground. The symbol in Andyn's otherworldly vision faded and went dark.

The lich muttered and pointed a fist at her. A triple-forked bolt of lightning stabbed out at Andyn, who pointed at another glowing symbol. The bolt shredded into little sparkles of electricity and floated to the ground around her.

"What?!" spat Margoth.

Andyn detected a hint of doubt in her voice. "All things are possible to

243

those who Serve the Holy Way," she replied.

Margoth screamed and brandished her staff, advancing with a series of whirling motions and shouts of arcane words.

This is going to get very exciting. Andyn realized with a start.

"Hold firm and wait for your opening," came Alyssa's voice in her head.

The next few minutes became a wild maelstrom of magic. Andyn dodged and deflected clouds of fire, globs of acid, veritable storms of fire-darts, buffeting blasts of hot, fetid wind and sizzling bolts of lightning.

Grasping stone hands burst up out of the earth. She used another symbol, empowering Eleison with a blinding light, then smashed through them.

She tumbled away from ghostly nightmare beasts. They slashed her with ethereal claws, pincers and tentacles, bruising and battering her but not breaching her chainmail. She touched another symbol and a surge of energy coursed through her. She thrust her hands to the side. A blast of light suffused the area and the spectral beasts shrieked and writhed, dissipating like morning mist.

Margoth followed relentlessly, throwing spell after spell. Andyn felt her left ankle twist as she stumbled from a sudden pit that Margoth churned up out of the earth. A few of the lich's shadow bolts made it through her shields and ripped into her body with pure cold and intense pain.

Grimacing, Andyn feigned weakness. When Margoth strode forward with a triumphant expression, she stepped in to meet her, Eleison glowing with golden fire. Margoth's expression turned to shock as Andyn swung her holy weapon.

Margoth blocked with her staff. Andyn spun, swinging down at her ankles, then up at her head, then back towards her midsection. Margoth retreated, blocking each attack. Andyn flicked another attack at her head and when the lich blocked with her staff, Andyn kicked her legs out from under her.

Margoth rolled just in time to avoid getting Eleison planted in her chest, then spun back to her feet, hissing with anger. Andyn touched another symbol and placed her hand on her side and then her ankle. Silver light washed over her, removing the pain and cold and Andyn stood tall, feeling refreshed and whole.

"Who are you?" demanded Margoth. "No one has ever defied me for this long.”

“Not true, Queen of Kher Mardil,” replied Andyn, eyes flickering over the various symbols that still glowed in her other vision. “I believe Alyssa defied you just this way, long ago.”

“Alyssa isn’t alive anymore!”

Andyn suddenly stopped and regarded Margoth.

“Neither are you, Your Majesty.”

Margoth stared at her in shock and, Andyn thought, a little fear. “Untrue! I stand before you, wreathed in power! I live forever!”

Andyn smiled. “No. You cheated death with your pact with evil powers, prolonging your exit from this world. You are no more alive than a withered twig that lies beneath the dead tree.”

Margoth screamed and leaped forward, lashing out with her staff and spitting magic words. Andyn blocked the staff with Eleison. Not even caring if she got hit, she stepped in and punched Margoth in the face with a gloved hand. The lich-queen staggered back. Andyn slammed Eleison into her leg and shoulder and barely missed landing a blow on the vile crown as the lich twisted out of the way.

Zhinia Margoth actually looked like she was panting. With a savage swing at Andyn, she darted back and slammed the point of her staff into the ground, starting a low chant. A swirling void of darkness grew in the air next to Andyn.

A horrid, putrid stench issued from the vortex and Andyn felt the pull of force from it. She saw a flaming, hellish landscape in the base of the vortex and a shadowy, horned figure with four glowing red eyes advance towards her.

She set her mouth in a firm line and touched another symbol. “Heavenlight,” she whispered.

A ball of pure radiance shot from her hand and struck the vortex, blasting it into shards of darkness. Margoth reeled, struck by some of the fragmenets.

Time to end this.

Andyn Eleandir held up her hands to the sky and began to sing.

Wow! I sound really good today, she thought in a distracted sort of way.

She sang a song of praise to Verian, thanking him for his bounty and blessing and the love of family and friends in her life. A dozen other voices, pure and glorious, joined with hers from some unknown place. The melodies and harmonies blended into beauty so intense it brought tears to her eyes.

Margoth held her hands to her skull and screamed, writhing and contorting. She tried to bring her staff to bear but Andyn swung Eleison and slapped it out of her hands.

With a final luminous note, she completed the song and a shaft of light burst out of the sky. It hammered the lich-queen into the dirt.

***

"She's winning," Saren breathed.

Terenil smiled and hugged her more tightly, hovering in the smoky air.

***

Andyn looked down on Zhinia Margoth, struggling to rise.

Here was the person responsible for the massacre at Westhaven, for the attacks and slaughter and misery all along the borderlands, the one likely responsible for the Whispering Death that took Janey and Rose Lomin and so many others in Evendale and Terenai, the one who had razed Deran from the northern border to this place on the plains near Sun Lake. This was the one who had ultimately been the reason her husband had died—and the one who had just killed all her closest friends.

"This is for you," she said between clenched teeth, hefting Eleison and feeling the sting of tears in her eyes. "For Dar, Eric, Buck, Connor and Hlerv."

"Stay your hand," said Alyssa's voice. "Give her a chance."

Andyn halted in mid-stroke, amazed. "Why?"

"Because eternity is forever."

Time slowed. Andyn sighed, letting her hand drop. Another presence entered the area, a presence that occupied the same place as Andyn and yet not. She saw her reflection in the dome.

Another figure superimposed itself over her image. It was a tall human woman. She only a pure white robe with a silver belt and had golden hair with a hint of red.

"Is that you, Alyssa?"

The image smiled. "One and the same."

Zhinia Margoth coughed and wheezed from her crouch on the blackened earth. "You're dead," she managed.

"Not so. I live with my Lord and Savior forever, Zhinia," Andyn/Alyssa said. "It's all I ever wanted. Peace, love, happiness, acceptance, joy. You can have this as well, if you repent."

"Repent?" gasped Margoth. "Repent of what? Of making my own reality, of advancing knowledge, of filtering out the unfit and the rabble from society? Of creating order out of the jabbering masses of fools? Of creating a nation ruled by those with the intelligence and knowledge to truly know what is to be done? I should say not!"

Andyn/Alyssa shook her head. "Look at all the misery that your pride and selfishness has caused. No amount of perceived order is worth that. Give up your pride and sin, cousin, and take my hand. Choose life, that you may have it in the full."

Andyn's mind reeled in shock. "Cousin?" she asked Alyssa.

"Yes," came Alyssa's voice, tinged with a great sorrow. "We were like sisters once. She is of my own family, my own line. To my shame."

Margoth shook her head. "That is an empty dream, conjured up out of nothing. It is a collection of airy legends promoted by those seeking to limit those of us who have more ability and intelligence. I am Zhinia Margoth of Kher Mardil! I bow to no god! I command and all obey! I say what is to be and it becomes real, by my word and my will! I am the master of my fate! I alone!"

Alyssa's voice sighed. "Show her."

Andyn/Alyssa nodded, using another symbol. A shining mirror of air coalesced before Margoth. Somehow, from the back side, Andyn could see the image in it.

A young woman crouched on the ground, a brown-haired human who looked very much like Alyssa. The lich-princess stared up at the image in shock.

"No!" raged Margoth. "That person is no more!"

Before Andyn could make another move, Margoth thrust both hands forward. A fiery mangle of lurid lights in purple, pink, red, green and sickly yellow shot out at the mirror. The mirror reflected the lights back at the lich, but they transformed to silver and gold.

Margoth froze in the midst of that brilliance, unable to move. The pinpoints of light in her eye sockets winked out and the crown fell from her head. Both arms fell slack at her side. Zhinia Margoth, Princess of Kher Mardil and High Priestess of Garon-Zith, keeled over like a fallen tree and thumped into the earth.

Andyn let her hands drop to her side. Margoth's crumpled form shriveled and disintegrated.

"I'm sorry," she said to Alyssa.

Alyssa sighed again. "Don't blame yourself," said Alyssa's voice. "I also failed. But she chose her own fate and it was her own pride and hatred that destroyed her."

A golden mist formed in front of Andyn and now Alyssa stood before her. Her red-gold hair reminded her of someone, as did her beautiful, gentle features.

She looked at Andyn with such affection that she gave a little sob.

"Now, now, don't cry, child. All will be well."

Andyn's eyes darted around the area, lighting on the still forms of Dar, Buck, Eric, Connor and Hlerv.

"But Alyssa, my friends," she whispered, her voice breaking. "Margoth killed them."

"And you have still other magic available to you via the Crown. You placed a Preservation Net on them, yes? Time has stopped for them."

"You mean...?"

Saint Alyssa of Tor Haldin smiled. "Yes. The God who rules the Universe commands both life and death. Call your friends back. They will hear you and return."

"Really?"

Alyssa smiled, stroking Andyn's cheek. "Really," she replied, her form fading. "You have done well. Go, be reunited to them. And know that God is pleased with his beloved daughter."

Tears streamed down her cheeks as Alyssa's image faded away. Hardly daring to hope, Andyn ran to her friends.

"Dar," she said, lifting him up by his shoulders to cradle him in her lap. "Dar, come back. Please come back. Don't leave me."

Her heart leaped with joy as his chest began to rise and fall. She laid him carefully back to the earth and rushed to Eric, Buck, Connor and Hlerv in turn.

"Eric, return to me… Buck, come back. Our work isn't done. Connor, I'm here. Come back… Hlerv, it's me, Andyn. Please come back."

The still forms of her friends stirred.

"Please come back to me…"

Their eyes opened. The dome of glittering light faded and vanished.

***

Gorlak crouched low to the ground, remembering Vorquul's instructions. He slithered up behind one of Ulgrut's guards, hiding in the shadows. He drew out the magical, cold iron dagger, eyes locked on Ildrisana.

"Not possible," whispered the dark elf queen.

Gorlak's heart pounded in his chest and he licked dry lips. How could a single half-elven priestess conquer the mighty Zhinia Margoth, glittering crown or no? That mere slip of a girl had hammered down the most powerful of undead sorcerers—

—and somehow raised the Grey Riders from the dead.

The golden dome of light faded.

Two figures floated down out of the sky and alighted next to the priestess. One of them, a half-elven officer, drew a silver sword and murmured words of comfort. Blue light glowed on the bodies of the Grey Riders and they stood, shaking their heads and lifting their weapons.

The second figure, a woman, unfurled ivory bat wings and drew a glowing sword and shining dagger. Her dark eyes swirled with rainbow colors as she glared at Margoth's troops.

A chill of terror ripped through Gorlak. He remembered a time long ago when a goblin shaman had summoned a daemon to deal with a rival. That daemon had looked a lot like this one, except the one here on the field had ivory wings and horns, not deep red like the one from long ago. He re-membered the screams, the blood, the horror. His hand trembled and he dropped the dagger.

Cursing himself for a fool, he retrieved it with shaking hands.

"Aha! They are weak!" rumbled Ulgrut, the ogre chieftain. "We can take them."

"Yes!" hissed Vorquul. "Attack now we will!"

The Ja'al cleric, Zanilor, lifted his shield and hefted a mace that flamed with pink light. "You fools. That's the White Demon."

"What do I care, demon or no?" barked Zirta. "We are many and they are few."

Gorlak crept low to the ground, looking for a gap in Ildrisana's guards. He used a dead ogre and a human corpse as cover.

One of the Riders, a gnome, stepped back from his comrades as they grimly readied weapons. As Gorlak watched, the gnome reached into his armor and took out a tiny bag, then put a hand into it. He pulled out a crowned helmet of dead black that seemed to suck in all the light near it.

Gorlak's heart skipped a beat. He had an odd feeling that this was some-thing very important.

The smaller, dark-haired human Rider with a sparkling black sword spotted the gnome. "Hlerv!" he called. "What are you doing?"

"What I have to, Dar," answered the gnome.

The others turned at his call.

"No!" cried the half-elf woman. "Hlerv, don't! It's evil!"

The gnome shook his head. "It won't carry more than one person now that Margoth is destroyed. I have to do this on my own, Andyn."

"Wait!" said a half-elf male. "We can help you!"

"I'm sorry, Eric," said the gnome. "This is my fight, my vengeance, my inheritance."

He put the helm on his head. Instantly, a whirling cyclone of shadow and mist surrounded him and he vanished.

Ildrisana drew back to her black-armored guards. She reached for her wand and a sizzling green disk of fire leaping up around her. Gorlak thought she looked nervous and unsure— an unusual sight.

"Now!" bellowed Ulgrut. He lumbered forward with his personal guard.

"Za'Arak Volchuul!" shouted Vorquul, leading his goblin troops towards the Riders. Next to him, the Kaftu queen Zirta let out a long howl as her pack mates charged, weapons raised. Goblin shamans, elf wizards and Kaftu witch doctors gestured, sending waves of fire, jets of acid or beams of red light at the Grey Riders.

The woman called Andyn looked pale and wan, but serene. She raised a hand as if touching something in the air. A golden screen of light pulsed out from her, surrounding the Riders, the daemon and the half-elven man with the silver sword. The spells of Margoth's allies broke on that golden dome like water dashed up on rocks. Andyn wavered, putting a hand to her head.

"This is folly!" screamed Zanilor to Ildrisana.

She shook her head. "They are still weak! We can take them!"

She held out a clawed hand and three sizzling balls of lightning shot out at their enemies. The man with the silver sword made a motion with his hand. The sword glowed and the lightning balls veered off course, slamming into the ground in clouds of sparks.

Kaftu, Ogres, and goblins swarmed at the Riders in a wave of steel and magic. The Riders drew back near the half-elven woman and the White Demon, their weapons shining with bright light and flame.

Gorlak watched, biding his time, eyes flickering to Ildrisana even as he watched the battle. The Riders and their two new allies slashed, struck, dodged and wheeled in an intricate dance of death. They cut down ogre warriors, goblin commandos, Kaftu rangers and dark elves alike. Andyn remained at the center, wearing the star-bright, silvery crown, touching the air before her as if pointing at some unseen letters. Each time a Rider or the half-daemon or her mate took a hit, a flare of blue light rejuvenated or healed them.

In the forefront, the half-daemon girl swirled like a tornado of light and steel and ivory wings, dropping her attackers until she stood knee-deep in the slain.

Face contorted in rage, Ildrisana unloaded a spear of blackest night at her. The daemon snarled, her eyes glowing red as she hurtled forwards. Her armor flashed and the dark spear shattered. Her dagger blazed like the sun.

Gorlak gasped and fell back, momentarily blinded. Ulgrut roared a challenge, his eyes maddened. Vorquul shrieked a curse, joining him in a charge. They leapt in, swinging with mace, battle axe and dagger, using every skill at their disposal.

Gorlak's jaw dropped. He had never seen such a display of speed and ferocity. Ulgrut never stopped moving, his deadly axe missing the woman by mere inches. Vorquul lashed out, changing direction frequently, leaping in and out, somersaulting and dodging. The combatants disengaged, the daemon using her wings to dart up into the air. Vorquul's sides heaved, he bled from a half-dozen wounds and Ulgrut leaned on his axe, limping.

The man with the silver sword arrived below the daemon and she floated down to him. He gave her a quick glance.

"You'll have to get those looked at, Saren," he said, eyes flickering to her cuts and bruises.

"Just a scratch, Terenil," she replied in a husky, sultry voice.

Gorlak shot a look at Ildrisana. The elven queen still shot magic bolts at Eric and the halfling, facing away from Gorlak. Her guards didn't even look in his direction.

The Riders, though wounded, stood amid a field of dead enemies. Eric now supported Andyn. Terenil and Saren looked by far the more fit and able to fight.

Gorlak remembered his instructions from King Vorquul. *"If Margoth falls and it not go well for us, at least we take the elves down. Strike when queen not looking."* He saw his opening and leaped.

"For the *Za'Arak!*" he shouted. "Slay the elves!"

Either she heard him or had some magical spell in place to warn her. His stroke with the magic iron dagger missed its mark between her ribs and slashed her hip and flank instead. She screamed in agony, slapping at him with a hand that sparked with electricity.

Daggers of pain lanced into Gorlak. He hurtled through the air, landing with a thump on a dead Kaftu.

"Treachery!" the queen screamed as she staggered to the side and fell onto a dead ogre. "We are betrayed! Elves to me!"

Gorlak's vision faded. He angrily shook his head to clear it.

Vorquul and Ulgrut leaped in at Saren and Terenil. The pair gave ground and defended, moving in an elegant dance, covering each other's backs and coordinating their movements. Vorquul, slowed now by his wounds, made a critical error and over-lunged, hitting Terenil in the shoulder with his mace, but received the full length of the silver sword through his heart.

Ulgrut swung, then grabbed Saren by the leg as she fluttered back, and yanked her in towards him. She obliged, letting him jerk her towards him, then impaled him through the eye and temple with her two blades. He tottered as she jerked her weapons out. Ulgrut fell with a heavy thud.

A different, wavering howl rang out. With bleary eyes, Gorlak saw Ildrisana retreating with her guards as Kaftu turned their javelins and arrows at the ogres. Goblins yelled and swarmed forwards, laying into the elves. The entire area became a maelstrom of chaos.

Somewhere in the melee, an errant quarterstaff hit Gorlak in the helmet and everything went black.

***

"My Lord DeGrance," rumbled Bishop Bannister. "I suggest a sortie now."

DeGrance hefted his greatsword. "I do believe you are right, Excellency."

The gates of Hillton swung open and, with a great shout, the besieged Deranese swept out, led by the Fire Eagles and Blue Ravens.

They hit the disorganized army of the Dark Rider like an avalanche.

***

He dimly heard voices, as if from a great distance. Next he heard footsteps, heavy boots, the jangle and clank of mail and armor, and the fluttering of banners.

His sense of smell told him he lay on a battlefield: blood, offal, burned things, sweat and other carnage of war.

He remembered the battle, his task, his attack on Ildrisana, partially successful, and then…

"Hey, this one's still alive," came a man's voice.

Small deft hands bound his wrists and ankles. Dirt and gravel crunched next to him.

Damned sunlight!

He squinted up. A halfling with dark hair and dark eyes sat next to him.

Dar, the human in bright armor with a long sword on his back approached next, accompanied by Eric and Andyn. The men held her up with sheltering arms. Even as tired as she looked, Andyn held herself with the bearing of a queen. The shining crown emanated waves of subtle yet earth-shattering power. A taller, lanky human with a golden sword and steel shield followed.

Dar shook his head. "I'm amazed anyone survived all that, Eric. Your sister is a machine of destruction."

Eric helped lower Andyn to a sitting position on a large rock. He grinned at Dar. "Tell me about it. We tried giving her time-outs and grounding, but it didn't take."

Andyn shouldered him with a tired smile.

With a start, Gorlak recognized the smaller human as he crouched down in front of him. He remembered a group of freelance mercenaries who had just liberated young dragonlings from the clutches of Gorlak's former employer, Halkith.

"I know this one," Dar said.

"Really?" asked Buck. He hefted an odd helmet in his hands, one with a diamond attached to a peculiar arm-like structure. "They all look alike after a while."

Dar watched Gorlak with narrowed eyes as the goblin struggled to sit up. "No, I know you, don't I?"

"Yes, you know me," answered Gorlak.

The Grey Riders looked so shocked he was momentarily proud of himself.

"Sweet angels," said Eric. "He speaks Humana."

Dar smiled. "In the forest near Whitehorse, right?"

Gorlak nodded.

"How is it you know Humana?" asked Andyn.

"I work for Aalre and Halkith," Gorlak replied, keeping a wary eye on her. "I adviser, translator, courier, sergeant."

"So how did you end up here?" asked the halfling.

Gorlak shrugged. "You Riders kill Aalre, Halkith. I have no job. I search for mother-tribe, find work for King Vorquul. I do job again: aide, translator, courier, this time captain."

"We won't hurt you," said Dar. "Will you stay here and not run?"

Gorlak laughed. "Where I go? Your army has field."

The one named Buck chuckled. "Good one, goblin! Untie him Connor. He won't go anywhere."

"But be nice," admonished Andyn, fixing Gorlak with gorgeous amber eyes. "He's been through a lot."

Gorlak watched in amazement as the Riders all sat around him. They, the slayers of the mighty Zhinia Margoth, sat on the ground with a goblin prisoner. They could have just turned him over to a lowly private.

"I'm Dar, this is Buck, Eric, Connor and Andyn."

"Where is other small one?" Gorlak asked.

They exchanged glances and Gorlak wondered.

"He, um, left," said Andyn. "What's your name?"

"Gorlak."

"Do you know what Margoth was trying to do?" she asked. "Why attack Deran?"

Gorlak mulled over the councils and discussions he had heard over the course of weeks and months, particularly the last few. "Not sure. I not king. Know that Margoth wanted a Helm or something. It get her close to human king. Maybe she kill him and get lands."

The Riders exchanged a look.

"That actually makes sense, knowing Margoth," Andyn mused.

"But the rest doesn't," said Connor. "Could she actually think she would take over Deran?"

Gorlak made a face. "Maybe Ja'al want it. She want something else. Maybe they trade later."

The Riders looked at each other.

Eric nodded. "That's pretty smart, Gorlak."

Despite the oddity of conversing with his sworn enemies, Gorlak felt a surge of pride. He shrugged again. "Maybe not. I just goblin captain. Not king. Not talk to Ja'al in councils every day."

The crown on Andyn's head seemed shinier, almost glowing. Her eyes measured him and though he found it disconcerting, he wasn't afraid.

"What do you think of working for the Ja'al?" she asked.

He made a face and spat. "Think they know everything. Treat *Za'Arak* like slaves, like dirt. They arrogant, losers."

Buck chuckled again. "Despite what I see, I'm beginning to like this guy."

"And Margoth?" she persisted.

Gorlak shuddered. "Glad you smash her into dust. She very… wrong."

"What will you do now?" asked Connor.

Gorlak felt a sinking feeling and looked down. "Prison I think. No one care about one goblin."

"Would you ever work for the Ja'al again?"

He shook his head.

Andyn smiled at him and he felt suddenly warm and peaceful. It was unfamiliar, but he liked it instantly. "Wait here a moment."

She stood, closed her eyes and whispered a word. The crown glowed again and a mild blue light coursed over her body. She opened her eyes, looking a little better.

"It won't last that long," said Eric.

"Long enough to get me through this and into a bath and bed. There are wounded who need healing," she replied, walking away from them.

Gorlak saw a group of people gathered in discussion, their armor shiny and bearing weapons that glowed with magic. A portly human with a beard and mustache smiled at her, his armor covered by a hauberk with the symbol of the Christ-god. Andyn bowed to him and began conversing with him and two other figures, one of which was the half-elf named Terenil and the other…

Saren…

Horror and fear paralyzed him. He couldn't tear his gaze from the half-daemon with the ivory wings who slew so efficiently and effectively.

A hand touched his shoulder and he looked up. Eric smiled at him. "What's the matter?"

"Daemon woman…"

"Saren can look scary sometimes but she's all right, believe me."

Gorlak shuddered, dropping his eyes. "King Vorquul's shaman summon one of those to kill rivals in the tribe: warriors, women, children. She wants to kill me. I am enemy. She hate me!"

He squeezed his eyes shut at the memory.

"Gorlak, don't worry," said Eric, sounding as kind as Andyn.

He opened his eyes and looked up.

Eric smiled. "That's my half-sister. I can assure you she doesn't hate you. She hated Margoth, for sure, but not you. You can't hurt anyone. She isn't mean, I promise."

Gorlak's mouth dropped open. His mind whirled, trying to come to grips with what he had just heard. "You? Sister? What?"

Andyn continued her conference with the couple. Eric waved to the Saren, who smiled and actually blew him a kiss. She waved back, not at Eric, but at Gorlak. He sat stunned.

"It's a long story. Don't worry. She looks scary but she's actually very kind and loving."

Gorlak had heard the word 'loving' before but never in relation to any of the daemon-kind. He watched Saren and the others for a while. The more he watched, the more his terror and loathing melted away.

Saren smiled and hugged Andyn, then left, hand-in-hand with Terenil.

Gorlak couldn't believe his eyes. *What is this strange world now?*

Andyn returned to Gorlak and held out her hand. "I have a proposition for you, Captain Gorlak. How would you like a new job?"

Chapter Seventeen- To Serve the Holy Way

"You were right, Mother. I should have been an engineer."

Dar Cabot smiled at his mother as she entered his pavilion.

She gathered him into a tight hug. "Yes, you scoundrel. You should listen to your mother."

"Or," said his father, entering the chamber with a broad, rascally grin, "you should listen to her about everything else except your career."

Elizabeth Cabot gave her husband a sour look. "You're not helping, Stephen."

"I know." The grin remained as his father put his arm around her.

Dar hugged them both. "It has been quite a wild ride."

"We're just so glad to see you're okay. They said something about that horrid Zhinia Margoth killing you but that's obviously a false rumor."

Dar looked into his mother's eyes. "No," he said. "That part was true. The part about Andyn using the Crown of Saint Alyssa to raise us up again—that is also true."

His parents' eyes widened in horror, then in wonder.

Elizabeth reached up to cup his face. "Then, God sent you back to us."

He smiled. "Yes, Mother. For what purpose, I'm not sure yet."

His mother stared into his eyes, then shook herself briskly.

"Let's have a look at you," his mother said, holding him at arm's length and examining his new uniform with a critical eye. She ran her hands over his deep green doublet with the gold chasing and gold band at the collar.

She stopped, eyes pensive, as she traced the symbol of Saint Kira's Order, a rose and mace worked in silver and red thread on the front of the cloth.

"You actually look presentable," his father said, sounding impressed. "They even made sure the trousers matched."

"New boots too," said Dar.

"Your grandparents would be proud," Elizabeth Cabot said in a soft voice.

Dar felt the pain and regret again, then sighed and steeled himself. "They are proud, Mother. They told me so."

She gasped and put a hand to her mouth. "You found them?"

"Come here, both of you, and sit down," Dar said, motioning to a couple of camp chairs by his bedside.

They sat. Distracted for a moment while he tried to figure out how to tell them, Dar's eyes roamed over his pavilion. A mobile apartment sent from Oakmoor for him and for each of the Grey Riders, it came complete with a main room, antechamber and bathing room. The bed looked like a normal one for a home, except that it was collapsible and the three flexible mattresses rolled up easily. Orderlies could pack it in a matter of minutes.

He brought himself back to his parents, smiling at them.

"Yes, I found Grandma and Grandpa."

His mother reached for his father's hand. "I don't expect they were alive, from your expression."

"No, Mother." Calmly, taking his time, he told them about finding his grandparents as wraiths enslaved to the Helm of Shadows. He related their battle and the damage they did to his friends. Finally, he told them how he broke their evil geas long enough for them to tell him how to free them by destroying them.

Her hands tightened on her dress and Stephen held her close. She blinked rapidly, tears in her eyes. "I knew the most likely outcome was that they were dead, but this…"

He took her hand. "Mom, I'm so sorry. If there was a way to bring them back, I would have. They just seemed so forlorn. There was no other way."

Elizabeth let out a deep sigh and smiled though her lip trembled. "I understand, sweetheart. Part of me always hoped that they could come back alive. But how did you manage it?"

Dar brought Rindara Starblade from the weapon rack. He drew the weapon out. His mother and father gasped.

"What thing is this?" Stephen breathed.

"A sword of the Elohir, from Celestia."

His mother wiped at her eyes and nodded. She stroked the blade gently, watching the stars glitter in the dark metal.

"Did they suffer?" she asked so softly he almost didn't hear.

He put his arm around her. "They did not. I saw them after I released them, Mom. They looked just like I remembered them, when they left us to go on their quest. Then they looked up into a shaft of light. They were so happy. I'm sure they didn't suffer at all."

Elizabeth nodded again, then burst into tears and leaned into Stephen. Dar joined his father in holding her.

She pulled herself up and smiled at him. "I'm being silly, I know. They are free of that horrible thing and you're the one who set them free."

She kissed him. "I'm so proud of you."

He felt a lump in his throat. "I did my best, Mom. I wish I could have brought them back to Forester."

"So do I."

A light bell rang outside the pavilion and Elizabeth stood taller as Stephen and Dar released her. She turned away, drying her tears and straightening her dress as an orderly opened the tent flap to the antechamber.

"Dar Cabot? I am sent to assist you in preparing for the audience with the King."

Stephen raised an eyebrow at him. "Servants?"

Dar shrugged. "I've gotten used to it for the past week or so. King Phillip won't let us join in the mopping-up efforts, so we've been here resting and going to so many meetings with various people that I'm going stir crazy. But it's nice having the extra help," he added with a smile at the orderly, who nodded.

Stephen nodded. "Just don't let this get to your head, boy."

Dar grinned back. "Who, me?"

His parents left and the orderly helped him change into his chainmail armor. He added a breastplate, greaves, pauldrons and dark green leather gloves with gold piping. Over this, he draped a hauberk of Saint Kira's Order, again dark green with the Order's symbol worked in silver and crimson and gold piping. Rindara Starblade went into its scabbard on his back.

The orderly brushed off his clothing and boots with a professional efficiency, bowed and left.

Dar took a deep breath and walked out of the pavilion.

"Nice clothes," said a voice next to him. "Going to a coronation or just showing off?"

Dar gave Eric Indidarc a look of mock disdain. "At least I have something to show off."

Eric wore a white hauberk over his chainmail, the front worked with the gold angel-wings-and-sword symbol of Saint Michael's Order. His longsword hung at his hip and he wore white boots.

These Dar noted with interest. "Guess who's going to get muddy boots at the first opportunity?"

Eric nodded. "After this is over, I invite you to the attempt."

They strode over to another set of pavilions. Buck Bydecy and Connor Lomin emerged from their temporary dwellings. Buck wore a deep grey hauberk marked with the sign of a kingfisher bird and a wave over his banded mail. Khelios shone at his side. Connor had his trademark black leathers and the new sword Tiuz.

A massive pavilion dominated the hill nearby. The royal standard of Deran fluttering from a flagpole. A table stood in front of the giant tent and rows of chairs sat on the earth of the churned battlefield. Dar saw a set of boxes of burnished wood with silver chasing on the table.

Knights of Saint Michael and Saint Raphael stood guard around the perimeter. A trio of griffon-riders circled overhead on patrol.

"Well, at least you clean up nicely," said a familiar alto voice.

Dar turned. Andyn Eleandir sauntered up to them, a cheerful smile on her face. Her golden hair, braided and looped over her shoulder, lay on a rich purple hauberk with the seven silver stars of Terenai. She wore brightly polished chainmail and carried Eleison at her belt. On her head, the Crown of Saint Alyssa shone with a nimbus of holy fire.

She had never looked more glorious.

He felt a pang of longing, seeing another half-elven girl in his mind's eye, one with red-gold hair and amber eyes.

"It took three squires to wrestle Buck into the bath," reported Connor.

"Four," retorted Buck.

"You look great, Andyn," said Eric.

She blushed. "It's amazing what the attentions of a good maidservant can do."

"Grey Riders?"

They bowed to Sir Colin Parker, who bowed in return.

"Please follow me for the ceremony," he said, not smiling, but Dar detected a twinkle in his eye.

By now, the chairs in front of the royal pavilion were almost full. Dar saw Lord Nolan and Lady Ellen, their children Timmy and Alice, Lord Jalek and Lady Riti of Dorn's Hall, Caridan Jas and many other people he didn't recognize. Some of them had writing boards and either sketched furiously or made notes on papers. Seamus and Miriam Lomin sat in the front row next to Brendan and Cerys and Deena and Darren. Darren currently was involved in a long explanation to Jack Bydecy, sitting next to Alfred, Buck's father. Dar's parents chatted quietly with Melinor and a handsome, golden-haired couple who could only be Andyn's parents.

A knight in a black hauberk embroidered with a golden chalice opened the tent flap and stepped next to the table. "All rise for Their Majesties, King Phillip the Second and Queen Ahlana the Third, Sovereigns Royal of Deran, and their noble guests," he announced.

Colin led the Riders to the side, in line with the table, as a dark-haired man in his late thirties strode out with a dazzling raven-haired woman on his arm. They both wore white trimmed with dark blue and the arms of the Royal house, a cross and crown under three stars, worked in gold on the front. Gold crowns shone in the late morning sunlight on their heads.

The Riders bowed with the rest of the assembly. King Phillip smiled and nodded, as did the Queen. A brisk wind ruffled the flags and pennons, warm with summer.

Others filed out of the pavilion behind the King and Queen: a slender elven man wearing robes of grey and red, a halfling in a black velvet doublet and trousers with a silver chain of office on his breast, a blonde human woman in sea-green with the arms of Astarel worked in gold on her tabard, a burly, bearded man with the livery of Saint Michael's Order, a brunette with the livery of Saint Kira's, and an elderly human in a black cassock and Roman collar with a purple skullcap lined with white.

"Honored guests," proclaimed the knight, reading from a scroll. "Kindly attend. We are gathered by Royal Decree on this field of battle to recognize and reward the efforts of those free-lance warriors known as the Grey Riders, sergeants-brevet all, in the service of Lord Nolan Hanford, Baron of Forester."

Dar felt the butterflies start as he looked across the crowd. So many of them! They all looked rather important, judging from their finery. He picked out Terenil and Saren immediately. The Countess of Tallemar looked stunning in a deep purple gown. She winked at him.

He felt himself relax.

"The Grey Riders will approach Their Majesties and their guests."

Colin Parker led Dar and his friends to the long table in front of the King and Queen. Dar bowed with the other Riders, right on cue.

King Phillip addressed the assembly. "First order of business is deferred to Edward Cardinal Simpson, Papal Nuncio to Damora. Your Eminence?"

The priest with the purple skullcap smiled and bowed to the King and Queen, then moved in front of the table.

"Andyn Fallbrook Eleandir, I understand you have something particular for me."

Andyn bowed low. "Yes, Holy Eminence," she replied. "Saint Alyssa of Tor Haldin bids me provide you with this."

She removed the crown from her head and knelt before the Papal Nuncio, holding it out to him. He regarded her and the crown silently for a while, watching her with dark eyes. The crowd murmured.

"You give this to me freely, without reservation? As the finder of the Crown, it is legally yours to do with as you please."

Andyn nodded. "Yes, Eminence. I—"

Her voice faltered. She dropped her gaze to the churned earth and Dar thought she might cry. She looked tired and worried.

He wondered if the Crown, because of its great power, also placed a burden on whomever wore it. He remembered Andyn after the battle, moving among the wounded, using the Crown to heal those she could. She had wept when she realized there were some beyond her help—she had spent much of the relic's energy in defeating the Dark Rider. He had helped Eric get her to a cart. She was so weak she could barely stand. Eleven hours later, after the rising of the sun, both Andyn and the Crown emerged recharged.

If I had all that power, I'd go crazy trying to decide who to help.

Andyn raised her head, eyes shining. "It was given to me by a very holy woman. I pray that I might serve Verian faithfully enough to be like her someday. I have wielded it for a short time and… it is not meant for me."

Edward Simpson regarded her quietly for a while. "No, dear lady, by your words and actions, you testify that you are among the few who could wear it without sinful pride. Your humility and spirit of righteousness are evident to me. Still, if the Saint herself bid you relinquish it to me, I will keep it safe until it is needed."

Something in the Nuncio's tone caught Dar's attention. The Nuncio's eyes flickered to someone in the assembly.

Dar froze when he realized the Nuncio had looked directly at Saren DeMey. Saren returned the Nuncio's gaze calmly.

Why?

The Nuncio accepted the crown and opened one of the boxes with a whispered word, then placed it inside and murmured another word. The box closed, then vanished in a sparkle of gold and white.

Andyn looked relieved and a bit sad at the same time.

"Thank you, Andyn," said Edward with a smile. "You are a credit to your house and your faith."

Andyn rose and returned to her place with the Riders.

King Phillip bowed to the Nuncio, who returned to his place. "Honored guests," the king continued, "witness now that it is Our Royal Will that these Grey Riders receive honors commensurate with their sacrifices and courage in ending the scourge of the Dark Rider Zhinia Margoth and bringing peace to Our land."

"The honors are to be awarded by the following guests," Ahlana announced. "Lady Emily Greyfair of the Royal Court of Astarel, Countess Greymark, for Buckminster Horatio Bydecy; Mister George Windrain, First Minister of Defense of the Republic of Evendale, for Connor Tiberius Lomin; Colonel Lord Sir Roderick Danforth, Baron of Stillwater and

Knight Commander of Saint Michael's Order for Eric Daniel Indidarc; Lady Sir Kathryn Roberson, Baroness of Fairview in Eldir and Knight Commander of Saint Kira's Order for Darius Richard Cabot; and His Grace the Duke of Eleth-Anor, Knight of the Diamond Gryphon, Rakshan Aluin, cousin of His Imperial Majesty, Brion IV, of Terenai for Ardyn Josette Fallbrook Eleandir."

The woman in the sea-green livery stepped around the table in front of Buck, holding a golden coronet of three points. Likewise, the other dignitaries moved before the honorees, holding circlets of their own, or in the case of the halfling, a shiny golden brooch about twice as big as a gold piece.

"The Grey Riders will please kneel," the knight in the dark livery announced. Dar heard the ruffle of cloth as the audience rose. Dar knelt.

Dar closed his eyes. "Marcus the Fourth, King of Astarel," Lady Greyfair intoned, "does will and decree that Buckminster Horatio Bydecy is now a Sword-Knight of Astarel."

He heard the hiss of steel. "You are Sir Buckminster, Knight of the Royal House, a title that will transfer to you, your house and the heirs of your body in perpetuity as long as the line of Bydecy shall endure. Arise, Sir Buckminster."

Dar heard the halfling's voice.

"As a Republic, Evendale does not confer titles or knighthoods. However, we do reward our faithful sons for service well-delivered on behalf of all good people. For your courage and selflessness, the Republic of Evendale is proud to bestow you the Medal of the Faithful Protector, one of the highest honors we can give. If you have need of it, speak the word I will give you and a sword of light will spring up to defend you or anyone else near you."

"Eric Indidarc," Colonel Danforth rumbled. "King Phillip of Deran informs the Order that you aspire to join our number in our mission of protection, service and sacrifice for the People of God. By your efforts, you have shown that you already are well-versed in the principles we hold dear. By the authority of my office as Baron of Stillwater and Knight Commander of the Order, I hereby name you Eric Daniel Indidarc, Knight of Saint Michael. Arise, Sir Indidarc."

Dar fought butterflies as he heard footsteps on the ground before him. "Dar Cabot," Lady Kathryn said, "for years you have served in our Order as a Squire Aspirant, seeking to prove yourself worthy of the trust of the peoples of the lands in protecting and aiding them."

Hands placed a circlet on his brow. "By the authority of my office as Knight Commander of the Order and Baroness of Fairview, I name you Darius Richard Cabot, Knight of Saint Kira."

With a hiss of steel, he felt the touch of a sword on his shoulders and head.

"Rise, Sir Cabot of Saint Kira's."

He did so, opening his eyes. Lady Kathryn, an auburn-haired and plain-looking woman with startling green eyes, smiled at him.

The Duke of Eleth-Anor actually chuckled as he stood in front of Andyn. Ralshan could have been twenty years old, a hundred and twenty, or two hundred. Like all elves, he seemed in the bright vigor of young adulthood. He wore a gold, nine-pointed crown with rubies.

"Never in my wildest imaginings could I have thought that the daughter of our loyal and faithful servant Colonel Eleandir would be in this place, at this time, doing great deeds for the betterment of all. Yet here you are, my child."

He took a gold circlet with purple gems from one of the boxes and placed it on her head, then laid his hands there and closed his eyes. "By the honor of my house and of the Elven people, in the name of our Most August Emperor, long may he reign in justice, and in the name of the most Blessed and Holy Verian, I name you Andyn Josette Fallbrook Eleandir, Knight of Mindra and Lady of the Empire. This title and its honors will remain with you and all the heirs of your body and their assigns, as long as the House of Eleandir shall endure."

He took both her hands in his and gently kissed them. "Welcome, Lady Andyn."

She nodded, eyes shiny with tears.

"Remain here a moment," he continued, moving to a tiny silver box to draw forth a brilliant object that scattered rainbow reflections everywhere.

"Upon the recommendation of their Most Serene Majesties, Phillip and Ahlana of Deran, by his Holy Eminence Edward Cardinal Simpson of the

Christian faith, and by his Imperial Majesty Brion IV Aluin of Terenai, my Royal Cousin, I am authorized to award this to you."

He pinned the object to Andyn's tunic as she watched him with wondering eyes.

"Receive this emblem of that most rare of Orders, an accomplishment and honor due to only a few persons on Damora, a feat made remarkable due to the extreme dangers and mortal peril faced in earning it. Lady Andyn Josette Fallbrook Eleandir, I name you Lichslayer and Light of Justice. Long may you be a sword of virtue striking down Evil in all its forms."

Dar felt dizzy.

The Lichslayer title was held by less than twenty people in all the Northern Alliance. Even Melinor didn't have one of those. Only the rank of Demonslayer was more prized, and he knew there were only a handful of people in the entire world with *that* title.

"The Grey Riders will please face the assembly," announced the knight with the black surcoat.

Dar turned around. He thought it was going to be a close contest on who would burst with pride first: Melinor, his mother, or Saren.

"Sound the trumpets! Hail the Grey Riders!" shouted the knight.

In answer, trumpets rang out from around the area in a complex melody and harmony. The people applauded and cheered. Dar could only smile shyly, watching Deena and Darren Lomin hopping up and down in their excitement. Timmy and Alice Hanford stared at him with shining eyes.

The crowd quieted as King Phillip stood forth with his hands raised.

"Honored guests, everyone is invited to a feast in honor of the Riders Grey, to be held on the lawn outside the city gates of Hillton, courtesy of our host, Count Marcel DeGrance. I will see each and every one of you there."

The trumpets blared again as King and Queen and the notables reentered the royal pavilion.

Dar's eyes went to his friends, still hearing the cheers of the crowd and feeling every eye on them. Even resplendent in their finery, with freshly awarded emblems of their renown, he couldn't shake the image of a dirty, desperate and scared group of freelances who went forth to their doom knowing they might not see each other again. Yet, here they were. They looked as awkward as he felt.

Unbidden, a smile came to his lips.

Buck gave one of his trademark grins in return and clapped his hands together. "So, what's for lunch?"

***

She awoke in the morning sunlight, whispering his name, her dream still hovering in her mind.

"Dar?"

Megan Alenar sat up in bed and stared at the light shining in through her balcony windows.

Just like the others but now different.

Previously, her dreams of Dar and his friends featured impressions of them being in danger, menaced by shadowy figures in a dark wood or a ruined tower. This one was more clear.

She shuddered.

She heard a knock on the door to the adjoining suite.

"Megan?"

"I'm up, Brandi. Come in."

Her sister opened the door and peeked in, her strawberry-blonde hair falling in waves over her shoulders. "Did I wake you?"

"No. I just woke up."

Brandi padded in and dropped on the bed next to her. Megan could tell something bothered her.

"Another dream?" she asked.

Brandi nodded. "Just like the last few but different. More clear, strange, frightening and joyful all at once."

Megan nodded. "Mine too."

Brandi twisted the hem of her shift in her hands. "I saw Eric and Dar and the others on a shadowy field, menaced by a skeletal queen."

"So did I."

Brandi looked up. "Did Andyn have a golden crown?"

"Yes. And everyone fell except her and then, I don't know, a swirling of light and dark? Then a flash of brilliance and the skeleton shattered on the ground."

Brandi sighed. "I think maybe we're just wondering and hoping in our hearts that they will find a way to destroy Zhinia Margoth and that they'll be okay, but worried that they might…"

"Die?" Megan choked out past the lump in her throat.

Brandi's turned away to the sunlit balcony instead. Megan took her hand and the sisters sat quietly in the morning, listening to birds chirping outside.

They heard a knock at the outer door.

"Are you up? And decent?" her uncle asked.

Brandi gave a roguish smile. "Yes. And we're always decent."

Megan suppressed a giggle.

Next they heard Daphne's exasperated voice. "Agreed. But are you clothed?"

"Of course," said Brandi. "Come in."

"Good," said Daphne as she swept into the room, already dressed for the day. "Because we have some wonderful news for you."

"What do you mean?" Megan asked, shooting a glance at Brandi.

Stephen plopped down in a chair. "We received word through our sources here in Meridian of a great battle fought near Hillton in Deran, and a great victory won. It is said that one Dark Rider fought seven of Grey."

Megan's heart skipped a beat. Brandi whirled to her uncle.

"You mean Eric and the Riders?"

Daphne nodded, reclining on the bed with them and taking their hands. "Yes. A lich named Zhinia Margoth was defeated and destroyed. The prophecy has come true."

Megan suddenly felt as light as a feather. She was sure that she could fly to the sun if she so wished. She held her hands in front of her mouth in prayer and closed her eyes.

"Thank you, God! They won, they won…" she whispered.

"Yes," said Daphne. "You will see them again."

Megan sat quietly, overcome with so many emotions. Brandi leaned against her, eyes closed and a peaceful look on her face.

Daphne put her arms around them. "I know, Megan. The life of a free-lance is uncertain and dangerous, as you know, but the Lord watches over us."

"It's more than that," said Brandi. She told Daphne and Stephen of their identical dreams.

"Sometimes, girls," their aunt said, shaking her head. "You scare the daylights out of me."

Megan smiled. "How do you think we feel?"

"Well," said Stephen, "They will have quite the tale to tell you when you meet again, as will you."

"Speaking of which," said Daphne, holding up a white envelope. "This came back with the dispatch bag from St. Martin's along with those two letters you were so interested in. Our new assignment."

Brandi opened her eyes. "Which is?"

Stephen nodded. "Find survivors of the royal houses of Torosc and, if possible, find out how to return them to their thrones."

***

"That was some party," Eric said.

Dar continued cinching the harness on Virasi. "I'll say," he replied. "Everything was delicious, the wines were amazing, and the desserts, well, I don't even know the names of some of the dishes they served."

Eric chuckled, leading his pegasus, Niveral. "Connor did."

Dar shrugged. "Halfling."

He leaned on his saddle. "I see that Puup somehow managed to make it back again."

Eric nodded. "I swear that pigeon will outlive all of us. Unless Connor gets desperate for squab."

Dar smiled. "Halfling."

They both laughed.

The wind ruffled the manes of their mounts. Virasi looked at Dar with a dark eye, as if to prod him to say something.

They stood on a high knoll near the battlefield, a place of ruin no more. Two weeks of hard work and industry by the people of Hillton, Forester and Sun Plains turned it once again into a clear space along the highway to the city by the lake. In time, the grass and plants would grow back.

The pegasi… well, suffice it to say that the governments of Evendale,

Deran and Terenai spared no expense in finding the flying horses and bringing them to Hillton to be reunited with their masters.

Connor, Buck and Andyn brought their own pegasi out, putting on their harness, saddles and saddle bags. Each of them now possessed a common gift, safely stored in their saddlebags: Queen Ahlana's own seamstresses provided them with light grey caparisons for their mounts, emblazoned with a black pegasus at the shoulder and decorated at the hem with their names and titles sewn in gold thread in Ecclesia, Veriani, Elven and Dwarven.

For high feast days, parades, and occasions of state, the King told them at the celebration feast with a twinkle in his eye.

As far as the celebration went, the Crown had paid for not only the party with the honorees, their families and the dignitaries, but also for a general feast for the people of Hillton, Sun Plains, Forester and Dorn's Hall, a development met with gratitude by a traumatized population.

Dar's eyes drifted northward. A day after the awards ceremony, the fallen defenders were carefully and lovingly sorted and prepared for burial. Large wains of honor carried them to either the National Cemetery in Oakmoor, the graveyard at Saint Anne's in Forester, the hillside at Sun Plains, or the burial cairns at Dorn's Hall.

He thought of a particular grave at Saint Anne's for Father Ander. He felt a pang of regret. By now, the peoples of those places were back at their ruined communities, left to figure out how to rebuild after the invasion.

So many. All because of Zhinia Margoth's pride and ambition and unwillingness to let go. Seven hundred forty dead and almost fifteen hundred wounded, not to mention the six thousand dead goblins, elves, ogres, Kaftu. What is worth that?

Dar took a glance at the nearby city as his friends approached. The pennons of Hillton county snapped in the breeze above the towering walls.

He knew. It was worth the safety and lives of those who had not perished. Father Ander would have agreed.

Hell, I was willing to die, and I did, in order to defeat Margoth. Most of the dead would say they were proud to contribute to her downfall.

So why did he feel guilty that the Crown of Saint Alyssa had been used to raise him and the other Riders? Part of it was the fact that the Crown's power was limited and could be depleted in a day, to renew the next morning. Part was just not understanding why he still lived while others died.

He sighed.

"Me too," said Eric.

Dar remembered his friend stood next to him and he looked down at the ground sheepishly.

"Is it that obvious?"

Eric gave him a playful push in the shoulder. "You think you're the only one having to deal with survivor's guilt? Think again. Andyn, especially, has a lot to deal with."

"Did I hear my name taken in vain?" she asked as she, Buck and Connor joined Dar and Eric.

"Always," replied Eric. "And don't you forget it."

The Grey Riders held the reins of their steeds, silent. Five sets of eyes rested on Eric.

Eric waited a moment before speaking. "I'll say it again. You don't have to do this. They're my family."

"Yes, we do," said Buck. "You're part of *our* family."

"And I have a duty to prevent what happened to Larad from happening to anyone else," said Andyn with a determined look.

"Besides," offered Connor with a straight face. "What else are we going to do? Perform at dinner parties? Take up needlework? I mean, the Spectral Sword of the Devoted Defender is a good conversation-starter, but even that gets old after a while."

Eric smiled and Dar knew it was settled.

"And Hlerv?" Eric asked.

Dar set his mouth in a firm line. "We'll find him. The Order of the Three Magi promised to help. We'll find him and get him out of whatever mess he's in. We owe him that much."

Buck vaulted into the saddle. "Then I say we get started."

Dar hoisted himself upon Virasi. "Good. It's about time we did something other than eat and drink, sleep and annoy the locals."

Andyn gave him a bright smile. "Riders up!"

Dar spoke to Virasi and the pegasus beat his wings, sending up a cloud of dust and dried grass. In the span of a few heartbeats, they rose from the ground and up into the air.

Dar turned in the saddle and waved his arm. They raised their hands in salute and wheeled to join him. The sunset to the west beckoned.

The Grey Riders flew to meet it.

Epilogue

Silvervale held a rightly-earned reputation in Meridian. Mansions and stately manors lined the curving streets of a hilly suburb overlooking the lake. They marked the homes of some of the city's (and the nation's) most successful and wealthy families. Well-tended trees and groomed lawns abounded near tinkling fountains and ornate fences of wrought iron or dwarven stonework.

In the shadow of the bushes and trees between two of the manors on Bright Street, a darker shadow gathered. In a swirl of deepest black and a hint of purple sparkles, a figure coalesced in the hidden place.

Handor, scion and heir of the House of Lervion, leaned his hands on his knees as the nausea faded. When he could straighten up, he immediately lifted the dark helmet from his head.

The figure outside the Chamber of Decision had warned him of the aftereffects of the helm. Hlerv regarded the headgear in his hand, feeling a twinge of revulsion but also fascination. The thing glistened with a sort of dark swirl embedded in the metal.

I am the master of this. The Advisor, so he called himself, told me what to expect and how to use it. So far, everything he told me has come true. Well, no magical item is going to master me. Besides, Margoth is destroyed, so now it is mine.

He flexed his other hand. His limbs felt light after using the Helm of Shadows, and tingly, like little pins and needles. Another after-effect, the Advisor had told him. Nothing to be worried about.

A thrill of elation surged through him and he smiled.

He shook his head to clear the last of a lingering wooziness, then raised his eyes to an impressive edifice across the street. In the twilight, he saw the magical lamps glowing on either side of the gate. The crown of the gate held his family heraldry: a sable badger on a tawny background with one claw upraised, its mouth opened in a snarl.

His eyes strayed to a window on the second floor, on the north side, now lit from within. He knew the window and the rooms well. He half-expected to see his sister standing on the balcony, looking out over the lake, as she often loved to do.

Instead, a guard with metal armor and a crossbow stood there.

One of Beol's dwarves. he thought with a scowl.

Hlerv knew Beol Torander well: a dwarf, half-brother and confidant of his father, given the keys to the manor, trusted and well-known.

Beol the Back-stabber, Beol the Betrayer, Beol the Murderer, Beol the Manipulator… Yes, the Ja'al would have welcomed you into their ranks.

Hlerv cast a spell of seeing. A quartet of symbols on the fence, walkway and side lawns glowed in his sight. He smirked. Getting past all that would be easy, pitifully easy, with the Helm of Shadows. The hard part would be getting Hannah out.

He thought about Beol's connections, the bribes he had paid to various and sundry magistrates and the men at his command. And behind it all, he mused on how Beol had managed to get together enough resources to pull it off in the first place.

He took out the Quartermaster's Bag and slipped the Helm back into it, then flipped up the hood of his cloak. Keeping to the shadows, he headed down the street towards a less reputable part of town.

In his wake, unseen by him, the plants where he had stood began to sicken and wilt.

Appendix - Glossary

<u>Aalre</u> - A beautiful, evil elven Ja'al wizard, she served a Ja'al leader named Halkith (q.v.) as both subordinate officer and mistress during his quest to find the pegasi of Whitehorse Peak. She was killed by Tholi (q.v.) and Kindri (q.v.), grandchildren of Iron Thunder (q.v.)

<u>Agent</u> - A spy, bounty hunter or thief, depending on context and the particular agent's morals and ethics. Connor Lomin, an agent, tended more towards the "spy" variety. Most agents provide a stealthy component to the groups they support. In military terms an agent would be part of a reconnaissance unit.

<u>Alenar, Brandawyn (Brandi)</u> - One of the original Grey Riders, a half-elven female, trained as a soldier and combat medic/corpsman. The older sister of Megan (q.v.), she and her family were persecuted for their Christian faith and eventually fled their homeland of Torosc under tragic circumstances. During her time with Dar Cabot and his friends, she fell in love with Eric Indidarc. Reserved but kind and devoutly religious, Brandi is quite pretty, with red-gold hair and violet eyes, but doesn't see herself as attractive. Brandawyn is also ambidextrous. Her pegasus is named Amicus.

<u>Alenar, Daphne</u> - Ranger knight and agent of the forces of good in the Realms. The only sister of Megan and Brandi's human mother, she spirited her nieces northward away from Torosc to safety. Sometimes thought of as overly serious (like her niece, Brandawyn), she served as a devoted mother-figure to the sisters after the death of their parents. Her brother is Stephen, a scholar and wizard.

<u>Alenar, Megan</u> - Another of the original Grey Riders and sister of Brandawyn Alenar, she attended college in Terenai and graduated as a wizard and scholar. Possessing red-gold hair like her sibling, Megan is friendly and outgoing, somewhat vain and impetuous, yet fiercely loyal and brave. She is also very attractive, with strawberry blonde hair and amber eyes, and is fond of baubles and fancy clothes. With her sister, she fled persecution in Torosc to arrive in Deran.

<u>Alenar, Stephen</u> - Uncle of Brandawyn and Megan Alenar, he is the younger brother of Daphne Alenar. Despite being a scholar, Stephen is also a skilled warrior and wields potent magic in battle. He likes to tease both his

sister and his nieces but regards them with deep and abiding affection

<u>Alvindor</u> (Dw. "*high council*") - Multi-racial metropolis (pop ~ 100,000) in Gorostol (q.v.). Occupying the top of a mountain ridge and the hills and plains directly below it, the sprawling city boasts several excellent universities.

<u>Arachnia</u> - Evil elven goddess of poison and assassination. One of the gods of the cult of the Ja'al, Arachnia is worshipped chiefly by dark elves (q.v.).

<u>Argus (Sergeant)</u> - Burly and bearded, Argus is the assistant to Lieutenant Altus Volan (q.v.) of the Ja'al Skullhead Legion.

<u>Astarel</u> - Kingdom to the north of Deran, along the coast. The homeland of Buck Bydecy, it is a seafaring nation with a robust navy and an eclectic society comprised equally of elves, humans, dwarves and halflings.

<u>Athor</u> - Large town (pop. ~ 10,000) along the northern border of Deran. It has a substantial garrison (1 augmented regiment) and efficient police force.

<u>Bannister, Arthur</u> - Grey-haired, portly Christian bishop of Hillton, Deran. He is a friend of Count DeGrance (q.v.) and a veteran of battles against evil forces.

<u>Bydecy, Buckminster (Buck)</u> - Another of the original Grey Riders, he traveled south in search of employment as a caravan guard and met Eric Indidarc, Dar Cabot and the rest of the Grey Riders. A tall, rangy, sandy-haired human warrior and free-lance, Buck is a native of Tyler, Astarel. His easygoing nature is often mistaken for boredom. His father is named Alfred and his brother is Jack. He has a sister named Summer.

<u>Cabot, Darius (Dar)</u> - An original Grey Rider and native of the town of Forester on the northern border of the kingdom of Deran, Dar ran afoul of Ja'al goblin troops in the wilds and headed back to town for help, setting the events of *Whitehorse Peak* in motion. A young, dark-haired human male, he is a ranger/scout and adept in the woods. As someone skilled in woodcraft, Dar seeks to determine the fate of his grandparents, who disappeared while searching for an ancient relic in the Wilderness. He rides a pegasus named Virasi (Elv. "*white star*")

<u>Cabot, Elizabeth</u> - Dar Cabot's mother. Her parents were the reason

that Dar decided to study to become a free-lance mercenary so he could discover their fate.

<u>Cabot, Stephen</u> - Finance clerk and accountant residing in Hillton, Deran. He is Dar Cabot's father.

<u>Coastwatch</u> - Seaside town in Torosc where the Alenar sisters were born and raised.

<u>Crossed Swords</u> - Guild of assassins based in Deran and Terenai. Founded and ruled by the Hylar family, the Crossed Swords are often used by evil forces to eliminate opposition. Eric Indidarc's real family name is Hylar and he is a son of the guild master; he escaped his former life and was adopted by Melinor Indidarc (q.v.)

<u>Daemon</u> - Evil to the core, the otherworldly race of daemons spend most of their time trying to overthrow the Elohir (q.v.) or conquer various regions of Damora. They are known as the Fallen because legend has it that they were originally Elohir who turned to the side of evil and worship of themselves (and the Dark One). While many Daemons look like nightmarish beasts, some are very attractive and almost human-like or elven in appearance. The overriding philosophy of the Daemons is that Damora is a free zone, ripe for the picking. Daemons are also known as the Fallen Ones.

<u>Damora</u> - Imaginary world setting for the Grey Riders novels. The fourth planet orbiting the star 82 Eridani, it is roughly 1.15 times the size of Earth and possesses climate regions and flora/fauna similar to Earth. The parent star is a G5V spectral class, main-sequence yellow star approximately 20 light years from Earth. It has two moons, Kaliri and Diometrius, which provide both tidal forces and substantial moonlight for the planet's surface. The technology level of Damora approximates the High Middle Ages of real life, with significant differences due to the use of magic and scientific advancement.

<u>Darlon</u> - Major city in Northern Deran, pop ~ 70,000. Home to people of many races, creeds and professions, it is a trading center and university town. Ruled by a duke, it controls trade, borders and access between Deran and the northernmost nations of Astarel, Elder and Rokon.

<u>Dark Elf</u> - General term used for elves who have left the religion of the Elven god Verian (q.v) to throw in their lot with evil, usually in the cult of Arachnia. Dark elves have all the magical talents, beauty and intelligence of

their brethren but no morals.

Darkwood Drake - A type of wingless dragon, darkwood drakes are stealthy, cunning, cruel and magically skilled. They jealously guard their territories and are often worshippers of Arachnia (q.v.).

DeGrance, Marcel (Lord) - Count of Hillton, Deran. He is pedantic and a bit of a scholar with a massive library but also fiercely protective of his county and its people.

DeMey, Saren - The half-sister of Eric Indidarc by adoption, Saren DeMey was found by Melinor Indidarc as an infant and raised by him and his wife, Anne. A devout Christian, Saren appears to be a complete contradiction in terms as she is half-daemon but fights for the forces of good. Dark-haired and dark-eyed, she transforms to a bat-winged, horned half-daemon at will. As the wife of Terenil, the Earl of the Oakmoor (q.v.) suburb of Tallemar, she is a Countess of Deran.

DeMey, Terenil - The half-elven husband of Saren, he is an earl and the ruler of Tallemar, a suburb of Oakmoor, Deran. A skilled wizard and soldier in his own right, he is adaptable, thoughtful and unfailingly kind. His devotion to Saren is unquestioned.

Deran - Constitutional monarchy in the northern lands of the Western continent of Damora. A nation built from the remnants of the Esten Empire, Deran is also a meritocracy, where nobles are elected by their peers and the legislature based on merit and ability more than noble connections. Deran has an advanced network of roads, potent military, and several universities. The seat of the Christian Church, Saint Martin's Town (St. Martin's) is in Deran.

Detlef - The young half-elven clerk and assistant to Edward Cardinal Simpson, Papal Nuncio to Damora.

Donnervassilianelikilandra (Drac. *"Thunder-iron-first-tribe-wizard"*) - The draconic name of Iron Thunder (q.v.).

Dorn, Jalek - Dwarven baron and ruler of Dorn's Hall. A seasoned soldier, he is committed to both fighting evil and protecting his people. He is an ally of the Baron of Forester.

Dorn, Riti - Dwarven baroness of Dorn's Hall and the mother of three. She is married to Jalek and is determined, clever and ferocious in defense of her people.

<u>Dorn's Hall</u> - Small (pop ~ 530) community of dwarves north of Forester, Deran (q.v.). It is home to Jalek (q.v.) and Riti (q.v.) Dorn, lord and lady of the Hall. The dwarves are allies of Lord Nolan Hanford of Forester and run a brisk trade in raw materials and finished goods. The town is significantly wealthy for its small size.

<u>Durant, Janos</u> - Former commander of a fortress near Shadow Lake and Twinspire Mountain.

<u>Dwarf</u> - One of the major races of Damora. The term "Dwarf" comes from the ancient elvish word, *duarfaen* (Elv. *duar* = 'stone' + *fae/ fey/ fej* - = 'magic', literally "those of stone-magic"). A typical dwarf male is about four feet six inches tall. Dwarves tend to be burly, sturdy or muscular for their size and can live for almost two hundred years. Males are often bearded (though not all are). They are generally honorable and appreciate strength and resolve in others. Their main talent, as indicated by the name bestowed on them by the Elves, is in stonework and metallurgy.

<u>Dwarfshire</u> - A town in Evendale with almost equal numbers of dwarves and halflings. One of the few areas with accessible minerals in the halfling nation, it has a peculiar character because of the mix of races. Many of the gnomes (a mix of dwarf and halfling) in Evendale come from the region.

<u>Ecclesia</u> - The official language of the Christian Church on Damora, it resembles a mix of Latin and Greek. Its most common use is in holy enchantments and blessings.

<u>Eleandir, Andyn</u> - One of the Grey Riders, Andyn was added to the group while on her way to Forester. A priestess of the Elven god Verian and a wizard, Andyn has honey-blonde hair and amber eyes, a trim figure and a marvelous singing voice. Rather impatient and quick-tempered, she nonetheless displays unwavering faith, mercy, warmth and a nimble mind. She is a widow and seeks her husband's murderer with fierce resolution. Her pegasus is named Medianox (Lat. *"midnight"*).

<u>Eleison</u> (Gr. *"have mercy"*) - The name of a powerful magic mace found by the Grey Riders near Twinspire Mountain. It strikes against evil with holy power and amplifies healing magic.

<u>Elethor</u> (Elv. *"dolphin tower"*) - Elven high priest of the Orchard Temple

in Glen, Evendale, friend of Seamus and Miriam Lomin, and agent of the Empire of Terenai tasked with liaison duties to Glen in watching the Wilderness for signs of evil activity.

<u>Elf</u> - One of the major races of Damora. The term "Elf" comes from the ancient word for their race, *Ellfaen* (Elv. *ell* = 'life' + *fae/ fey/ fej* - = 'magic', literally "those of life-magic"). Elves are more slender than humans and possess intriguing eye colors, such as aqua, amber or violet; they also have a slight point to top of the ear, though this is not usually pronounced or even noted if the ears are concealed under hair, hat or helm. Elves tend to be a bit more reserved than the other races and have more of an affinity for magic of all kinds. They possess skills for getting along well with animals and have a remarkable talent for healing trees and plants.

<u>Elohir</u> - Denizen of the planet of Celestia (the 5th planet of the 61 Virginis star, a single G6 spectral class, main-sequence yellow star approximately 28 light years from Earth). Sometimes called "Celestials", they appear to be winged humans. Skin color covers the range of typical shades seen in humans (porcelain, tanned, brown, yellow, dark brown) and their eyes are black with a silvery sheen. Their beauty is often described as 'unearthly'. All possess potent magical and martial skills but are usually reluctant to meddle in the affairs of Damorans. They are uniformly kind, wise, honest and just. Elohir live extremely long lives (~ 1000 years) if not killed in warfare with their evil kindred.

<u>Entropy Globe</u> - A magic spell that causes disorder in any material it strikes, causing it to fray and fall apart.

<u>Esten Empire</u> - An empire formed of various kingdoms controlling much of the known world during the second age of Damora (known as the Imperial Age and denoted in calendars by the letters IY (for Imperial Year)). It fell after over a thousand years of rule due to infighting, a breakdown in the social fabric and the influence of evil.

<u>Evendale</u> - Small halfling nation south east of Deran and northeast of Terenai (q.v.). A republic, Evendale consists of seven districts or counties, each of which have a prescribed number of representatives (aldermen) and senators who draft laws that are approved by the High Minister, another elected position. A land with mild climate and productive farmland, Evendale nonetheless has a border with the Wilderness, which means the

halflings are always on vigilant watch, having been invaded by evil tribes from the wild lands multiple times. Its capital city is Lakeview.

Eye of Truth - A magical diamond, the Eye of Truth is actually a sort of lens that allows the owner to see the true nature of things and people. It can detect evil or good auras, see through illusion and discern truth from lies. It was crafted by an ancestor of Buck Bydecy. Buck has a special metal structure on his helm that holds the Eye and allows him to use it hands-free.

Faldanor, Andareth (Lord) - Half-elf healer and wizard, retired. He and his free-lance group, the Four Silvers, defeated the evil wizard Galchimor in the wilderness near Evendale, mapping the route to Twinspire Mountain which is eventually needed by the Grey Riders.

Fallbrook, Larad - The deceased husband of Andyn Eleandir (q.v.), Larad was assassinated by agents of the Crossed Swords Guild (q.v.). He was a carpenter by trade and childhood friend of the Eleandir family.

False Mirror - A magical spell that puts up a screen to reflect back an image to the viewer of what they saw previously or what they expect to see.

Farfield's Lethargy - A magic spell that makes the target disoriented, slow, and uncoordinated. Named after the wizard who devised it, Edward Farfield.

Fendir - Dwarven priest of Kurental (q.v) and assistant/advisor to Jalek Dorn (q.v.)

Firedart - A magical attack spell used by wizards and sorcerers. It is essentially a small projectile of flame with a detonable core that looks rather like a tiny comet and has a limited range (about 100 feet or so). It produces the effect equivalent to a 9 mm pistol bullet and rarely misses.

Fire Finger - A magical attack spell that looks like a beam of fiery light with a small globe at the point of attack. It has the approximate effect of a 7.62 mm incendiary rifle bullet.

Forester - Large town along the northern border highway of Deran. Forester is ruled by a baron and controls trade along the borderlands. Its defining feature is the central town proper, which is surrounded by a tall, well-built palisade with giant, living trees as its guard towers. It is the hometown of Dar Cabot (q.v.)

<u>Garon-Zith</u> - Ancient religion from the Paragon Age (q.v.) that held such views as eugenics, child sacrifice and ritual prostitution as precepts. By the time period of *Helm of Shadows*, it had been eradicated. Zhinia Margoth (q.v.) was a high priestess of the religion.

<u>Ghai-zhal</u> (Gobl. "Surface slug") - Goblin term for human.

<u>Ghai-zhal-ik</u> (Gobl. "Surface slug snack") - Goblin term for a halfling.

<u>Ghoul's Kiss</u> - A magic spell that burns the target and has a chance to induce paralysis. It is rarely used by any but evil practitioners.

<u>Ghost Hammer</u> - A magic attack spell that sends out a blunt-force projectile of kinetic energy which dissipates upon striking. It is akin to being hit with an eight-pound medicine ball.

<u>Ghost Creeper</u> - A vile and noisome growth, ghost creepers are semi-sentient and have the ability to reach out an weaken victims with a type of poison. They also set up a wailing noise if any non-evil creatures are nearby.

<u>Gnome</u> - Half-breed race resulting from the marriage of halfling and dwarf, gnomes possess features from each parent: natural affinity for stone and the underground from the dwarves and a cheerful disposition and natural talent with all things organic. Somewhat taller than halflings but shorter than dwarves, gnomes are industrious and found in all the known lands. They usually have dark hair, tan-to-dark complexions, and brown, amber or grey eyes. A typical gnome lives about 180 years or so.

<u>Goblin</u> - Short, half-simian creatures who often serve as foot-soldiers for the forces of evil, looking somewhat like horned chimpanzees. Extremely agile and able to use any available weapon that is sized for them, they are also good at hiding in shadows. They dislike sunlight. Their social structure is usually in a hierarchical monarchy, with the chieftain or king of a particular tribe wielding absolute authority. Goblins particularly hate dwarves since the two races compete for underground areas and resources. They are capable miners and are about the size of a gnome or tall halfling (a few inches short of four feet tall).

<u>Gorf</u> (Gob. "*Lump*") - A goblin word for an Ogre. An obviously derogatory name, it expresses the disdain of the goblins for Ogres, who often abuse goblins if they can get away with it.

<u>Gorlak</u> - A goblin sergeant and aide to the Ja'al (q.v.) forces in *Whitehorse*

Peak. Originally attached to Lady Aalre (q.v.), he is more mentally adept than the average goblin and an original thinker. By the time of *Helm of Shadows*, he is a captain and aide to a goblin king

<u>Gudarti</u> - The evil goddess of torture and suffering, the seductive and sadistic Gudarti is a member of the Ja'al pantheon.

<u>Half-Elf</u> - The offspring of a union between an elf (q.v.) and human, half-elves are a mix of their parents' heritage: magically talented, strong, adaptable and capable of learning new skills quickly. If it were not for the fact that they are noticeably larger than elves by a couple of inches in height, they would be indistinguishable from elves due to their predilection to inherit their elven parent's eye color, hair color and ear shape. Half-elves live to between 100 and 150 years.

<u>Halfling</u> - The smallest of the races, halflings (from the elven for "those of hearth magic" - *haliv-fae*) prefer pastoral villages and countrysides to large cities, though they are at home in any setting. As adaptable as humans, halflings have a talent for craftsmanship (with things other than stone) and farming. They are known for their skill in the kitchen and the durability of their finished goods. Their hair color (blonde, brown or black), skin color (porcelain to dark brown) and eye color (blue, green, black or grey) remind the other races of miniature humans. They live about 100 years or so.

<u>Halkith</u> - A human cleric of the Ja'al cult (q.v.), Halkith was a commander of troops in a set of bases in the Wilderness near Forester, Deran charged with a mission of capturing the pegasi of Whitehorse Peak (see Book 1). He was killed by Dar Cabot near the Border Highway.

<u>Hanford, Ellen (Lady)</u> - Baroness of Forester and wife of Lord Nolan, she is dark-skinned and dark-eyed and comes from the nation of Targanon far across the GreatSea. Kind, determined, gentle, and a bit absent-minded, she is nevertheless a fierce defender of the weak and a person of high morals. As an accomplished wizard, she has extensive experience battling the forces of evil.

<u>Hanford, Nolan (Lord)</u> - The titular ruler of the Deranese border town of Forester (q.v.), he is the person who originally hired the Grey Riders (q.v.) for their first mission. A tall, middle-aged man of trim physique and piercing dark eyes, he is also a paladin (q.v.) and a member of the Christian Church. He is married to Lady Ellen Hanford and has two children (Timmy

and Alice).

<u>Heritage Stone</u> - A magical item, a Heritage Stone is used to prove paternity and lineage. It uses magical analysis of DNA from a blood sample to ascertain the relationship of the subject to a predetermined DNA pattern associated with a target family or person.

<u>Hillton</u> - Fortified city (pop ~ 27,000) in the center of Deran positioned on the shores of Sun Lake, a very large body of fresh water on the plains near the center of the country. It is ruled by a Count. Due to its position on the plains, it is a major trading center and hub for agricultural areas nearby.

<u>Hlerv (Handor Lervion)</u> - A gnome wizard and spy, he joined the Grey Riders in *Eye of Truth* and helped them clear Buck Bydecy's name and avenge the murder of Andyn Eleandir's husband. Secretive and somewhat aloof, he is nevertheless loyal, resourceful and intelligent, possessing a sometimes wry and sardonic sense of humor. Despite the openness of the other Riders, he is not comfortable sharing any information about his past. He has a penchant for chemistry. Connor Lomin (q.v.) lets him ride on his pegasus, Phantom.

<u>Human</u> - Humans on Damora (q.v) are much like real-life people of the planet Earth, with the exception that they can use magic in the same manner as elves, dwarves, halflings and other denizens of the fourth planet of 82 Eridani. Humans are energetic, adaptable, learn quickly and are endlessly curious about Damora and its people, flora and fauna. They live in all climates and places that will welcome them. The origin of the word "human" has no Damoran equivalent as it does not translate from any Elven or Dwarven syntax.

<u>Humana</u> - Language of the human race on Damora (q.v).

<u>Indidarc, Eric</u> - One of the original Grey Riders, Eric is the adopted son of Melinor Indidarc (q.v.) a famous wizard. He meets Buck Bydecy (q.v.) on his way to Forester, Deran to seek his fortune as a blank-shield freelance mercenary guard. Able to use magic and martial weapons with equal proficiency, Eric is cheerful, optimistic and friendly. He treats everyone he meets with the same courtesy and kindness, whether a beggar or noble. Eric has violet eyes and blond hair and is a half-elf (q.v.). His pegasus is named Niveral (Elv. *"snow blade"*)

<u>Indidarc, Melinor</u> - High Wizard of the northern kingdom of Deran,

nobleman and confidante of royalty in the Kingdoms of the Northern Alliance (q.v.). He adopted both Eric and Saren (q.v) after his own children were grown. A formidable ally and genius with knowledge of magic, science, medicine, literature and history, Melinor is fluent in several languages. A kind but somewhat absent-minded man, he is singularly focused on thwarting evil plots in the known lands.

<u>Irial</u> - The halfling god of harvests, craftsmen and home, Irial is a benevolent deity who sometimes counts elves and humans among his adherents. The precepts of Irial are hospitality, kindness, courtesy, respect for people, animals and nature, and steadfastness in the face of hardship, whether caused by nature or evil designs.

<u>Iron Thunder</u> - An elderly dragon who lives near the Deran borderlands and the town of Forester. He was the guardian of the pegasi herd (which eventually were found by the Grey Riders) and kept them in temporal stasis as part of a clan vow made by his grandfather to the last good Emperor of Esten. He is a friend and ally of the Grey Riders and has two orphaned grandchildren who he is fostering. The Grey Riders sometimes call him "Grandpa".

<u>Ja'al</u> - Also known as the Manipulator Church (for their penchant for twisting words, lying and otherwise using others callously for their own ends) the Ja'al are one of the evil religions on Damora. The cult is a polytheistic religion worshiping a number of harsh and cruel deities. The precepts of the Ja'al are world domination, rule of the strong over the weak, eugenics, personal gain at the cost of others, and treachery.

<u>Jas, Caridan</u> - Elven wizard under the tutelage of Ellen Hanford (q.v.). He has a tiny Companion Pin of a sparrow named Alicia.

<u>Jered</u> - Large southern nation allied with Torosc (q.v.) and Morlan (q.v.). It was established by pirate warlords after the Paragon Age (q.v.), who selected their ruling king via trial by mortal combat. It is the home of the Viper criminal enterprise.

<u>Kaftu</u> - A race of hyena-folk similar to the creatures of African legend. Their society is matriarchal, with males only used for mating, brute labor and some specialized tasks. The balance of each tribe is female. They are cunning, vicious and greedy and view all other creatures as either obstacles or food.

<u>Kaljirre</u> (Dw. *"sky mirror"*) - Beautiful lake near the Gorostolian capital city of Meridian.

<u>Kenwall</u> - A suburb of Meridian, Gorostol.

<u>Kher Mardil</u> - The ancient name for the domain of Zhinia Margoth (q.v.). Its location has been lost to antiquity.

<u>Kindriana (Kindri)</u> - Dragon and granddaughter of Iron Thunder (q.v.).

<u>Lake Silverdown</u> - Large freshwater lake in Evendale near the capital city of Lakeview. Silverdown is a very beautiful and picturesque area and a popular resort destination.

<u>Lich</u> - An undead wizard. Liches are created when a wizard or sorcerer makes a pact with Dark Powers in order to forestall his/her own death, gaining immense magical power and undead status in the bargain. They perpetually exude an aura of terror but are greatly harmed by holy spells and items.

<u>Lightning Spear</u> - A magical attack spell, it sends out a thin stroke of lightning from the caster's hand. When used by a skilled practitioner, it can burn through armor and hide and skin, and can be deadly if the user is powerful enough.

<u>Lomin, Brendan</u> - Halfling banker in Glen, Evendale, he is the brother of Connor Lomin and is married to Cerys. His two children, Deena and Darren, are keenly interested in the exploits of their uncle Connor and his friends. As survivor of the Whispering Death (q.v.), he cannot raise his voice due to the aftereffects of the disease, which he contracted while assisting his wife in caring for the sick.

<u>Lomin, Cerys</u> - Halfling healer in Glen, Evendale, she and her husband, Brendan, took serious risks trying to assist victims of the Whispering Death. A pretty and bright woman, she is rather quiet but friendly to Connor's friends.

<u>Lomin, Connor</u> - Another of the original Grey Riders, Connor is a halfling who hails from Evendale (q.v.). Serious but with a somewhat ribald sense of humor, Connor appears stoic and sober most of the time. He is knowledgeable about traps, curious about ancient ruins and secrets, and wields a broadsword, a rather heavy weapon for a halfling. Dark-eyed and dark-haired, he has a muscular build but has an almost uncanny skill for

moving unseen. His pegasus is named Phantom.

Lomin, Darren - Halfling boy, age six at the time of *Helm of Shadows*. He is the son of Brendan Lomin (brother of Connor Lomin, Grey Rider). A rambunctious and curious fellow, he aspires to be a hero warrior like his uncle Connor when he grows up.

Lomin, Deena - Halfling girl, age eight at the time of *Helm of Shadows*. A precocious little girl, Deena is talkative, a good artist, and the boss of her younger brother.

Lomin, Janey - Deceased wife of Connor Lomin. She and her mother-in-law were at odds before her wedding to Connor due to several differences, not least of which were her friends of somewhat unsavory reputation and the fact that she was pregnant at the time of her wedding. They eventually reconciled not long before Janey perished in a plague from the Wilderness known as the Whispering Death (q.v.).

Lomin, Miriam - High priestess of the Heather Temple in Glen, Evendale and wife of Seamus. She is the mother of Connor Lomin and his brothers Brendan and Kendall (the latter of whom is a student of magic at the University of Lakeview, the capital of Evendale). A very proper halfling woman, she is nonetheless keenly fond of her children and grandchildren and struggles to balance her official persona with her motherly one. She is sixth in line to the High Patriarchate of Irial.

Lomin, Rose - Deceased daughter of Connor Lomin, aged just less than a year. Only a few hours after the passing of her mother from the Whispering Death, Rose died. Connor Lomin sometimes dreams of her.

Lomin, Seamus - Husband of Miriam Lomin. A free-lance warrior in younger days, he is a quiet but friendly man and sees much without saying much. He is currently head of security for the Heather Temple in Glen, Evendale.

Margoth, Zhinia - A former Paragon Queen (q.v.) who used fell and evil magics to transform herself into an undead sorceress (a lich) to avoid death near the end of the Paragon Age, Margoth is vicious, conniving, and cruel. Her ultimate goal is unknown, but her forces range about near the borderlands of Deran, causing havoc. She has intimate knowledge of the Song of the Grey Riders (q.v.) since it seems to mention her; secretly, she fears its fulfillment since it implies the Grey Riders will be her doom. She appears as a skeleton with pinpoint eyes of purple light, clothed in rotting royal robes and wielding a skull-headed staff. Her standard is a fanged skull with a crown of flame.

<u>Melissa</u> - An Elohir (q.v.) warrior tasked with watching for the Chosen to arrive at Twinspire Mountain.

<u>Mens Motus</u> (Lat. *"mind move"*) - A spell of telekinesis.

<u>Morlan</u> - Populous and wealthy nation south of Torosc (q.v.) ruled by a line of wizard-kings. It is allied with Torosc and Jered.

<u>Navarre, Colleen (Captain)</u> - Cavalry officer and commander of Beta Company, Third Regiment (the Fire Eagles), Third Division, Royal Army of Deran.

<u>Neralia</u> - Evil goddess of child sacrifice, murder and domination, Neralia is one of the members of the Ja'al pantheon. Similarities between her church and the defunct worship of Garon-Zith (q.v.) have led some to speculate that the two goddesses are one and the same.

<u>Northern Alliance</u> - A multinational alliance similar to NATO in the real world, the Alliance is composed of Deran, Astarel, Rokon, Eldir, Evendale and Terenai.

<u>Oakmoor</u> - The capital city of Deran, home to over a quarter of a million people. Oakmoor is based on three large hills at the confluence of the East River and Lonmar Rivers. It has several suburbs in addition to the main city proper.

<u>Ogre</u> - Large, human-like creatures with fangs and odd-colored hair, ogres are brutish, violent, and not particularly smart. Their leaders are usually the more intelligent members of a particular tribe. Some of their number are smart enough to use magic. They are usually over seven feet tall and three hundred and fifty pounds. Used as shock troops by the forces of evil, Ogres are also greedy and fearless.

<u>Oldur</u> - Captain of the Guard at Dorn's Hall (q.v.)

<u>Overlook</u> - City in Gorostol along the northern border, pop ~ 50,000. Rich and plentiful mines are nearby in the mountains and hills.

<u>Palatine</u> - The capital city of Astarel (q.v.). It has a population rivaling that of Oakmoor (~ 250,000 not including suburbs).

<u>Paractus</u> - A magical medallion like Stealth (q.v.), Paractus is much more powerful. Its owner, Daphne Alenar, can summon a magical construct in the shape of a massive giant owl, nine feet tall at the head and sporting a saddle capable of bearing two riders.

<u>Parker, Colin (Sir)</u> - Aide-de-camp to Lord Nolan and Lady Ellen of Forester. He is a member of the Order of St. Michael (q.v.).

<u>Puup</u> - Buck Bydecy's pet pigeon who somehow manages to avoid getting killed despite being in or near several battles.

<u>Quartermaster's Bag</u> - A magically enchanted bag that can hold as much material as will fit into two large bowls but can shrink to the size of a belt purse when a keyword is spoken.

<u>Ridanmir</u> - Darkwood Drake and sire of Thulrin (q.v.) and Ziskar (q.v.).

<u>Roadwardens</u> - The equivalent of the Highway Patrol of Gorostol (q.v.).

<u>Saint Martin's</u> (Town) - Major port city in Deran (pop ~ 80,000). It is the seat of the Christian church and the base of the Curia, the ruling council of Christianity on Damora. The Papal Nuncio (q.v.) makes his residence there.

<u>Saint Thomas, Order of</u> - Christian order of musicians, artists and writers who try to counter propaganda that is subtly introduced into society by the forces of evil.

<u>Saint Michael, Order of</u> - Christian military order of knights and warriors dedicated to protecting the innocent against evil.

<u>Sarith, Mary (Lady)</u> - Lady and ruler of Sun Plains, Deran.

<u>Selaan</u> - Evil god of seduction, slavery and lies, Selaan is alternately male or female as the need suits. He/she is part of the Ja'al pantheon.

<u>Shadow Lake</u> - Medium sized freshwater lake in the wilderness east of Evendale. It lies in the shadow of the local mountains, one of which is Twinspire (q.v.).

<u>Shark Bluff</u> - Coastal city (pop ~ 30,000) of Gorostol with a somewhat shady reputation.

<u>Shriek</u> - A magical infantry sword found by the Grey Riders near Twinspire Mountain. It makes its wielder more stealthy and does great harm to

undead.

Skullhead Legion - Paramilitary guard force in the service of the Ja'al cult leadership. Known for their brutality, greed and utter disregard for life, they are often used as shock troops. They are fanatical and fight to the death.

Song of Kudath - Ja'al propaganda poem found by the Alenars during their quest in Gorostol.

Starsilver - A light and strong metal similar to titanium alloy (Ti-6Al-4V) but stronger and with a greater amount of flexibility. It is very expensive and is often used in the fashioning of armor.

Stealth - Eric Indidarc's enchanted familiar. Summoned from a magic item called a Companion Pin, it transforms to a realistic hawk upon command. When active, he gives Eric the ability to see through his eyes as he flies high above.

Sting of the Scorpion - A magical attack spell that sends out a spear of green light into the target. It can penetrate armor and brings with it any one of several optional poison effects.

Storm Force - A defensive spell that casts up a spherical globe of high pressure, bursting out around the caster and hurling enemies backwards or breaking projectiles.

Sun Lake - Body of fresh water near the Deranese city of Hillton.

Tamsan - Ja'al Skullhead infantry spearman, attached to Lieutenant Volan (q.v.). He is very tall and has dead eyes.

Terenai (Elv. "*Realm of the Elves*") - The hereditary homeland of the Elven people, Terenai lies due south of Deran and also shares borders with Evendale (q.v.), Gorostol and Merdail. A verdant and fruitful land, it is heavily forested in places. It is ruled by an Emperor (or Empress) and is the oldest of the nations on Deran. Its capital city is Mil-Tereth (Elv. "*King's Palace*").

Tholios (Tholi) - Dragon and grandson of Iron Thunder (q.v.)

Three Magi, Order of the - Secretive order of Christian mages and scholars in service of the Papal Nuncio (q.v.). Composed of extremely skilled practitioners, it counts Melinor Indidarc as one of its number (and he is one of the few publicly acknowledged members).

Thulrin - The brother of Ziskar, he is the larger of the two Darkwood Drakes but not as sophisticated. He comes off as a bit petulant.

Tombfire - Evil spell that enervates and drains its target of life, eventually creating a skeletal servant or zombie after death.

Tor Haldin - The city of Saint Alyssa.

Torvu - Another of the Ja'al pantheon, Torvu is the evil god of corruption and the undead.

Tricky Sprite - A spell of misdirection and illusion, it tries to fool the viewer into thinking that sprites or pixies are flitting about nearby in the shadows, distracting the target from their current task.

Troll - Large, brutish bipedal creatures similar to ogres but taller and heavier. Trolls are hairless and can have four arms rather than two. Somewhat related to giants, they are considerably less sophisticated. They prefer mountains and forests and will kill and eat anything edible. Cruel, greedy and selfish, they can nonetheless be outwitted by smarter creatures. Some more intelligent of their species can learn to use rudimentary magic. Trolls have the unnerving talent of being able to blend in with trees and rocks by merely holding still and often use this ability to ambush the unwary.

Twinspire Peak - A mountain in the wilderness east of Evendale (q.v.) near Shadow Lake (q.v.) it holds secrets related to the Helm of Shadows (q.v.). Dar Cabot has a medallion taken from a Ja'al wizard that depicts the mountain.

Tyler - A major city of Astarel (q.v.) located on the coast just north of the border with Deran (q.v.) It is known for its large harbor, excellent fishing fleet and naval base. It is the hometown of Buck Bydecy (q.v.).

Ulgrut - Ogre Chieftain and ally of Zhinia Margoth.

Umchak (Gob. *"gnawers"*) - Goblin word used to describe Kaftu, playing on the idea that all the hyena folk do is lay about chewing on bones like common dogs.

Urmum - Goblin word for "Elf", both used in the singular and plural sense. Translated literally as "Glowing Thing", probably due to the fact that elves live in sunlight and are adept at magic.

<u>Vampire Rose</u> - Semi-sentient evil plant with the power to hypnotize victims. They are mobile and will use their thorny branches to cut open their hypnotized prey to release blood, upon which they feed.

<u>Verian</u> - Elven god of forests and nature (from the Elven "Veri" meaning "Lord" and Verian meaning "Highest Lord".) Followers of Verian worship in open structures usually in groves or copses of trees. The organizational structure is somewhat loose, with a council of high priests and priestesses making decisions of doctrine and teachings every year. Andyn Eleandir (q.v.) is a priestess of Verian.

<u>Viper</u> (slavers) - An organized criminal group hailing from Jered (q.v.) specializing in human trafficking and drugs.

<u>Volan, Altus (Lieutenant)</u> - A Ja'al Skullhead (q.v.) officer with a hidden past and a dislike of his commanders. He is slender, perceptive and agile. He is adept at dealing with the uncouth and brutish troops who very often make up the bulk of a Skullhead force.

<u>Vorquul</u> - The King of the Whiteskull goblin tribe, Vorquul is highly intelligent, politically astute, a deft negotiator and an iron-fisted despot, embodying almost Machiavellian qualities. He is one of Zhinia Margoth's allies and an accomplished scholar and field marshal.

<u>Vrixus</u> - A lecherous and conniving Skullhead scout under the command of Altus Volan (q.v.).

<u>Ware, Killian</u> - Christian dwarven free-lance mercenary, an agent (q.v.)and friend of Dar Cabot's grandparents.

<u>Westhaven</u> - Ruined Deranese town destroyed by Halkith's (q.v.) troops in their search for the pegasi that the Grey Riders ended up recovering. Its inhabitants were massacred.

<u>Whispering Death</u> - A magically-induced plague infestation originating in the wilderness near Evendale (q.v.) and Terenai (q.v.). It killed many thousands before a cure was found by the Church of Irial. Survivors have damaged vocal cords and cannot raise their voices above a whisper.

<u>Whitehorse Peak </u>- A large mountain north of Forester, Deran, so named because its geology and snow-fall pattern reminded the people nearby of a white-maned horse. It is the home of Iron Thunder (q.v.) and the site of the recovery of the pegasi (as described in *Whitehorse Peak*) that the

Grey Riders own at the time of *Helm of Shadows*. Its dwarven name is Kelematris (Dw. "*Mountain -Horse*").

<u>Whitepine</u> - Small town (pop ~ 700) near Deorfast, Deran. It is the home of Melinor Indidarc.

<u>Widmer's Corner</u> - A small town in northern Gorostol (q.v.) near the highway leading from Terenai (q.v.).

<u>Wit's End</u> - Small (pop ~ 800) village along the northern border of Deran.

<u>Wizard Scan</u> - An analytical spell, it is used by magic workers to gauge the intensity, type and origin of enchantment on a magic item.

<u>Za'Arak</u> - Goblin word for their race, loosely translated as "The Rulers".

<u>Zanilor</u> - Ja'al general sent with a sizable force of troops to support Zhinia Margoth. He appears witty and urbane but is very observant and calculating.

<u>Zirta</u> - Pack queen of the Shadowrunner clan of Kaftu (q.v.). She hates ogres almost as much as she hates elves. Her clan is a rival of the Longfang clan, another Kaftu tribe with an ambitious queen.

<u>Ziskar</u> - Darkwood Drake of the woods near Twinspire Mountain. She has an incestuous relationship with her brother, Thulrin. She loves to toy with her victims.

ABOUT THE AUTHOR

A route to fantasy fiction through the aerospace industry may seem an odd one to take, but PG Badzey has been writing stories since grammar school and has never stopped even though his path took an unconventional turn for someone interesting in writing. A trained systems engineer, he kept up with creative writing and coursework throughout a career working on the C-17 airlifter, the International Space Station, the Delta IV Rocket and the James Webb Space Telescope. He has enjoyed and been influenced by JRR Tolkien, C.S. Lewis, Katherine Kurtz, Christopher Stasheff, Terry Brooks and C. Dale Brittain, to name a few. Previous publications include short stories published in *Dragonlaugh*, an online fantasy humor magazine, and the publication of the first two novels in the *Grey Riders* series, *Whitehorse Peak* and *Eye of Truth*. PG Badzey has studied martial arts for many years, mentors a high school robotics team, and is active in his parish community. He lives in California with his wife and two sons.

Find out more about the World of the Grey Riders at
https://pgbadzey.wordpress.com!

All the Furs and Feathers

Book 1 in the Cat Tales Series

Eileen O'Finlan

Print ISBNs
Amazon Print 9780228624172
LSI Print 9780228624189
B&N Print 9780228624196

Dedication

To all of Smokey and Autumn Amelia's furred and feathered friends.

Acknowledgments

I would like to thank everyone who helped make this book a reality: Jude Pittman and everyone at BWL Publishing, Inc.: cover artist, Michelle Lee, editor, Nancy Bell, and fellow BWL author, Eileen Charbonneau, for her always exceptional content editing.

Thank you to all who read, listened to, and commented on early drafts of *All the Furs and Feathers*, particularly Cindy Kazanovicz, Wendy Stafford, Eileen Charbonneau, Patty Duffy, Tom Kelleher, and the wonderful members of my writing group: Lee Baldarelli, Janice Hitzhusen, Barbara Lammachia, Jim Pease, Pam Reponen, Rebecca Southwick, Cindy Shenette, and Jane Willan.

Thank you to Don Lutz for designing my new website. Don, your expertise and patience are greatly appreciated.

Huge thanks to my biggest cheerleader, Katie Kelley.

A special thank you to Kathy Leal of Blushing Bee Naturals, my inspiration for Tamarind and Tonk's Treasures.

A very special thanks goes to Ruth E. Brouwer, cat mom of Arnold P. It was Arnold P. who brought Brussels sprouts to a Catster© party. He came up with the idea of playing with them and told everyone not to put them in their mouths. RIP Arnold P.